Y0-CZP-195

STELLAR WARNING

The sky enlivened with beating wings. Falizians, led by Evaladyn the Mistress, circled overhead. She descended, hovering over the pool, her four sets of wings stirring the air. The sun caught briefly on her scales iridescent green rainbows. Her long neck supported a large head which shook nervously. Two luminous blue eyes splayed with silver took in all the surroundings at once, yet devoted her attention primarily to Stefen. Her wide beak, narrowing to a sharp, bent point, opened. Melodious words ran out in a jumble.

"A thing touched the land. From the stars or from the sun. One of your kind emerged from it. He howls at night. Oh, Stefen, I fear for you, for he is angry and rages. He must be very dangerous."

Other Avon Books by
Susan Coon

CASSILEE

Coming Soon

CHIY-UNE

SUSAN COON

THE VIRGIN

AVON
PUBLISHERS OF BARD, CAMELOT AND DISCUS BOOKS

THE VIRGIN is an original publication of Avon Books.
This work has never before appeared in book form.

AVON BOOKS
A division of
The Hearst Corporation
959 Eighth Avenue
New York, New York 10019

Copyright © 1981 by Susan Coon
Published by arrangement with the author
Library of Congress Catalog Card Number: 80-69900
ISBN: 0-380-77842-4

All rights reserved, which includes the right to
reproduce this book or portions thereof in any form
whatsoever except as provided by the U. S. Copyright Law.
For information address Richard Curtis, 156 East 52nd
Street, New York, New York 10022

First Avon Printing, June, 1981

AVON TRADEMARK REG. U.S. PAT. OFF. AND IN
OTHER COUNTRIES, MARCA REGISTRADA, HECHO EN
U.S.A.

Printed in the U.S.A.

10 9 8 7 6 5 4 3 2 1

For my Father, Alexander H. Fassbender,
who loves to read.

Loneliness, spawned at the beginning of time, at the birth of awareness, gnawed holes in the soul of a Great Intelligence destined to war, unvictoriously, with His weaker brother. Out of His need came the fortitude and ingenuity to create a Lover. Her fragility was unparalleled in the Universe and teetered precariously in defiance of physical laws. The foreign energies released in her presence by errant travelers jeopardized her stability and worsened the chaotic time when she passed between the two warring powers.

Chapter 1

THROUGH THE EYES OF HIS SON, PADREE looked older and wiser than his years. He had seemed so much younger the last time the double moons appeared side by side in the sky.

Stefen choked on tears clogging his throat. He lifted the old man's head, wincing at the hot perspiration brought by the fever, and held a drinking cup to Padree's shriveled lips.

It was not the first time his father had been taken into the clutches of the fever. But this time, Stefen was afraid, more afraid than he had been in all of his ten short years. The gray pallor had taken on a chalky hue around the age lines deepened by suffering.

The old man wheezed, coughed and tried to sit, managing to do so only with Stefen's help. His hands shook as they sought the smaller ones. Blind eyes stared straight ahead, frightening the boy. "Stefen? That you, boy?"

"I'm here, Father."

"Remember what I've said these years." Panting, "When you've grown into a man, you must go back. Go to the Forbidden Place. Remove the amulet . . . throw it inside. Don't you go in. Oh, never, never do that. And never go back to that place again." Trembling, he reached for the boy, his bony fingers twitching wildly. "Promise me! Promise you'll do this, boy."

Stefen sniffed, realizing his father had bowed to the fever, and with that, death. "I, I promise."

The bony fingers clawed at the boy's small arm. "Not before manhood. You must wait . . . eleven Passages, Stefen. Eleven."

"I'll wait. Please don't die, Padree! Please don't leave me alone." The old man's grip tightened, then faltered.

"You hide from the enemy if he comes." His words were a rasp in the wheeze rattling out of his lungs.

"I won't let them see me. They won't steal me from the Virgin." Wiping the flood of tears to the side, Stefen managed a composure beyond his tender years.

Padree sighed heavily, slumped and fell back to the sleeping pads. "Sorry, Stefen. So sorry." His breathing labored erratically. "Annalli, it failed . . . you were right. Annalli!" he cried out with the last of his strength. A yellowish flow from the sides of his eyes cut through the moisture clinging to his temples.

Then silence.

Padree's protruding eyes stared at the crude thatch ceiling. His mouth gaped and his tongue was frozen over his bottom teeth. The bony fingers of his right hand were wrapped around his son's arm.

Stefen sank to his heels and let the tears roll down his cheeks, marked by an occasional sob. His left hand began to throb. He pulled his arm free of the corpse. The gnarled hands were gently folded over his father's hairy chest.

Stefen sat in the aura of death, feeling it heavy in the small enclosure, wondering what he should do, where he should go and how he would survive without Padree. A million questions entered his mind. There was no one left to answer them. They were all gone; all dead for different reasons.

Annalli, his mother, had died giving birth to a sister who did not live long enough to be named. It seemed that Padree began to die then, too, bit by bit, day by day. There had been others, a long time ago. But they, too, were dead; victims to the hostile jungle and the monstrous creatures that dwelled there.

Once, someone had said there were others living on the Virgin, but no one mentioned them again. Who were they? Where were they? Panicked by the prospect of living totally alone, Stefen fought to remember what had been said. It was too long ago, too vague.

Chirping sounds invaded the hut turned graveyard. A genuine panic for the immediate put him into motion. One last glance at Padree, and he snatched a pouch belt and filled it with anything considered useful within his reach. He was almost at the door when he turned back, ran to Padree and lifted the overstuffed moss pillow.

A thirty-centimeter blade on a curved golden handle laid sheathed in a silver case. Stefen glanced at the old man, feeling approval, grabbed the knife and ran.

Outside the chirping noise was deafening. The ganids were clustering, ready to feed on the death inside the hut. North of the small clearing there was a bright-red swarm making short flights from tree to tree. Their translucent wings caught the sun in a thousand colors. On the ground a dozen scurried on spindly legs in circles generally aimed at the hut. The red bodies were the size of one of Padree's fingers with a long stinger added to the tail. Considering their size, the mouth was vicious in comparison.

Stefen ran hard, trying not to step on any. The pouch grew heavy in his right hand and the knife helped to counterbalance it in his left. Arms pumping, strides long and stretching, he entered the jungle path to the lava flow. The nacki vines were alive with the red ganids, chirping, darting from leaf to leaf, making short flights to the ground.

They rushed over and around him, landing on his head and chest. He did not dare to swipe at them, lest they sink poisonous stingers into his flesh. Fusci ferns slapped his thighs. Putch trees dropped right-angled branches down to graze the top of his head and scrape off a ganid or two. There were a dozen of the red insects crawling over him as he ran toward the black tongue. One crawled onto his face, waving the stinger in front of his right eye.

He cried without knowing it, thinking only of the nebulous safety of the Passage shelter half a kilometer away, of Padree being consumed by the ganids, of his future—alone. The chirping seemed to be all around him, louder and louder, as one settled over his ear. Dozens of suction-cupped feet clung to the insides of his sweaty thighs, moving steadily up and down his legs, looking for an open wound at which to feast.

The jungle thinned. Wainor bushes shook their small yellow leaves in the breeze. Shanuts, nearly ripe, hung on black branches. Stefen ran, attempted a leap over a low bush and caught his foot. He went sprawling through the prickly wainor and skidded to a halt against the lava flow.

Lying there, the pain flourished in his chest, stomach and legs. He did not move except to breath. And that he did with achingly slow movements, though his lungs burned and sent his brain dire threats of oblivion.

The ganids wiggled and scurried over and under him.

3

Most of them abandoned him as not quite dead or fit for proper consumption. A few were not as choosy.

Stefen pressed his eyelids so tightly together that he did not think they would ever open again and gritted his teeth. One by one the lingering ganids took a hunk from his body and sauntered away to eat.

It was close to dark when the jungle noise changed pitch. The ganids quieted and disappeared. Slowly, Stefen got to his feet. The scrapes and scratches rubbed in dirt over the partially covered lava had begun to scab.

Remembering the precious amulet around his neck, he quickly checked it. The sunburst with a beautiful woman in it was cracked. The blood and dirt ground into it would wash away, but the crack would never heal. Padree had warned him time and time again that the amulet was a sacred thing the possessor guarded with his life. The fierce pounding in his head worsened.

He gathered the pouch, knife and amulet and started up the flow toward the waterfall he named Crystal Curtain. If only he could last that far. The cave behind the falls was cool and dry. It was safe. It was the Passage sanctuary.

One foot moved in front of the other over the weather-smoothed lava. The first moon rose, turning the five-petaled orbi flowers a glowing yellow to illuminate the jungle. Soon the second moon would turn the rest of the opening buds a brilliant white, brightening the undergrowth where they flourished into a false day.

The hint of his name in the gathering dark stopped him cold. He looked around frantically, knowing he was totally alone.

Ten meters ahead stood two fenwapters, a male and a female. Below and behind the flow, kervemith roared awake to prowl the night. There was no place to run and no energy left in his aching limbs.

In the bright moonlight, the male edged closer and raised onto his hind legs, claws retracted. He was a fuzzy creature with thick, short fur pale gray in color. Three eyes ran in a line that never seemed to stop near the top of his pan-shaped face. His mouth was another line Stefen had seen take shape long ago when two fenwapters fought. Jaws, filled with teeth, had popped out of nowhere. Two holes above each shoulder alternated opening and closing

4

where the creature breathed and heard the most insignificant sounds. He was small, less than a meter high.

Stefen held his ground, clutching the knife that was too big in his hand. "Get away from me."

The male paused while the female angled off the path and over the side of the flow to come up behind Stefen. The male gave ground as the female neared, forcing Stefen onto open ground away from the sides and high foliage. His head thumped as though someone were steadily pounding on it with a rock.

They followed a flat ridge up to the Crystal Curtains, which spilled into a clear pool that had no water flowers, and therefore no worm vermin. The male fenwapter circled to join his female. Both prodded Stefen onto the ledge at the giant lava spill.

The boy tried to watch them and where he was going at the same time, finally having to give up on the fenwapters. If they wanted to do him harm, they had their chance.

The rock was moss-slippery. The water felt good, washing his wounds, stinging clean the dirt-crusted scrapes. He entered the cave and gathered a handful of light-green moss which acted as a healing agent. After covering the ganid wounds, he watched the two fenwapters at the pool's edge through the Crystal Curtain.

"When I'm a man," he muttered belligerently, "I'll never be afraid. I'll make them all obey me, and I won't have to hide from the old enemy. I won't hafta run away. And I can go look for people. And I'm gonna find them if they're here. I'm gonna find 'em!"

Chapter 2

ELEVEN TIMES THE VIRGIN WAS SEDUCED BY the weaker sun in the binary system. She kept faith with the strong one, enduring the perpetual daylight as her axis wobbled through the Passage between the two ominous powers. During the journey there was no safe place upon her surface. The land opened and swallowed great segments. The seas rolled and thundered. Rain fell constantly. Volcanoes erupted out of flat ground, belched molten rock and grew majestically into black clouds laden with rain and ash.

And each time, she was soothed and lauded by the strong sun who loved her. The clouds rained themselves out, as though a power wrung them dry. The jungle flourished at an accelerated rate to heal the scars of trauma. Stability returned, as it always did after a sudden cold period. But the sun's smile upon the Virgin who existed in contradiction with the rest of the Universe warmed her again, ending the annual ninety days of chaos.

The services were short, regal and too familiar to those attending. Lozadar cor Baalan knelt in front of his parents' caskets, stone-faced to the world, grieving with soul-wrenching pain inwardly. The black-curtained room had seen too many deaths over the past score of decasets. Only one had been resultant of natural occurrences.

A devastating movement underway methodically eliminated the chain of Rulers in succession, one after the other. Lozadar eyed those around him with rightful suspicion. He was the youngest to approach the throne for more than four hundred standards, being just over twenty-five of them himself. Trust was a luxury ill affordable at the present, considering that a standard earlier he was twenty-third on the succession list and highly unlikely to have even to put in an appearance at the palace capitol.

In an hour he would stand in the sacred place, accept the crown and responsibilities, knowing the very act made him a marked man. Of course, not all those in line for the crown were dead. Some, he suspected, had found ways to contrive their demise before becoming actualities. Their names were known in all sectors, never spoken, their cowardice known, the disgrace born by their families. A few had managed to turn up freshly dead a standard after their funerals.

He reached out to touch the cold, smooth hardwood richly carved with the cor Baalan crest, wondering how he would escape the assassins and how he could protect his sisters. While they were not in line for the crown, they were in the same jeopardy that touched each of the leading houses in the Seven Worlds Federation. Whoever led the Insurrectionists commanded a healthy respect.

The most sophisticated warning detectors and devices were incapable of stopping an attack. Followers threw their lives away as easily as one would toss the garbage into a converter. Fanaticism, in an age of freedom and advanced technology, was difficult to understand, especially when the cause or reasons were as hidden as their identities.

Across the room stood Corinda dez Kaliea, the friend now destined to be his wife as a matter of alliance and protocol. He hoped the marriage would not get in the way of their lifelong friendship. If any could be trusted, Corinda could. But skepticism managed to put a veil over her, too. She nodded, as did her cousin Lisan and father.

Lozadar returned the gesture, and noted that for a thin man, Lisan was strikingly handsome. A flair for excitement clung to the man like a battle uniform under an energy-charged metal-studded cape.

Lozadar recalled the list of succession. Four more funerals until Lisan's coronation.

He turned away, leading his sisters out of the room and down the stone halls of the capitol house where the Rulers lived and the laws were made.

The palace reeked of age and death, though the air was purified and warm. The hollow sound of his boots against the polished stone floors matched a void in his heart. Prepared as he was for an attempt on his father's life, he had not expected the violent manner in which

8

death had claimed him and the sleeping woman at his side. The floor was pressure-sensitized. Lasers mounted on top of watch sensors were suspended from the ceilings, set into the walls and at ankle level throughout the room.

Still, they had been killed by something unpredictable and crude. The device tossed into the chamber proved to be a powerful enough explosive to blast out two walls and destroy all the elaborate precautions. It cost only three lives: his parents' and the attacker's.

He went to his designated room and changed for the coronation. Fortunately, it would be a short, simple affair, there having been too many of them in the last standard to justify anything but a brief ceremony loaded with armed guards and any dignitaries who happened to be in residence.

The ritual was a trimmed version, which still seemed terribly long to Lozadar. He did not want to be Ruler, nor did he feel prepared for such a vocation in the areas of both temperament and education. As the crown settled onto his head, he looked at Corinda. She still wore black. He approved. It symbolized how they both felt. The countless childhood hours spent sharing dreams on a quiet lawn or in the corner of a busy social affair brought them too close for the existence of pretense.

What both feared for nearly six decasets was a reality snaring them into walks of life incompatible with what they wanted. Worse was the knowledge of how briefly the ensnarement might last.

He stepped down from the elevated throne dais with Captain Oranda, his father's personal bodyguard, at his side. Oranda had lost better than twenty kilos since the former Ruler had taken the throne. Although he tried, Lozadar could not fault the man.

Corinda managed a faint smile when he approached. Conversations of a solemn nature hummed through the ornate expanse of the throne room, which had seen more coronations over the past two millennia than any cared to count. Lozadar turned to Oranda and whispered, "Keep an eye on the girls. Tell them to stay together and near you."

Captain Oranda nodded understanding and departed. Two men, each easily as big as the Captain, moved in as replacements.

Corinda took the arm offered to her, eyed the dignitaries and spoke through clenched teeth. "I feel like you've been invited to dinner at the Cannibal Festival on Weiaah and the desert is clinging to your arm—in gala black."

"We need to do some talking later. Privately."

"Watch what you say in this vulture nest. If you collected all the listening devices in the palace, you'd have enough to fill this room." She nodded to four men engaged in a hushed but heated conversation. They were visible through a temporary split in the crowd. "See? The vultures gather to make wagers and divvy up the spoils."

"Maybe I'll fool them all and survive." The idea appealed to him greatly.

"Then they'll hang you as the perpetrator. We can't win, my friend." She turned to him, eyes moving rapidly in her head. "There's no way out for either one of us."

He put his arm around her shoulders and nodded gravely. When he looked up, the administrators and dignitaries were coming their way. The reign of Lozadar cor Baalan, Ruler of the Seven Worlds, had just begun.

Stefen sat on a ledge in the pool filled by the Crystal Curtains. Andazu lumbered forward on his hind feet, carrying a wainor branch heavy with shanuts to the water's edge. The fenwapters had grown to their full height of a meter and a half while the boy had grown into a man of almost two meters. Stefen took the branch, pulled off a shoot and handed the rest back. Andazu settled beside Kachieo and cracked nuts. Stefen blew on the bright little yellow leaves, making them twirl-dance on their short stems. A ganid crawling along the near edge of the pool flexed all three sets of wings.

"Andazu," he said, tilting his head at the insect.

"Umph." The fenwapter turned almost imperceptibly and struck out with his claws at the ganid. His speed was always a startling thing when he appeared so relaxed. Nodding a thanks, he split the ganid in half and gave the head section to Kachieo.

The threesome shared a camaraderie which had evolved during the growing years and blossomed with maturity. At times, days passed with no spoken words. A bridge of thoughts meshed until words were unnecessary. It was something they worked at with a great amount of effort.

There seemed a barrier which might tumble at any time. It held steadfast through each endeavor.

Stefen leaned back on his elbows and tossed the wainor branch aside. "It's past the time I should have gone to the Forbidden Place. I'm leaving tomorrow. It'll be difficult to find it after so long." Head back, he watched two falizians do a mating dance in the sky. Their thin bodies were graceful as they came together, only to have the female coyly shy away. The male became more ardent in his complicated pursuit. Their transparent wings made a fluttering in the air as each of the four sets beat to the intricacies of the ritual.

"That is why you labored on the nacki leaves." Andazu cracked three shanuts by placing them between his claws and closing the stubby fingers of his forepaws.

Stefen looked at his hands. Callus on top of callus covered his palms and fingers around the sides. Even so, his hands ached from processing the leaves into a soft, durable material suitable for packs.

Kachieo ripped the branch again. "Esse suspects you are up to something." Looking around, all three eyes in different directions, he said, "He will be here soon. Will you tell him?"

"Yes." The water lost its appeal, since it had already wrinkled his lower body to the consistency of a dried batina. He climbed out to join the fenwapters at the edge. "You are welcome to travel with me." It was more a request than a polite gesture.

"We go," Andazu said in the pure pronunciation of his language.

"It will be long," Stefen responded in kind, the low, guttural tones coming easily out of his throat. The growing years had taught him many facets of survival, the most important of which was the ability to understand and form methods of communication with those sharing his demesne. The fenwapters' patience and teachings were the greatest help. He learned to listen to the falizians and the kervemith, and on the rare occasions when a yaxura ventured up from his underground realm for a jaunt, he listened to them. All knew of the friendly zuriserpants, Lords of the Great Sea beyond the landmass. The pilgrimage to the Forbidden Place would take them near the Great Sea. Perhaps he would see a Lord.

The falizians ended their ritual and settled in the top

11

of a putch. The right-angled branches made it an ideal mating spot. Heavy nacki vines, leaves half as large as Stefen was tall and flowers a bit smaller, gave them privacy. Their delight carried through the jungle and shook the fotigs growing on long stalks out of nodules on the putch branches.

Watching, Stefen felt a pang of jealousy.

Sensing his need, "After the Forbidden Place, we will search for the people your ancients mentioned." Kachieo offered half a dozen cracked shanuts to him.

Stefen smiled, took the nuts and clasped Kachieo's foreshoulder. "They were not truly ancients, as your ancients are. I don't even know where they came from, only that they were here and I am left. Perhaps the Forbidden Place holds answers for some of the questions."

A roar from the near jungle momentarily drowned out the gentle sounds of the Crystal Curtains.

"Esse," Stefen muttered.

The big kervemith had never attempted to utter Stefen's language, though he understood a great deal if it was spoken slowly. Speaking it was an impossibility because of the fang arrangement in his snout. Upper and lower ivory protruded above and below his mouth for fifteen centimeters when the mouth was closed. Many times they had tried to communicate without words. It was a vaguely successful enterprise.

Spotted-green-on-gold fur ran four meters of body before dwindling into the solid green of Esse's powerful tail. Its length equaled that of his body. Six muscular legs with five claws imbedded into each of the mammoth paws held him to a total height of two meters. A hooked horn extended thirty centimeters from the middle of his forehead. Two electrifying blue eyes, constantly moving, were surrounded by an extension of the whiskers that began at the snout. Head lowered, he moved to drink from the clear pool. The sleek lines of the predator's build and muscles rippling the short fur coat promised his bite to be worse than his horrendous growl.

The slurping noise paused. Esse licked his fangs and afforded Stefen a long glance, unblinking.

Stefen stared back, a slow smile creeping over his face. It was the closest the kervemith ever came to showing affection. Tolerance, patience, yes. Those were frequent, but not the supreme luxury of his undivided attention. The action both pleased and touched him.

Esse moved closer, skirted the vigilant fenwapters, came around to the other side and lay beside Stefen. Impressed by the show of affection, Stefen stroked the enormous head between the two pointed ears and above the horn.

"I leave tomorrow, Esse," he snarled as best he could to make the beast understand. "I'll miss you. We have been friends a long, long time."

His right forepaw clawed at the lava beside Stefen's leg, turning the black/red stone bubbles powdery white. "You will return before Passage?" the huge animal communicated with snarls.

"I can't say. I also want to search for any others of my kind living on the Virgin. I may be gone a long time." The scope of his undertaking settled into a harsh reality. There was no way of telling how long it would take to search the planet, which was what he would do before admitting defeat. It could take an entire lifetime.

A streak of light, brighter than the strong sun, flashed through the sky. A bellow, louder than the collective effort of the kervemith, shook the trees and ground. A roaring fireball hurled across the zenith, commanding the attention of all those on the Virgin's lighted side in these latitudes.

The fenwapters clung to each other, heads tilted to the east as the phenomenon disappeared. Esse, too, gave it his semidivided attention. Stefen recoiled, watching with a sneer while he scratched the kervemith a bit too harshly. Esse shook his head in warning.

"What was that?" Kachieo asked fearfully.

"I think it is my enemy," Stefen answered quietly.

The packs were filled with the treasures of his life: legi-slates of data he had read over and over, his mother's most cherished possessions, a map box Padree favored and Stefen could only partially operate. There were several handfuls of gold jewelry and a mishmash of small boxes and orbs that he knew would yield the rest of their secrets if he worked hard enough at them.

Kachieo and Andazu each wore a pack the size of Stefen's. They checked each other's burden, fondled one another intimately, reassuring themselves that all things would return as they were the day before and nothing would touch them as long as they were together.

Stefen made one last search of the cavern behind the Crystal Curtains, his home for more than half his life. Nothing was left untethered. Mentally, he said goodbye to the place and moved through the water and across the ledge and joined the fenwapters.

Several dozen of the furry creatures fawned over them, speaking in short, choppy phrases, wishing them well, promising to fix a place for the lazy sleep during Passage. One by one, Stefen recognized them as visitors brought individually to the pool. The slight changes in color ranged from an obvious light brown to pale gray. Both ends of the spectrum existed in the pair accompanying him.

He tucked the fiber-wrapped amulet into the last whole shirt in existence. It had once belonged to his father and was small on his large-muscled frame. As long as it covered enough to protect him against the sharper leaf edges it was fine. Fingering a hole near the collar, he thought dismally of working on more nacki leaves to fashion another.

The greatest treasure he possessed was strapped to his right thigh. Wiggling his shoulders to work the pack into a comfortable position, he flexed his hand and stroked the knife. Over time and countless practice sessions the blade remained sharp and gleaming.

The fenwapters closed around him, touching, petting, stroking, as though he signified a relic out of their ancient's oracles. Stefen enjoyed the affection and felt a new sadness for leaving the safety of the Crystal Curtains area. Here, he roamed the jungle day and night without fear, played with the fenwapters and occasionally a kervemith or two.

Esse roared from where the lava warred with the jungle. A second roar, not as deep-toned, followed.

The fenwapters withdrew from around Stefen, leaving him in front of Andazu and Kachieo. The main body scrambled up the lava to the top of the falls.

Esse led Asa, his mate, onto the black tongue. The green spots in her coat were richer, the gold fur brighter. Her noticeably smaller size did nothing to diminish her ferocity. The females of the species were keener hunters than the males. She hung back, her head never encroaching upon the space ahead of Esse's foreshoulder.

Puzzled, but pleased to see the kervemith one last

time, Stefen waited for Esse to approach. The fenwapters on the upper falls silenced, poised for flight and combat simultaneously. Glancing around, it suddenly occurred to him why Andazu had been chosen as their leader. None of the others had managed to overcome their innate fear of the kervemith to cohabit the same ground.

The sky was enlivened with beating wings. Falizians, led by Evaladyn the Mistress, circled overhead. She descended, hovering over the pool well out of reach of both the kervemith and the fenwapters. Her four sets of wings, invisible in the rapid movement, stirred the air. The sun caught briefly on her scales, iridescent green rainbows. Her long neck supported a large head, which shook nervously at the kervemith. Two luminous blue eyes splayed with silver took in all the surroundings at once, yet devoted their attention primarily to Stefen. Her wide beak, narrowing to a sharp, bent point, opened. Melodious words ran out in a jumble.

Stefen cleared his throat and asked for a slower rendition.

"A thing touched the land. From the stars or from the sun. I know not which. But it has defecated one of your kind. He howls at night.

"But, Stefen, he does not seem the right mate for you.

"I fear for the land. I fear for you.

"Does not your species have two kinds?

"Oh, Stefen, I have so much fear, for he is angry and rages. He must be very dangerous." She paused to inhale.

"Perhaps he is my enemy," Stefen said quietly. "Or perhaps his enemy is also mine."

"He has cursed the Deity."

Stefen's mouth opened, soundless. The kervemith stopped moving. The fenwapters recoiled. Andazu snarled.

"He cursed the Deity? Are you sure?" How could any man dare to curse the Deity who protected them from the Passage fury with his strength? A benign and loving Deity who made the clouds sweat on the jungle and made the flora abundant. The Deity was sacred. He ruled the weaker sun and both moons. Curse the Deity? An unforgivable transgression!

"Stefen, he is one of your kind. You must make the determination or we will have to make it for you. He speaks some of your first tongue which we have trouble understanding. You must make sure, for we do not wish to act unjustly."

Thumbs tucked into his braided tendril belt, Stefen nodded, inwardly uncertain and excited at the prospect of another like him upon the Virgin. "I'll observe and make a decision before going to the Forbidden Place."

Evaladyn veered right and joined her fleet. As quickly as they had appeared, they emptied the sky.

The Forbidden Place would have to wait. Stefen felt the first twinges of guilt. It had already waited too long, and why he had put off going directly after Passage was never quite clear. Much as he desired to know his origins, he also feared the answers waiting at the Forbidden Place. Why else would it be forbidden? Yet, if the enemy had sent one to find him, it was more crucial than ever to learn about himself and the enemy.

Deep in thought, he started down the lava flow and turned east, the fenwapters at his side. Esse and Asa followed, silent, vigilant.

Chapter 3

WITHIN THREE REVOLUTIONS THE ENTOU-
rage was beyond the heart of the home jungle. Evaladyn
flitted through aisles of heavy growth, guiding them toward
the Deity Curser. They spent a day in the putch trees,
evading the grabber moss spread across the ground. Stefen
cut a stalk of fotigs and dropped it into a sparse patch.
The moss shot up around the stalk and totally engulfed
it before pulling it into the bed. The action lasted less
than a hundred heartbeats.

Using cut vines, he breached gaps between putch
trees that the kervemith leaped effortlessly, and the fenwapters hurled themselves across and sank their sharp
claws into the targeted branch as a stop.

The fourth night was a true night as the Virgin moved
behind the powerful sun which shielded her from the
jealous weaker one. In a hundred days they would need
to find a place for hibernation and stock it for the long
Passage duration.

Stefen listened to the jungle—chirping ganids, the
distant waking of the kervemith and falizians nestling
in the heights.

The cracking of an old putch as it split down the middle
filled the night. A yaxura made a trip to the surface.

The noise traveled with the fragrance of orbi flowers
preparing to bloom for their respective moons. It was the
restful part of the night for the jungle. Stefen squinted to
get a glimpse of the yaxura, which was partially obscured
by deep shadows. Twelve meters long and four high, it
snaked along the ground, ingesting ganids trying to flee
from a decaying fern tree remnant of the last Passage.
From the hundred-plus meters above the jungle floor the
yaxura still looked awesome.

Stefen grabbed a dangling vine the size of his forearm,
tugged and swung to the next putch tree. Below, the

yaxura vented his external lungs and dove into the ground. Ahead, light flickered against the nacki ceiling woven over a small clearing. It was an eerie manifestation, foreign to the Virgin wilds.

Stefen moved down the perpendicular branch he had used as a stop and tied off the vine. It was a straight walk of nine paces until he had to go around another rising branch. The light touch of his feet on the slippery bark was responsible for his silent approach. The heart of the tree was open above the center leader which had snapped into a jagged growth Passages ago.

Through a maze of fotig stalks, withered nacki leaves curled into tight rolls and putch leaves, he saw a man sitting crosslegged beside a fire.

The fire was as intriguing as the man. He had not seen one in a small, controlled area since Padree had died. The man cooked ganids on a sheet of twisted metal held over the flame. The smell was vaguely familiar and brought back memories of his parents when he was small and they were healthy.

Across the clearing Esse was perched on a fat limb. Asa was above him and slightly to Stefen's left. Andazu and Kachieo were in separate trees on his right. They watched for half the night, long after the man slept fitfully on the ground and the embers were dim among the clustered rocks.

Stefen worked the kinks out of his muscles while climbing down to another branch. Once at the edge of the clearing he was well behind the Deity Curser. On the ground, belly down, the knife went between his teeth. Elbowing forward, his eyes were fixed on his target. Barely breathing, he became a part of the Virgin's night, blending with the jungle and the soft earth. A kervemith was no more deadly than Stefen when he stalked his prey.

The front jungle erupted. A giant tree creaked and groaned, listing dangerously to the side until the nacki vines stabilized it. Kachieo tumbled, striking branch after branch, claws extended to grasp at the limbs. The yaxura bellowed oxygen into the air and retreated into his freshly made hole.

The man sat up straight, his knife in hand, facing the dazed fenwapter who was struggling to get on all fours. Andazu swung from limb to limb, unable to get to his mate fast enough.

18

Kachieo floundered closer to the Deity Curser. He began to rise, braced on one knee, slowly getting to his feet. Left arm poised slightly away from his body, he flipped the knife into a stabbing position and started to move around the firepit.

Andazu loosed an ear-splitting scream.

The man spun toward the sound.

Stefen sprung. His left arm flew at the man's wrist, and and pulled it high behind his back. The knife just behind the jawbone below the right ear-stantly, the man froze and dropped his weapon.

dazu bounded to the ground beside his mate, quickly g her over and running his immense paws over her ction. She moaned and garbled enough words to m know she would be all right.

er out of here," Stefen ordered, feeling the man hard rigidity at the sounds of the fenwapter ing languages, "Esse! Asa! Come down." knife away, applied pressure to the ed to the ground. The man was pulled the firepit. Stefen squatted behind, feet de, a good distance between the man's back and his chest.

He felt rather than heard or saw the kervemith on each side of him. For a split second, he relaxed.

The Deity Curser seized the advantage, lunged to the left and grabbed Stefen's knife. Once Stefen released the man's wrist, the element of surprise increased.

He fought to pull away by using brute strength. When it failed, he shifted positions and found himself being hurled through the air and over the man's shoulder. He fell squarely in front of the Curser.

In a heartbeat, he was on top of Stefen. The knife caught a glint of starlight as it trembled midway between the two. They struggled, putting pressure on each other. The outworlder gained, only to be pushed back. His desperation to thwart the nighttime attacker did not bow easily to the exhaustion trembling through the muscles under his distended veins. Grunts and raspy breathing filled the breach between them with tiny beads of moisture.

Esse snarled loudly.

The invader flinched.

Stefen threw his arm and torso to the left, pushing

right with his legs. An upward heave unseated the man. "Stay, Esse!"

Stefen rolled to his feet, listening to the man grope for his knife. The urge to spring as a fenwapter or kervemith became tempered by caution. This was a man who capitalized on the smallest fluctuations. He could be expecting it, Stefen mused, and already have the knife.

Circling the stone firepit, he listened for the man and smelled fear in a strong perspiration foreign to the night. In the quiet, the man breathed loudly.

Stefen grinned. "Esse, back to the jungle."

Feeling the kervemith depart, Stefen also retreated the black shadows of night, leaving his opponent in the clearing. Quietly, he moved up a putch watched.

The first moon started over the horizon, bring the yellow light of the orbi flowers to bright and cast a soft illumination on the trem ing his knife. Alone.

The man turned slowly, listening, jungle, sweat running down his face. eyes flashed as he looked in all directions versary. The second moon was well into the sky before he took a step toward the dead fire. With a head-shaking shrug, he dropped crosslegged and waited for dawn.

Stefen watched the outworlder for the entire day as the man hauled his meager belongings north, fighting the dense jungle every step of the way. He looked around constantly, knowing there was something formidable dogging him.

The five in the trees took turns resting, eating and occasionally napping. The fenwapters played and disappeared for a while for the privacy of mating. It was a leisurely day for them.

At times, Stefen wondered how the Deity Curser had managed to cover the distance since Evaladyn's horde first detected him. It was amazing that his ineptitude in the jungle had not killed him.

By nightfall the man showed definite signs of exhaustion. He did not bother to make a fire and ate the two small ganids he found raw. His bundle served as a pillow. His knife, approximately the same size as Stefen's, filled his right hand.

Before moonrise, Stefen crept up on the man, stealthily blending in with the fusci ferns and high moss grass. His breathing melted into the breeze, never stirring the fragile greenery out of turn. Carefully, movement duplicating the heavy rise and fall of the snoring body, the bundle was slipped out from under the dark head. Packed moss replaced it. Stefen slunk back to the ferns and passed the bundle to Andazu.

Moving in on the opposite side, he watched the man for a long time in order to gauge the depth of fatigue evident in the sleep. Gingerly, he took the tip of the knife between his thumb and forefinger and slipped it from the Deity Curser's hand.

Morning sounded with an irate barrage of curses. The man shook his fist at the sky, swearing revenge upon the scum who had placed him here to die in torment.

Stefen understood most of the garbled words. They were of a language whose purity belonged to the past. It took several hundred heartbeats for him to realize that he no longer spoke the language of his parents. The years and the multitude of jungle vernaculars had forced an evolution into it. Words like these had not been heard for more than eleven Passages, and only overheard by him. Padree had forbidden cursing and swearing in his son's presence.

He watched, enthralled by the rantings, relearning words and emphases. Gradually, he noticed incongruities about the man. The richly embroidered garb, now torn at the fringes, did not coincide with the powerful build of the man waving his shirt in the air, muscles rippling with each movement. The manner in which he had worked on the jungle the previous day displayed a fine skill with the knife, but an unfamiliarity with rugged terrain. He did not seem to be afraid to work himself to death, and might accomplish that end if he did not employ some labor-saving methods, such as traveling through the trees where the jungle was too thick. The Deity could not be too offended at this man's alleged transgression, or He had great patience, Stefen decided. The man had not run into any grabber moss yet.

Stefen climbed down to the lowest horizontal branch of the tree, squatted and observed the man closer.

Eventually, the man spotted him. The shirt fell to the ground, his arms loose at his sides, knees slightly bent.

His eyebrows lowered over a topaz stare which bored holes into Stefen. Fingers together, palms out, he motioned for Stefen to come and face him in the light of day.

Grinning, Stefen refused, head shaking.

"Who are you?" The words came harshly through clenched teeth.

Thinking, speaking slowly while searching for the correct pronunciation, he said, "I am Stefen, Judge of Man upon the Virgin. All the land you see, I claim. Why do you trespass? What do you seek? Me?"

Fleeting bewilderment turned into disbelief, then incredulity. "I am Lozadar cor Baalan, Ruler of the Seven Worlds." Snorting, "At least I was for three days." Hands on hips, "Trespass? Not by choice. And what I seek, I don't think you can provide."

"Tell me."

Lozadar grinned, turning his head slightly. His change in attitude indicated an end to his anger and a strong desire to find something to hope in. "How about a starship? Nothing fancy, just something spaceworthy?"

Brow furrowed as he tried to comprehend the request, Stefen shook his head.

"Oh, well." He sighed, exhaling the hope that was too good in the first place. "I didn't think so. How about a flask of wine and a good woman?" Lozadar's grin broadened. The change allowed his despair to show. In spite of the grin, he looked defeated.

"No," Stefen answered wistfully.

"I'll settle for my knife and the bundle you—ah—borrowed."

"You have been accused of cursing the Deity."

Perplexed, Lozadar's grin faded. "I've cursed a lot of things and a score of people, but I don't remember taking on anything called a 'Deity.' "

Stefen glanced beyond the man to where Esse and Asa stood, waiting.

"Mind telling me what a Deity is?"

"The Deity is the benign lifegiver and protector. He is the true sun which the Virgin is faithful to during Passage. He is the supreme force which helps us live here. Without Him, there would be no life on the Virgin. To curse the Deity—"

"Look, I've been through a lot in the last thirty days. I've become the Ruler of the Seven Worlds because of the succession lines. That lasted three days. Of course, as soon as that happened, I was supposed to marry my oldest and closest friend because of her genealogy.

"My family has been murdered—atrociously. And I've survived abduction, laser fire, blindfolded battles, just to be dropped here." The words tumbled out without thought, needing to be spoken to someone. "Now, this isn't the first time in history this has happened. It couldn't possibly be. It's just the first time it's happened to me.

"Consequently, I've cursed a lot of things, none of which even vaguely resembles what you're describing. But if you want to accuse me of cursing your Deity, go ahead. I can hardly stop you. You're in charge. I was sent here to die, so you may as well do what you're going to do. I yield." He threw his arms up in the final gesture of defeat.

"You do not seem like a man who yields this easily," Stefen said cautiously.

"Easily?" Lozadar put his head back and laughed. It was a sad sound, bordering insanity. The red around his eyes heightened a sense of unpredictability about him. His hair, matted by filth, parted above his eyebrows and dripped perspiration, which ran down the sides of his face and into the dark growth ranging the remnants of an olive complexion. The tension in his stance strained his body visibly. "I know you've watched me. Do I look as if I can survive here without even a knife? Hell, I'm a pragmatist." Jerking his thumb back, "Are those the executioners?"

Stefen was still trying to analyze "pragmatist" as he considered the man's behavior. Finally, "If you were not cursing the Deity, what were you doing?"

A quick shrug preceded the answer. "I don't know. Probably showing my appreciation and gratitude for the ride here and the luxurious accommodations awaiting the former Ruler of the Seven Worlds."

"You are not ruler here!" The quick speech neither matched the voice timbre nor the sporadic hand gestures. It was confusing.

"That is quite true, so I didn't expect much." Sitting, "If you don't expect much, you aren't often disappointed." One finger raised, "However, that does not always work either. I didn't expect you. There anybody else around here? How about a higher court?"

"I do not know 'court,' but there is no one here except me. I wait for the old enemy and wonder if he is you."

"Since we just introduced ourselves, I can hardly be classified as an old enemy." Lozadar relaxed, preferring a conversation with the man in the trees to his friends breathing down his neck. "If there are no people here, how did you happen to choose this place to retire?"

"Retire?" Another strange term not covered in the the books he owned or explained in childhood.

"Sorry. How did you get here? And why the hell am I asking all these questions if I'm not losing my mind?"

Unsure of what else to do, Stefen answered, "My people are dead for eleven Passages. I am all that is left."

After a thoughtful moment, "Do you have a heavy schedule, or can we talk outcast to loner for a while? I'd hate to die not knowing if I'm crazy."

Stefen regarded the man for several hundred heartbeats, trying to dissect the idiosyncrasies of his personality, the sarcasm and overall good nature totally unbecoming a man in his position. Eventually, he conceded his lack of knowledge where his own species was concerned. The Virgin's children were another matter. They would not wait long for a verdict. And the enemy was cunning. Padree had said so often.

Chapter 4

Stefen listened to Lozadar's tale for half a day. At times, Lozadar paused for hundreds of heartbeats, visibly shaken by the account which exposed his soul to the loner in the trees. A week of treachery left him all that remained of the House of cor Baalan. Stonily, he related the tale of Captain Oranda, Chief Protector of the cor Baalan House and those who had once composed it.

The Insurrectionists' propensity to strike when the victim was lulled into a fleeting sense of security was well known. Admittedly, Lozadar did not think such a state could exist after the coronation. But the sustenance of an attitude ripe with suspicion and fright lasted only so long before his normal personality made a chink in the armor protecting him.

However, Captain Oranda did not possess such a basic flaw in his character. He was born mistrusting both the medic and his mother. That attitude grew stronger after the deaths of the elder cor Baalans. It was a virtue, once engaged by loyalty to either a person, cause or house, that made him one of the most dedicated and valuable Protectors in the realm.

Other than a serious nature, there was nothing else spectacular about the super-soldier. He had been around all of Lozadar's life, looking much the same over the last twenty-four out of twenty-five standards. The last standard had aged Oranda well beyond his years. It also honed his mental skills as his role of Protector became more than a title he took seriously. The twins, Chalate and Corry, were as special to him as they had been to their parents, products of a reblossoming of the love affair the elder cor Baalans always managed to keep excitingly alive.

He stood out in a crowd, never managing to control the blond mop stretched into a neatly trimmed beard cut low as fashion presently dictated. As though size happily wedded silence, Oranda was a presence controlling the most potentially unruly gathering; strong, yet gentle to the privileged few he loved in his lifetime.

He had been in the chamber with Lozadar when the Insurrectionists exploded the lock bolts on the door. Immediately, he went on the defensive, firing his Lat-kor at the flood of humanity surging through the door. Their numbers had been staggering. They had crawled over one another, firing through their own masses to score a hit in the royal chamber.

An overpowering stench lingered in ghost senses whenever Lozadar remembered the smoke and blood carnage oozing through the massive metal-core wooden doors.

Oranda kept firing, edging closer and closer to his Armco rifle, carrying a double power pack fully charged. He hit the most dangerous attackers charging over the cadaver pile, careful to conserve his supply, never off target.

He yelled: nonsensical words to the Insurrectionists, well-defined instructions to Lozadar.

Wall decorations, furniture, thick carpets and the bed were aflame. The room heated to an unbearable temperature. Fire retardants flooded from the ceiling. The chemical mist proved to be to the enemy's benefit. Combined with the smoke, it stung permeable membranes, teared the eyes and clouded vision.

Lozadar found his own Lat-kor and fired, trying to fill the gap while Oranda picked up his Armco. Six bursts laid waste to the whole corridor and the room beyond, taking with it the men trying to get into the chamber.

Oranda took advantage of the pyre-induced lull to shove Lozadar into the connecting passage opening at the rear wall. He stood prepared to shoot until the wall closed.

For a few breathable seconds, it was completely dark in the tunnel. The scratching sounds Oranda made were inconsequential to Lozadar. Each time he blinked he saw again the stringy tissue clinging to an exposed bone—an arm bone, he thought, the humerus. The elbow and shoulder lay somewhere else.

The gore repulsed him. It denied him anger and spontaneous retaliation. Shock, he thought, trying to put the world back together all at once and be a part of the life-and-death battle going on all around them. The total absence of light lent a false security in anonymity.

"I'm going to check on your sisters." Captain Oranda's voice carried the same calm, positive assurance it carried when times were good. The tone acted to fortify Lozadar. "You're safer here than anywhere else in the palace. I don't think I can get you out right now. Lordy! There's a lot of those bastards, Loz."

Abandoning the formalities required in public, the Captain's huge left hand plopped onto Lozadar's shoulder in reassurance. The action scared Lozadar enough to make him jump. These were troubled times, and Lozadar was still more of a nephew or son than the Ruler of the Seven Worlds.

When Lozadar reached out to get his bearings, Oranda was gone, silently on his way to the twins. He waited, the darkness washing over him like a satin oil; comforting, soothing, at first, then stifling, pressing in on all sides, the sounds leaking through the old masonry wall billowing a new sensation of fear which tried to smother him.

His right hand shook as he ran it through dark-brown hair he expected to be white or gray by the time the night was over. A jumble of voices, hard-soled boots on the old stone floor, and the rustling of metal-studded capes, all came through a corridor on the left he had not known existed a few minutes earlier. Frantic, he looked around for a magical direction light to point the way to safety.

Moving cautiously, he spread his hands wide and felt the wall. Silently, he turned to slide along the sides. It was cold in the passage, yet he perspired heavily. Jelly replaced his bones. Anxiety sapped his strength until the Lat-kor weighed as much as a corpse. A nonviolent man by nature and subdued by culture, Lozadar wanted to avoid a confrontation with the Insurrectionists for a number of reasons, the least of which was his inexperience with hand-to-hand combat.

Methodically, he continued moving, not caring where the corridor took him, just making sure he kept a good distance from those exploring the escape passage behind him. It took a sharp turn. He stumbled, caught himself and followed the turn, afraid his clumsy actions were heard.

A new urgency flowed through him. He hurried, hoping for another side passage to further confuse the marauders. The offshoot dead-ended. Heart thundering in his temples, he used both hands to grope for a trip. One of his touches produced a click. A small door swung open.

He ducked through, pushing it closed without letting it click back into the lock. After a few seconds his eyes adjusted to the familiarity of the dimly lit room. It belonged to his sisters, or so he thought.

He moved out of the shadowy niche between a huge fireplace preserved from the ancient times, and an ornate entertainment center. Trying to listen and look in all directions, he did not pay much attention to where he was going. Something reached out to trip him. His own weight hurled him forward. He stumbled awkwardly for several steps before recovering. Mentally, he cursed and glanced back to see what it was.

Captain Oranda lay writhing on the floor, both arms strangely twisted where there were no joints. Agony deformed his features. Blood spewed from out of his mouth where his teeth had once been. The abundance of the blood obscured a score of additional head wounds. Holes, three centimeters in diameter, had been burned through his legs in circular patterns. Lozadar looked away, nauseated. There had to be several dozen just where he could see.

Bile filled his throat. He tried swallowing the foul taste, unsuccessfully, then bent and pulled the Captain by the cloak ties on his shoulders until he was out of immediate view behind the entertainment center. He gagged several times as new, uglier wounds were exposed. The man was alive. For now.

Oranda's lips moved, his eyes imploring, jittering, then begging Lozadar to listen to his soundless mouth.

"Shhhh, I'll come back. You're going to be all right. By God, you'd better be. I'm not cut out for this." Adjusting the cloak into a pillow, "See? You should've taught me this kind of stuff when I asked. Now I have to wing it." He managed a smile and turned away before it became a wince. "I'll do all right, Oranda. You weren't my only source of learning, just my best one."

The words summoned a false confidence. He stepped out from behind the entertainment center.

The pale-blue wall coverings flecked with tiny white flowers were splattered by crimson, drying to brown stains. He stared at the walls, able to pick out subtle distortions in the patterns flaking away. It was easier to fix his gaze on the wall than on the source ahead. Bits of flesh, he realized, strips, like hide. . . .

He threw up the bile accumulated in his stomach. The retching continued, convulsing, as his eyes took in the sisters on the floor.

The escape door banged open.

Lozadar remembered hearing it and ignoring the danger.

The Insurrectionists swarmed over him, dragging him closer to his sisters, forcing his head down to inspect the little patch of skin on Corry's arm where her birthmark remained intact.

Lozadar paused, unable to describe what he saw in detail, blotting it out as though by not looking at it, it had never happened. Pressed by Stefen, he mumbled, "Rape" and a clinical definition.

The killing Stefen could understand. Padree had taught him the necessity of killing when threatened or for food, shelter and the requirements of life. But needless assault? That was foreign to the Virgin.

"Do not the females of the species go through the ritual and mate with any who choose them?" Stefen asked, perplexed by the social mores Lozadar implied.

The question left the outcast speechless, then made him laugh the first genuine laugh since before the nightmare began. "Oh, there is a ritual," Lozadar said, still chuckling, "but it would take a long, long time to explain it to you, Stefen. A very long time, and then it would change with every woman you met."

A knot inside Stefen formed and tightened. Was it possible that if people were found on the Virgin none of them would want to mate with him? It was a horrifying thought. Peering down his nose at Lozadar, "Never laugh at me."

In surprise the smile vanished and Lozadar stood below the tree to gaze up at Stefen's emotionless face. "I wasn't laughing at you. Apparently there is a great latitude of misunderstanding between the world you know and the one I did. I was laughing at how germane the term 'ritual' is, and the mistakes I've made, the chances I had and didn't take. . . . It really is a ritual, yet there is no set pattern.

"Perhaps it is the same kind of misunderstanding which gave you a reason to believe I cursed something you hold precious.

"No, Stefen, I'm many things, but not malicious enough to deride a God I don't know, nor to intentionally offend those who have not wronged me. I've been on the receiving end of that too often."

Evaladyn led the falizians into the treetops and hung in the air, awaiting the judgment. An unnatural quiet befell the jungle, keeping even the independent kervemith in place. This was not the time for petty power wars wherein a creature was killed or survived. It was a period of tenuous peace in respect for the Virgin and her lover, the Deity, Giver of Life.

Stefen swung down from the tree and faced Lozadar, who was almost his height. Calmly, "Should your life be spared, would you be willing to prepare for the Test of Worth? Would you be willing to subject yourself to what the Virgin deals to you?"

Lozadar opened his mouth, but Stefen continued. "Should you agree to this, you will wish yourself with your sisters long before you are. And, if you betray me with words, and you are my enemy, there will come a time when I will know. Then you will wish you had spoken now. So I ask, are you my enemy?"

"No, I am not your enemy."

"Did you curse the Deity?"

Lozadar thought about it for a few seconds before deciding on total honesty. "In truth, I don't know. If I did, it was not done knowingly or consciously."

Stefen nodded, seeing what he considered truth in the man's unguarded expression.

Shrugging, "I was angry and cursed many things I personally held sacred. For that, I'm ashamed, which is a big thing for me to admit to anyone. Looking at you, I know my life as I knew it is over. Whether or not another way exists is up to you. That doesn't excite me a hell of a lot right now. But there are a few things you should consider.

"The doors of trust and friendship swing both ways.

I told you my origin. There would be large gaps of understanding between you and me. It could be very trying. You would have to bend, too. If you don't think you can—hey, end it now. I'll go easily. Later . . . well, who knows?" He sank to the ground. Depression and fatigue seeped into the marrow of his bones.

The man was a host of incongruities, beaten, yet courageous, openly emotional, yet callous in his ability to analyze, considerate of the opposite side of a question; the question of his life. No, he did not make sense in the realm Stefen knew. He studied the man—dethroned of his birthright, isolated from his civilization, removed, forever, from those he loved either by distance or death. That part of the man he could understand, sharing a rebirth of his own isolation. He tried to measure the inner strength of the dejected outworlder withdrawn to some inner hell on the ground before him.

Many of those in the settlement had been physically strong, but their spirits had been weak. They did not embrace the Virgin. The price for their disparity had been death; there was nothing to live for without that belief. She was an unforgiving hostess.

For half a heartbeat, he wondered what made him so different. The colonists had shunned him as though he carried the death fever which befell so many of them. Others wandered, some ran, into the jungle, where the beasts dealt a swift death. Inwardly he smiled, remembering his trial of survival lasting eleven Passages. The worst had come right after Padree's death.

He focused on the outworlder, empathizing more than he cared too.

Lozadar did not look up.

If this is my enemy, he is truly formidable, Stefen concluded. *He has been in circumstances like this before, or perhaps he is used to wielding much power, and this is a ploy to find my strengths and weakness. It would not be unlike the kervemith stalking his prey. Yet . . . he seems to accept he may have offended us and cursed the Deity, even without knowing himself.*

Finding no quick resolution, he turned, snarled at Esse and climbed the putch to its highest branches, where Evaladyn waited.

"What is your judgment, Stefen?"

Balanced on an extended limb, he reached out and

31

stroked the Mistress's face, soothing her. The thin branch bounced with each movement. "It is difficult to say. There is a great area of no understanding. He is very alien, one of my kind, yet not my kind. I believe him when he says he did not curse the Deity with foreknowledge. I also believe him when he does not deny the act."

Evaladyn shivered, the complexity of the situation too great in the black-and-white world of the falizians. "Either he did, or he did not."

Stefen smiled. "What do those who heard him say?"

"They cannot be sure. Their grasp of your language is loose. The man does not speak properly!" She eyed the kervemith glancing up at them from both sides of the outworlder.

"He will live, Evaladyn. He will be readied to face the Trial of Worth. If he doesn't survive it . . ." He shrugged.

"If he does, then we know the Deity smiles upon him, in which case he is forgiven or innocent.

"Besides, I would like to learn from him. I think there is much he can teach me in relationship to my own kind."

Stefen was silent for a moment, watching Lozadar, sitting dwarfed by the kervemith. Evaladyn nudged him gently. "If he is my enemy and survives, I will have loosed a terrible thing upon the Virgin. Men will come by the thousands with their machines and rape the land, just as Lozadar's sisters were." Looking into the blue eyes, "Impossible to understand, this thing called rape. The Deity would become angry and no longer look upon the Virgin with favor should the machines change her surface and litter it with false bones or metal mountains. I have lived in a false shelter made from scavenged pieces of ships. Outworlders cannot live here without them—at least, they do not choose to."

Rubbing his forehead with both thumbs, fingers laced into a pyramid, "I don't know, Evaladyn. I can't say, 'Take his life,' for he has already suffered greatly and may be innocent. Too, he could have been guided here by the power of the Deity." He glanced at the sun riding the western sky burdened with black clouds bringing the daily shower.

Evaladyn moaned sympathetically at the Judge of Man. "It is one thing to allow him to live for the test, but, Stefen, please, do not take him as mate!"

He smiled quickly, keeping his head low. "I would prefer one of the opposite sex, Evaladyn. While the need is great, I believe I would find more satisfaction with a female. Perhaps the falizians will assist me in locating any other of my kind upon the Virgin."

Evaladyn flexed her wings as a warning for Stefen to retreat. In a flurry, the horde responded and disappeared into the wind. "We will seek, Stefen. But you are unkind to make me worry about you."

Stefen climbed down, wondering if his own mother could have been any more protective than Evaladyn over these last seven Passages.

Moist, hot breath from the kervemith pumped down on Lozadar, suffocating him by degrees. He stood, stealing a glance at the largest one, decided he liked it better when he couldn't appreciate their awesome size. Somehow, the preparations for becoming either Legate of the cor Baalan House or Ruler of the Seven Worlds, had failed to include survival techniques, except those which he had been able to coerce out of the seasoned Colonial Federation Army generals and the reluctant Captain Oranda.

With nothing else to do but watch Stefen in the trees, he found it surprising to feel a pang of envy for the absolute simplicity the man enjoyed on this hostile world. The Virgin he called her, Lozadar mused. Appropriate.

The planet had been known about for centuries, though why it had failed to fall into one or the other of the two mighty stars pulling on it was a mystery which defied all known logic and physical laws. It was teeming with life—another unnatural phenomenon. At best, it should be a burned out cinder, void of atmosphere, parched down to mantle rock and pitted by meteors.

Exhaling sharply, which drew a longer than usual glance from both kervemith, Lozadar thought about the two moons—the greatest inconsistency of all. But the moons brought reminders of night. And night brought horrible nightmares and memories into a vivid reality.

For an instant, his mind flashed back cruelly to Antition.

The twins were sprawled on the blue carpet. Blood everywhere. *My God! How can there be so much blood*

33

in two frail girls? It was on the divans, floor, walls, tables, even splattered on the high ceiling.

His stomach pitched as it had then, rolling up into his throat as the marauders seized him and threw him onto the floor between them. They were two slabs of raw meat, slivers of skin peeled away, legs splayed wide, Chalate's left one dislocated at the hip and twisted.

A half-crazed youth, bolstered by drugs that made his eyes dilated and red with glaze, knelt and began fondling Corry's adolescent breasts. Lozadar slapped his hands away and was hauled up by several of the older men, who encouraged the youth to continue.

Lozadar heard himself screaming; threats, curses, animal sounds.

Then they were all looking at him. The cold steel of the leader's knife drew blood from beside his left ear. A defense mechanism silenced him.

"You livin' here so fine, you have any hole you want ta fill. Us . . . well, we don't live so good. Our women get worn out quick. We gotta share them. So, you don't mind so much if the boy there humps hisself dry on one of them, do ya? It isn't as though she's objectin'."

The laughter burned in his mind.

"And I think you ought to watch. Ya might learn something. Besides, if you don't, you won't see anything else so long as you live. The Iron General wouldn't like that too much. He's partial to his precious colonies, an' the Ruler here done helped him out."

Laughter, foul laughter, pungent breath . . . Iron General. Iron General. Stuhart Myzillion—the Iron General —the man to hate with all his being. *God! how could I have been so wrong? How could I have picked the wrong people to trust all my life?*

"Are you all right?"

Before him stood the clear hazel eyes of the jungle man. Lozadar nodded, his brain burned with resurgent hatred.

"Put your fear aside. Your life is mine, for a time. I'll work you hard."

"There's no fear left in me, only pain and hate," he whispered to no one.

Stefen felt uncomfortable and jumped up to grab the low branch of the big putch. "Come on."

Esse and Asa whined jointly. Stefen whined back,

sending them a small distance from the outcast. They stayed close enough to prevent an escape.

Rain began to fall. Lozadar concentrated on the present. The trees were slippery when dry. Wet, they felt impossible. He watched where and how Stefen placed his feet, then tried to duplicate the moves. He lacked the agility and grace of a kervemith which Stefen possessed. Branches slapped at him. They cut his skin where his clothing left it exposed. The leaves made delicate slices along his ankles, reminding him of his sisters. For the millionth time he wondered why he was alive. It would have been better to have been killed . . . but perhaps that was the whole idea behind this form of execution.

Slowly, it dawned on him that whoever the traitor was in Antition's tightest circles, he knew his prey well and sought to break each member of the presiding royal family before death alleviated the torment.

Following the fenwapters and Stefen, he dimly thought of them as his future, denying simultaneously, that the future would be worth living with the emptiness and hate embroiling him.

They moved through the trees, crossing on nacki for the rest of the day. By the time they descended into a clearing ringed by moss Lozadar's hands were lumps of bloody skin where thin calluses made by his knife handle were pink and swollen underneath. His ankles and feet were a swollen mass covered by fine lines and caked blood.

Stefen took Lozadar's bundle from Andazu and tossed it to the ground. "Make fire."

He rummaged through it, brought out an instone, struggled to his feet and pulled down dried putch leaves and empty fotig stalks. In lieu of rocks, he scraped out a hole with a sharp branch and set the kindling in the center. He pushed the side of the instone. A flame jumped at the crumpled leaves and ignited.

Stefen dropped dead pieces of branches from high in the trees and brought down a stalk of fotigs. In silence, the branches were built into a pyramid over the kindling and sorted off to the side by size. Lozadar stared at his hands and feet denying the new sources of pain.

The moss at the edge of the clearing looked fresh and crisp. Little beads of moisture on top of the green puffs would be sufficient to clean his hands. He started toward it, hoping it possessed some kind of natural healing agent.

Stefen tossed one of the larger fire branches at the bed just in front of Lozadar. The moss pillared into the air, engulfed the flaming wood and slurped it into the ground, then looked as though nothing had happened.

Lozadar, stunned by the swift display, recovered and continued toward the bed. How easy, he thought through the black depression rolling in waves, piercing his being, a depression that only built and never receded. So easy. So quick. So final. It hurts no one and offends nothing.

The green lured him as the night tantalizes the day with a colorful dawn.

Chapter 5

CORINDA DEZ KALIEA WATCHED THE CHRONometer floating in the wall. "It's about that time," she muttered, shifting, relacing her fingers in her lap for the fifth time in as many minutes. She counted off the seconds and watched the door when the double zeroes flashed.

Part of the wall disappeared. General Myzillion hesitated, then strode through. As the door closed behind him, he arched his leg over the second chair in the quarters which had been his. He settled in and folded his arms over the scrolled white back.

For several moments no words were exchanged. The quiet became so absolute that a faint hum from the air-purification system filled the gulf between them.

The three-decaset journey, spiced with several battles that she knew about and a half dozen that she did not, had taken their toll. She was ghostly thin and pale, her olive skin transparent. But there was still a bright spark in her eyes. Stuhart Myzillion used those gray beacons as a gauge. If they dimmed . . .

He refused to think of that happenstance. "Look, I've got—"

"There are some—"

The flurry of words ended as abruptly as it began. Each was more than willing to let the other speak first. Corinda studied her hands some more, took a deep breath and began.

"I've done a lot of thinking." An empty laugh nearly stopped her cold. "Suppose I did accept your explanation for, well, for why you were in Antition. And I acknowledge the apparent debt I would then have to you for getting me out of there. You've never told me why you did it, or what you want. I mean, why me? I'm nothing to you. The House of dez Kaliea doesn't pay ransom or rescue fees. That's common knowledge." Morose, she found a smudge on the floor to stare at. "We let them keep—"

"You would not have liked the alternative. I found Loz's sisters. Death was the best thing to happen to them."

Corinda's mouth opened, then closed again. She could not meet his straightforward gaze while remembering them as they were in the garden the morning before they died.

When she did focus her attention on the man across the quarters she saw him in a different light, one filtered by a screen catching her hostilities. A big man, easy to see in any room or on an open battlefield, he was fair-complected, with the washed-out traces of a million freckles in childhood. The temper attributed to those with golden-red hair had been tamed somewhere along the line, though she did not want to see it loosed in her direction. Bottled, it was bound to be awesome when released.

On the positive side, he was a brilliant strategist when it came to close fighting against the Insurrectionists who attempted to raid the colonies. Consequently, he had become somewhat a legend. Not one successful attack had been waged against the colonies for over two standards. He did what he did well.

He straightened in the chair, suddenly looking authoritative. "We've received a message from main Colonial Fleet. I've got to leave for a while. You'll be taken care of. In fact, I've made plans for you to be taken down to the surface of 4724Y to get some exercise. I'd like to see you looking more as you did in Antition, Lady Corinda." He glanced at the chrono and stood.

Never had he cut his visit short before, even when they were staring matches. Alarmed, Corinda suddenly found a thousand things to say in order to keep him. The isolation of the quarters became stifling when he headed for the door and bowed a formal goodbye.

She jumped to her feet, reached out and touched his arm. "Will you be gone very long? You are coming back, aren't you? You're not going to just leave me . . ."

Off guard, he began to smile. His reaction embarrassed her to silence. She turned away.

"I'll be back as soon as I can. I've got a battle to plan and fight." Bitterly, "A battle for a government who won't give the colonies the sweat off their . . ." He sighed heavily. "I'll miss our staring contests, Corinda."

Without turning, "If you resent the treatment from the Seven Worlds, why do you go fight for them?"

"Ya gotta believe in something to make life worth while. I believe in the colonies and want to see them incorporated into the Seven. It's a mutually advantageous move.

"Besides, I'm going to die someday, and who's going to fight back the Insurrectionists then? We need the military supply and support. We don't have the manufacturing capabilities, and won't for at least ten standards. The Seven need our resources and brainpower. And there was—I hope somewhere is—a man I believe in more than the government.

"Goodbye, Lady Corinda."

The door had closed before she turned around to stare at it. "Good luck, Hart, both in the battle and in finding Loz." The next hour passed in trying to find the reasons why she spent so much time resenting and defying him instead of speaking. Looking around, it was better than Antition was now.

"In your world, is there honor in dying the death that makes your enemy happy?" The fire warmed Stefen from the chill sweeping along the ground. Lozadar's aberrant behavior disturbed him. Andazu and Kachieo nestled up on both sides, each wide-eyed at the stranger and fearful of something they could not comprehend.

Lozadar paused, contemplating the smooth green death arrayed before him like a good night's sleep lasting forever.

"Why don't you save yourself for the Virgin's Test of Worth?"

The green took on tiny distractions. The moss was not smooth. It was millions of minute tentacles growing out of one another in intricate patterns. The ends were sharp, like the needles of memory puncturing his brain. The horrors he had survived and witnessed were so much clearer in the wake of his painful hands and feet. Muscles he did not know existed pulled and throbbed after less than a full day with Stefen and his unusual traveling companions. How would he survive a decaset of days, let alone tomorrow? For what? To be stranded with no hope for revenge? To be the subject of some jungle man, his strange gods and animals? That was living?

Stefen cracked a fotig with his knife handle.

The intensity of the noise jarred Lozadar. The moss sea lost some of its lure. The menace it represented became enthralling. Were he alone the green might have claimed him earlier without foreknowledge of death or a conscious decision. Inwardly he sneered. The humiliation of ignorance would have lasted only seconds. A new idea crept out of his despair.

"Stefen, can you teach me the jungle? Can you teach me how to live here?" His voice was a shaky whisper loud only in its indecision.

A sliver of fotig pulp paused in front of Stefen's mouth. "Yes." He popped the food in.

"When? How long will it take?" He sounded a bit stronger as he stood barely out of reach of the grabber moss bunching and heaving at the shore.

"I'm still learning." Another fotig left the stalk with a snap. "The land changes with distance. I haven't explored much beyond my home. I'll teach you what I know as quickly as you can learn it." Glancing up, "If you do want to learn, you had better step back before the moss finishes piling for a lunge."

He hesitated, still indecisive, watching the moss form a hill cluster at the edge. Nodding slightly, he stepped back, memorizing the intricate patterns of the moss, the size and shape of the tentacles and the smooth even color of green death.

The fenwapters unwound their trembling extremities from one another and relaxed. The hideous death of the grabber moss was abhorrent as well as terrifying to them. Nonverbally they soothed and consoled one another for the fright experienced at the thought of another grabber-moss victory. High in the putch branches, Esse roared.

When Lozadar turned, head hanging, the torment on his face made Stefen look away. The familiar aura had not presented itself to him for many Passages. An indifference to life and death hung over the outcast, the same sensation many of those in the colony had displayed before they sickened and died or ran into the jungle. Only now he recognized it for what it was and wished he did not know its face.

Lozadar ate slowly, idly gazing around the clearing,

staring at the moss for long stretches of time. Sleep came before the moons rose. The whimpers and tears shed by the slumbering man kept Stefen and the fenwapters awake half the night, until the nightmares subsided and exhaustion beset Lozadar's sleep.

Stefen nestled in with Esse and Asa while the fenwapters stood guard. Occasionally a chotiburu squealed when it fell victim to a waiting kervemith on the prowl. He watched the outcast curled into a fetal ball and tried to understand why anyone would contemplate yielding his life while his enemy lived.

The days passed painfully for Lozadar. The fenwapters and kervemith grew restless because of the slow pace they were forced to maintain for his benefit. Side jaunts and chotiburu hunts became their norm, changing day shifts much the same way as they divided up night duty.

After the first ten days, a decaset, Lozadar's physical and mental health took a sharp turn for the better. Hands and feet swollen and bloody with blisters had begun to callus over. Adroit maneuvers evaded the sharp leaf edges which otherwise would have flayed the tissue from his bones over the distance the entourage had covered.

A quick learner, he remembered details down to the subtlest variations. Stefen felt an ambiguous hope for his survival. It was strangely comforting to have a companion of one's own species, even one as alien as Lozadar cor Baalan.

Evenings were spent around the fire Lozadar habitually made. When pressed hard enough by Stefen, he spoke briefly of his home, the worlds he had visited, the plans he had once had, but never about what events shaped his coming to the Virgin or about being the Ruler of the Seven Worlds. Talking about the good times deleted the need to think about their outcome. Lozadar had never been a particularly extroverted individual when times were stable. He enjoyed listening. After reciting the day's lesson, asking questions of Stefen and assimilating the answers, he learned about the Virgin's world.

In a brief time, a fast kinship grew between the two. Lozadar found himself no longer just tolerated by the traveling companions who guarded the night, then ignored as soon as possible. They too were becoming part of his circle.

The second decaset of days moved faster. They took to the land as often as possible for Lozadar to learn the flora. Twice they encountered yaxuras. The second one approached Stefen, who did not give a centimeter of ground for the duration of the confrontation. Not until several days later did Lozadar venture to ask the hundreds of questions he had about the encounter.

Stefen had few answers.

By the third decaset, they traveled through the trees and on the land at a speed the fenwapters and kervemith could comfortably tolerate. Evenings changed patterns. Lozadar practiced uttering the strangled sounds of the fenwapters and the snarls of the kervemith with Stefen as interpreter. Early mornings, the fenwapters schooled him in using the trees to their fullest value and the kervemith and Stefen taught him the principles of being one with the land on which he hunted. Their subtle personalities became distinct as he worked with them.

Though the outcast learned quickly, he lacked finesse, something only time and practice could impart. Yet time was not plentiful. Stefen watched the sky change daily as the second sun shone brighter and the nights shortened. He also watched for Evaladyn, who had not maintained such a prolonged absence during the time he had known her. Silently, he worried.

The forty revolutions which had passed since Stefen had postponed judgment on Lozadar became a time both cherished as turning points. During that interlude, the outcast learned many things, mostly the value in living. Stefen taught many skills, but received little practical knowledge in return. Stefen's confidence enhanced a visage of superiority over the outcast, but failed to impart understanding. He was no closer to comprehending the human species than on the first day.

Lozadar talked more frequently, but with a reserved joviality, as though being sidetracked would cloud the path to his newfound goal to survive.

Instinctively, Stefen feared Lozadar. The outcast's world was complex, alien, and the motives of his people were shrouded in ambiguities uncomprehendable to Stefen. Little things Lozadar took for granted stymied him. It never occurred to Stefen that people did not mate for life once ritual was set. Nor did it make sense to him that young ones were taught how to live by strangers—away from their parents.

The time to go to the Forbidden Place was at hand. Stefen argued internally whether or not to take Lozadar with him. If he possessed some idea of what might be found there, the decision would be easier.

He sat beside the fire, pulled a long strip of chotiburu meat from the bone and stared vacantly at Lozadar, wondering what to do with him.

The long twilight cast by the second sun flashed brightly above the trees. A roar, much louder than the one at the Crystal Curtain, shook the jungle. The kervemith roared back in unison. A second, third and fourth followed.

Stefen watched Lozadar peer into the trees, unable to see the shapes heading the lightning bolts. He returned to eating, looking up once to meet Lozadar's eyes when the noise yielded to the agitated jungle sounds.

"Sounded like four scouters. I can't tell whose they are —mine, or the enemy's."

Stefen remained silent, angry that men with their awesome weapons, low life codes and alien mores would taunt the Virgin sky. Worse, he felt powerless to prevent it.

The sky roared alive again. The lights were brighter this time and seemed to match the sound better. It was close and the light was constant.

Stefen smothered the fire with dirt, hoping the wind created by the craft would disperse the smoke and not betray their location. The din subsided.

"They've landed." Lozadar's tone was emotionless. A gleam in his topaz eyes became fierce. "Let's go see who they are."

Stefen grabbed his arm and jerked. "If they are yours, you are not free to go to them. The Virgin has yet to test you, outcast. Until she does, you are my responsibility. I will kill you if I suspect a betrayal."

Lozadar took in Stefen's threat, shivering inwardly. He had no doubt that Stefen could, and would, make good his words. He felt the slim hope of rescue beyond the next rise fade. Even if it was there, he could not utilize it.

"You agreed. Your word cannot be rescinded." Stefen watched the man struggle, his conflict visible, his duty divided.

Lozadar sighed heavily, finally nodding. "I gave my

43

word. I'll stay as agreed. If they're mine, would it be permissible for me to speak to them? Perhaps they could return after Passage?"

"No. If you survive the test, you will belong to the Virgin. If not . . ." Shrugging, his head tilted to the right, "You will be dead."

"I, ah, see." He cleared his throat. "Tell me, if they are my enemy, will I be permitted retaliation?"

"Unless provoked by an assault on the Virgin or on us directly, there will be no action taken against them. We stand to gain nothing and to lose much."

Lozadar thought about it for several minutes, digesting the hidden meanings in such a plain statement. The simplicity of Stefen's world was almost too complicated. "Would you prefer I stay here?" he asked flatly.

After several hundred heartbeats of careful consideration, Stefen admitted the lure of spaceships over the next rise was too great to pass up. "It's time you earned your way. Thus far, all the teaching has been onesided. We have given our knowledge to you. It is time for you to give us some information about your world on a firsthand level. Tell us what we see. Explain how it works. Your word pictures leave us in too much doubt and ignorance."

Commands went out to the beasts, ordering them to spread out and keep watch as they traveled. Halfway up a putch, Stefen told them to keep a sufficient proximity to Lozadar so he could be killed if he tried to break toward the ships. Stefen employed the pure forms of their languages, an act which piqued the outcast's attention, since he did not understand any of the symbolisms.

They moved silently through the trees, down into a ravine and up over the rise. From a lofty perch in a giant putch, Stefen saw four triangular ships resting in a flat, freshly denuded patch at the bottom of the hill. The dull glare of the second sun reaching into the western horizon added to their alienness. Markings, written in the Old Language of his parents and hardly recognizable, were etched in black on the right sides of the flaring triangles. They were pictures of what Stefen suspected as suns and a tracer circle of seven little dots and two big ones.

He beckoned to Lozadar. The climb, which seemed horrendously loud to him, could not be heard beyond the highest branches. The fenwapters and both kervemith turned to watch. Andazu fluttered a disgusted sigh to indicate his displeasure with the outworlder he considered a "klutz" in Lozadar's own word. He and Esse exchanged brief sympathetic glances, their camaraderie reaching an all-time high over the last forty days.

Lozadar studied the foursome, jaw clamped shut, a muscle spasm twitching in his right cheek.

Stefen pointed to the clearing and started down, leaving Lozadar to follow at his own pace. A head motion sent Andazu back to accompany the outcast. Stefen moved over lateral branches, skirting the uprights and taking advantage of the ones perpendicular to the ground. He crossed from putch to putch, catching glimpses of the kervemith on either side, staying where the growth was the most lush and the shadows the darkest. The strong scent of orbi flowers preparing for the moons to rise permeated the fat blossoms of vines oozing a peculiar scent all their own. Yet over the familiar smell of the jungle came a malodorous pungency which offended him.

Burned putch splinters lay dead with the skeletons of vines seared away for the landing ships. On the fringes of the immense clearing, loban and fusci ferns drooped and whithered, half dead, their delicious fruit broiled into ruin. Wainor bushes dropped their shanuts and turned as black as their bark. The shanuts lay open for the ganids to swarm over them. The distinctive chirping of the red insects below made Stefen more cautious. His approach slowed.

Only parts of the ground were visible through the heavy foliage. Broken vines had fallen to be a curtain hiding the ships ahead. Sound, garbled by the wind and distance, wound through the growth. He heard a noise in the rear left, figured it was Lozadar, but checked as a precaution.

Kachieo moved ahead on the right, working through the upper-middle branches more than twice her body width. Esse took to the heights, his keen eyes able to detect the slightest movement below. Asa moved in on the lower left, venturing out toward the clearing fringes in order to find a good vantage point.

Andazu trailed Lozadar until dismissed to cover the left flank. The outcast worked for more quiet as he encroached upon Stefen's limb. When he reached the flat spot where Stefen watched the four ships, he was struggling to control his breathing so it would blend into the breeze. The intensity of his gaze never wavered.

He's learning, Stefen thought, watching the way Lozadar sensed and felt his way over the limb without having to look.

Upon reaching Stefen he pointed to the closest of the four ships. "That's the one to watch. They aren't expecting any trouble or they would have landed so their engines faced inward and their weapons outward," he whispered.

Studying them, Stefen understood and grinned.

"But the front one," Lozadar continued, pointing at a series of circles ringing the sharp point of the triangle, "has weapons available and can fire without jeopardizing the other ships. Notice how large the insignia is on the side?"

Stefen nodded, seeing the discrepancy for the first time.

"The size designates it as the command ship. That's the one to watch."

Stefen motioned Lozadar to follow. They moved laterally to the end of the branch. Stefen cut a vine, tested it and swung to the next tree. He threw it back for Lozadar and kept going, hearing him follow. Around them, the other watchers moved as a silent force.

The place Stefen chose to view the ship was well camouflaged by nacki leaves and blossoms withered by the landing heat. With Lozadar at his side, a jumble of mixed emotions, he waited to see what would happen.

Just before the weaker sun disappeared completely in the west and the orbi flowers began to open, so did the hatch of the command ship. Four men led a woman circled by another six men out to the clearing.

She glanced around nervously, chin up and seemingly ignorant of those wanting her to hurry. For an instant, Stefen looked into her face, or thought he did. The thirty-meter distance left a margin for error. Stefen's heart rate increased nonetheless.

One of the men guarding her gave her a shove as he stumbled over a bough. She caught herself before falling flat in the giant toothpick carpet.

A man in the advance guard ordered the men to spread out and give her room.

Stefen began to memorize her: long, dark hair bunched into a knot at the nape of her neck, white and crimson robes over pants of the same hues. The flowing material swished when she walked. Her eyes were an indiscernible color, and the major features of her face were beset with worry and defiance simultaneously. Smiling to himself, he knew Evaladyn would approve the choice of her as a mate. The smile vanished. How would he get her?

He looked at Lozadar. Was this his enemy?

Lozadar held to a thin branch so tightly his knuckles turned white and veins distended up his arms and into his neck. Several times his mouth moved before he spoke. "Corinda dez Kaliea, daughter of the Coralis Legate . . . my intended wife."

Chapter 6

STEFEN GLARED AT LOZADAR; HATRED bludgeoned his emotions. It was irrational. And he knew it. With effort, the sensation dimmed, but would not fade completely.

Below, the detail scanned the clearing and trees, nervous, uncomfortable in the quiescent, dense surroundings. The ganids stopped chirping. Gradually they formed a red barrier two deep on the ground directly under Stefen. The normal play of the wind in the trees and vines sounded loud beyond proportion. Fotigs clanked against one another to produce a hollow dirge.

The invaders kicked away splinters of debris along an uneven path carved out by the two leading men. Corinda divided her time between watching the ground and gazing at the jungle. She did not share the obvious trepidations or fear the silence.

The regolith moaned, rearranging the top layer just enough to make a difference. Shriveled nacki leaves trembled and fell, crumbling into a million pieces as they struck the lower branches, so much confetti raining on the ganids. The brown flakes caught by the breeze fluttered through the air, disintegrating the curtain hiding the watchers in the trees.

Quickly, Stefen ordered the fenwapters and kervemith to retreat into the protection of the green, change elevations and hide.

A curious yaxura poked through the ready-made kindling between the eleven outworlders and their ship. Two white eyes, located half a meter from his upper lip, worked independently to survey the devastation. His black, leathery skin was heaped with dirt and a few shards of putch trees imbedded in the clumps. His toothy maw opened to a full four-meter diameter, belching oxygen and dripping corrosive saliva which burned holes in the ground. Small pillars of pungent smoke rose from the contact points. His bellow paralyzed the aliens just beginning to regain some composure.

As the echo faded, Corinda's convulsive giggle floated in the aromatic breeze. She watched her guards with an amused satisfaction, as though there were some private measure of justice she enjoyed.

The yaxura moved farther onto the land. His short, powerful legs worked in alternating rhythm. Head swinging from side to side, he bellowed again, flinging saliva in all directions.

The closest man, a young captain, unstrapped the fine thong which held a shiny, long Lat-kor to this thigh. Carefully, his fingers closed around the curved segment and pulled the barrel out of the three spring-grippers fastened to his leg.

Corinda stopped laughing and ran at him, screaming, "He hasn't done anything! Leave him be! Please! Leave him be—"

A second officer caught her around the waist before she reached the man taking a bead on the yaxura. She scratched, kicked and screamed, until another man helped to subdue her. Her screaming interested the yaxura, who turned to gaze at her with his enormous left eye.

Baby yaxura, the size of Corinda, wiggled out of the adult's back pouches. There were three of them writhing and jerking around the debris close to the parent's feet.

Cordinda renewed her warnings, freeing her hand to wave at the beast.

Stefen motioned for Lozadar to stay put, then disappeared on a lateral course through the trees. For an instant, Lozadar had no choice. The speed and agility Stefen displayed left him feeling more inadequate than he ever suspected was possible.

It seemed there were still a few isolated pockets of life who had not heard about the dangers brought by the outworlders. Running, swinging, free to hurry without the burden of his charge, Stefen found a position low to the ground and near enough the clearing to distort the sounds he made.

From the right rear, another bellow reached into the clearing, followed by a second, the pitch slightly higher.

The yaxura children scurried back to the pouches located near the flatter rear back of the adult. He bellowed, returning the call.

Corinda quieted and pulled her arm away from one of the guards long enough to push hair and tears from her face.

The yaxura crept backward toward his hole, watching the strangers blighting the Virgin's skin.

There was a blinding flash of light. Then a second one.

The yaxura roared in agony. Two smoldering holes in his side, one near the head, the other just above ground level, oozed a silver-brown sap.

Corinda went wild. A strength her frail appearance denied set her free. She ran at the creature, trying to shield him with her small body. "Hurry! Keep going! Save your babies!" The sobs from a hurt deep inside of her punctuated her phrases.

The beast heaved volumes of oxygen, listening to the bellow beyond the perimeter. Dazed, the yaxura slowly sank into the hole, turning to rest one eye upon Corinda and the other on the guards clad in white and maroon.

Two of the colonial soldiers ran toward Corinda, weapons drawn. She calculated the fringes, trying to decide whether to hide in the jungle or be a party to more death. Her eyes found an anomaly in the low branches and stopped their scan.

Stefen felt as though he should be able to reach out and touch her, lift her out of the clearing and away from the reprehensible outworlders whose heinous lust for the blood of trusting creatures she did not share. Behind a veil of dirt-splattered tears, he saw a pristine beauty and a pain he yearned to assuage with his own desires.

For Corinda, the bearded man crouched on one knee with his hands cupped over his mouth seemed an illusion. A bellow rocked out of the flesh megaphone. When it ended, she heard the final heave of the earth as it crashed into the yaxura hole. She turned to see that the beast was safely gone. When she looked back, Stefen was also gone. His disappearance left her stunned and composed.

Soldiers took each of her arms and hauled her into the ship. Twice she looked over her shoulder into the trees, vainly attempting to recapture the image.

At the ramp, she stared condescendingly at the man who had fired on the beast. "Murderer," she hissed. "Isn't there enough death taking place this very moment in the

Gredenvald System? You've killed a helpless creature who did nothing—absolutely nothing!—to you. If that's the colonial reaction and answer for anything threatening, may the gods help the Seven if you're admitted.

"This is his world. Not yours. Not mine. Not the mighty General's or anyone else's!" Her voice rose with the color in her cheeks, the tide of emotion cresting into a massive wave. Pent-up hostilities and tears gushed out unrestrained.

Two more yaxuras surfaced, rudely jolting the clearing and unsettling the westernmost ship.

The young Captain picked up Corinda, staggered as the ground heaved again and carried her into the ship. He returned with his weapon drawn and yelling orders at his men to get inside. The last four started up the ramp.

Five more yaxuras surfaced in the center of the four-ship diamond. The ground took on the pitch of an angry ocean, trees, debris and even ships being tossed back and forth to satisfy the beasts' curiosity.

It was all that any creature caught in the perpetual quakes could do to hang on. Rifts opened and closed, dropping portions of the ground several meters.

The soldiers grabbed the guard rails that shot out of of the ramp, drew their weapons and began firing. The Captain's orders directed them into an efficient operation.

Kachieo swung through the trees, screeching a warning of her own at Stefen, who was perched just over two yaxura.

Stefen screeched back, moving through the trees cautiously to avoid attracting attention. The kervemith moved also, trying to intercept the excited fenwapter. A special kind of hysteria which flourished with each movement possessed her. Andazu chittered in the heights, warning Kachieo to hide before the enemy struck her down with the deadly light.

Arms wrapped around a perpendicular branch, legs spread to straddle the more solid one near the trunk, Lozadar watched the young Captain pinpoint the new sounds crisscrossing the middle tree level. His stomach jumped while his perch remained still. A helplessness set him hugging the branch until an old fotig stalk hole drew blood from his chest. He could not help watching the scene he knew would unfold as the natives converged.

The Captain lifted his Lat-kor to the trees, sighted carefully and followed the furry shape whose flapping back pack made a perfect target when she did not bother to seek cover, then fired. Upon his command, the rest of the soldiers fired upon the yaxura.

In less than a few heartbeats three yaxuras lay partially exposed on the ground, unrecognizable as anything but a charred mass of malodorous flesh smoking into the fires overhead.

Kachieo tumbled through the branches, striking the fat ones with bone-breaking thuds, spinning off and plummeting to the ground where the ranks of ganids waited. Her body bounced and flopped, twitched for a few heartbeats, then was stilled in death.

Andazu uttered one perpetual scream carrying an agony and disbelief over the fate of his beloved.

The soldiers fired in all directions, steadily retreating up the ramp and into the ship. Flames erupted along the perimeter, licking the putch trees and providing more fuel for the inferno.

The ship's door retracted, permitting the soldiers to hurry in as soon as they were near. Corinda's anguish could be heard over the crackling of the fires. The instant the door closed for the last time the ramp retracted.

Engines burst into life. Bypassing the warmup starters, the main thrusters kicked in and ignited more of the land.

The ganids turned into a red river with tributaries rushing into the jungle. They hopped and flew away from the fire, leaving Kachieo and the yaxura feast for a later, safer time.

Stefen swung through the trees, slid down a series of branches and stood near Kachieo in the shadows. There was nothing left of the nacki pack. Twisted pieces of Annalli's jewelry and two of his father's strange orbs were burned into her body. The remainder of the contents were strewn through the branches she had struck on the way down.

Heat swelters distorted everything in all directions, its source so massive and intense that Lozadar considered it hell itself. The protestations of the yaxura were lost to the roar of the fire and the drone of the ships lifting skyward. They moved in unison, the right-flank one turning slightly to fire down at the clearing to set the remaining ground into flames.

53

Stefen grabbed Kachieo's body, flung her across his shoulders and started climbing. Over the fire's thunder, he called to Lozadar and told him to return to camp. Handicapped by the dead weight, it was all he could do to make it on his own without perishing.

Before he cleared the rise Andazu, Esse and Asa flanked him once again. The noisy pyre was distant behind them. Lozadar's clumsy efforts carried through the smoky breeze.

Black clouds boiled over the horizon and mingled with the smoke. Twin flashes of lightning, followed by the thunder of a displeased Deity, released torrents of rain unseasonal to the Virgin. The stench of the ruined jungle ripe with death was offensive in the small air spaces between the large raindrops hurled out of the sky.

The last strains of light vanished, obliterated by the clouds. Stefen dispatched Esse to guide Lozadar, not quite trusting the man's abilities to ensure his survival. Death had claimed enough this day without a careless mistake by the outcast.

The rain beat down until after they had reached the campsite. Stefen gazed at the dead fire from which the dirt had been washed off. It reminded him of the ugly wounds the enemy had inflicted. He kicked at it, splattering mud in all directions.

Andazu whimpered and eased his mate off Stefen's shoulders.

On all fours, hunched over the depression, Stefen picked up a couple of charred sticks poking out of the fire's grave and hurled them one at a time into the jungle, each one with more vehemence, digging and sifting through the mire until all of them were gone. Knees spread, he chopped at the mud with his knife and purged the recess carved into the Virgin of any and all evidence of its former purpose. Anguished sobs ground out of his mouth and were lost in the frenzy of chastisement. Again and again, he plunged the blade into the soft ground, covering himself with flying mud, bits of ash and greenery.

He blamed himself for Kachieo's death. She was always a bundle of protective clumsiness in a tense situation, more concerned about him or Andazu than herself. *I knew that,* he wailed silently while groaning aloud.

He hacked at the hole, erasing every black piece of

54

charcoal from the land, working out the hate and blame to a livable level, physically exhausting himself.

Asa's snarls brought Stefen partially back to the reality of Kachieo propped against the tree. Andazu stroked the stubble of burned fur soaked with blood and washed by rain, the color gone in the anonymity of night. The fenwapter crooned the melody of his Ancients. The hymn tore at Stefen's soul until it brimmed with grief and guilt. Settling beside her, Stefen put his arms around her and cried for the good times that were no more and were never to be again. The gentle fenwapter's eyes, horrifyingly still, gazed at the emptying sky where the stars tried to peer through the jagged slits in the black anger to witness the emotional maelstrom.

Stefen could not halt the chaos. A million memories of the growing years paraded through his mind. The Crystal Curtain opened once again, the soft fall of water into the clear pool a distant song luring him home. He saw the five of them there, relaxed, happy, untouched by the threat from the outworlder. There, in the early years, she was the peacemaker when the tempers of the young fenwapter and the arrogant human were at odds and pride was at stake. Even then, he thought he and Andazu would have killed each other without her intervention.

Sadly, he remembered Kachieo's baby, born at the wrong time—during Passage. She had spent that one with him, braving the falls, and forcing Andazu to do the same by her actions. When the babe took so long to be born, nearly killing his mother, they worried about his survival. The worry ended with the child's life before the third nursing. Kachieo defied Passage, went to the outside and buried her dead baby. It was long after the next Passage before she was well again. Her barren state was never spoken about openly between the three of them, though once Stefen heard her implore Andazu to take another mate and she would go to the jungle with his blessing. Andazu had become furious with her. The subject never came up again within Stefen's earshot. Yet, sometime after that, he knew he took the place of her lost child. It was ridiculous to indulge her—but he did.

Now, it seemed that part of the mother figure he saw in her was real.

She was gone.

And he blamed himself, knowing he had let her think

of him in danger from the outworlders' weapons. He had not stopped to consider her reaction and the cost.

Suddenly he wanted to go home. Forget the Forbidden Place. Forget the old enemy of his father. Just go home. Be safe . . . unhurt . . .

He sat quietly with Andazu, who also held onto the lifeless body in an unspoken reluctance to yield up the dead as dead. The sky cleared and the orbi flowers lit the night in splendor for their moons.

Grunting, huffing, Lozadar made his way down the tree and into camp. Esse remained in the heights to keep watch. Asa discreetly forced Lozadar to keep a distance from the two making their farewells to a loved one.

Lozadar hunkered down against a putch across from the three. He wondered at the loss he felt and the remorse which could not be resolved by an explanation. In the brilliance cast by the flowers, he saw the dirt-laced sorrow on Stefen's face and the clear paths where mud had been washed by tears.

He winced.

Nothing masked the man's emotions, nor did he try to manufacture a screen.

For the first time he realized how different he and Stefen were, a difference far greater than the light-years separating their homeworlds. The candor of Stefen's world knew no controls or restraints when it came to honest emotions.

He felt ashamed that his upbringing had not permitted him to grieve for his family a fraction of the measure he experienced. No, that needed to be buried, lest it be taken for a sign of weakness. It was an unspoken, unbreakable edict of civilized society.

Yet, before him was a man—perhaps five standards younger than he—he deemed to be stronger and more disciplined than any he had encountered.

He wondered if it was symptomatic of all of his feelings. Was he an emotional cripple in a universe filled with them? Head on his knees, he hoped not, but feared the conclusion was true. Was civilization really civilized and good?

Eyes closed, he recalled the way the colonial soldiers had ignited the jungle; needless destruction. Fearful men. A small party of four ships floundering in an inexplicable part of the galaxy—a bad place for superstitious men, unless they were hiding. With Corinda aboard, they were probably hiding, he concluded. Afraid, they responded to the smallest threat with violence, despite their training. Was it a standard answer, born and bred of his civilization? He remembered countless reports of survey teams scouting new worlds beyond the perimeter of the central Seven. Each contained proposals on how to be rid of the indigenous life forms considered potentially dangerous.

Lozadar wanted to be sick.

No. The colonials are no different. How could we expect them to be? "Such a waste," he whispered to the ground. "The saints are dead and the gods are myths, unconcerned with imperfect mortals."

After a time, Andazu and Stefen wrapped Kachieo in fresh nacki leaves and bound them with orbi blossoms ablaze in the night. Esse came out of the trees and began to dig with his front four paws.

The trees quivered slightly. A yaxura surfaced in the midst of a heavy orbi patch. He came out of the ground to eye level. The maw was closed as far as it could be; half the distance.

Stefen walked confidently to the edge of the brilliant tangle.

A low series of throaty growls came from the yaxura. Stefen nodded, waded through the flowers and extended his hand to touch the acid-drooling beast.

The yaxura slunk back into his hole. There was a rumbling, then silence.

Stefen returned to his friends and spoke quietly while exchanging touches that consoled and reassured them of a physical caring and safety. Lozadar's vigilance went unnoticed. The name "outcast" carried home a new meaning when he thought about it. Esse nudged the fenwapter, who reached out for support against the lowered ivory horn. Stefen placed Kachieo atop the kervemith's back.

Flanked by Stefen, Andazu and Asa at the rear, Esse carried his burden across the clearing and through the sea of bright flowers. For a few moments they disappeared into the black hole created by the yaxura.

When they filed solemnly back into the clearing, the ground rumbled again. The yaxura worked the soil and filled the hole. From the center of the circular island came an obsidian monolith. As the sun broke the eastern green, the carmine-streaked black marker stood as a reminder and a guard over the place where Kachieo's resting spirit joined her Ancients.

Stefen bellowed into the dawn, a note of thanks and shared commiseration for the Virgin's losses.

The yaxuras bellowed back from every direction, the force so great that fotigs and nacki flowers shuddered and fell out of the trees.

Lozadar turned away, ashamed of the worlds he once ruled and took great pride in, confronted by his own ignorance of what had been of real importance.

The lights were set on dim to match the black depression Corinda felt. It was a slaughter, she moaned, seeing the probing eyes of the bearded native in the trees. The miasmic stench of his fired world clung to her clothing. Bruskly, she stood and pulled the garments from her body.

Naked, she plopped onto the edge of her bed and drew the blanket into a ball on her lap. She hugged it, rocking back and forth, seeing the jungle man etched on her inner eyelids. It felt as though he watched, accusing, judging, and wanting something from deep inside of her. In the few seconds they had seen one another, he had been able to touch a chord only Hart knew was there and stroked reluctantly, as though he could not help it.

"It stinks. All of it—Antition, the conspiracy tearing up people's lives, the protective captivity, the jungle . . . and me," she whispered, "the great House of dez Kaliea."

She tried to think about the beauty covering the soil of the virgin world they orbited. A hundred shades of green blended harmoniously for as far as the eye could see in any direction. There was a raw, unsettled flavor in the air which tantalized the adventurer with a subtle promise of a reward.

Flashes of light. The aura of death. The smell from her clothes became stifling. Again she saw the green world erupt in flames, heard the beasts roar in surprise and agony, experienced the same feelings of horror when the chittering ball of fur in the trees fell, hit branches, disappeared and reappeared—bouncing on the ground as a wall of flames reached up to the sky.

"It was just on the screen," she murmured, pleading with a part of herself to believe the words. "It wasn't real. It wasn't a sentient being. It couldn't have been." A rage of denial sent the blanket ball whapping against the wall. She gazed into the mirror and saw soot and dirt from the Virgin clinging to her face, hair and hands. Repulsed, she slapped the wall control and kicked the door for not opening into the sanitary chamber fast enough.

She stood in the light bath, vaguely hearing the warning buzz, not caring if there were side effects to a prolonged stay in the cleansing rays. She wanted to feel clean again.

Staring at a spot on the wall, it didn't seem possible to be clean again. Life had changed too drastically and would never revert to a point where there was even a chance.

Lozadar's image commiserated with her. A friend. "Oh, Gods of the Universe, the value of one friend is infinite, even if I would have to marry him. . . ." She laughed sadly, the sound lost in the warning buzz. "Compromises. All of life is a compromise. No wonder I can't get clean!

"And death. Kill it! Kill it all! Don't let it live—it might be harmful. It might attack!" She repeated the words over and over, hunching forward with each rendition, until she was crouched on the floor and crying. The jungle man's eyes watched inside her head, yearning and angry simultaneously.

Chapter 7

KACHIEO'S DEATH BROUGHT A CHANGE TO the established patterns of daily living. Now, Stefen sought to learn from the outworlder instead of teach. During rest periods and evening quiet, he pried knowledge from Lozadar which the outcast did not know he possessed. Questions by the hundreds were asked and answered, solidifying a unique friendship with a semblance of mutual understanding.

Stefen assimilated what he did comprehend, accepted facts as being the way things were on the alien worlds, and resorted to memorizing characteristics when he could not find logical roots behind the information. A determination to prevent the outside threats from marring the Virgin became fortified by his anger and a silent vow for retaliation should they try again. He would know the enemy and be prepared to do more than watch next time.

No longer was the way to the Forbidden Place approached via detours or filled by precautions against the outcast. Stefen's mind was fixed upon Lozadar's future. The obligatory pilgrimage to the place of his father stood in the way now, preventing them from getting on with the business of judgment and the outworlder. But, while he liked his companion, he could not bring himself to wholly trust any individual nurtured in the strange, hostile environment of the far worlds.

Lozadar adapted to the jungle better each day. No longer were his ventures through the trees marked by noise. He too seemed lost in thought most of the time.

A decaset later, they rose with the first sun. Esse and Asa were restless and paced the clearing they chose to camp in. Gleaned bones of the chotiburu they had shared the night before were in a heap in the center of a small firepit Stefen had reluctantly allowed for cooking.

In truth, the spicy raw meat turned his stomach, making it easier to bend his will toward Lozadar's requests.

This morning felt different from the others since the funeral. The breeze hardly stirred. The jungle sounds were distant, subdued from the usual morning exuberance. Stefen started right into the trees, leaving the others to catch up at will. He knew they were close to the Forbidden Place. Gradually, markers prodded his early-childhood memories. The mountain in the north rose, bare and pointed to the very tops. Calderas puffed easy spirals into the cloud-flecked sky. More cycle trees, which lost their leaves well before the turn of Passage, mingled with the putch, giant ferns and nacki vines.

He did not know what to expect, though he was sure he would know it when he saw it. Looking down at Lozadar struggling up to the first branch, he felt a pang of guilt. He tried to assuage it by telling himself it was better to be overcautious where an outworlder was concerned than to be betrayed. "Don't expect much and you won't often be disappointed," Lozadar had said the first day. In some ways, he knew he expected a great deal from the outcast.

The sky erupted with noise.

Stefen braced against a perpendicular branch and craned his neck at the royal blue flayed with morning orange. The enemy was back, streaking silver threads against the dawn. Heart beating fiercely, he locked his jaw and clenched his fists.

"Esse, Asa! Take Lozadar and find a shelter. I'll return later."

Esse balked, but acquiesced after a round of snarls.

"Go with them, Lozadar. There will be no death on my mind today—unless you choose to defy the kervemith." The desire to see whose forces ripped the morning blazed in his companion's features. For a heartbeat, he was tempted to relent and allow Lozadar to chase his metal birds with the kervemith as the safety valves. Head shaking, "It is best this way. They'll protect you." He shed his pack, checked Andazu's and threw the extra to Lozadar, replacing the needed one on the fenwapter.

Lozadar slung the added baggage over his shoulder, turned toward Esse, paused and glanced back. "Stefen?"

"Yes?"

"Would you believe me if I said I understand how you

feel?" Looking back at the empty sky. "I've done a lot of thinking. . . . I'm not sure I want to go back to spend the rest of my life handing down dictates and living under a shroud of . . . " He snorted, then smiled quickly. "What say we go find out if there are any others, after you do what you have to do here? I could still go for the woman or the wine—preferably both."

The spark of easy friendship kindled. "Yes, Lozadar, we'll do that. Evaladyn has been gone a long time. She's searching." A white grin in his sun-streaked beard lit up his eyes. "She fears I'll choose you as a mate."

"Must be that irresistible sex appeal I was cursed with at birth." He turned to follow the kervemith down the branch lanes. "Offhand, I think you'd better hurry up and do what you gotta do, so we can go looking. I have a history of getting married—I should say mating—with my friends, if that tells you anything."

The generous grin half masked by Lozadar's stubbly beard set a new desire of expediency into motion. He would miss Lozadar. He and Andazu watched until they disappeared below the heavy growth and set out toward the volcanoes.

Soon, they were forced to the ground, around patches of grabber moss, through trees shrunken in size. The vegetation grew sparse and diminutive. Stefen loped over coarse lava disintegrating with time and the elements. Ferns slapped at his thighs, grabbed his breeches, whipped his flesh. Arms pumping, he skirted open steam fissures ringed by a poisonous brown moss trying to establish itself in a linking pattern over the black corroded rock.

He ran for most of the morning, ducked under low branches, avoided shadowy hazards and found the eroded strip where the jungle met the volcano to be the best path. Above, rocks lay precariously on one another, ready to tumble into the creeping foliage at the slightest provocation. Fresh flora was sweet in his nostrils. Running, free from the outcast, free to choose his own pace, which Andazu matched easily, he tried not to think about anything but the delicious sensation of being a part of the Virgin.

Up, over jagged lava tongues, down into the valleys where rock moss ate up the shadows and along the joining trails of two volcanoes struggling for dominance he ran. Heavy steam belched out of long, open chasms like so many secret fires unearthed by force.

Before the first sun set, he was approaching the sea and open jungle on his left. The briny spume of waves crashing against the lava cliffs filled his senses. He ran harder, sprinting to the finish, delighted by what graced his vision. Perspiration soaked his hair and beard, then dripped off to roll down his shirt and breeches.

He slowed at the jungle fringes, letting the pain of the run crest. Slowly he bowed under low-ceilinged vines laden with blossoms and fruit clusters. He pulled a nacki fruit away, split it with his knife and bit into it. He chewed the bittersweet pulp, kept the juice and spat out the bulk.

Andazu chittered ahead, bringing Stefen to investigate. A small pool capped by water flowers bubbled out of the ground. A stream flowed over a smooth depression and found its way to the cliff's edge, where it joined the sea fifty meters below.

Delicate flowers spread over the water, six flaring petals trimmed in fine lace. At the center grew an equally fragile-looking formation of three stamens swimming in a cup of amber nectar.

The clear water gently rippling at the edge betrayed the depth of the pool and the presence of water vermin who fed upon the flowers. The vermin ranged from a centimeter to three meters, thin and active. Andazu sighed audibly, gazing at the intoxicating nectar in the flower cups.

"On the way back," Stefen told him, bending over the falls to capture a drink of water without risking the paralyzing sting of the vermin.

Below, the waves thundered. Stefen swung over the cliff and worked down the face until the spray reached up to cleanse him. In shadow, he found a recess worn smooth by the relentless storm waves. He called up to Andazu and settled in.

The place he chose to rest for the night was located on a rugged point of the escarpment midway between the sea and the land. He watched the water swell powerfully, crest and splatter against the lower cliff. It made him feel small and insignificant in the face of so tireless a force.

Andazu joined him, carrying a stalk of fotigs tied to a

nacki cluster slung over his shoulders. He too settled in and watched the great water with more terror than awe.

Off in the distance zuriserpants lifted their eyes on the ends of long tentacles to watch the escarpment. They became brazen, humping their masses of aqua-blue spectrumed dorsal fins in the longshore current.

Stefen watched, wanting a better look, but impressed by what was evident in their size.

As quickly as they came, they disappeared. The evening changed sounds. A roar louder than the ocean asserted itself, ever increasing.

Anxiously Stefen sought the open sky for a direction. He saw nothing, yet the familiar noise grew. On his hands and knees, he approached the edge, glanced up and immediately retreated.

He reached for Andazu to keep him hidden. "They're directly above us and coming down to the ground." Dismayed, he knew he should have counted on the enemy's return. The area above was everything Lozadar said a tactical crew would want for a landing site or temporary base. The sea bordered the east to the north and south. High volcanoes and lava tongues protected them at the west, all around to the sea. A spear of guilt sent him wincing. Lozadar had spoken accurately. He had explained until Stefen understood, giving freely of himself.

He glanced at Andazu. "We may be here for a while. It's a good thing you brought food. Lozadar warned me and I didn't listen. When the time came, I didn't heed his warnings." He tried to recall the proper profanity to use for a time like this and couldn't select a word to sum it up.

Andazu rumbled a curse of his own and cracked a fotig with his claws.

A hundred heartbeats later the noise died. The rock felt ominous above them.

Those on the colonial ship had little use for the pangs of conscience Corinda's mere presence brought. They preferred to forget the interlude on the planet as part of a bad dream; at worst, an extension of the war raging in the Gredenvald System. General Myzillion's return with news of a questionable victory which only temporarily fought back the conglomeration of unmarked ships of a wide vintage cheered morale for a brief while. The true enemy was still a faceless, brutal entity.

On the rare occasions when Corinda attended a general assembly or dined in the officer's mess, she maintained a stoic attitude. The young Captain displayed his gratitude for her silence by showing her his skills with the ancient chivalry perfected by his ancestors. The performances carried no weight with her and annoyed the General enough to inquire what the Captain had in mind.

General Myzillion sat in his old quarters. Across the small expanse was Corinda. Even with his eyes closed he knew where she was from the faint traces lingering in the scent pockets of her tunic robe. Expressionless, he listened to her version of what had happened during his absence.

Her monotone account faltered several times. He waited, allowing her to regain her composure on her own, needing the time to find a way to explain why he would not bring any of the men involved up on charges.

Finished, she sought understanding and found stone, the very substance that made him the commander of the legends. He rose, hands clasped behind his back, and avoided her gaze. "It's a judgment call, Corinda. Admittedly, we are a species in trouble when the only response to a threat is violence. Were it peacetime, I could probably call for an investigation." Turning to look straight down at her, "However, what you saw was a tiny sampling of what normal inhabitation procedure is—according to the Exploration Manual written by the Seven Worlds Government.

"I would be questioning not just the events of that planet back there, but the entire ethical code of the Seven's terraforming policies. Just how many points do you think I could score for my cause that way?

"No. I don't approve. Maybe I would have reacted differently from Captain Gevek. Maybe not. I wasn't there. But from reviewing the records, I'd say we were lucky not to sustain damage or casualties." The ice congealing over her made him stop.

"Hart. I saw a man down there. He was in the trees. He called that big thing back into the ground. And he saw me." She shuddered and gazed at the wall. "He saw me," she repeated in a whisper.

Shaken, General Myzillion paused directly in front

of her. "Are you sure? You know, you were pretty upset." One straight-on glance and he changed tactics. "All
right. Did you recognize him? Could it have been . . . no.
I suppose that's too much to hope for."

"At first, I thought it might be. The coloring was similar." She stood, crowding him, forcing him to step back.
"It really doesn't matter now, does it? The jungle became
an inferno. Nothing—no one—could have survived."

The general paced quietly for a while, sorting, disas-
sociating himself from the growing feelings he had for the
woman. He clung to the ragged edge of analytical judgment. By the gods, she played havoc with all the stable
elements which had ruled his life successfully for so long.
He found himself staring at her, part of him considering a course of action and weighing the options, the other
undressing her.

Corinda felt the intensity of his attention and took advantage of it by positioning herself seductively on the
bunk and looking back through a veil of black eyelashes.

The game was out of character for them both and soon
ended when the general laughed. "All right. What do you
want, Corinda? Ya know damn well I can't disprove you
any more than you can find someone to corroborate what
you claim to have seen."

Serious, "I saw it, Hart. You can't change what I know
by trying to intimidate me. I saw a man in the trees, and
your men killed him along with the indigenous life in the
clearing."

"What do you want? I can't very well call the first
lady of the House of dez Kaliea, pro-tem to cor Baalan, a
liar, can I?" He slumped against the wall. "I wish I
didn't believe you."

Corinda rose to stand directly in front of General Myzillion. She was rigid, her voice not quite as hard as she
wanted it to sound. "I want to go back there, Hart. I want
you to scan the whole planet for human life forms." She
smiled faintly. "I'll bet there have never been any scans
run on it. In fact, I'll bet we find some interesting things
there."

"You win, Corinda. We'll go back." Gruffly he turned
away, pausing at the door, his hand hovering over the
manual release. "You could have told me what you
wanted, told me what you saw, and your conclusions.
You're not dealing with the hierarchy of Antition."

For a second he looked over his shoulder, the hurt inside him apparent. Corinda hid her surprise.

"But then, I guess it really doesn't matter to you, does it, Corinda?" The door opened, swallowed him and closed.

"Damnation, Hart, I'm afraid it does and I can't afford you." She stared at the door for a long time, holding her hands tightly folded on her lap to keep them from touching the intercom to call him back. For as long as possible, adherence to her original decision was mandatory.

By the third day the enemy enjoyed the freedom overhead. Stefen was totally oppressed and thought constantly about Lozadar's tale of captivity in the enemy ship which brought him to the Virgin. He doubted he would have survived such restrictions, or been able to withstand the debasement inflicted without striking back, and therefore playing into his enemy's hands. Desperate to be out in the open again and on his way to the Forbidden Place, he made up his mind.

He and Andazu crept out onto the escarpment and descended low into the spume where the rocks were worn slippery. It was hard work demanding an intense concentration from Stefen. Constant glances at the heights slowed him. When the ocean paused for a few heartbeats, the voices and laughter of the land occupants reached the climbers. Stefen tried to put them out of his mind, abhorring their presence.

The fear Andazu emitted was stifling. Water was his nemesis almost to the degree of those overhead. The time spent at the Crystal Curtain made him familiar with it and quite tolerant—there. But a whole ocean nipping at his claws sent him across the escarpment at twice the speed Stefen could manage.

The fear was shared by Stefen and magnified by the thought of capture. If they did not kill him, they would imprison him in one of their metal ships. Death seemed a preferable alternative, an honorable death in the line of battle against the Virgin's enemy. Padree's enemy.

Half the short night passed in muscle-straining agony. Stefen no longer felt his fingers and had to resort to double-checking each hold visually. His knees were bleeding onto his torpid feet, which often slipped out of the niches he wanted them in. Checking upward, he thought they were far enough to begin the ascent. Andazu was nowhere to be seen.

Laboriously, he moved up the face, salty spray hurting the scrapes and bleeding contusions over the front of his body. Near the top, the air was warmer.

A bloodcurdling screech rifled the night.

Stefen froze, gooseflesh rising over his body

"Andazu . . ."

The squall came again.

Stefen could not move quickly enough over the lip. Continuing his momentum, he rolled into a cluster of fusci ferns and pulled them around him. A few heartbeats of rest and evaluation and he was ready to move.

On his elbows and knees, trying to ignore the stinging dirt grinding into open sores, he penetrated the dark. An artificial light glowed ahead. It was no fire, he thought, edging closer; the light was far too even and did not flicker.

The lights were aimed at a fern tree. Tatters of vines hung down to the ground around it, isolating the tree.

Two men holding lights in one hand and weapons in the other were all Stefen could see. He peered to the south, calculating their distance from the main body. Testing the southwesterly wind blowing up the coast, he decided to gamble that Andazu's panic had not reached the main body.

The two separated, weapons raised, and approached the fern tree.

Stefen chose the larger, quieter man and followed him through the ferns. In a flash his knife filled his right hand. Scowling, he was determined that Andazu would not go the way of his beloved mate. There was no dignity in a death caused by an outworlder's weapon. Honor demanded a one-on-one confrontation. But the enemy possessed no such concept of honor.

Stefen hurried to circle the man.

A flash of light preceded an agonized scream which died to a moan. The center of the fern tree lashed violently, then was still.

"Did you get him?" the larger man asked.

"I think I just wounded him. It wasn't a clean shot. I'm moving in closer."

Stefen listened for the second man's location, feeling his ungainly footsteps upon the earth. Through a veil of fronds he saw his gray form gazing at the fern tree, the light held up, the weapon lax at his side. He noted the tendency of the man's right foot to turn inward, the shallow breathing which left his back almost still and the slow response of his reflexes to the other man's changing light beam.

Stefen grinned wickedly. Barely breathing, he turned the knife over in his hand and held the dull side, the point in his fingers.

Like a hungry kervemith, he sprang to his feet, startling his prey. The enemy's mouth opened, his eyes wide and bulging. Stefen hurled his knife.

It thunked point first into the man's heart.

Stefen slapped the outworlder weapon away and grabbed for the light, catching it only after it wobbled on the high fronds. The man clutched at his chest with both hands, his fingertips clawing as though trying to dig out the steel impaling his heart. He teetered dangerously toward Stefen.

"Hey! Hold that thing still, will ya?" came the other man's irritated voice.

Stefen cleared his throat slightly and tried duplicating the dead man's tone. "I tripped."

"Watch where you're going."

The dead man crumpled on his knees and pitched toward Stefen. Holding the light steady, he caught the man, turned him and reached for his knife. It came free with a flutter of blood and air being exchanged in the corpse. Carefully, he wiped the sides off on the man's shoulder, placed the blade between his teeth and retrieved the weapon. He sucked in his stomach; the waistband of his breeches gave enough for the barrel to slide down his back.

Armed with the light and the knife, he continued to circle, checking the origin of the second beam and the ground for the place he wanted the two to meet.

"Maybe we ought to chop down the tree. One blast ought to do it," came the baritone again.

"It might get away," Stefen answered. He moved away, shone the light wildly and called out, "Help me. I'm stuck in a hole."

"Where are you?"

"Straight across from you. I dropped my light and can't reach it." Stefen placed the light in the center of a heavy cluster of loban ferns fat with batinas. He retreated a dozen meters and waited, watching the light move toward him.

"Can you see me?" There were strains of nervous tension in the timbre of his voice.

"Straight ahead."

"Are you sure? You sound funny . . . yiiee!" The light flew into the air. Brilliant flashes shot into the dark sky as the man's weapon fired spastically. A second scream, half muffled, culminated in wild thrashing. Then silence, marked by the thud of the light hitting the ground and bouncing.

Stefen moved halfway around the fern tree before addressing Andazu in fenwapter. "How many? Two? Can you get down or should I come for you?"

Andazu's voice was weak. He confirmed that there were only two and he would not require assistance. It took several hundred heartbeats for him to climb down.

Stefen waited near the base after rolling the first man's body into the grabber moss. He paused, then threw the lights in after them. Grinning, he decided to let the enemy wonder what had happened to their comrades.

The grin faded when he saw Andazu. The fenwapter's left forelimb dangled uselessly, forcing him to move on his hind legs. The heat had seared the open flesh around the bone. Andazu's three eyes looked in divergent directions, seeking an object to settle his pain on. Heavy breathing seethed through his extended snout, filled with teeth ready to tear through anything with enough stupidity to provoke him.

Stefen removed his shirt. The amulet slapped against his chest. It struck him as odd that he had never thought about the pendant as the reason for going to the Forbidden Place. Yet it was the sole reason for the journey.

He wrapped his shirt around Andazu's wound, encasing the dangling paw-hand in the center. It did not seem likely to grow back together. Gently he tied off the ends, touching the fenwapter as little as possible.

They moved north as fast as Andazu could hobble on three paws. Pained by his friend's suffering, Stefen wished that Esse were not so far away.

Chapter 8

THE CAVERNS GROWING TINY STALACTITES cramped Lozadar. It was not that the area was small. On the contrary. Several times he considered exploring it. A concern over getting lost prevented him. Neither of the kervemith appeared willing to find him in that event. For the first time since his arrival, he was bored.

The admission brought a smile. Much of his life was spent being bored by one inanity or another. Of late, he considered his lot as Ruler of the Seven Worlds. He did not have the proper temperament. No . . . besides, there was too much time wasted on formalities and inconsequential ceremonies.

It had always been like that. How often had his father given him the same lecture, started in childhood, about personal restraint and self-control? The words came back, spoken by a man who understood the desire to explore, to live on independent terms and to be free of the birth shackles he had no control over.

He stared at the wall without seeing it, wondering why it had taken the death of his family and the ensuing hardships to recognize the conflict his father had lived with on a daily basis. *Of course he understood*, Lozadar mused. *He had the same wanderlust, the same drives—just more discipline...*

Somewhere between the time he had reached maturity and the day he had assumed the title and responsibilities of the cor Baalan House, he had hoped for a chunk of space to assuage his inner discontent. Ships left twice a decaset for alluring places, half-tamed planets, unknown adventures and the glittering recreation ports spread across the Seven Worlds and their colonies.

He picked up a pebble and threw it at the wall.

"Well, here I am on an untamed planet that shouldn't physically exist, and I'm damn bored. *Bored*," he shouted, rousing Esse. He wished for Corinda. She understood. She shared the outrage at the way protocol and government functioned in mountains of etiquetted futility. *Corinda. Yes, she understands a lot,* he decided. *Perhaps that's what drew us together as children. We're a great deal alike.*

He threw another pebble, saw it strike and dropped the rest.

Stefen's pack drew his attention. Idly he reached for it. Stefen never went into the packs for food, clothing or anything else, he realized. Curious, he unlaced the ties and threw the flap back.

A history orb rolled into the cradle of his legs. Esse snarled, not caring for the idea of an outworlder going through the Judge's pack. "It's all right. I'm not going to take anything." The beast settled, guardedly. A few decasets ago Esse would have shredded him without warning. "Progress . . ." he began, then stopped when he activated the orb.

The sequencing seemed wrong. The orb had been put together in a hurry by someone apparently unfamiliar with the process. Snatches of events began but did not end. He turned it off, then on again, hoping the intermittency was in the activation device.

He set it aside, making a note to ask Stefen about it later. The choice between an old-style book and a neatly wrapped softened nacki package was easy. The cords were strong, the knots tight. He worried at them for an hour before they came loose. The more difficult the task, the more intriguing it became for him.

Inside the soft wrap was a necklace. Four rich strands held an elliptical pendant—the dez Kaliea crest—suspended in the center. They came together at a point where an invisible clasp held them around the wearer's neck. The monetary value of such a bauble was enormous. It was possibly the one thing the House of dez Kaliea would ransom, with a possible bonus for the fate of Annalli dez Kaliea. Dumbfounded, he gaped at the glittering rocks. Stefen had said his mother's name was Annalli, but names like that, like Stefen and Padree, were so commonplace.

Lozadar pondered over the jewels for quite some time, during which Esse changed places with Asa, hunted a couple of chotiburus and brought back dinner for the three of them. Absently, Lozadar went through the motions of making a fire, gutted the piglike cadaver and finally ran a spit through it. The kervemith made short order of the innards, lapping up all traces of blood. They preferred the insides raw, but found small quantities of cooked meat a delicacy.

As though clarification might be found in the crystalline sphere, Lozadar opened the book. The jewelry could have come from any source—not necessarily Annalli dez Kaliea.

A delicate script, something rare these days, graced the inner confines of the book. There were several entries which Lozadar read while the meat burned. When finished, he repacked everything, knowing that as Ruler of the Seven, he was the sworn enemy of Padree eal Kaul, founder of the Insurrectionist movement.

He wished to turn back time and never have invaded the secrets of Stefen's pack. Yet he could not help thinking about the Insurrectionists of eal Kaul's day and the twenty-year terror they had inflicted on the colonies.

Is eal Kaul really dead? he wondered, trying to pull a strip of meat from the chotiburu's steaming haunch without burning his fingers.

Stefen said he was. But the old bastard was not incapable of leaving his kid to fend for himself. What does anyone know about total deception at age ten anyway, anyone of Stefen's naive character? *Or maybe he did love his kid,* Lozadar mused, *and he's really dead. Stefen has him immortalized.*

Thinking of the whole mess, which he was helpless to do anything about, conjured up Corinda in the clearing. She did not appear to be mistreated, nor did their manner toward her indicate anything but respect.

He put his head in his hands. Nothing made sense, nor was it likely to as long as he stayed in the caverns. He turned to Esse, who was regarding him with restless glances. "You know it's been too long, don't you? He said it wasn't far. They should have returned by now."

Esse turned away, looked back and snarled quietly.

"Yeah, you know." Lozadar picked up another handful of pebbles and tossed them one at a time at the target scratched into the wall.

Stefen tucked clean nacki leaves around Andazu and fed him nectar from the water flowers to deaden the pain.

The cave they occupied was deep and well protected by santi ferns. Poisonous fruit rotted on the ground outside. A trickle of fresh water leaked through a split in the lava to collect in a large pool.

Piles of batinas, fotigs and nacki were mounded near Andazu's head. His fur was wet with fever perspiration, though he shivered often.

Stefen checked the wound. He did not know if it looked good or bad, but there were no signs of festering. The fever worried him. Fenwapters were generally not susceptible to the malady which struck down his own kind.

Squatting, he watched Andazu for a sign of change.

"Go," the fenwapter croaked.

Stefen shook his head.

"Go."

Stefen looked into the middle eye, which was bright and glazed by fever. "I do not want to leave you alone."

"I was alone before we met. I do not need you now." The chitters and moans came hard, further exhausting him.

Reluctantly Stefen rose. "I will go, then. But I will not be gone long, Andazu."

The fenwapter's eyes disappeared. He turned away, embarrassed by his frail condition.

Stefen backed out of the cave and arranged the ferns into a natural array. He checked in all directions, listening, then crept away, still vigilant.

He ran for two kilometers at full speed toward a black obsidian mountain, more anxious than ever to be done with the death promise Padree had extracted. Now was a time for the living. Their need was surely greater than the dead's. Rain drizzled out of gray clouds to make the stone treacherous. He slowed further at the sight of an opening in the otherwise smooth escarpment. A wad of mist puffed out in breathing rhythm.

Stefen came to a panting halt in front of the maw and stared at the black formation that ate the light with its density. The texture was incongruous with the exterior. The entrance was shaped like an enormous eye, upswept at the sides, high in the middle and wide horizontally.

It was not at all what Stefen had tried to visualize.

Watching it, a feeling of insignificance rolled over him as the mist lapped his toes. An expectation of power stilled the air and halted the rain. It poured into the jungle on three sides of the black dais. He sank to his knees humbled by the presence around him. The mist churned faster and faster in the eye, now holding a tighter control and not allowing a churl to escape. It seemed proper to say something, but he could not think of the right words.

Inexplicably, he rose and moved close, drawn to it, yet fearful. Padree's words careened off the walls of his memory. ". . . never go in . . . never go back . . ." The pull faltered. His curiosity hesitated. Trembling, he untied the wrapping from around the amulet. The gold shone brighter and brighter, glowing into a ball he could not look at.

The mist took on subtle pastel hues in the core. Entranced, he slowly lifted the chain from around his neck. For an instant, it felt as though a great burden rose from his shoulders. He gathered the woven strands of light composing the chain in his right hand and let the golden ball dangle at the end of the brilliance slipped between his index and forefingers.

Vibrant yellows, piercing reds, rich blues and a pure white swirled rhythmically out of the center of the eye. Greens and browns formed independent whirlpools at the sides. The vortex turned black.

Stefen gathered the light into his hand, turned slightly, then hurled it into the center dilating to swallow the colors. From the sides, brown and chartreuse mist gushed out to encircle him.

He wanted to run, afraid as he had never been afraid in his life. Every nerve in his body tingled. His head began an angry pounding. The mist encompassed him. It became difficult to breathe.

He tried to fight the inundation of his senses, not wanting to hear the soft hum in his ears or smell and taste the bittersweet fragrance inherent in the shroud. Even with his eyes closed he was in a world of red and black, perpetually changing, exploding with soundless velocities that touched the distant stars.

A sensation of floating through the maelstrom implied movement, yet he did not believe in the lingering spots of lucidity, that he was walking. It was impossible to move otherwise. The mist fingers of color touched his body, caressing in hues to evoke intense pleasure and soul piercing pain, simultaneously.

Visions coalesced.

His parents—younger than he thought they had ever been—stood hand in hand at the Forbidden Place. He wanted to reach out and touch them, call to them, have them look his way. The stone had more flexibility than he. They were garbed similar to Corinda dez Kaliea and the outcast Ruler.

He listened, as though the scene were taking place for the first time; he was a part of the rock's molecular structure from the beginning of time.

When the vision ended, he wanted to be ill. Bent, he retched futilely.

The mist hurled him upright. Bile caught in his throat. He felt unclean, used. The love held so close to his heart turned inside out to become hatred. The mist continued playing with his emotions until he achieved a state of indifference with a remote smattering of understanding.

Gradually, he abandoned himself to the mist. He felt as though he was going to sleep regardless of how hard he fought it.

When he woke, he was deep inside the Forbidden Place. The mist was gone. The walls radiated a shiny cold. He ran from the black bowels out to the platform, wanting to be away from the evil Padree had warned him about, but afraid the taint had already rubbed off on him.

His clothes were in a heap where the mist had taken him. The amulet lay on top. He gazed at it for half a hundred heartbeats, then into the obsidian cavern and recognized the implications. "No," he whispered, "I will not be a piece of flesh to be bargained for. I am not my father's son to be sold and used as a payment. He can pay his debts. I will pay my own! I am my own man. Do you hear? My own man!"

He swept up the amulet and again hurled it into the ominous maw of the Forbidden Place. The sound of metal on stone was loud and echoed louder and louder, reaching out to the jungle, beyond the highest putch, into the sky and beyond. The clouds sped away, parting furiously, until the Deity looked straight down upon him. The day turned a blinding white.

He screamed, hiding his eyes, cowering into a fetal ball around his clothes. The light seared the rock beyond his immediate area until it too glowed.

He lay trembling, whimpering, till long after dark. But

the dark he experienced was not that of night. He blinked a hundred times, rolled on his back and screamed louder. The agony of hot rocks against his flesh was secondary to the knowledge that he was blind.

The land pitched and rolled, thundering on the three levels of earth, sky and bowels. Putch trees cracked and split, crashing through heavy vines, thudding down to smash the delicate ferns below. The land opened at the edge of the obsidian dais and slammed shut. Steam jetted fifty meters into the air.

The violent cacophony was so tremendous that he did not know where to go. He opened his mouth to scream a submission. No sound passed through his frozen vocal chords.

The noise grew, jumbling together in one continuous bombardment that crescendoed and fell abruptly into silence. Stefen threw his hands over his head and felt his bald scalp. Groping in the silent, dark world filled with pain, he touched clumps of his hair lying on the stone. Hurriedly, he touched his arms, chest and groin. Not a hair remained on his body.

Shakily, he came to his feet. For a moment, he straightened, a naked man in the light and presence of the Deity and his Virgin lover.

He nodded, knowing he would have to make peace with them, but not until he made his own internal peace could it be attempted. It was not a time for compromise.

He bent to pick up his belongings, expressionless, steeled to hide the thunder in his brain. He held them in his left hand, the outworlder's weapon awkward in the bundle. His right hand remained extended as a feeler. He turned toward the steam and sought a passage through.

Overhead, Evaladyn flew out of the clouds, calling and whistling. She dove, seeking attention. The horde filled the sky, playing tag in the steam vapor.

Stefen followed the heat to a small break. He rushed through, unable to stop once he started. The steam scalded parts of his flesh. As he ran, nacki leaves cut his thighs until he collected his wits enough to put on his breeches. Sharp fotigs poked into the tops of his swelling feet and popped the heat blisters. Ferns grabbed at him and the putch branches tripped him. All that he had once deemed familiar and friendly turned hostile. He tried to recall whether or not there were any grabber-moss patches between the Forbidden Place and Andazu's shelter.

Falizian scouts went south, others to the west and still more splitting the difference between the two directions. Evaladyn dispersed the entire horde in search for the fenwapters and kervemith. Her distress at Stefen's condition infected her horde.

Stefen fell again and debated whether or not to get up. He attached his knife to his breeches and found a tendril with which to tie the Lat-kor to it. He used a gnarled stalk, once laden with fotigs, as a locater in his right hand, keeping the left out and free.

Evaladyn dove into the putch trees, tightly folded her wings back and snaked her head to the sky. More of the roaring beasts who defecated men onto the Virgin were coming through the sky.

She resumed calling to Stefen.

Chapter 9

STEFEN WANDERED IN A DAZE. UNAWARE OF the night-darkened land or the glorious sunrise of the new day, he went in circles. Eating was sporadic and controlled by a separate part of his consciousness. He no longer experienced hunger or thirst, those pangs far too subtle in his collected agonies to gain attention.

Overhead, Evaladyn watched, lamenting, wings fluttering nervously. Often she soared into the sky, trying to ease her anxiety with exhaustion. She kept calling, knowing he could or would not hear, not knowing what else to do.

The volcanoes along the southern and western lands erupted. They hurled fine ash into the clouds in huge quantities. The clouds themselves gathered and built, holding back their burdens of moisture until the Virgin should allow their release.

To the east, the ocean rolled, boiled and pitched. The scent of brine reached far inland and mingled with the storm threat electrifying the air.

The presentiment that the Deity and the Virgin were going to vent their ire upon the land brought the yaxuras to the surface often. Their roars were lost on Stefen. Occasionally, they surfaced close enough for him to catch a whiff of pure oxygen. Their sojourns into the light tore the jungle, pocking the lush floor with holes gouged deep into the Virgin's crust.

Stefen faltered at the rims of the deathtraps, falling often while poking frantically with his stick in the loose dirt for solidity. The burns ached so deeply in his flesh that he would have cried aloud if he had had the voice or any tears left.

Despairing, he considered pausing for a rest, but felt he would never get up if he did. For a while he could not remember where he was going or why. Yet he knew he would die if he stopped to ponder the whys and wherefores of his fate. The ground would swallow him if the trees did not pounce on him or the sky did not strike out at him again. There was a spark of anger which fed his survival instincts, vowing a revenge upon the powers inflicting the torment upon him. Through the black maze shimmering across his brain he felt sad that all his loves had become hates.

Andazu's image came and left, cajoling him onward. *He does not need me,* Stefen bitterly reminded himself, wishing he could rest. *I cannot help him now. I cannot even help myself.*

Just past noon the odor of rotting santi fruit assaulted him. He debated its importance, knowing it was significant, and traced it to a cluster of ferns. He stood at the edges of the fronds, knees quaking, muscles jerking in his calves and thighs.

The clouds churned. The day turned as dark as the night.

Evaladyn spread her wings and screeched hoarsely at Stefen. Her melodious song was gone, her voice damaged beyond natural repair.

The walking stick became a probe through the ferns, tapping at the base rock, moving to left and right, groping for the top. Stabbing in a frenzy, he hit air and toppled into the ferns.

He crawled through the green, crushing iridescent blue flowers and rotten phosphorescent fruit. Once the frond padding gave out he stumbled to his feet. He hit his head on the ceiling and bent over, then fell several steps before his balance totally gave out.

Chest heaving, finding no position which offered a relief, he reached out and found Andazu. The furry creature was asleep and beyond the fever crisis. He left the fenwapter and groped for the water trickle; his bloody hand, worn through the skin, left a trail on the floor.

He rolled in the stream, feeling the cold pull the heat from the burn splotches, wishing he could be numb from head to toe—especially his head! He lay down, exhausted, and tried to calm his mind.

The Deity spun in space, shooting prominences out with fury. Pores opened and spread into numerous sunspot pairs on the lower hemisphere, their magnetic fields increasing by thousands of gauss. The immediate temperature lowered in the black centers. Polarity reversed.

The Lovers empathized with each other, consoling, assuring, bitter at the turn of events, despondent at their choice of a Champion for the delicate Virgin.

Man made his way through the galaxy, tainting, mauling, mutilating all he grabbed. He never accepted what was and always changed it into something it was not meant to be. He took what looked ugly to him and made it beautiful. He also soiled that beauty with abominable machines, artificial structures and his own brand of weather. And their method for forming the perfect Champion to hold back the onslaught of technology and ruin had been in error.

The Virgin contemplated her fate, then cried. She projected the seizure of her ores from their deep, secret places, the release of her treasured gases and fuels, the plunder of minerals scattered generously over her surface and through each level of the crust. She saw her skies change to the smoky hue of a thousand settler fires as they built on the land. These things she could adjust to and live with. But she foresaw the change in her orbit that would not permit her the close proximity to her Lover. There would be no more Passage. After the years alone during the solar maelstrom as the envelope gases from the weaker sun passed them by, her orbit would change, the life on her surface would die, and then, after the final degradation, man would come—unless he was stopped now, for he would never live in harmony with them.

The Deity stormed, flaring out to the weaker sun, who observed with a cold dispassion.

Stefen would be their Champion and learn more than the tiny insight from the Forbidden Place that his was an aggressive species who could demolish the fragile balance preserving the Virgin.

It was so little, what they asked. . . .

Esse crept into the cavern, growling and snarling. Asa stood quickly and snarled back, her exquisite muscles rippling under her rich coat. Outside, two falizians sang an anxiety-ridden conversation.

Lozadar stood, flanked by kervemith. The entrance was cut off by their bulk. He tried to catch the gist of their conversation and the reason for the rare truce between the beasts and the falizians hovering just inside the cavern. Thunder banged above the jungle, sending its echo to bounce around the limestone walls. The effect vibrated his heart and sent gooseflesh up his backbone in anticipation.

The kervemith circled. A high note from a falizian sent them toward Lozadar. The sudden intensity of their gaze was frightening. Never had he seen the eyes so still. At the same time he was transfixed by the clarity in their blue eyes. Esse managed to halt time.

Asa moved behind the outcast and nudged him toward Esse. Lozadar lost his fascination and found the good sense to be afraid of what was happening. Rain beat the jungle, slamming the ground so hard that it battered the orbi vines and stripped ripening berries off the fern trees and fuscis.

Esse turned so that his and Asa's bodies enclosed the outcast.

A multitude of green spots on gold formed an oddly shaped wall more formidable than any Lozadar had confronted. Below their combined bulk a mesh of hefty legs flexed. The sound of their claws on the smooth stone became unreasonably loud. Quickly, he wondered if something had happened to Stefen and the Virgin's creatures had arrived at their own decision of what his fate was to be. Worse, could they hold him responsible for an unknown tragedy?

Esse hunkered onto his forepaws, lowered the center and finally lay completely down. Lozadar grabbed the packs to keep them from being crushed and put them on to free his hands.

Asa sidestepped, forcing him closer and closer to the other giant kervemith. Worried, Lozadar glanced from side to side, trying to find a way out. Esse's head turned to look at him on the right. Asa snarled on his left. The small space evaporated quickly. He was up to his chest in kervemith, with Asa pressing over his head to the rear.

Preferring to die quickly, he wiggled his left leg free and crawled onto Esse. It seemed better to have the kervemith strike once with his jaws than to be slowly crushed.

Esse rose, rocking him. He grabbed desperately at the short fur, shook his body and spread his legs over the side of the front midsection. The speed Esse accelerated to forced him low over the beast's back. Arms spread, he bounced forward until he found a hold just below the powerful neck. His feet pressed against Esse's sides, not reaching halfway around the mass of rhythmic legs stretching into the jungle.

Feline, graceful motion spanned the yaxura holes in single leaps as the kervemith followed the two falizian scouts in the trees. The jungle became a blur on the peripheral edges of Lozadar's vision. Rain pounded out of the sky with such velocity that it stung his skin and hurt his scalp.

The falizians had difficulty when the jungle ended and they no longer were able to make use of the trees as bastions against the wind. The lava mountains were shrouded by black and gray clouds. Lightning flashed, striking the lower elevations angrily as the sky bellowed. In the rear, trees crashed and split under the force of the storm. Lozadar was tempted to look, but did not dare divert his attention from the task of remaining on the kervemith.

They climbed to a narrow path between two volcanoes rising out of the ground at impossibly steep angles. Lozadar glanced in the noisy direction when they slowed, saw rows of elevated steam vents and put his head down. *This place is fitting of the ancient myths of hell,* he decided. Although the path was wet and slippery and the rain fierce, Lozadar calculated Esse's speed in excess of three hundred kilometers a standard day. He speculated on the kervemith's capabilities without him on his back under good conditions. It seemed a good idea to stay close once they stopped.

Lozadar lost track of time, and still the ride continued. It seemed darker. And cold. How could it be so cold in the midst of all the steaming gaps in the earth? The rain slackened and the wind tossed it around in sideways patterns. Volcanoes rose out of the ground on all sides before they hid in the clouds. Their rumbling blended with the thunder. Esse watched the skies and waited for the falizians.

Lozadar relaxed his legs and arms. They no longer seemed to know how and immediately started to twitch. His stomach growled. The rain turned into sleet. Shivering, he shook his head and grinned. Water dripped off his nose and chin. *Here it is, at long last—the life of adven-*

ture, he mused. The Virgin continued to defy every law his world adhered to.

The smell of perspiration worked into soaked kervemith fur filled his nostrils. He stroked the beast at the throat where his hands almost reached when he stretched out atop the green pelt.

Asa snarled into the wind.

The three of them watched the falizians battle turbulence and descend out of the clouds. They looked too heavy in the cold air. The green of their scales took on a dull luster. They tilted, being thrown by the currents howling above the quieter nook occupied by the kervemith.

Asa moved beside her mate to create room for the falizians. Lozadar watched, remembering Stefen's lessons. The falizians seldom, if ever, landed on the ground, and never in open space. What he was seeing was a rarity that might never be shown him again.

When they did land, exhausted, both sank to their bodies as though they lacked the strength to stand. The far one flexed her wings, showing deep tears in them and ragged, translucent edges on both the frontal sets. Her eyes never wavered from the watching kervemith.

Lozadar kept stroking Esse while they waited. Time cycles no longer existed; only the wind and the rain pushing rivers along the paths and low spots held any significance.

The falizians croaked out a few notes, flexed their wings and labored into the air. The kervemith followed along the second of three paths separated by lava and ash mountains.

Night came early under the clouds. The pace slowed to a fraction of what it had been during the day. The falizians took turns leading, calling over the storm to the kervemith scaling angular sides of the last volcano before the jungle softened the land and the ocean smoothed the cliffs.

Stefen lingered in the vision which the Virgin and her Deity had imposed upon him at the Forbidden Place. Annalli and Padree stood majestically before the mist, each afraid, and that fear so great Stefen felt it also.

Eloquently, Padree requested a place of sanctuary for his group. He spoke about the discontent lying in the stars, the inability for them to find peace among the developed worlds and their need for a refuge.

The Deity and the Virgin listened, pleased and saddened simultaneously.

And Stefen gazed upon his father, watching him change from the image he presented the outer world, seeing the inner man guilt-ridden, ruthless and void of honor. He saw a man whose deeds ranged from the reprehensible to the despicable. Yet, he also saw a man who loved the woman at his side, the woman he stole from one of the Ruling Houses, the daughter and firstborn of the Coralis Legate.

Stefen's mind balked, knowing he could not deny what he saw and knowing that was not the man who loved, cared and raised him. The stronger his refusal to believe what the Lovers put before him, the more they showed to him.

The callousness with which Padree eal Kaul raped and killed a young woman colonist after plundering her settlement sent Stefen into convulsions. Again he saw his father at about his own age rip the woman's tunic dress off her body. She cried softly, trembling, her hands folded across her small breasts, slightly bent at the waist and her legs shaking, but pressed together. Padree grabbed her hands, spread her arms out to the sides and laughed. A quick foot sweep dropped her to the ground, screaming.

Padree lunged on top of her, slapping her until the sounds abated. Her face was unrecognizable under the blood. Wide-eyed, sobbing quietly, she turned her head toward the white caghplast wall splattered with her blood while Padree explored her breasts and kneed her legs apart. He fumbled with the front of his breeches, leered at the woman and tried to penetrate her. It was difficult at first, but the third thrust broke her last line of defense. She screamed in agony and struck out with fists and fingernails.

Knowing what followed, Stefen too screamed in his world of silence, not wanting to see it again, not wanting to believe the vision, not knowing why this was being done to him.

Padree caught the woman's left hand at the wrist and held it. Using both hands, he bent her fingers back until they snapped. Conscious, the woman became still. Emotion left her face. Her eyes closed, squeezing tears out to run through the blood on her cheeks.

When Padree's need was filled, he stood and fastened his breeches. Cursing at the red stains across the front, he used the shreds of the woman's dress as a cleaning rag. He tossed it at her when finished, then calmly drew his Lat-kor and fired it into her stomach. The wide scan made a hole in the pavement where her rib cage had been.

The act was one of the hundreds of visions running individually through Stefen's mind. The violence was foreign to him, and he felt as though it was a crime of total degradation, not one of sexual offense. The people were strangers wearing familiar masks. The worlds were of another time and dimension, their cultures more alien than the outcast's.

He could not comprehend that the gentle, caring, loving man who had been his father—thoughtful and protective—was this same vermin capable of the heinous acts the Lovers depicted. Yet he knew there was truth in what he was forced to view. The Virgin did not lie. Nor did she know subtlety or innuendo. Suddenly, he felt that he knew too much, not a bit of which he wanted to know. Acceptance was out of the question without reasoning.

Annalli stood before the Virgin. She asked for the life she would never see again. Hardly more than a child, she was frail, unaccustomed to primitive life-styles and uncertain of her future. Violence was an abhorrent thing to her. Fleeting visions of her childhood and a genteel upbringing wrapped in luxury surrounded her presence. Annalli emanated a soft-natured naiveté in total contradiction to Padree's character.

It was the puzzle which Stefen dismally knew he had to solve and accept before he could find peace with either himself or the Lovers. *Impossible,* he groaned inwardly. Almost as impossible as being able to accept himself as part of a bargain, predestined to the role of the Virgin's Champion.

Chapter 10

IT WAS A TIGHT FORMATION. NINE SHIPS FOL-
lowed General Myzillion's Commander-Flight Mark IV
speeding towards 4724Y.

Five ships fired their front thrusters and fell behind the
others. The four continued, their course unchanged. Moments later they jumped and came out a few hours from
4724Y. The other five also jumped. Their destination was
Antition.

He sat at the com, uneasy and more than a little unhappy
over the obligation Corinda had thrust upon him. There
were anomalies in this part of the quadrant which were
better left alone, that planet being foremost on the list.

Another time, another place, the contradictory reports
and odd changes since they had last visited would incite a
fever and the near edge of panic. The crew mumbled to
themselves and their instruments quietly, concerned over
the drastic inconsistencies and the effect of the tremendous
magnetic and solar storm on directional equipment. Tension rode the upper air level in the spacious room.

The side door opened. Corinda made a first-ever appearance at the center. She looked composed and felt rattled as she sought the General.

He gave her a small sign of recognition, raised his hand
slightly and motioned her over to the elevated chair he occupied. Unobtrusively, he smoothed his uniform jacket.

Corinda found more confidence with each step and just
a little hope for the search she wanted. She reached the
General, but before she could say anything a siren wailed,
the lights went out, leaving a dull-blue glow, and a voice
called out.

"Insurrectionist forces leaving 4724Y gravitational well
on midrange scan zero-three at zero-one-five degrees.
They have read us and are closing. Contact in one-niner
minutes."

A brief pause in his oration left a void. The siren droned on for several minutes, covering the flurries of reports and acknowledgments exchanged by the crew and their commander.

The nineteen minutes flew by and dragged at the same time. The anticipation of being the object of an all-out attack did not sit well with Corinda. Experiencing the skirmishes and battles tucked in her cabin was one thing, but to stand on the bridge besides the com and watch it happen—it was horrifyingly exciting.

For the most part General Myzillion forgot his guest, being far too busy planning an attack and countermeasure. Her hand on his shoulder startled him. "Get back to your cabin, Lady Corinda. It's better for you there."

"Safer?"

"During a war there is no safe place on a Mark IV. You're riding on a first-class target."

"Then I'm staying."

"I haven't got time to argue. Strap yourself into one of those seats by the console and stay out of the way."

She started to say something about his opinion of her, but saw that he was already engaged in another conversation with one of the ten voices perpetually coming through the speaker on his armrest. She hurried to the only empty seat in the center and strapped herself in tightly. Heart thudding, she waited. Now the time dragged.

There were five Insurrectionist ships. The center ship was larger than the Mark IV. Screens all around the command center were alive with different views of the enemy bearing down on them.

"Two minutes to range." The young man next to her spoke with an impartiality Corinda found unnerving. Inwardly, she felt as though there were two minutes left in which to totally panic.

"They're still accelerating," he continued.

"Good," replied General Myzillion. "One pass. Right wing and rear, hold your fire, save your energy."

Two instant confirmations came through the wall speakers from the other ships.

Corinda watched breathlessly as the Insurrectionists approached. A tiny circle on the enormous center ship fascinated her and eased some anxiety.

"Full deflectors engaged," came another calm voice from across the bridge.

She hardly heard the words flowing freely around her. The ships changed angles and grew on the screens. The emblem took shape, almost recognizable. The ship moved.

A flash faster than the eye could register was picked up by the alarms. The close range made the clanging useless, as it had already hit, the light faster than the sound. Three drones hung where the Insurrectionist ship had been, each with a small thruster to slow acceleration and keep it out of the way until needed.

The Colonials retaliated. The Mark IV sent burst after burst, concentrating on the front-and-center ship, hitting the same spot to break down its defenses.

"Give him a double charge followed by a negative-ion blast," the General ordered.

Within half a minute the front ship disintegrated. Corinda stared at the screen in disbelief. It was just gone— no fires, no explosion, dead without a whimper. How many men and women? Shivering, she trained her attention back to the new lead ship.

Damage reports trickled in.

The ship on the left side of the leader teetered, hurled through space by its own momentum, which was great enough to escape the sun's pull. The illumination of its skin died, indicating it was totally disabled and only time separated its inhabitants from their destinies.

"Tempting. So damn tempting," General Myzillion muttered at the com.

"This is Captain Gevek at rear. We can trail and attempt retrieval—"

The ship became a flash of light. The space next to the center was empty, a victim of her leader's policies.

The screens filled with the bellies of the Insurrectionists as they passed overhead.

"Go for the big one," Myzillion ordered.

Left and rear poured out all they had and could not inflict major damage. They pursued with firepower until their effective range diminished.

The lights came on, bright by contrast. Corinda unstrapped the harness holding her to the chair and rose, unsettled. Wordless, she left the bridge, headed for her cabin. She wondered how many of those on the four bridges had studied the emblem on the Insurrectionist command ship and recognized it.

She did not look back even when the General called her name.

Directed by Evaladyn, Lozadar parted the broken and smashed santi fronds and crawled into the dank opening. The abrupt darkness took a little while to adjust too. He paused, hearing the kervemith snarl anxiously outside. He crawled toward a lump surrounded by nacki leaves.

Carefully he touched the mass. It was fur. "Andazu?"

The fenwapter moaned and rolled toward him.

Lozadar pulled at his wet pack and tugged on the left strap, which felt grafted to his shoulder. He rummaged through it in the dark until he found the instone. It went between his knees. Next he took one of the nacki leaves, rolled it up tightly and cut the bundle in half.

He lit the end.

The sudden brilliance made the fenwapter turn away. "Andazu, what's wrong? What has happened to you? Where's Stefen?" He spoke slowly, pronouncing each syllable with Stefen's emphasis. As he started to look around, he noticed Stefen's shirt wrapped around the fenwapter's forelimb. He found a niche in the wall rock for the torch and gently unwrapped the shirt.

Andazu watched, coming out of his shock-and-fever-induced stupor. He uttered a word which Lozadar interpreted as "enemy."

Three centimeters of solid flesh held the hand/paw onto the forearm. The hair was burned away. The stub was partially cauterized.

Lozadar took a deep breath, placed his hands on his knees and exhaled loudly. Shifting his gaze between Andazu and the wound, "You were very lucky. But not lucky enough. When the rain stops, this has to be worked on. It will hurt very much."

Andazu labored to sit, lifted his left forelimb and held the hand/paw so that it would not dangle.

Lozadar lost his appetite.

The hanging limb would have to be cut away and the rest of the stump cauterized. The light was bright enough to see the flesh dying around the claws. They could not procrastinate too long before attacking the problem.

Morosely, he picked up the torch and walked hunched over into the back part of the cave. He did not have to go far before discovering Stefen lying in a trickle of water.

Stefen flinched at his touch. His eyes opened, as did his mouth.

Lozadar refrained from additional contact. He spoke softly, asking what had happened, when, who, and received nothing in response. Examining Stefen, he found steam burns near his shoulders, across his back and on his feet well up his calves.

He turned away, agitated, irate and helpless. It took two tries before he cleared away the lump in his throat. "Andazu? Stay with him, but don't touch him."

The fenwapter lumbered forward on three limbs, whining at his friend.

"Not do," he said emphatically.

Lozadar scurried back to the entrance, where the falizians and kervemith waited impatiently. The lightning and thunder no longer waged a perpetual siege upon the sky. The rain fell straight down. He walked several dozen meters, hands clasped behind his back, while he searched for the right words.

The group followed silently.

He gazed at the followers, feeling their intensity and concern blend with his own. Beginning with the fenwapter, he conveyed what he thought had to be done when the rain stopped and presented an explanation of why.

Esse whined.

Asa's big head swung toward the cave.

Lozadar sighed, thinking that they at least understood the words.

"Stefen is inside, too." He watched the river he was standing in grow wider. "I do not know what happened to him." Briefly, he described Stefen's condition, adding that he did not think Stefen was aware of what was happening around him.

He had nothing more to say. He did not know how long he stood there. When he looked up, the others were still waiting. Shrugging, "We will do the best we can for him. It might be temporary." The words carried more hope than he felt.

Annalli sat on a carrier in the shelter behind the Crystal Curtain. Pale and golden, she appeared thinner than when she had accompanied Padree to the Forbidden

Place. Her regal demeanor delineated her as special, above the women huddled in the midsection with their men. Her fine dress was worn by another, the seams bulging and the hem tattered.

Padree sat on the floor, leaning against the wall, dozing.

A man rose from a stone game he had been playing with four others and approached Annalli. Wordless, he grabbed her wrist and pulled.

She shook her head and resisted. "Please. Let me go."

"In case you haven't noticed, we share everything here, including you." His pudgy smile through a sparse beard made his eyes twinkle.

Without opening his eyes, Padree spoke. "Not her. Pick one of the others. She doesn't get shared."

"What's this? The rules suddenly change? If you hadn't snatched her we would be back in business by now. Since we're all payin' the price, I want to sample the goods. We're entitled! Each and every one of us."

"No." Padree's voice was low and brought the attention of the rest sitting in the section.

"I say we vote on it," the man insisted, jerking Annalli to her feet.

"No vote. My word is law here." Padree looked half asleep, his eyes closed.

Annalli, panic-stricken, gaped at the man towering over her. When her captor turned to address the group, she pulled free and fell back to the carrier.

He turned back, enraged, and slapped her so hard she went sprawling on the floor.

Padree opened his eyes. There was a flash of light and the putrid smell of charred flesh. The man crumpled to the floor. Annalli's muffled sobs were the only sound in the shelter for several minutes.

"Get him out of here," Padree said. "Any more of you want to try what he did can expect the same thing." Crouching beside Annalli, he stroked her head and gently turned her so she could sit up. Blood ran out the side of her mouth. Padree tenderly thumbed it away.

Stefen found himself in a world of eyes—his father painfully looking at Annalli; suspicious, angry, understanding eyes from all over the shelter focused upon them; Annalli looking back at Padree in confusion and gratitude.

There was no outrage over this one of his father's killings. Searching through the muddled vision, Stefen likened it to the killing of the two who had attacked Andazu. He became nauseated as he realized he took lives with no more concern or guilt than his father. His inner ear heard the outworlder being engulfed by the moss. So much confusion. Was killing wrong?

Lava crept over his shoulder. Was it lava? Or was it someone touching him? There seemed little difference. Questions and answers dissolved into a chasm of pain.

It rained for two more days. When the clouds parted, the Deity looked down upon the ravaged jungles of the Virgin. The shreds of her green raiment mirrored a desperation born of the Lovers.

Remnants floated upon the seas to be bashed against the cliffs. Kilometers of broken and torn nacki vines were draped over fern and putch trees, hanging down over the matted jungle floor. With the warmth of the suns came the pungent odor of rotting fruit lodged in the rubble. Swarms of ganids chirped and flitted over the heaviest deposits and gorged upon the feast.

The volcanoes quieted, leaving only faint traces of smoke to curl into the bright day. Streams ran through the jungle in beds carved deeper after each Passage.

Lozadar built a fire outside the cave. Andazu watched, flanked by Asa and Esse. He checked his knife, went inside and returned with Stefen's. His went on the edge of the fire where the rocks glowed red in the shadows.

Evaladyn and two other falizians flew over the trees, each carrying a delicate water flower in the front leg sets. She hovered away from the fire. Wind generated by her wings fanned the blaze and sent embers into the sky with the smoke.

Lozadar ran over and took a flower, careful not to spill any of the nectar. The flowers were so large that he could handle only one at a time. He made three trips, placing each of them beside Andazu.

The fenwapter drank heartily, focusing two of his three eyes on the knives and the fire.

When the time came Lozadar took his knife and ran it through the blue part of the flames several times. He felt as though his body were made of porcelain, and tiny hammers were making his stomach ring.

The fenwapter had passed out, having drunk too much too fast. Lozadar wondered if the nectar caused a hangover. Andazu would have enough pain to cope with even if it did not. A flat rock pulled out of the fire and cooled became the operating platform for Andazu's hand-paw. With one swipe he cut the clawed section free. It rolled to the ground.

Immediately he grabbed Stefen's knife with his shirt wrapped around the handle and pressed the flat edge to the bleeding area.

The hiss and stench were revolting. The blade covered the whole area. After he was done, he sat back on his heels and looked up.

"Evaladyn," he called, finally remembering her name. She hovered above and behind the kervemith.

"Would you send someone for another batch of the flower stuff? He might need it when he wakes." Both knives went on the ground. Straightening, he placed Andazu's forearms over his chest, took a deep breath and scooped him up. He was heavier than he looked. Lozadar struggled to get him into the cave. The multitude of ganids were too close and too easily tempted by the aroma of damaged flesh.

Inside, he maneuvered Andazu into a premade bed of moss, fronds and a nacki-leaf sheet. The fenwapter curled into a ball, holding the mutilated stub away.

Stefen lay on a similar bed beside the water.

Lozadar wiggled slivers of nacki fruit into Stefen's mouth. They always disappeared, though he never saw him chew.

He kept Stefen naked to make the cleanup of his bodily functions easier. The air seemed to be good for his burns, also. Layers peeled away from his splotches. The uglier he looked, the better Lozadar felt and the more hope he had for a recovery.

Outside, he picked up the knives. The two kervemith kept a split vigil, one in the trees, the other near the entrance. Looking around, Lozadar pictured the oasis of jungle smashed between the sea and volcanoes as it was before the storm. The image of an angry, powerful giant who had vented a great rage upon the land came to mind. But the pristine beauty of the place could not be abolished. Already, new buds were opening on the nacki vines and the fragile orbi plants lifted to the sky.

Gradually he gave up questioning why the land had such a drawing effect upon him. Giving up hope for going back had come easily—too easily. He tried not to think about that aspect. The lonely days when the smallest sound had brought fear had vanished. He missed Corinda and maybe several others. It surprised him to realize how few friends and close relationships his birthright had afforded.

Loyalty to a person or an ideal, such as the kind the Virgin's indigenous creatures held for her and Stefen, was the rarest commodity in all of the Seven Worlds. Here it abounded, molded by an unseen hand and cemented by a morality that the finest weapons of civilization could not disintegrate. He thought he had known a man who possessed such an ideology—the Iron General, who was responsible for the brutal slaying of Chalate and Corry. What had happened to him? Was nothing incorruptible? No bond of trust or friendship sacred? Unfortunately, he did not know how the war affected him. What he did know was that hatred flourished where respect and trust had once dwelled.

He stroked Asa, marveling at how quickly the adjustment evolved. He had thought he would miss the luxury, convenience and comfort which had surrounded him all his life. "The price was too high. If you gotta take the responsibilities and pains that go with it, it's too high," he muttered. "We've got plenty to eat, a place to sleep, good company. . . . Now, when Stefen's better"—a pat on Asa's shoulder—"we're going to search for the people he wanted to find. Another decaset and—"

Esse snarled. Asa backed into the brush.

"No!" Lozadar watched three ships cross overhead, circle and spiral down to investigate the smoke from the fire. He held his breath, hoping they would think it was a new vent from the volcanoes, anything but a man-made fire. He crouched back and squatted between Asa's forepaws while the sound of the ships bombarded the land.

Chapter 11

THE SHIPS DIPPED LOW OVER THE TREES AFTER swooping down from the sharp angle created by the volcanoes. They leveled off and pulled up over the sea. Their close maneuvers bespoke battle veterans at the helm, each knowing how close the other was and working the formations by a sixth sense acquired over years of survival. Silver isosceles triangles filled the sky with noise, heat and an alien luster of burnished metal.

Lozadar's heart hammered so loudly that he thought Asa might try to silence him. For an instant, it stopped. The insignia (it went by so fast) was familiar. Breathless, he waited for another formation to pass, this time from the sea.

Nondescript colors made a distinctive pattern. The planet Coralis against a solid background belonged to the House of dez Kaliea.

They've come to look for Corinda, he thought. Maybe even for me. Immediately he wished that he had not seen the emblem. The war raging in his brain kept him immobile while half of him yearned to jump up and run out into the clearing, arms waving for attention. They would come for him.

Rescue.

And would it not be better for Stefen? Andazu? The medical mechanics and doctors would be able to effect a cure more quickly than the uncertainty of time.

Just a moment ago everything had been so clear and well defined.

Stefen. He winced. He could not begin to analyze the extent of his problems, nor could he figure out their cause. The ominous Forbidden Place filtered back into his thoughts. It hinted of things he did not understand about the Virgin.

The ships loosened their pattern and spread. The middle one continued to scrutinize the area like a bird of prey that knew its quarry's hiding place.

Stefen and Andazu were not the only motives to crowd in. How else could he hope to find the bastards who had murdered his family?

He saw his sisters in his mind's eye. Anger leaped inside of him and his fists clenched. He wanted to torture their killers in the same manner and knew that would not be enough to quell his rage or compensate for their loss.

The battles for power among the Seven Worlds, the Colonial forces and other factions he could only guess existed were being waged on all fronts.

Head in hands, he wondered if coming forward and claiming the Rulership would diminish the conflict sufficiently for a peaceful compromise, or if it would merely bring about his death. Death held a different meaning since he had first confronted Stefen. *I want to live,* he mused, *and to be able to live with myself. Too many debts. I couldn't fake it long enough to find a compromise. Damn! I don't even know who the enemy is!*

He owed the Seven their rightful leader. His family was due revenge and justice. But Stefen had his word that he would not leave until judgment was passed—and after.

What did the future hold for him in any one of those circumstances? As Ruler he would never be free to indulge in the wanderlust that had filled his dreams as he grew up. There would be a satisfaction in knowing he was doing what he had been somewhat trained for on a lesser scale—a hell of a challenge!

Looking at his hands, he wondered how he could make decisions affecting millions of lives when he could not make one for his own now.

A tableau of his family materialized. Again, he heard the bass voice behind him quiet those standing around his sisters. They deserved justice and he deserved revenge. It was vowed to them posthumously.

He became aware of Asa. He liked the jungle creatures without understanding them. They understood him. Some of the time. But to live out the rest of his life with them? What if there were no others living on the Virgin? Suppose Stefen never recovered?

Lozadar cringed, trying to envision Stefen as the vegetable he was now for all of his life—the muscles atrophying, the skin lax on his bones, the lifeless eyes moving lethargically and possibly seeing nothing.

Shaken, he reached out to steady himself against Asa.

The sight lingered. He blinked hard, trying not to see the magnificent jungle man, once in command of his life and the realm about him, reduced to less than nothing.

The middle ship hovered over them, gradually lowering.

Now! If you're going to do it, do it now! They'll recognize you at this close a scan! Get out there! Move!

Yet he held tighter to Asa, as though to prevent himself from moving. *The civilized world would be another kind of captivity for Stefen,* he thought. *He's better the way he is here than whole there. He'd be a novelty, and I'd be in no position to help him. Who knows how long it would be until things settled down—provided I lived so long.*

He shrank against Asa's foreleg, hugging it tightly. "I owe him something," he whispered into the noise. "At least the same chance to survive as he gave me."

The decision to stay with Stefen did not sit comfortably. None of the options would have. But it was one he could live with himself by making. Over the years he had heard of too many species who had died off when removed from their home planets. The new environments were always made to the exact specifications, but the inhabitants knew the difference. Each time, they sickened and died. Stefen was that kind of species, a class unto himself. His territory could not be synthesized anywhere.

He loosed his hold on Asa and laughed, realizing that the decision he had made was indeed a fortunate one. Asa would probably have killed him with one swipe of her paw if he had made a break for the ship.

Patting the spotted leg he moved farther along the inside track and tried to shield his body impulses in case they were scanning on the ship. Given enough time and exposure to the creatures of the Virgin, those in the ships could decipher his readings from Asa's, but they would have to learn enough about the planet first to know the readings were faulty.

If they were doing a deep scan, they would pick up Stefen. *Too late to prevent that,* he mused.

Unexpectedly, the ship rose, veered south and joined the other two heading out over the ocean. After they departed the sounds lingered in Lozadar's head as one solid hum without a fracture in the rhythm.

"Evaladyn! Evaladyn!"

She flew out of a putch and hovered over the clearing.

"I need six lengths of strong but thin vines to go around the kervemith. Can you get me that? And I need moss. Lots of moss. And a couple of very soft leaves—the big ones. Fast as you can." He watched her disperse the horde into work groups. "Good. Very good!"

He ran around the fire and picked up all of his belongings, paused, then went back for Andazu's paw.

Next, he called Esse and laughed when the big kervemith came out from over the cave, figuring that his and Asa's readings would be close enough to buy them some precious time. Anything they picked up of Stefen's would be mingled with Esse. "Wish I'd thought about that earlier, but I'm glad you did."

The laughter caught in his throat. "How could you have known?"

Esse uttered a throaty sound that hinted of laughter—kervemith-style.

A pang of fear crimped his stomach. How had the kervemith known to go to that spot? When had he moved out of the trees on the opposite side? It was a deliberate act, purposeful and effective. He wanted to think of it as a coincidence, but there were fewer coincidences on the Virgin than anywhere he'd ever visited.

Shaking off the eerie sensation, he addressed Esse. "You've just been promoted to beast of burden in the Judgment Day Army. I'm afraid we can't pay much, but we're heavy on IOUs." Patting the chest fur where it peaked in a stand-up pattern, "We can't stay here. We are going to run. I don't care where. Follow Evaladyn or choose a place. I'm putting Stefen on Asa. Andazu and I will ride on you. If we run into trouble, you're also head warrior. I'll take care of Andazu, and we can get off fast.

"Stefen's another problem. He's got to be strapped on." Turning away, "Lord, those burns are going to hurt." Looking above the fangs at the twitching blue eyes, "It's the only thing I know to do. If they"—glancing at the sky—

"were only curious, two fly-bys would have been more than enough. They're more than interested." The need to explain persisted, though the technological gap was insurmountable, since he could not begin to expound on the workings of the machines he had taken for granted all his life.

He waved his hand in exasperation and went to make preparations.

She kept the lights at their lowest setting. The thought of seeing her reflection on a shiny surface or in the mirror was abhorrent. Regardless of how the facts were slanted, the implications remained unchanged. The House of dez Kaliea had become extinct, because there was no one left to head it, or it was and had always been a part of the movement to overthrow the government holding the Seven Worlds together.

Corinda saw the emblem blazing on the main ship each time she tried to close her eyes and escape the reality. The shame of her family's involvement with the Insurrectionists equaled that which she felt for preferring the extinction of the House. The latter acknowledged the death of her father, the Coralis Legate. There was no painless alternative.

Her eyes puffed, though she did not cry.

Objectively, it made sense for the Insurrectionists to want an in with the House of dez Kaliea. What other house built ships equal in quality and speed? Or even attempted to dabble in shipbuilding? What other house had the connections, assigned ports and interstellar routes?

Objectivity had a price she had not counted on. Even in the last days of Antition's glory the upper echelons of the great houses had not been subjected to security measures or screening at the palace. One helper in the right place would lay the entire capital open to siege. Was that what had happened? she wondered blackly. "By the gods, not my family. Please! Some other family. Not mine. Not mine." The last words were a whisper. The odds were seven to one it was hers.

"Why?" she asked the wall she was facing.

The door opened. Light poured in from the corridor, offensive, and bright. General Myzillion palmed it closed immediately. Saying nothing, he assumed the chair he always occupied and watched Corinda's back for signs of life.

More than an hour passed, neither moving. "Go away," she said quietly.

"I think we ought to talk about it."

"There's nothing to talk about."

He rose slowly, started for the door, then turned back and sat on the edge of the bed. "Corinda," he started.

"You knew! Didn't you?" She flipped onto her back and glared at him.

General Myzillion closed his eyes and nodded curtly.

"Why didn't you tell me? Why did you let me go up there and, and . . . My God! Didn't it bother your men to have a . . . a relative of the enemy on the same bridge?" The tears finally came. "All that my family has tried to achieve in the last four hundred standards is being used against the empire—isn't it?"

He looked at her sympathetically, not sure what to do or say, only wanting to comfort her.

She reached up and grabbed his uniform near the shoulders and tried to shake him. "Answer me! Is it?"

He gathered her up and placed her in a sitting position facing him. "I'd like to say I think the ship was stolen—"

"Not that one," she interrupted. "That one wouldn't be stolen in a million standards. It has a character control helm and can be operated only by three people in the whole galaxy."

"—but I can't," he continued as though she had never spoken. "We've been seeing too many emblemed ships for it to be a spoils raid. The older Insurrectionist ships are being maintained and updated too well for there to be anything but at least a partial involvement of dez Kaliea operations and ports."

Reaching out to brush away her snarled hair, "Corinda, would you have believed me if I had told you? Would you have believed anything like that unless you had seen it with your own eyes?"

Head hanging, "No. I don't suppose so." Abruptly, her head came up. She glared accusingly at him. "But you could have done something to prepare me."

"What?"

"I, I don't know. Something. Anything." Her hands covered her face as the tears ran freely through her fingers. "The whole damn world has gone to hell." She sobbed.

His arms went around her and held her to his chest before his mind had a chance to think about it. The warmth of her body added to the image of frailty clinging in response. A damp spot on his shirt grew as she sobbed.

He soothed her, speaking softly, alternately holding her and stroking her hair onto her back. Eventually she was quieted, content to embrace him and be the recipient of his stroking.

"You're like a rock," she said after a time, "physically and emotionally."

"No, I'm not."

She looked up and saw his conflict through a veil of tangled dark hair. "Hart?" She met his mouth eagerly, freeing her left arm to move up his chest and around his neck. It did not seem rational to feel so totally depressed one second and charged with excitement the next. The hands moving deliberately over her body took on a different meaning and tone, adding to the enjoyment of a moment detached from despondency.

Breathing heavily, Hart eased her away. He was confused and a little embarrassed. "I, ah . . . I had better be going."

"Please, don't leave yet."

"I have to, Lady Corinda." His fingertips almost touched across her shoulder blades.

"Because I'm Lady Corinda dez Kaliea of a Ruling House?" Seeing his nod, "It usually happens the other way," she said, half smiling for an instant. "Will you stay with me until I go to sleep? Hold me for a little while?"

"I don't think . . . "

Corinda stretched just far enough to reach his lips with hers. Her arms coiled around his neck, pulling him down and pressing her body against his.

Initially, he pushed against her ribs and pried her back a few centimeters. Her arms tightened, forcing her breasts into his chest. Her tongue on his lips, teasing, taunting, became more than he could resist. *How often does a man get attacked by the woman he loves?* he wondered.

Slowly they undressed one another, exploring, appreciating, touching the reality filled with a beauty shared.

They made love without speaking, lest the words break the spell each cast over the other.

Hart stayed until she slept, then rose, covered her and put on his uniform to face his troops.

Lozadar sat on top of Esse. His knife was on his right hip, the Lat-kor on his left. The packs were used as side rails around Stefen's moss-and-nacki-padded body.

They moved away from the campsite. The fire smoldered in white embers. No sooner were they into the jungle than yaxura bolted out of the ground and demolished all signs of occupation.

The kervemith were content to let Evaladyn set the course. By the time of first sunset they were deep into volcano territory and on a northwestern heading. The pace was much slower than the one which had brought Lozadar to Stefen. They paused only long enough for him to check Stefen and turn him to even out the pressure on his new flesh.

After Andazu woke he spent his time watching Asa's burden. It seemed to take his mind off his own pain.

They traveled through the night and rested during the hottest part of the day. Night travel offered more safety, for they could detect ships coming though the skies before they could be spotted with a ground search.

By the fourth day Stefen looked good. New skin grew over the red splotches covering his feet and ankles and across his shoulders. Andazu slept beside him daily.

Lozadar worked on the paw-hand, cleaning the tissue away from the bones and whittling on a dried chunk of wood.

The land changed often, yet stayed the same within its changes from barren rock to impenetrable jungle floors. Lozadar did not know where they were headed, nor if in fact there was a destination. It suited him fine to be moving and having to watch for hazards below and the ships in the sky. Life was easier when he did not have to think about what he was doing, what he should be doing or what lay ahead.

Deep in the world of imagery Stefen played, experienced and was many entities. He became the dynamic force changing hydrogen to helium in the core of the Deity, atom by atom in uncountable quantities, yet knowing of each transformation as it took place. He stood in the eye of a storm churning over the Deity's northern hemisphere, the chromosphere lashing about him, spicules licking at his body, unaware that he was invincible. Suspended in the corona, he experienced the emotion-packed power of a flare; frustrated needs, desperate wants and the soft cajoling to the Virgin to stay with him.

In the quiet umbra of a large sunspot ulcerating the southern hemisphere, Stefen viewed his Deity over the countless millennia it took for the Virgin's birth and evolution. It was a patience only a lonely lover could possess.

Below, rock boiled in glowing patterns over the Virgin, leveling the mountains which tried to form in the cooler places, filling the chasms down to the mantle. Gradually, a transformation occurred. The rock solidified, not quiet or satisfied with its placement and constantly on the move over the molten peridotite convections separating the core and the crust. Once tenuous stability commenced, subtle changes began in the form of bacteria, atmosphere, different bacteria and the beginnings of growth patches over the surface.

He took part in the wonder the Virgin floundered in upon waking into consciousness. The simple delight of seeing her creator, the Deity, and the instant recognition of their unbreakable bond, warmed him. Her origin flashed over the vision as debris hurling through space were gathered a piece at a time, painstakingly selected and coalesced until the mass was sufficient.

As the only planet the Deity grasped in His realm, Stefen partook in the first Passage, knowing the fears, the torment and damage the pull of the weaker sun inflicted. A yearning to sooth the Virgin until the tumultuous phase was exhausted sent him rambling and aching to do something for her. Simultaneously, he knew this was a thing of long, long ago, before the ganids, before the zuriserpants, kervemith, fenwapters, chotiburus and the others in the chain. And before man.

The jungles grew and creatures filled the seas, some of them walking upon the land, perpetually in a state of change and slowly becoming recognizable. Peace dominated his senses, assuaging all anxiety, pain, yearning. He felt surrounded by warm emotions as the Virgin embraced the Deity during Passage to make that time a cherished congress between them.

The Virgin imparted the communion she held with the maturing children of her surface and below. The function of each species unfolded, all to her maintenance and benefit. In turn, she cared for them, supplying food, shelter, warmth and territory for all with the blessing of her Lover.

Stefen accepted what was thrust upon him, not needing to understand anything but the emotional bond shared by the Virgin and the Deity. A limbo descended over him, during which time he wondered if he would experience a love and caring such as the one he was privy to. There was so much to absorb, and so long as he remained on this plane there was no pain or punishment for the claim pressed against him which he denied.

Again, the jungle surrounded him. Man came in a deluge of fire. An enormous ship imbued with rocks sat on the land and emptied its cargo of people, battered, wounded and frail. It seemed that their journey had been generations long and destined for some other planet. The end had been reached for better or worse. The ship died and was swallowed by ensuing Passages. No others came for many, many more Passages. Stefen lost count of the cycles speeding into a blur.

There was balance and peace during the first men's sanctuary time. They adapted or died. Inwardly, Stefen's hopes soared in the knowledge that there were others of his species on the surface.

The mood of the vision changed. It grew ominous and black. More ships came through the voids of space and sought out the Virgin. The lead ship settled near the Forbidden Place. Padree stepped out.

The vision abruptly ended in a swirl of black and red. Anger boiled through Stefen's veins and pain inundated his senses. It pulsated, bouncing him up and down, lashing at him through padded throngs, lasting forever.

Chapter 12

LOZADAR HAD LOST TRACK OF THE NUMBER of nights they traveled. Stretched on a moss bed, he tried to account for them and settled on a maximum of ten, maybe twelve. Until the evening prior, time did not matter. Today, he hoped the falizians had a destination and that it was close. What he suspected the last few nights was now a certainty. Just how long the pack of kervemith had been stalking them he did not know. While they did not attack, they had made their presence known by confronting Esse at dawn.

Andazu did not seem concerned once the exchange of snarls began, but Lozadar considered a coronary arrest quite likely. The encounter rattled him to a point where he found it difficult to climb the rope up Esse's back.

Thinking about it destroyed his chances for sleep. Perhaps he was not the adventurer he had once thought he was.

Stefen rolled and tried to sit. This first sign of voluntary motion excited Lozadar. He hurried to his side, guided him upright, then handed him a strip of day-old cooked chotiburu. "Hey! You're ready to join the living again?" The jubilation in his voice alerted Esse overhead.

Stefen fumbled the meat up to his mouth and ripped off a bite.

"Say something, will you?" Lozadar settled in front of him.

Andazu lumbered forward on three paws and leaned close to Stefen. All three eyes showed as his head cocked from one side to the other.

Stefen stopped chewing and dropped the meat. Slowly, he put his hands on the fenwapter and felt his head, chest and foreshoulders. He groped down the left side and came in contact with the stub. Head hanging, he let go.

Lozadar talked excitedly, slowing when he realized

Stefen was not paying attention. In an effort to distract him, he waved his hand in front of Stefen. Not a blink. The eyes remained stationary.

Stunned, he folded his hands in the cradle of his legs and watched Andazu and the Judge of Man. A small place inside him grew totally numb and spread mercifully. The worst was not over with Stefen's return to consciousness.

Andazu backed up a step and squatted facing Lozadar. "Not see. Not hear. Not talk," he managed with an obvious struggle.

Both looked back to Stefen. He had found the meat strip and was eating again.

"Understand me. Sometimes, maybe."

The fenwapter spoke rarely and only when it suited him. Lozadar was grateful for the sharing of knowledge. He pursued, asking, "You can communicate with him anyway?"

Andazu gave an indifferent shrug and cracked a fotig with his foot claws.

"Did he say what happened to him? Or how? Anything that might help us help him?"

"Not enemy. Friends. He say 'No' to Deity. Deity get angry."

The color drained from the outcast's face while he prayed that he had not inadvertently cursed a being with power enough to make him like Stefen. "Is there . . . is it permanent?"

"Not know." He groomed his chest with the claws of his left foot and scooped out the inside of the fotig with his rough tongue.

"Andazu, thanks for telling me." He watched Stefen for several more minutes, then got onto his knees. "Okay. Maybe you can't see or hear me, but that's not going to stop me. I can't help you with the mind, especially since I'm not sure I'm playing with a full complement most of the time. But I can make sure you keep in shape, just in case . . ." Turning Stefen, he put his hand on his left shoulder, stretched onto his stomach and continued, "This is a push up. Three hundred a day ought to be a cinch for you."

Lozadar executed three perfect ones, then maneuvered Stefen onto his stomach. Using his hands and positioning Stefen's arms, he started him on the excercise.

"No! Keep your rear level." He pushed down on Stefen's buttocks and lifted on his chest. It took the better part of the morning to go through the program Lozadar devised. Stefen was content when they finished. He lay perspiring, half smiling with his eyes closed.

Lozadar leaned against a putch and pulled out the block of wood he worked on daily with his knife. He did not notice when Stefen's eyes opened and his placid expression changed to one of alarm.

Stefen was at the Crystal Curtain shelter again. There was a fire glowing halfway down the open expanse. Annalli lay on a makeshift pallet of rags, moss and dry ferns. The sounds of her panting filled Stefen's ears and sent his heart racing. Padree crouched between her legs. Perspiration glistened on her white flesh.

A bedraggled woman with stringy black hair washed her hands in the air and fretted openly.

Annalli groaned and screamed through clenched teeth. The mound in her stomach moved lower. She used both hands to push the babe toward the exit.

"For God's sake, Padree! Let me help. It's taking too long. We've got a med-kit. At least use it." Her voice was shaky and abnormally high.

"I cannot. It has to be done this way." He gave a pleading look at the woman for understanding, then to Annalli. His voice was husky. "Do you think I like this? Don't you think I'd turn her over to you if I could? We've made our bargain with the powers that be here. There is no way out except death. I, for one, am not ready to die. Neither is Annalli."

"But the child, Padree. Think of the child. He's having to fight too hard." She squatted to look him in the eye.

Padree snorted. "Don't worry about him. He's not going to die. This is just the beginning of his fight for life. Just the beginning."

Annalli grunted long and low, pushing with her hands and abdomen. She panted quickly, then strained again. A bloody little head emerged. Now she breathed as though she had just run halfway around the Virgin.

"Keep pushing!" the woman yelled.

Padree cradled the head in his hand and waited.

Annalli pushed again, moaning and finally uttering a scream as the little body slipped into Padree's hands.

Following the woman's instructions, Padree tied off the cord and cut it with a sterilized knife—the same knife Stefen now possessed.

He watched himself take the first breath of life in the arms of a man so dear to him in death, a man he did not know. Wrapped in a clean square of cloth, he was passed to his mother. She was soaked with perspiration and crying. The tears were not for the pain she suffered, rather a mixture of joy and an extreme sorrow he did not understand.

Annalli put the babe to her breast and talked quietly to him. "The little miracle. You're so small and your burdens will be so great." She wiped the perspiration from her face and managed a smile. "You're beautiful, Stefen, so beautiful. You'll be a great Champion."

Stefen screamed a long, silent, agonizing "Noooool!"

The vision became a tableau and turned black.

Anger impelled a temporary end. Motionlessly, he raged, storming the four corners of the Virgin, demanding a reason for the conspiracy against him even prior to birth. He, who had more intelligence than any of the Virgin's creatures, did not have free will to choose his destiny?

Betrayers! Users! he ranted. *I was never more than a bargaining tool? Less than a chotiburu haunch to a fat fenwapter? You deceived me, Padree! You used me just as you did that girl you raped and killed. Only I was your own flesh and blood. You bought your solitude with my life, protected it with my future and left me unprepared.*

There was much pain in the way he saw his evolution. The entire reason of his existence laid bare an open wound which festered angrily.

"It is a better life than you might have had, little one," Annalli whispered, kissing his head before she covered it with the corner of the wrap.

The woman who had been watching went to work with clean rags and boiled water left to cool beside the fire. She washed Annalli tenderly, the dark expression of disapproval deep in the lines of her face. Head down, she said, "I was there when you were brought into the world, Annalli. Your mother called you 'little one.' By the gods I never thought your firstborn would be greeted by these conditions. That monster Padree has changed you, Annalli, and I don't like it one bit."

"It's not him, Deedra. It's this place. It's changing all of us, and there is nothing which will stop it. There is a quality about the land I can identify with. Someday my son will tame the beasts, conquer the jungles and unite the chaotic forces for the benefit of the gods ruling this planet."

"That's a pretty tall order for a boy only minutes old, Annalli. Are you sure he won't mind doin' that in his spare time?"

Padree took the babe and started toward the entrance.

Deedra dropped her rag into the bucket of warm water. "Where're you going with him?"

"Let him be," Annalli said and placed her cool hand on Deedra's arm. "He does what must be done. There is no choice involved. The commitments cannot be changed or broken. Stefen will be safe."

Beyond the waterfall forming the Crystal Curtain the sky was blood red. Ash from hundreds of volcanoes hung in the heavy clouds, hiding them from the wrath of the weak sun. Warm water splashed onto the small babe's face, washing away bits of pink tissue. Padree walked deliberately along the ledge and out to the lava tongue.

"It is done!" he yelled at the boiling sky. "Here is your future!"

Instantly, Stefen was no longer there. He was in the heart of the Deity feeling the hope and pride and appreciating the beauty of himself as a baby. The soft Virgin presence abounded with the tender attributes of motherhood by proxy.

Stefen wished the vision would end. When it did, abruptly, he wondered whose child he was—Padree and Annalli's or the Virgin and the Deity's. For while he may have been birthed of the woman, he could not help feeling that he was never hers or Padree's. He had been sold into bondage before conception.

The kervemith pack shadowed the travelers at night. In the distance fenwapters called and Andazu answered back. Occasionally the sound of a chotiburu fighting a losing battle for his life shattered the night.

The days took on a routine when Stefen was cognizant. His body was a bit paler than when Lozadar had first met him, and thinner. Otherwise he maintained his naturally formidable outward appearance. He took to the exercises and worked far beyond the outcast's expectations. Lozadar usually joined him until he had his fill and ultimately proclaimed he was not a glutton for physical abuse.

A decaset after Stefen's first response, Lozadar called Andazu over to him. He held out a contraption which encased the original claws.

Unable to understand its function, Andazu shrugged.

"What we have here is called a prosthesis." He took the hairy forearm and held the jointed wood to the stub. Using the right forearm as a measurement, he nodded. "I'll have to take a little more off."

"How go?"

"You have the advantage of being both dexterous and intelligent. That will help you to overcome my inexperience at making one of these. It's an artificial paw for you. See this little pin?" He pointed to a thin metal rod near the joint. "Push it in and the wrist—whatever you call it—doesn't move."

After a demonstration he handed it to Andazu. The fenwapter worked it both ways, fascinated. Lozadar strapped it to the forearm with a lattice made of tendrils, looped it over the opposite shoulder and tied it.

"Try it out for a while. You're healed up pretty well. It will get sore, though. You'll have to get used to it and toughen the skin up. Let me know when you've had enough and I'll take it off and work on it some more. Later, we'll look for a rig you can handle yourself."

The fenwapter gazed at him for three hundred heartbeats. Lozadar tried to decide whether he had made the apparatus because he felt guilty or because he genuinely wanted to do something for the lonely fenwapter. He did not know.

Stuhart Myzillion stood outside the exercise-room door and watched Corinda move through a series of dancelike gymnastics. It was heartwarming to see her partake in the few benefits of ship life. Members of the crew neither solicited her company nor shunned her if she requested permission to join them.

However, that veneer of civility would evaporate if they were made aware of the motives behind the Gen-

114

eral's search of 4724Y's ghosts. And the General knew the time was short before questions were asked which required answers. Thus far he was grateful for their co-operation and treasured their silence.

"Corinda," he called, then waved for her to join him at the door.

She flipped over the lowest of three parallel bars, spun in the air and landed on her feet, bowing to him. When she stood the smile she wore masked the shadows under her eyes. She walked over to him and stood so close that if they inhaled simultaneously they would touch, then saluted.

"Good morning, General. What can I do for you?" In a whisper, "Or what can we do for each other?"

The intimation made them both uncomfortable and dampened the light spirit seldom seen in Corinda's attitude these days. She stepped back and folded her hands, picking at her thumbnails for something to focus on.

"I should not have said that. I'm sorry."

Tersely, "Yeah." He took her arm and guided her toward the officers' lounge and mess hall. "Look, I know I made a promise to you, and I want to keep it. We're also fighting a damn war. So I have a problem. Maybe you can help me solve it."

There are no solutions to our problems, Hart, she thought. Out loud, "You want me to forget the search just when we've made some real progress? There are people down there, Hart. We'll find him if he's alive. It's not as though he can catch the closest hop and be there, I mean."

He stopped in the hall and turned harshly on her. "I know what you mean, Lady Corinda. I want to find him as badly as you do. I want to get on with building the colonies, not sit on some backwater planet looking for a gem in a slag heap." He turned away, changed direction and started down another corridor.

Corinda ran to catch him and grabbed his arm with both hands. Surprised, he turned around quickly, throwing her off balance. "You're right. We had better talk, and now!"

Moments later they faced each other in Corinda's quarters. "It's not just the search, is it, Hart? You want to be away from me. It's safer that way, isn't it?"

"I'm needed in the Antition sector."

"You're needed here!" Leaning forward on the edge of her bunk, "Just because I was born to a house doesn't mean I'm long on wealth and short on brains, General. I've seen the scans on the planet and the beginnings of enemy bases. You can't ignore that, either.

"Want to do something for the war effort? Destroy the bases. Plunder their supply caches. Call in reinforcements, because they'll be back. If there is one dez Kaliea involved, believe me, they won't let that much money wrapped up in munitions and rigging go to waste. How do you think we got to be so stinking rich?"

He rose and began pacing. "I've considered it. Tell me, what are you going to do if we find Lozadar alive?"

Corinda looked away, unable to bear the sight of him while she spoke. "Same as before. Marry him."

"What if he's dead?"

"I don't know. Mourn the loss of the best friend I ever had, probably. Then . . . I don't know, Hart. The way things, look, I'd be free to do as I chose. But he's alive. I know it. And he's down there."

He paused and looked at her, wishing Lozadar was as dead as last winter and feeling guilty for having such a thought. Corinda gazed back. He saw a struggle in her eyes which matched his own. It was a hell of a price to pay for loving the wrong person. While he would never trade the joy of the night they had shared he knew it would have been better had it never happened.

"A decaset, Corinda. Sorry, that's all the time I can spare. Meanwhile, we will be doing recon and destroy runs on the storage depots they have started."

He towered over her when she looked up. "I . . . I guess that will have to be enough, then," she murmured, noting the deepening of the lines in his face and the tinge of gray in the gold and red of his hair.

"Hart, I . . ." Looking down at her hands, she could not finish. When she looked up again he was gone. "I love you, Hart, and it hurts me too," she said to the door.

He stood on the other side of the door for a moment and cleared his mind of the aching lust she always incited.

He began walking, calling up snatches of unrelated information from his memory and sorting bits and pieces in a new light.

Little things began to fit into place for the General.

The more neatly his speculations filled the jigsaw border, the more likely it was that she was right: Lozadar was alive. Lisan dez Kaliea was a greedy, ambitious man. He was likely to attempt to hedge any gamble where the House of dez Kaliea was concerned. It would not be sufficient merely to control from the outlaw fringes. He was in line for the crown, but could not take it and hold it without arousing suspicions.

"Sure," he muttered, scowling, "what better scapegoat than Lozadar and the Colonials. That way he can confiscate the House of cor Baalan holdings and keep Corinda in line—long enough to get her to sign away her claims to save Lozadar."

It hurt to see how well her cousin had played her. At the same time, it felt great to know he had upset Lizan's well-made plans. "The bastard has to find Lozadar in order to use him against Corinda, and Corinda is still an ace," he said to himself.

His pace quickened. He smiled. Misery had lots of company.

Two nights passed. The motley entourage traveled toward a chain of uplifted sedimentary mountains. Jungle worked to soften the jagged thrust bragging layer after layer of colorful deposits. Both moons were on the decline, and the first rays of light crawled over the eastern horizon. Evaladyn flew in circles partially visible through breaks in the highest putch where the stars peeked down. She called out the same five notes repetitively. The melodious lilt of her voice was still pleasant, but it had roughened since her ordeal at the Forbidden Place.

Esse and Asa paused and listened, heads up. Andazu looked ahead, trying to see through the maze of vegetation. Lozadar watched all of them, not knowing if it was time to stop traveling or if they were about to be attacked. As far as he could determine there was nothing to indicate a reason for Evaladyn's excitement.

The dawn became thick with falizians, calling, singing, pairing into mating rituals and dances filled with an intricate beauty.

Stefen was expressionless at Asa's head. He was strapped into a sitting position with tied lengths of fotig stalks as a support. He was aware of something happening and gradually managed to wring the significance of the halt out of Andazu.

The kervemith began to descend along a lateral direction, choosing the opportune branches to keep a steady pace. They came to the end of the jungle and leaped to the ground.

Lozadar gaped, blinking hard to make sure he was seeing reality.

At the opposite end of an immense clearing the size of a landing field were structures built out of stone and wood. The tops were slanted, thatched with small grasses and tiny ferns. Behind them a mountain rose straight up, then bent over the structures as though it had been pulled and shaped by a giant hand to protect them. It was eerie the way it thinned at the ragged edge. Nothing was sharp on it. It was not rounded either, but flowed like a stone wave into the air. Black splotches in the layers hinted at dozens of caves.

More mountain rose beyond that and melted into a chain which lasted forever.

A shrill yodel sounded an urgent warning. Fires burst into being between the buildings. Figures moved hurriedly in all directions. A few angry cries mingled with loud syllables and shrieks of joy.

The travelers changed positions. Esse and Asa moved shoulder to shoulder toward the light, their paws silent upon the land, heads level to respond to the slightest aggression. Lozadar's heart pounded out a steady flow of hope to the rest of him. He wished Stefen could see the people gathering behind two heavily robed individuals standing between the two foremost fires. A quick count totaled at least twenty-five adults and three little ones.

The kervemith approached guardedly.

Decisive, Andazu changed from Esse to Asa and held onto Stefen, thus becoming his eyes and ears. Sometime between the ataraxia of the Crystal Curtain and the present the final barrier tumbled.

Esse halted ten meters short of the fires.

A silence clung to the ground. Errant smoke wound through the air over the kervemith's heads, then moved upward, spurred by the spitting and cracking of the fire.

Sunlight grew strong enough to melt some of the shadows bathing the clearing. The falizians settled into the tops of putch and fern trees. The trailing pack of

118

kervemith roared in the sound of morning with a startling finality that made Lozadar look back. It struck him that they were gone for good.

Lozadar took a deep breath and climbed down. He stood between Esse and Asa and nervously stroked his mount's foreshoulder.

An aged man whose face was a mass of wrinkles in the soft firelight adjusted his thick green cloak and lifted his long walking staff. "Who is it seeking the Leatez?"

"I am Lozadar the Outcast." Raising his right hand, "This is Stefen, Judge of Man upon the Virgin."

"Does he not speak for himself?" A gnarled hand flexed roughly over the detailed carving on the staff.

"No. I speak for him at this time. Whom are we addressing?"

The man in the green cloak was called Aviea, Bespeaker of the Leatez. The heavy-set woman with the comfortable-looking face and gray-white hair was the Leader, Basea. She watched the men with an eye that took in the slightest fluctuation of breathing.

"We have sought others on the Virgin and are so glad to have found you. It has been a long, tiring journey. Perhaps you could spare us lodging?"

Aviea and Basea conferred privately while the others watched the strangers.

Lozadar surveyed the gathering and concluded that the entire population had turned out for the event. It was a small, fearful population, too. There was a noticeable gap in the age range. It appeared that a whole age group ranging from thirty to fifty was absent. Odd, he thought. There were oldsters in the group. They were the ones hanging back. All of them shared one great characteristic. They gaped at Stefen with an awe Lozadar had not seen evidenced anywhere, for any man.

One adolescent boy in the crowd divided his time between Stefen and him. He returned a feeble smile when Lozadar acknowledged him. On his left was a striking blond girl. She wound her hand into that of the dark-haired woman beside her and visually worshipped the Judge. The dark-haired woman met Lozadar's eyes without a smile or a flinch.

"There have been omens from the sky. Bad omens," Aviea said, scratching the source of the long wisp of beard hanging down to his waist. His arthritic fingers worked nervously.

"There is a great battle going on in the civilized quadrants."

"Why do they fight?"

Lozadar cleared his throat, regretting the volunteered information. "It is a struggle for power. There have been many killings and abductions."

"Why do they bring their fight here?" Aviea asked incredulously and turned to Basea.

"Some of the ones who were abducted were brought here to die. I was one such man. I was Ruler of the Seven Worlds." The words gushed out, glad to be free. He glanced at the dark-haired woman. Her expression was unchanged and still accepting.

"Then why do you not go with the ships in the sky? Surely, it would not be difficult . . ."

"I am not free to go. I . . ." Again, his eyes met hers. It felt as though she could look into his soul and see the chaos and pain he lived with.

Aviea was speaking again. It was necessary for him to repeat the question.

"I asked why you are not free. Why do you bring your troubles here? Why do you expose us to dangers which are not our doing? Surely you know we cannot help you to return or to fight for your throne."

"I bring Stefen, Judge of Man, to the place he wished to find. Until he renders a final judgment I am not free and possibly will not be even then. He has been to a place called Forbidden and now spends his time conferring with the Deity and the Virgin." Lie, lie, lie, his mind flashed.

"Is true," Andazu said to him.

Lozadar was as surprised to hear the words as the Leatez were to hear a fenwapter speak. Half the population knelt immediately and pulled on those standing near them. The murmurs became a solid background sound.

Another quick conference and Aviea reluctantly bowed to Lozadar. "Please, accept our hospitality. What is ours is yours. Our women will prepare food and bring it to you." Left hand raised, "Kansi! Take our guests to the inner circle of the mountain."

The idea of living in a mountain did not sit well with

120

Lozadar. It was too restricting in comparison to the open jungle. "Bespeaker," he started with a respectful bow, "I believe the Judge of Man would prefer the access of the open jungle. If you have a hut we could use? We would be happy to camp on the open land within the clearing boundaries if that would be permissible."

"Most certainly. Kansi will see to your comfort."

The dark-haired woman came to her feet, approached Lozadar and bowed. When she straightened her smile was dazzling.

Andazu worked on the bindings and loosened Stefen. He climbed down under his own power, placed a hand on Lozadar's arm as they had practiced during their walks and approached the village.

Chapter 13

THE HUT INTERIOR WAS OPULENT IN COMparison to the exterior. Evenly spaced strips of tapestry hung on the walls. Complex stitcheries depicted the Virgin's jungle inhabitants. Double suns symbolized Passages so numerous they required a long time to count. Hieroglyphics punctuated each set. Those at the beginning bore some familiarity to an ancient script Lozadar remembered from a boring school lesson. Too late he wished that he had paid more attention.

Woven mats covered the floors. In the center was a square table supported by two gnarled putch branches touching the floor and the top in five places. The top reflected a dull luster on its irregular shape and fell off at smooth edges.

Straight poles came down into the center. These were moved and adjusted for the weather, creating a baffle for the smoke to always find a way out. The interior walls were drapery, tied back and parted to form private sleeping quarters. The corners were more circular than square and blended the walls rather than delineating them.

Kansi led them to the center and motioned for them to sit at the table. She looked at them often in quick glances which betrayed her nervous state.

"These huts are our peaceful-weather quarters." Twitching a smile, "Of course, there are still some who wish to remain in Sanctuary at all times." She turned toward the door and loosened a tie that held the stiff material pulled to one side. "I will return soon." The drape fell over the door behind her.

Lozadar situated Stefen and went to the door.

Outside, Esse lay with his head resting on his paws, eyes jittering in all directions. His mate was nowhere to be seen, having taken to the jungle to hunt in the short time Lozadar was out of sight.

Beyond the firepits and between the two gentle rises the near huts stood upon was Kansi. The sun darkened her arms to match the rich brown of the simple dress she wore. The hem, decorated with the same fine embroidery as the hut, swayed against her calves. Her dark-chestnut hair bounced between her shoulders from a thong securing it.

He watched her disappear into the caverns, noticing minute details about her. Head shaking, he tried to recall if any woman had ever impressed him quite as much. He went to Esse and unfastened the harness rig worn into the beast's flesh. Anticipating freedom, Esse cooperated eagerly.

The segments were spread on the ground and sorted by length, then tied off and coiled for future use. Occasionally he glanced toward the cavern for Kansi and took in the inquisitive stares of some of the younger villagers.

Esse lumbered to his feet, yawned and snarled. Asa sauntered out of the jungle. The packs strapped to her back bounced unevenly without Stefen's bulk to hold them in place. She assumed Esse's spot while he wandered into the jungle.

The network on Asa was more complicated, and the packs wrapped in moss and nacki had to be cut off. Lozadar hefted Stefen's packs, the source of a million unanswered questions, then threw them into the hut with his. "Asa," he said, praising, "you did a good job." He patted her face, then climbed on top of her to unfasten the harness.

She rolled playfully for him to slip the last part over her head, rose and stepped out.

As he coiled the final strands and prepared to lash them together he noticed Kansi and the blond talking with the leaders near the firepits. He could not make out the words. Aviea appeared stern and disturbed. Twice his wrinkled hand gestured in their direction.

Kansi spent most of the one-sided conversation nodding. Her wide-eyed young companion incurred Basea's displeasure when she smiled. She bowed a solemn repentance.

Lozadar grabbed up the two large coils and pulled them into the hut.

Andazu looked up from playing with his artificial paw and cocked his head.

"However you do it, let Stefen know we're about to have company, the kind he and I talked about. Tell him I said to mind his manners." The coil dropped with a thud.

A slight smile indicated the message had been relayed. Lozadar finger-combed his hair, straightened his ragged and soiled clothes and sat. "At least you don't have to think about combing your hair," he said to Stefen. "It's too late to worry about shaving." He leaned back against the side of the table and thought bleakly about the attitude of the Leatez when they had arrived. The sudden reversal bothered him.

The drape opened. Kansi bowed and introduced her companion as Tari, daughter of her sister. On the food-covered tray Tari set on the table were scooped-out bowls and slightly curved spoons. Kansi placed a pot in the center of the table, took off the lid and doled steaming portions of stew into their bowls. Tari went outside and drew back window-sized segments located behind the tapestries.

Lozadar ate, watching Kansi. Eventually she and Tari sat and nibbled at a bowl of shanuts.

"When you are rested I will take you to the basin where you may wash, if you would like. Later, the Leaders wish to hold conference with you.

"Tari has been chosen by Basea. She will take care of the Holy One during your absence. Please, you must give her instructions and define what limits she may not trespass."

The spoon was halfway between the bowl and his open mouth. He glanced at Andazu. The fenwapter nodded. He shoved the stew into his mouth, chewed and waited.

The fenwapter chittered, sobered and sat immobile. "He say, you tell."

Worry signs appeared around Stefen's eyes and he seemed to be concentrating, trying to see which way things were going. Lozadar dropped his spoon into his bowl, annoyed and amused with what he understood.

"Look, Kansi, Tari," he started, bowing his head to each and gathering his thoughts to find a resolution to his new problem, "there are a few things . . . well, I'm not sure it would be wise for Tari to be too, ah, friendly with Stefen just right now."

Tears of shame filled the young woman's eyes. She listened, unblinking.

"Wait a minute. You don't understand. Please, hear me out. I'm not expressing what needs to be said right."

Andazu spoke. "He say, not hurt, he no do. He wait longer. No hurt."

Relieved, Lozadar pushed the bowl away. "Everything's fine. She can stay. Please, don't cry, Tari. You'll be safe with him. He's given his word."

Perplexed, Kansi asked, "Why would Tari not be safe? He is the Holy One whom we have waited for for thousands of Passages. He is the Savior of the Land, a Child of the Sun sent to us at our hour of need. He will resolve the crises and thwart the vile threat to the Virgin's peace."

It took Lozadar a few seconds to form a reply. *Stefen had always said he was Ruler here,* he thought. *Why the hell shouldn't they worship him? It makes about as much sense as most things here.* Later he would seek a whole explanation from Kansi. Yes, that idea appealed to him. He would need a long explanation and have lots of questions. He gazed down at the center of a swirl in the tabletop. "As near as I can tell, I'm the first person Stefen has come in contact with for eleven Passages." He looked into Kansi's dark eyes for understanding and did not find it.

"Here, you have people around you all the time. Isolation is not a problem. There are ways of fulfilling your needs and drives through the community. When that alternative is absent in daily life, certain needs become quite pronounced. And the one thing I do know is that Stefen shares a—well—universal drive prevalent in the part of the stars I come from."

Tari grinned radiantly.

Kansi laughed, holding her hand over her mouth and obviously trying to be serious, unsuccessfully.

Lozadar did not laugh. Celibacy had never been amusing to him.

Stefen rose and went to the pallet Andazu focused on. The fenwapter followed and sat on the floor.

Kansi stopped laughing and looked horrified at the Holy One. "We did not mean to offend. Please," she said to Lozadar, "you must tell him."

Lozadar shrugged and nodded to Andazu.

126

"It was expected that you should desire the companionship of a woman. If we have misinterpreted what you said, or erred, please tell us so. If you do not wish to have companionship, please, also say this.

"Tari is virginal. She is our last maiden until the small children reach reproductive age, which will not be for at least another eight Passages. Aviea hoped she would find favor with the Holy One who speaks to the Deity." Finished, Kansi lowered her eyes and went about gathering up the dishes.

"He say, yes, please."

"You did not err. It was a misunderstanding—common enough when different cultures are involved. Tari, Stefen spends half his time in an uncommunicative state when he confers with the Deity." The term came easier than his personal description of what took place. "He does not know when he will be summoned, nor does he control his physical realm during that time." He leaned forward and took Tari's hand. "If something should occur that disturbs you, or you don't want to watch what is happening—leave. He will not be offended. He would not want you hurt by his hand while he is not in control. Understand? Andazu will be with him at all times."

"Is good, he say." Andazu rolled onto the pallet, shoving Stefen onto the edge.

"I have no fear of the privilege to serve the Holy One." Tari smiled with the sincerity only the innocent managed and the wise recognized.

The setup felt uncomfortable. It was too neat and too good to be real. Nonetheless, he rose and started for the door and glanced over his shoulder at the two sitting on the edge of the pallet. He needed time to think, time alone. He mumbled something to Kansi and started toward the jungle, not looking back until the sounds of the dishes on her tray were gone.

Andazu watched him go and conveyed what he saw to Stefen. Through the fenwapter's eyes he saw the woman at the table. She looked small and frail, afraid and courageous, prepared to handle any situation presented to her and inadequate all at the same time. The even, delicate features framed by her straight blond hair carried an edge of childhood which the ample body pressing against the seams of her soft brown dress denied. The cleavage at the generously scooped neck when she placed the remaining fruit bowls in order stoked his biological urges and made Andazu uncomfortable.

Immediately he walled the fenwapter out, apologizing, without allowing the rebuttal he knew would follow. Groping, he found clear floor space and began the workout which had become an enjoyable ritual. For all intents and purposes he ignored the presence of the third party in the hut and concentrated on counting out the leg lifts he performed with his hands on his belly and his head raised fifteen centimeters off the floor.

As he labored he thought of the Virgin and the Deity, trying to understand all that had happened during his life and how it related to them. While he loved the land and the Virgin's children and now understood the relationships between them, he could not envision himself a major, viable part of them. His lifetime was not equal to the blinking of an eye compared to the millennia they had existed. Nor was his ability and strength more than an atom in the core of the Deity's flaming body.

I am born of a woman who was imprisoned for her life and a man who refused to allow me to know his true self.

He rolled over and motioned for Andazu to sit on his shoulder blades. He started his pushups, thinking about all that the Lovers had shown him concerning his father.

Padree loved her, he decided. *But it is hard to believe he could change into the father he was just by loving Annalli. I would not have liked him as he was, nor could I have loved him the way I did. Does what he was diminish what he became? Or enhance it?*

He shook his head, answerless.

That was not what really made the difference. It hurts me, and I cannot understand why they would conspire, those four whom I loved, to predestine me before my first heartbeat. There is no more feeling involved there than in planting a fotig and waiting for the putch to grow large enough to strip away all of its fruit. But I am not a tree, nor am I a fruit to be eaten and defecated upon the land after its life juices have been masticated.

I am a man! I have wants and needs and dreams. And I am my own man!

Andazu tapped his head three times to signal the full count. Suddenly he wanted to fly through the trees on the nacki vines again and experience the freedom such an act imparted. He yearned for the feel of the bark under his feet, the cool waters of the Crystal Curtain and moss against his flesh and the solid company of his friends in the near jungle.

He plopped down on the edge of the bed, head in hands, elbows braced on his knees.

The Crystal Curtain changed. Uniformed men with Lat-kors and rifles walked up the lava tongue.

Stefen's abdomen tightened into muscle-rippling knots.

They entered his sanctuary, laughing and talking, turning over the containers salvaged from the tiny settlement Padree had established. The containers, fragile with age, shattered across the floor, spilling out their precious contents of dried food stored for Passage.

The human sounds gave way to those of gentle water spilling into the clear pool. It was music of a rare kind.

A flash of light and a soul-piercing scream ended the respite.

He saw a fenwapter falling out of the giant putch Esse usually occupied. The fuzzy coat was charred black against the normal light brown. It tumbled through the air . . .

Kachieo . . .

bounced against an upright branch . . .

Kachieo . . .

and fell free until she struck the lava and splattered . . .

DEAD. . . .

He was on his feet, teeth and fists clenched, every muscle rigid. Yet knowing he was helpless to prevent the nightmares from occurring even while he was in the midst of people did not ease him into resignation. He wanted to lash out and strike back.

He stood like a statue watching the soldiers led by a light, reddish-haired man burst out of the brush and attack the white-and-scarlet killers. Pieces of light flew in all directions, gouging the lava and rebirthing the fire which put it there. Trees erupted in flames from the long-barreled wide-angled rifles.

The speed at which the battle was decided was awesome. The white-and-scarlet-uniformed men fled to the jungle. Beyond the immediate fringes were falizians, fenwapters and kervemith, side by side in layers. For less than half a heartbeat Stefen wondered where the timid fenwapters had found the courage to approach one of the green beasts, let alone ride them.

They waited for the desecrators of their territory to flee into the deceptive safety of the brush and greeted them in kind.

The man in charge stood on the lava tongue below the spill point of the crystal pond and watched the fate of his enemy. He took off the goggles he wore and ran his hand through his red-gold hair.

The vision faded along with his burst of temper. Gradually he became aware of where he was and the impact upon the young woman. Using Andazu's senses, he saw her frozen to the table. When he sat down, she closed her eyes and sighed in audible relief.

The visions demanded a physical toll. He lay down and tried to calm the fresh agitation welling up inside.

Lozadar wandered around the perimeter noting only what was imperative to keep from getting lost and oblivious to all else. He pondered over the happenings since their arrival. The results left him skeptically optimistic.

He wandered toward the north for a while, trying to decide if any of the Leatez were to be trusted. Even the woman Kansi, who let his body know just how many hours he had gone without fulfillment, could be a tool of Aviea, and most likely was.

"Why not? What am I to her?" He slapped a stick against an empty fotig stalk and splintered it.

A roar unmistakably Esse's shook the ground.

Lozadar looked around, trying to pinpoint the direction. He ran to a low branch growing from a lateral overhead, used it as a catapult and balanced on a limb. It took less than a minute for him to cover the next two hundred meters diagonally to the upper-middle regions.

Through a veil of green-brown came a bitter exchange of snarls.

Up another fifty meters before plunging straight ahead, Lozadar pursued the source. His steps were sure as he crossed the slippery limb to get beside a vertical branch. He looked around it cautiously and saw open space.

Fifty meters below Esse crouched on a broken stub. Across ten meters of wide-open no-man's-land was another large male, who bore a marked similarity to the one who had confronted Esse during the journey. The stranger's spots were almost black the green color was so deeptoned. He pawed the air, lifted his head and snarled.

Lozadar did some fast calculating and figured the ivory he showed was enough for the handles of half a dozen swords.

Esse's responding growl raised the small hairs on Lozadar's neck.

Quicker than he would have thought possible, the stranger leaped across the open space to where Esse had been a split second earlier. Instantly Esse was on top of the aggressor. He dug his claws into the darker hide and roared a score.

The limb quaked and snapped. The beasts tumbled through a snapping vine mesh which palsied the trees. Their fall slowed, accelerated and slowed again before they became a heap of biting, scrapping fur trapped in the nacki.

Lozadar scrambled downward for a better view.

A flurry of motions sent the leaves flying in all directions. The trees vibrated and recovered from the trauma of the lost vines. The two squared off over the vines, snarling and growling, their usually twitching eyes still and intent upon the opponent. They paced out the clearing by moving in a circle. Always there was an equidistant gap between them.

Crouched, Lozadar held onto a sturdy vine with his right hand and a limb with his left. The behavior code of the jungle amazed him. The battle resultant of the confrontation had been postponed until Esse's foremost duties had been discharged. Were men only that civilized, Lozadar mused.

The stranger's fur was very dark. Maroon blood ran down his sides where Esse had left his prints. Tails flicking every which way, heads level, they circled for easily an hour.

The ritual lulled the outcast, gave him time to think about what was happening and to realize how tired he was.

Abruptly, the stranger charged Esse, head down for the horn to do its devastating work, paws hard to the ground and claws extended for traction. He thundered across the arena, bunching his muscles into the running thrust.

Esse turned, jumping into the air, back hunched, feet together and tail straight up.

The stranger's horn caught his right middle paw just above the joint. The fur split open and spewed blood down the aggressor's back as Esse landed, narrowly missing the tail.

To Lozadar's surprise, Esse lunged at a tree. His claws held him for a split second before he pushed off, twisting in the air, and came down in front of his opponent. Head down, he thrust, found the foreshoulder muscle and lifted.

The stranger roared with anger as the muscle came away from the bone and lay on his coat as a strip of fresh meat.

Esse moved to the opposite side of the clearing and waited. Idly he pawed at the ground with five of his six paws and made his area smooth.

The stranger roared again and charged. It was a reckless move born of pain and anger.

Esse instantly dropped onto his belly, hunched his shoulders and fixed his head for the blow. His horn caught his opponent's opposite shoulder. The velocity of the charge was so great the momentum jerked Esse's head back on himself. Rather than be run over by the pounding claws flailing at him, Esse sprang upward, lifting his adversary into the air. They battled for half a minute braced on their rear feet. The flurry of claws and extremities was too fast for Lozadar to keep score. Blood flew in all directions.

Suddenly, Esse was on all sixes, then on the back four, his horn embedded into the other kervemith's abdomen between the middle set of legs.

The roar was deafening. It choked off as the beast writhed senselessly against the ivory spear. He collapsed atop Esse, feebly scoring Esse's hide with his right forepaw and pouring blood out of his left shoulder. As a last struggle he sank his teeth into Esse's side and caught a fang on one of his ribs.

Lozadar watched until the stranger was dead and Esse had extricated the fang from his side. The kervemith stared at his kill for several minutes, not seeming very excited with his victory. He finally ambled away toward a spring Lozadar had seen en route.

Mulling over what he had witnessed and paying little attention to his surroundings, Lozadar descended the tree and headed toward the clearing. He could see the end of the foliage ten meters ahead.

A cord snaked around his neck and tightened.

He clutched at his throat and tried to get a finger under.

It might sever his head any second. He could not breathe and felt the panic of death hot in his lungs.

"Death greets the death bringer. The killers from the stars want you and they can have you, you slime. You demon who brings the death sleep to the innocent! You, who make the children suffer!"

Twisting and turning, he could not get free of the power riding his back and choking the life from his body.

Chapter 14

"MY GOD, HART! ARE YOU ALL RIGHT?" COR-
inda sank to her knees and examined the black slash of
flesh oozing a yellowish-pink gel.

"I'll be all right."

"Why haven't you gotten this treated? Why didn't you
have it closed? Have you become a devout masochist?"
Gingerly she picked up a ragged piece of his pant leg and
laid it aside.

The gouge was deep and had been packed with a salve
preservative before any of the filth had been cleaned out.
He moved aside and sat down. Determined to say what
he had to say and leave, he gestured to her bunk.

Reluctant at first, then resigned to the wisdom of a no-
contact policy, Corinda followed his orders.

He was silent for the several minutes it took to put his
thoughts into order. "Either there are two jungle men,
since it is impossible for one to travel from where you saw
him and have enough time to organize what we saw, or
the indigenous life down there could be sentient." He
paused, lowered his head into his left hand and thought
some more.

Watching him in a new light, Corinda was unsure of
what to make of his actions.

His hand went over the top of his head and caught behind his neck when he looked at her again. Still he did not
speak for several minutes. This was something totally new
for him. The colonies were rough, unsettled in parts, even
primitive by Seven Worlds standards in some areas. He
knew them and the life forms on each of the planets like
the crucial part of a battle plan.

"There was a slaughter down there such as I've never
seen." The monotone was a whisper, as though if he spoke
any louder he would hear himself. "We followed them
down and into an area near a dormant volcano." He

glanced at her. His eyes were vacant and did not really see her perched on the edge of the bunk and chewing her lower lip.

"There was something about the way the area looked, or felt—damn, I don't know. Somebody lived there once.

"There were dozens of those fuzzy creatures like the one Gevek shot down. They were on the backs of the most ferocious and biggest cats I've ever seen. In the trees and sky were green-scaled flying creatures who sang through the battle."

Caught in the reliving of the scene, he leaned forward and took Corinda's hand. "Once we routed the Insurrectionists with a show of strength they gave up. They ran into the jungle.

"I stood on a rise and watched them be slaughtered with no more feeling than they showed when they shot one of the furry things out of a tree. Those beasts did not kill them cleanly, not even the big cats. Some of the men took a while to die.

"I ordered my men out. Those cats were all around us. Damn! They were big. Nobody panicked and fired." The deadpan tone halted. He blinked and looked down at her hand in his. Black soil from the Virgin was ground into his flesh. Her olive-toned skin looked sterile by contrast.

"You were right," he whispered. "They knew who to kill, when, and how to tell the difference. They took Gevek. How could they know? How?" His head drooped. "We could hear him screaming as we boarded the lighters.

"Corinda, I couldn't stop them. There were hundreds of them . . . hundreds. They only wanted Gevek and the ones who were with him. You had to see it to believe it. They sorted us like feed animals and selected the ones they wanted. The rest of us were allowed to return to the ships.

"It was a vengeance thing for them. That's the only part of the whole incident I understand. It had to be. We were so outnumbered."

His head lifted. Moisture rimmed the bottom of his eyes, dammed by an invisible wall. "I have never felt so . . . so helpless . . . no, so impotent, in my life.

"You were right. I was wrong. Gevek was wrong. And now it scares the hell out of me."

Corinda wrapped his hand in both of hers and raised it to her lips. She kissed each finger tenderly and pressed

136

his hand against her cheek. There were no words to ease the torment he had experienced. Well-meaning, tender words could not unsay what had been said or bring back the dead.

Bruskly he turned away, pulling his hand free, and slammed the table with his fist. "Damn it, Corinda! It's not fair!

"We spend our lives doing what's expected of us, doing what's right. Damn pillars of society! Hail, staunch defender of the *right* way of life! You're almost good enough to walk upon our soil as equals. Lay down a few thousand more lives and we'll take a tally!" The ugly sarcasm poured out as he reddened with anger and despair.

He turned ferociously on her, but his outburst was subdued. "I love you, Corinda, and we'll play it by the rules if that's the way it's to be. But down there is a planet that exists—hell, it thrives!—by not conforming to any of the rules. It shouldn't even be there."

There was an empathy in her expression which silenced him for a moment. "Damn, frustration and loneliness . . . are those the only rewards for us?"

"I know, Hart," she whispered beside him. She bent, holding his head, and found his lips. "The rules will be there always, but for now, let's live for us."

The need in his response was more than physical and demanded a great deal from them both. But when it was over there were no answers to his questions or resolutions to his conflicts. Gevek's cries filled his sleep.

Yelling and screaming slammed at the velvet quiet of Lozadar's world. He stood on a precipice over a rancid, forever-black chasm. Grotesque fingers writhed from the dark and reached out to him. Teetering on the edge . . . where were those voices coming from?

Light and dark images attacked his vision. The chasm was gone. His throat burned like ignited tinder. Air entering his lungs felt as though it were filled with tiny needles whose homing devices took them into each nerve ending. The inside of his head spun like an active gyroskin.

The voices were arguing. A woman? Kansi?

Too weak to stand, he rolled and looked around. His eyes would not focus properly at first. By the time they did and the pain in his throat and lungs had diminished, she was at his side. A strangled sound came out of his mouth when he tried to talk.

"Don't," she said. "Rest for a while." She fumbled in the pouch tied to her waist and brought out a concoction which she wrapped in a rag before placing it against his throat. "You're going to have a welt there."

When he could stand she helped him along a path he had not noticed before. He tried to watch the brush and her, not daring to speak yet and unable to get anything out of her without words.

They entered an arching growth. It was well trimmed and solid. The density muffled out the usual jungle sounds of chirping ganids, calling fenwapters and restless kerve-miths. It seemed odd that yaxuras had not devastated either the path or part of the living structure in recent times.

Uncomfortable and suspicious, Lozadar tried to look in all directions at once. The tunnel wound and turned toward the end, finally opening in a rock shelter on one side and nacki vines streaming down from high overhead on the other. A stream poured out of the rocks and filled a pool. The stream continued on the other side and ran into a second one gushing from the stone. The water carved a path through the foliage. Its sound filled the grotto.

Cautious, feeling stronger with each step, Lozadar followed the stream and left Kansi behind. It meandered for half a kilometer. From a putch over the gnarled mesh trying to swallow the fast-running water he saw the jungle's end. A lethargic river easily half a kilometer wide moved through the mountains between smooth granite walls. Judging by the height of the marks on the cliffs, the river was in its low season.

He tried to imagine it after Passage and the rains. It would be a torrent gushing to the ocean at horrendous speeds. The mountains rising on the opposite side were jagged and not mellowed by the elements as were the sedimentary ones where the Leatez lived. Squinting, he looked hard at the exposed cliff walls. Granite, he affirmed. Behind him rose an older chain. He searched for a reason to cover the anomaly of such a total delineation and decided they were two different places and the river ran through the connecting place; one massive crust fault.

Nothing seemed to have a definite explanation on the Virgin.

He climbed higher, exhausting his strength in order to survey the lay of the land. In the uppermost branches, which towered over the jungle, he saw the settlement. The top of the mountain formed a half arch like the second crest of a frozen wave. It too was thin at the leading edge and serrated. From the air the huts would not be seen until the right angle and low elevation converged. The clearing was an obvious scar on the land and likely to raise the suspicions of a half-trained scouter.

He descended, traversing back to the bathing pool where Kansi waited. She was in the water and scrubbing the dress she had worn. He tried not to watch the motion of her breasts in the water. Soundless, he left the tree, stripped and entered the water. The warmth turned out to be a surprise, and the water came up only as high as his waist. He washed, highly conscious of Kansi's presence, and kept his eyes on the trees.

He jumped, his heart in his mouth, when she came up behind him. She stifled a cry and fell back. A quick look at her and he shook his head, preferring to do his own washing and remain near his weapons.

Half successful at hiding the rejection, she moved to the other side of the pool.

"Oh, great Deity! Preserve us," she whispered.

Lozadar dropped his clothes and filled his hands with armaments while looking to see what had alarmed her.

On the branch he had used to enter the heights sat Esse. Lozadar sighed and set the weapons down. He motioned to the kervemith.

Esse bounded out of the tree to the water's edge in one motion, settled on his forepaws and drank. Lozadar used his shirt and began to wipe down the beast and clean his wounds. Fresh blood ran from a couple of the deeper ones by the time he finished. A few whines were the only comments Esse made. He ruffled the animal's head and whispered, "Keep watch and look for a good spot to retreat to. I don't think we're as welcome as they say—at least I'm not."

Esse yawned, licked at his whiskers and rested his head on his forepaws. He snorted, spraying water halfway across the pool, in a "you're telling me?" manner.

Kansi left the water and dressed. Lozadar followed suit without as much haste. He felt better knowing Esse was around. It would have been a risk not accompanying the woman through the dark tunnel to the settlement, but the confines were an invitation to whoever had taken a disliking to him. With Esse on guard, he could go without trepidation.

Nervously, Kansi broke the silence between them. "You are important in this place you come from, outcast?"

He shrugged and nodded, watching the walls that felt as though they were closing in on him.

"Do all the fire-spitting bird ships look for you?"

"I don't know," he answered with a raspy voice. "Why?"

"I'm curious. Our history does not speak of visitors from the sky." A pink flush crept up on both sides of her hair tie bouncing at her neck.

The fresh color of self-betrayal intrigued him. He had not broached the subject, so why would she volunteer a lie when she was so bad at it? "How long is your history?"

"Many thousands of Passages. It is said our origin will be revealed by the Holy One."

Lozadar almost laughed out loud. "What do you expect him to tell you? He was born here and lived most of his life without people."

"If he is truly the Holy One he will know."

Lozadar put his hand on her shoulder and turned her sharply, stopping them both. "And what happens when he finds out he's been betrayed?"

Her eyes widened with a vehement protest.

Lozadar shook his head and silenced her by pointing at his throat. "Who and why?"

"The Bespeaker will—"

"Oh, I'm sure he'll have a nice polished story. You were there. I want to hear yours."

The first glint of fear fell away. Kansi turned to stone. Her voice was emotionless when she asked, "Don't you trust our Bespeaker? It is our way that he will do all explaining, listen to all complaints and defense and pass judgments. He is the one who guides us in our wait for the Holy One. He—"

"Means nothing to me," Lozadar interrupted. "He's a politician."

"Have you any idea what you are asking of me, outcast?"

"Only the truth."

"Aviea will tell you—" she tried to insist.

"I've lived with accomplished liars who sell bits of their soul every day. He's the same. Now, you tell me what's going on here or I'm going to gather up your Holy One and we're leaving."

She met the anger without flinching and sounded relieved as she began to talk. "Hermi tried to kill you. I beat at him with a stick and called loud enough to make him think they could hear me. I followed you after you left because of him. He . . . he has suffered a great loss and is no longer the same. Some of us fear he will not have the presence of mind to come in for Passage shelter."

"Why does he hold me responsible? Or is that part of his insanity?"

"They came looking for you. A woman dressed in white"—she averted his gaze for the first time—"whom I did not know I hated until I saw you came asking for you."

"Corinda?" he asked, incredulous that she would have any say after what he had seen of her in the clearing.

Kansi walked several meters to a flat rock wide enough to accommodate them both. "They called her Lady dez Kally, or something like that."

"Dez Kaliea," he corrected absently, then followed her. Seated, she looked up at him. "They were not the first."

"What do you mean?"

"Before them came another ship. Hermi's new, young wife and his four daughters were taken. That was the first we heard of you. They took more than half the villagers when they left."

"I see." He stared down the tunnel, putting the pieces together in his mind.

"No, you don't." Agitated, she rose and blocked his view. "The lady gave Aviea a special box and showed him how to use it. He was to do something with it if you came. I believe it summons her. I do not know for sure."

"Was it activated when I came?" It was his turn to be worried.

Head shaking, "That will be decided when they talk with you."

Lozadar looked closely at her and stood, wondering why she was so willing to continue. "They can do some explaining at the same time."

Now she grew afraid. Instantly pale, she clutched at his

arms and tried to push him back. "Wait! Do not confront them with that. Please.

"We were visited twice more in less than six revolutions after the woman departed. Each was different." Hands gesturing in circles, "Their colors, the ornaments and decorations, all were different. There was a blue one and a gold. . . . The last was like the first. They took half our population again. This time, mostly strong men and young boys."

"And they did not take you either time? I find that amazing, pretty as you are."

"Tari and I took Adru, her brother, and hid when we saw them come down. Tari has an ability to sense danger. She pleaded with me to take them into the jungle, and I did. Seven of our people were slaughtered before the village bowed to their might."

Lozadar cursed under his breath.

"They wanted the woman and you." Poised, she folded her hands at her waist and met his eyes. "I do not understand what goes on in the far worlds we now know exist. But I do know it is not safe for you here, and I do not know how to help you other than to tell you what I already have. No one knows when they will return. Basea has proclaimed those forced to go with the outworlders as dead. She says we will never set eyes upon them again. They will turn hopeless and sleep the death sleep."

"Death sleep?"

"It is the sleep of the hopeless when the will to live has already died. There is a fever and then peace with the Virgin." She stepped aside.

"And what of Stefen?"

"They do not ask about him. They may not know of him. . . . You had best return before Aviea sends out searchers."

"What about you? Aren't you going back?"

She gazed down at her hands pressed so tightly that her knuckles were white. "I go into the jungle. What I have just done is a betrayal of my people. I have no home now." She turned back to the grotto.

Lozadar reached out and caught her. "I can't live with that burden, Kansi. Look, they don't know we've talked. Stay with me. I want you to." He pulled her against him, realizing just how much he did want her to stay. "For as long as I'm alive and you're with me on the Virgin, I will do my best to protect you. Also, I do not believe it is possible for me to leave here even after the Test of Judgment has been passed."

"You are asking for a bond between us?" Her dark eyes filled with surprise.

"Humph. I guess I am." For a fraction of a second the rigid social doctrines of his family, the years of structured lessons steeped in responsibility and the genealogy of the Seven Worlds, screamed at him in protest. It was vetoed by the tender feelings directed at the woman. The choice was his, and it was a choice not available to him under any other conditions. The bond she spoke of represented a strange form of freedom. Looking at her, he smiled, appreciating the guileless quality which betrayed her lies when she attempted them. *Lordy, but that's refreshing,* he thought.

"I cannot accept. It would be unfair to you. They sought to protect the populace by giving you me." She spun and broke for the pool.

She had already disappeared around a turn by the time Lozadar recovered. He charged after her, instantly conjuring what kind of fate awaited her alone in the jungle. Passage was too near. Where could she go and survive? What was so unfair? He ran around the curve, caught a glimpse of her before she disappeared again and ran harder, finally catching up with her just before the grotto. He reached out and grabbed her shoulder.

"Kansi!" He pulled her to a stop and turned her around.

She refused to look up. "I'm so ashamed. Please, let me go."

He gathered her in his arms, felt her trembling, and covered the side of her face with his hand and held her head. The kiss was laden with desire and a longing to ease desolation. When Lozadar released her, there were tears in her eyes.

"What is it?"

"I could not be a true part of your life." She pushed back, her fingers lingering on his extended forearms before dropping to play with her skirt. "It is doubtful that I can have children."

Stunned, Lozadar could only stare at her dejection. Upon recovery his first impulse was to laugh. He imagined himself trying to keep up with Stefen—and five stairstep kids trying to keep up with him. "Ah, considering the circumstances," he said carefully, maintaining a serious nature, "that might be best." He reached for her, saying, "Besides, maybe you haven't tried the right man."

Hope flickered across her face.

"Come on." He put his arm around her shoulders and started walking. "We'd better get back. Will you think about it?"

Nodding, she tried to match his step.

"I'd like you to stay with me at this little conference of Aviea's. Don't worry about a thing. I want to see Stefen before we go, though." He smiled down at her. "If things don't look the way I'd like them to I'll take your hand and squeeze it three times. Then you make some kind of excuse and get out of there. Go to Stefen and tell the fenwapter I sent you. Go with them and I'll find you later."

She was openly worried, but she nodded. "My destiny is clear, outcast. I will do as you say and not question. At least, I will wait until I know what my questions are."

Chuckling, "That is usually the best way. And my name is Lozadar."

"That means strange life and strong promise," she said, trying to find her smile again.

"You sure about that?"

"Yes. It is a good name."

"I always thought it meant do what you're told or you'll end up on a jungle planet with beasts possessing large mouths and larger appetites."

She grinned in disbelief.

He paused long enough to kiss her and relish her open response filled by a need, hope and desire of her own that she wanted him to assuage.

Together they left the tunnel behind and crossed the clearing to the Holy One's hut, where Asa guarded the door.

Chapter 15

STEFEN DIGESTED WHAT THE FENWAPTER related of Lozadar's experiences and assumptions while Kansi kept Tari occupied fetching water. Through the fenwapter's eyes he saw the outcast as a friend and felt ashamed of the way he had treated him and the mistrust generated by Kachieo's death.

Andazu gathered their belongings and placed them in the coiled harnesses beside the door. When Lozadar and the woman departed he ambled outside to Asa. The two perfected the appearance of play while communicating in the jungle vernacular.

A growing urgency to be rid of the shackles placed upon him by the Deity incited a mental frenzy in Stefen. He could visualize the ships coming out of the dwindling night to fill the clearing with eye-burning light and the stench of charred metal still hot from assaulting the atmosphere. The terror of the villagers offended his nostrils. Their whispers boomed in his ears. He saw the scarlet and white of the House of dez Kaliea and did not understand the significance. He tried memorizing the various insignias on the ships, knowing they would be important to Lozadar.

Straining, he tried to hear the words spoken by a thin man bedecked in scarlet as he conferred with Basea and Aviea. His inability to hear overlapped to kill the words. Yet the gentle throb of the engines came through, punctuated by the sounds of hard boots marching on the rock.

It seemed as though he was watching from a distance and existed in the midst of the strangers simultaneously. This new dimension of the vision was unsettling in its confusion. The reference point constantly shifted and distorted the sounds jumbling his mind. For a flickering instant, he saw Tari, Kansi and a boy watching from the jungle.

The scarlet-clad outworlder gestured with a flair that

fascinated one viewpoint and disgusted the other. Stefen tried not to usurp the conflicting tides of emotions. He concentrated on the main event.

Abruptly, the emotions coincided. Soldiers entered the Passage caverns and dragged out the villagers. They were kicked, pulled and brutalized. Aviea's daughter—he recogized her without knowing why or how—was thrown at the Bespeaker's feet.

Stefen found himself gazing into her trusting face. She did not look to be more than three Passages older than Tari. Fire reflected in her hopeful eyes as she sought the Bespeaker of the Leatez, then abject terror as the scarlet man banished her with a wave of his white-gloved hand.

A burly soldier, scarred on his left cheek, forced a young boy in the latter stages of puberty toward the thin leader. He said something, then grinned satisfaction when the leader smiled and nodded. The boy fought, pleading with his eyes at Basea, and was dragged onto the lead ship.

Yaxuras surfaced, roared their displeasure and ran for the depths when weapons turned the jungle into flames and expanded the clearing. The collective protests of the land creatures inundated the open land with noise so great the sounds of the engines were drowned.

Stefen took note of the fine points, trying to keep in mind that there were three visits and, according to Lozadar, at least three factions roaming the Virgin. The uniforms were not too different from those of the two men whose deaths he had caused. He found the vision slowed when utilized to absorb the details of change and difference.

A middle-aged man picked up a torch from the fire and began beating a soldier who was dragging a woman away. Her legs were scraped and bloody as she was pulled by the hair and she held onto her captor's arms with her nails, screaming for help all the while.

Embers flew into the air.

The man yelled and the woman tried to crawl away to the jungle.

A flash of light that left dark places in his vision blotted the scene. When his sight returned the man was dead. His body seemed to float through the air as the garish hole expanded in his abdomen. The death expression carried surprise, his mouth opened and his eyes wide. He landed in the fire, flinched, then stilled. Flames engulfed his clothing. A vile stench rose into the air.

The soldier came to his feet, swaying for several heartbeats, then rubbed his head where his hair had been singed. He bent, retrieved the torch and went after the woman.

She was crying and crawling, her legs trembling too much to support her.

Swearing, he caught up to her and prodded her with the torch. Her clothes caught fire instantly. She writhed in the dirt, screaming, trying to smother the flames, which were reignited by the soldier over her. She flipped onto her back, covered her face and stilled. A mound rising from below her breast to her pelvis gyrated.

The man with the torch paused, his hand raised in the air. He gaped at the struggling flesh, absently dropping the torch into the dirt.

Her hands came down as she pleaded and cried words Stefen could not hear. Blistered, black flesh grew over her neck and down to her breasts where her dress had burned into her skin.

The soldier nodded, unstrapped his weapon and fired at her. He stared at the mangled corpse for several hundred heartbeats, then slowly put his weapon back into his belt. Retching, he turned and stumbled back to his ship.

The tone of conflict changed. The captives moved resignedly as half the population, the cream, was herded into the ships. Seven bodies lay on the ground behind Basea and Aviea when the ships rose into the clouding night.

The sky opened up with the same fury vented upon the Forbidden Place. Large drops, one on top of the other, pelted the ground and sent the dust flying even as it settled from the whirlwinds created by the rising ships.

The Leader and the Bespeaker of the Leatez remained side by side as though rooted to the once-peaceful ground they occupied.

Stefen could not fault them for being tempted to bargain with Lozadar's life. He saw what they saw and knew he could not begin to experience their grief, their loss, nor would he want too.

Head in hands, he pondered over the vision. At last the Deity had hit a nerve he could not anesthetize with rage. People, the Leatez, to live with, companionship, a mate,

147

were a dream come true. To have the reality within his grasp only to find it jeopardized affected him.

The solitary life of the Crystal Curtain had not seemed so acute until Lozadar had entered his life. Now, with people all around, a beautiful companion sitting at his feet awaiting his slightest need, he knew isolation such as that would be unbearable again.

To love the friends of his realm was not enough. *They have always known that,* he realized. *Always. I need my own kind. I have found them. They need help and I am a hindrance.*

Deity, free me to help them. Let me go. Let me try. I yield. I will be a Champion or whatever you want. Defeated, his head sagged, his elbows rested on his knees with his hands folded into knots of white-tipped fingers against blue knuckles.

There is still much you have to learn and comprehend before you can accept such a charge, Stefen.

I accept now. You showed me vision after vision and now leave me powerless to do anything about them? My fate lies in the hands of an outcast who awaits the test. This is how you choose for the Virgin's Champion to live?

Ah, Stefen, Stefen, he has met his test and passed it long ago when he chose to stay with you. His heart is good. He struggles to make the Virgin home and accept all the conditions he believes I impose through you. They are easier than the ones he has lived with for his lifetime. He is a man volunteering for servitude because the freedom he knows is filled with the shackles of a responsibility he is not prepared to shoulder. There is no such thing as true freedom, Stefen. It is an illusion.

We have indulged you for eleven Passages and now it is time for you to know the bondage of duty and the weight of responsibility that freedom demands. Only when that is realized can freedom be truly assessed and appreciated.

There is one more vision for you to experience. When you comprehend the true significance, then you will be ready to begin training to champion the Virgin.

When? Stefen felt desperate to be mobile and whole again. It seemed that world events moved in total chaos.

When the time is right.

The communication ended.

Frustrated, he wondered how much more would have

to happen before the Deity released him. *I have abdicated everything,* he mused. *I am no longer my own man. Perhaps I never really was.*

Tari came to sit beside him.

He had forgotten her. She was shaking either because of nerves or fear. Perspiration soaked her dress and matted her hair. Lightly she touched his chest, took his hand and touched his chest again, then her own.

Understanding eluded him. She repeated the sequence.

Tari. She was the confusing emotionalism and distant viewpoint in his vision. The memories coincided with the lesson from the Deity. It was so unexpected that he did not want to believe it. Yet, logic denied any other explanation. There was a quality about her that put him on guard. She was a link with the Deity and saw the visions thrust upon him. He felt ashamed that anyone could see what lay inside of him.

Much as he wanted to reject her, he needed the solace of another person caught in the quagmire of circumstance. The word "patience" floated through his mind. *Patience,* he thought stolidly.

Tari clasped his hand in both of hers and pressed it to her face, nodding. Being so near to her diverted his thoughts to his needs and curiosities. He pulled his hand away and felt her rise from the pallet. The misery of being alone lasted only heartbeats.

Tari stood in front of him and placed her hands on his head, then knelt in the spread of his legs. He touched her, feeling small bumps rise over her skin.

Hesitantly, she brushed his lips with hers and relaxed her arms around his shoulders. Stefen found her mouth a second time to kiss her. It did not seem rational that such a small act could incite the reaction it did. Tari pulled on his shirt and slipped it from his shoulders. She moved aside for him to shed his breeches.

For several heartbeats neither was sure of what to do. Stefen reached out and found her standing beside him. Exploring, he kissed her again, running his hands slowly over the curve of her shoulders, into the valley of her back and across the mounds of her buttocks. Her breasts were firm against his lower chest as she molded her body to his. His hands moved to her sides, over her round hips, into the narrows of her waist, across the flare of her ribs and to the full sides of her breasts.

Unreasonably, his breathing duplicated the ragged edge after a long run. The sound of his heart in his temples took on a pulsation throughout the rest of him.

Tari backed away, holding onto his hand when she sat on the pallet. Stefen followed, taking her with him as he stretched out. He explored her breasts, lingering at the small peaks, moved on and caressed her belly into her crotch. At the same time her kiss took on more passion while her fingers memorized him.

He wrapped his arms around her, pulled her close and rolled, keeping her on top. She kissed him again, slipped down a bit and straddled him.

Hands resting on her thighs, Stefen felt her work against him to break the maidenhead. The temptation to force her down became greater with each of her attempts. Her thighs turned rigid under his hands. The depth both wanted came instantly.

Stefen used her, releasing pent-up need and urges, venting his frustrations and tensions which found no other channel of escape.

Later, after she brought a bowl of water to cleanse them, he felt guilty for not considering her during copulation. He hoped that he had not hurt her either physically or emotionally. The immediacy of his release left room for compassion. This time when he took her into his arms it was for her pleasure and his whims were secondary.

Tari slept on his shoulder, the thin nacki-fabric blanket drawn over her. On his back idly stroking her hair on his chest, Stefen thought about the oddities in the passion she shared with him. She looked upon him as though he were something more than a man, while he felt he was something less than that without his speech, sight and hearing. But there were things he saw clearly in the dark and silent world.

For thousands of Passages the Leatez had dwelled upon the Virgin in peace with the jungle environment, yet strangers to the beasts ruling the green-shadowed realm. He saw them as a people who had outwaited what they originally waited for. The Virgin had claimed them as her children and adopted them without truly adapting them.

The placid resignation Aviea and Basea shared as their world crumbled around them in the face of the enemy was hard to understand. He considered the vision again and found only one man who fought for his woman. The man did not fight wisely, nor did he assess the situation. These were a people who did not know how to fight, and all but three were too proud to run.

He wondered how a man, or a woman, could watch the taking of a child spawn, raised and nurtured under his care, and not lift a hand in protest. Initially, he wanted to think of the Leatez Bespeaker as weak. But natural selection upon the harsh Virgin weeded out the physically weak and the infirm. *So it is not a shortcoming of a physical nature,* he concluded. *It is of another realm and called passivity.*

He considered the other five deaths, finding them to be acts of panic and the doings of men similar to a crazed animal caught in the midst of the Passage maelstrom, rather than rational beings. There was no justice or dignity in needless deaths. Caught in a situation they could not understand, the Leatez resisted individually, never combining forces to help one another.

Faces of the scarlet-and-white-clad soldiers passed across his inner eye. Most were young, afraid and disgusted by the easy submission to the threats of one man. The conviction in their faces was frightening in itself. There was a uniformity in their expressions. Its meaning eluded him.

Power, he recalled Lozadar saying. *It is a power struggle and they do not respect the absence of absolute power in a people who do not need it.* The Leatez carry no weapons. They do not seek to conquer territory. Nor do they plunder the land for what Lozadar called the basics of technology and civilization. And they do not war on anything but the elements during Passage.

Surely they possessed knowledge of some forms of technology and the means to develop a more sophisticated life-style at one time, he mused.

Time formed a rolling display over the multitude of visions thrust on him. He saw their origin and the fate of the errant craft during the following Passage.

Tari shifted and draped her right arm over his stomach. His thoughts returned to her. There was no love, as he perceived love, between them. Worship and lust hardly constituted an emotion which fired his soul.

He wondered if that was how Padree had felt when he had raped the girl in the burning colony, then killed her.

He could not stand the thought of Tari being killed without sweating profusely. But he knew if she were killed, her loss would be no greater to him than that of any of the Leatez. She was the Virgin's child and would be mourned and missed. The mate he desired was an outworlder imprisoned on a ship of death.

Parallelisms to his father bothered him. He did not want to be anything like the man, but he could not help seeing the growing similarities.

Chapter 16

LOZADAR ACCOMPANIED KANSI INTO THE sanctuary. He carried himself formally as though entering the highest court in the land. Twenty-five meters inside, the walls changed from a natural character to the mirror gloss of hand-polished stone which highlighted the divergent layers of sedimentation. The amount of time and effort spent in finishing the stone impressed him.

Sounds of running feet and whispers leaked out of offshoot corridors lit by torches set into living-rock holders. In the distance, he saw straight-line rays of light pour through high openings in the outer cliff. The history of the Leatez clung to the walls in bas-relief accentuated by polishing the areas the artist wished to stress.

In a second hallway farther down on the right a woman stood on a stack ladder and cleaned soot from the apex of the ceiling. The rounded arch behind her gleamed as though alive and radiating an inner force. When she saw them approach she hurriedly climbed down and moved the stacked platforms well away from them. Covertly she eyed Lozadar with distrust from under the graying strands of brown hair matted to her damp forehead.

At the end of the main hall was a door and more halls leading away on each side. A child peeked around the corner on the right and suddenly disappeared with a protest to his unseen mother.

The door was one of the most exquisite works of art Lozadar ever had the pleasure of examining. Various textures and colors of both stone and wood were inlaid around a circular carving of a delicate, beautiful woman backgrounded by a radiant sunburst. Her hair fell to cover her nudity. The only adornment she wore was an amulet of herself.

Lozadar leaned closer. The amulet went on into infinity like two mirrors facing each other.

"That's familiar. I've seen it somewhere before," he whispered to Kansi.

"Where?"

"I can't remember. But I know I have." Straightening, "It will come to me."

"Don't think about it now." She glanced up nervously. His stony appearance did nothing to ease her state. "Ready?"

He nodded and recaptured his regal formality.

Kansi rapped softly on the door. It swung open on well-oiled hinges. Polished walls rich with wood sculpture, tapestries and carved tableaus were the first real display of luxury since Antition. He would have enjoyed browsing through the Great Hall's treasures.

A tincture of incense hung in the room. Two rows of elevated hearths spaced ten meters apart burned to give off light. The room felt cold for the amount of heat Lozadar figured they should be producing. At the end of the fire aisle Aviea and Basea sat on hand-carved wooden chairs which might have been well suited to serve as thrones on several worlds.

The Leader and the Bespeaker wore what had to be their finest robes of carmine braided with bright yellow. In contrast with the ornate surroundings they were the plainest objects in the room. Yet their age blended them into place the way an artist would balance off a holo-painting with the right dimension which distinguished him.

"Welcome, Lozadar cor Baalan. It is time we talked of the present, the past and the future." Aviea bowed slightly at the waist as he greeted Lozadar, but did not rise.

"Thank you. I am listening." He met the Bespeaker's rheumy eyes steadily while returning the stiff bow of formality exchanged by equals.

Basea raised an eyebrow. Aviea checked a thin smile and said, "It is you whom I hoped would tell us."

"There is little to tell. The past cannot be undone. It is dead. The present is always with us. And the future is an unknown which can only be speculated about and, therefore, part of the present." *Spoken like a true politician,* he complimented himself.

"Tell us of your world and the conflict it brings to the Virgin," Basea snapped. Her eyes became tiny marbles of ice as she hunched forward.

154

Kansi flinched and took Lozadar's hand for support.

"My world is as far above you, technically, as you are above the ganids," he said evenly, watching the effects of his words upon them. "Since my coming to the Virgin, I have also learned that we are equal to the ganids in many ways. I suppose it is the price we pay for a mass-production brand of civilization. Whereas the ganids will eat their own if they grow hungry enough, we kill our own if we are afraid enough, or if the prize is great enough.

"You ask to know what goes on in the far world. All I can answer is that it is a power struggle, perhaps the same one that has gone on since man's numbers became sufficient to have a divergence of opinion. Usually it is confined to words and an occasional skirmish. Other times it takes the form of an out-and-out war.

"Presently, it seems to be in-between. Men aren't willing to go to war until the reasons are clear-cut and well defined. War is a devastating thing when unleashed full-scale. It's still in the bargaining stage."

"Who does the bargaining?" Aviea asked.

"Whoever wants the power to rule the Seven Worlds and dominate the colonies."

"And who is that?" The Bespeaker was leaning forward in his chair also.

"I don't know."

"You are Ruler of the Seven Worlds and do not know who threatens you or who brought you and your vile hostilities to the Virgin?"

"I was brought here as a way to die, but I did not die." He sighed. "No. I do not know who leads the Insurrectionsts, just that they are my enemy. And here, I am an outcast bound to Stefen, Judge of Man."

"That is a problem," Aviea muttered, then leaned toward Basea and conferred in whispers.

Lozadar waited, feeling Kansi rigid and perspiring in the cold room at his side, watching the two old leaders and wondering how they planned to get information he knew they wanted without tipping their hand. It was a glimmer of the old days when he had sharpened his wits at General Assembly pleading the colonies' cause for admission.

Aviea straightened in his chair, cleared his throat and spoke. Loose flesh clinging to his jowls vibrated the white streamers of beard with the motion. "If you were free to return, would you be able to bring about a peace and keep the outworlders away from here?"

The stone mask of the politician playing with the leaders hid his surprise at the question. "I am not free. Speculation is a waste of time. Maybe you ought to be talking to Stefen instead of me."

Basea leaped to her feet, red-faced and shaking. "Why do you continually refuse to give him proper homage? He is the Holy One!"

"He is Stefen to me, until he asks me to address him otherwise. It seems you have expected him for some time. May I ask why you never went out looking for him?"

"It is written," Basea said quickly as she settled on her throne, "that when our time of need is greatest and the days before Passage numbered, a Holy One will come forth from the wilds. He will be salvation from the plague and thwart the demon upon the land."

Silently Lozadar wondered what scoundrel had written the words these people believed wholeheartedly. It seemed their religion, government and mode of living were all based on false promises. It was hard to imagine Stefen caring for himself in the jungle as he was, let alone assuming the leadership of the Leatez. Even if he were not afflicted by the multiple maladies of the Forbidden Place he was unaccustomed to dealing with people. A good leader needed to understand his underlings and be able to motivate them.

Mentally, he shrugged, realizing these people would follow Stefen out of religious obligation right into the pyres of Hell if that was what he wanted. *Fanatics were funny that way,* he decided.

"We will confer and speak with you again tomorrow, Lozadar cor Baalan. Please, ask the Holy One if he will accompany you." Aviea rose and bowed.

"I will do so, but he does not like closed places such as this." *God, I don't, and I'm calling the shots for now. Too easy to get trapped or walk into a trap.* "Perhaps it would be best to meet elsewhere?"

The Bespeaker and the Leader exchanged worried glances. Both nodded.

Kansi pulled on his hand to let him know they had been dismissed. He turned away and walked between the giant hearths, again amazed at the size of the Great Hall.

156

When they reached the ornate door Lozadar stopped and asked, "How is it that you know my full name? That's the second time you used it." He turned back to the thrones. "I did not tell you."

Basea paled, frightened. Aviea managed a smile and said, "Intervention of the Holy One among us is a mysterious and wondrous thing."

"That answers the sewage problem," Lozadar muttered under his breath, knowing it would be unwise to challenge them further.

When they departed the caverns he turned to Kansi and said, "Now that's how to lie. Did you see the way he didn't even break stride?"

"Perhaps he is telling the truth. Aviea is a holy man who also brings doctrines from the Deity and the Virgin. We have done well under his reign as Bespeaker." A troubled expression told the other side of her feelings.

"It's a good thing you don't have a treasury. He'd walk off with it."

It amazed him how basic types of people remained the same regardless of the circumstances. There were Avieas in every government he saw. With the religious power the man held, he was very dangerous as well as powerful. No man lied so quickly or so well without a lot of practice.

Kansi waved and called to a youth exiting a nearby hut. He waved back and walked hesitantly toward them, eyes focused on Lozadar. He appeared to be about thirteen Passages old. He bordered being skinny. His pale complexion was more noticeable next to Kansi's olive tone. His features were fine and delicate; most pronounced were his long-lashed brown eyes.

He bowed respectfully when she introduced Lozadar. "I was praying," he said.

"For what?" Lozadar asked, hoping he wasn't praying to Stefen, and glanced at the hut the boy had come from. It looked like the one assigned to him.

"To the Deity and the Virgin that they would allow the Holy One to find favor for our people through Tari. Aviea has pledged Tari's life for that purpose." He smiled quickly at Kansi. "She can be very determined and stubborn when her mind is made up."

"I see," Lozadar said noncommittally, trying to piece together what he knew about their culture. Regardless of the words, Aviea did not seem the type of man to willingly pass on the power he wielded to another, Holy One or not.

"Will you be taking the evening meal with me?" Adru asked Kansi.

She smiled, a gesture with no meaning. "No, my place is to serve our guests with Tari."

The look she gave Lozadar entreated him to speak. "You're welcome to join us, if it is permitted by your elders."

The boy's face changed from awe to total excitement. "I would be honored."

Adru sat quietly, taking in all that was happening around the table. Furtive glances at the Holy One grew brazen as the meal entered its final stages.

Stefen's hair had grown evenly over his body. It lay flat on his scalp, automatically forming a part on the left side. The steam-burn marks were a dull pink and hinted of handprints where the Deity may have touched him. The abnormal way he kept the fenwapter near fascinated the boy. The creature uttered no sounds and seemed to take in all that happened. How exciting a life the Holy One must have lived alone in the jungle with only his wits and tenacity to depend on! Adru was enraptured by the prospect.

In an effort to improve his understanding of the kind of people they were dealing with, Lozadar asked countless questions. The Leatez answered quickly, eager to please one so closely associated with the Holy One. Tari and Adru persistently referred to him as the Bespeaker, a title he did not want, but did not refute.

Their life-style was simple. Half of each day was given to meditation directed at becoming closer to the gods ruling their existence. A child participated after surviving his fourth Passage. From the end of one Passage to the beginning of the next they prepared for seclusion. Aviea secured each family group designated quarters, allowing them to gather as a whole three times during their internment. He summoned them individually to worship with him.

The scripture guiding their lives and rituals had been handed down from the First Ones. Their payment was great for not recognizing the gods controlling their survival. Only after the second generation did they begin to worship the ground they walked upon, the air they breathed and the strong sun holding them close when the weaker demon tempted the Goddess. Violence was an abomination which disturbed the Holies. Daily, they prayed for tranquillity across the land and her continued protection during the annual crisis.

At the halfway point between Passages a young boy was sent into the jungle to learn its ways. It was an honor to be chosen. Never had one returned. If he had, he would have immediately been proclaimed the Holy One and charged with securing a closer spiritual relationship with their gods.

With an air of impartiality learned in childhood and practiced ever since, Lozadar listened, piecing together why Stefen was immediately deemed a savior. He had mastered the jungle creatures and taught them his ways, just as the scripture predicted a Holy One would ultimately be able to do. They had been sending children into the jungle for better than four millennia, hoping one of them would walk out after a Passage and give them divine guidance. It did not seem far removed from human sacrifice, which some of the floundering and distant settlements had resorted to in past histories.

If the premise of a living God and Goddess was accepted, he theorized, it would make the entire unnatural existence of the planet understandable. And it would explain some of the reasons why Stefen and his jungle comrades shared the same belief as the Leatez even though there had been no previous contact. Stefen's condition substantiated that something existed. For a moment he wondered if they were correct and he was the one who did not see the whole truth. Mentally, he shivered.

He thought of four thousand children, lonely, afraid, unprepared, swallowed by grabber moss, attacked by a kervemith, ripped apart by a fenwapter, ingested by a yaxura or attacked by hundreds of red ganids, each claiming a piece of the find before a horde of chotiburus interrupted.

Stefen signaled an end to the meal and conversation by grabbing Tari's wrist and rising. The heartbeat of fear running over her face made her appear strained. It vanished as quickly, but not before it was noticed. Together,

159

they went behind the brightly stitched tapestry hiding their cubicle from the others.

There was an awkward moment of silence. Slowly, Adru came to his feet and stacked the meal remnants and utensils onto a tray. He thanked Lozadar for allowing him to take part, bowed and left with the dishes.

Lozadar remained at the table, oblivious to Kansi, thinking for several minutes. Her touch brought him out of his reverie.

"Let's go see if Esse has found anything in the way of another shelter," he said.

Kansi nodded, smiling. "It is almost rest time. If it is good, perhaps we can pause awhile."

Instantly Lozadar grinned, yearning for privacy and a leisurely time wih Kansi.

Chapter 17

ANGRY, STEFEN ORDERED ANDAZU TO STAND watch. Through the fenwapter's senses he had listened to the easy conversation Lozadar invoked from the Leatez. The contents did not disturb him, for any worship or service done for the Virgin and the Deity was commendable. But the ability to vocalize and draw words out of others was a gift he knew he did not possess even with all his senses functioning.

He resented the years alone when he might otherwise have been in the midst of people, learning the subtleties of interaction and relationship values. And it was irritating the way the boy looked sideways at him and spoke to Lozadar. *He is a boy,* Stefen fumed, *not a man as I was at his age. He would not last a day in the jungle by himself.*

At times during the meal, he was glad for the penance he served. It saved him from having to contribute and display his social ineptitude in the light of Lozadar's grace.

It did not seem right. This was his realm. The outcast sought to gain it for himself. He still wanted to be a Ruler.

He pulled off his clothes and reached for Tari. She was half a heartbeat slower in getting out of her dress. Hurrying, she tripped on it and fell toward him.

There was no thought involved in the reflex that hurled Tari onto the pallet and crushed the wind from her lungs. She became an extension of his ire.

Padree would have killed Lozadar had he been in a similar situation. In that, he deemed his father would have been right.

He sat on the edge of the pallet, his left hand kneading the soft flesh of Tari's stomach and occasionally roaming over her breasts.

It irked him the way he had been ignored at the meal.

It seemed that his presence had no more function than an empty fotig shell.

His fingers closed around Tari's breast, unable to become a fist. Small hands closed on his forearm. He shed them like shaking off a ganid.

He saw Padree as a child on a desolate planet where everything struggled to grow. The trees were scrawny and dwarfed. Red sand blew across the rocky surface in waves like a great sea which encompassed the planet. It felt old, older than anything experienced firsthand, and lonely. Isolated. Neglected. Shunned. Cold ached in the ground and wind in the fading night. Soon, heat would overtake the land and scorch the sands and mountains, against which a small settlement took refuge.

Padree crouched against a rock and peered over another one slightly above the domed habitats. He watched the sky where the last stars fled from the sand-fuzzed horizon. Shivering, he adjusted the face cloth tighter at his left ear.

Four pinpoints of light appeared in the dawn. For a while they looked stationary, but they grew steadily more brilliant. When they moved it was toward the mountains.

The boy withdrew a small signal box from his robes, pressed the sides and put it back. The domes below came alive with activity, though no additional lights were lit to change their appearance.

The ships hovered, sending sand and dust into the sky in churning billows. A man settled beside Padree and made quick gestures with his hands. Padree nodded. Stefen could feel him smile through his mounting fear.

The vision further infuriated Stefen. He saw no sense to it. There seemed little point in the exposure to his father as a child. He did not want to know the man in any different light than at the present. There was enough conflict and inconsistency shrouding the dead man.

Padree stood inside one of the ships, confronted by an officer dressed in a green-and-white uniform. Compassion oozed from the friendly-looking soldier. Off to the left, two guards hauled a man in white wrist and ankle bracelets out to the ramp. He had the same defeated look as the other prisoners brought to the settlement; nowhere to go and no way to get there.

The officer in charge repeatedly asked Padree who his

parents were, yet seemed to understand when he remained silent, knowing they would be sought out and subjected to another sterilization process.

He felt an uncertainty and a sense of duty war inside of Padree. Fright made the time pass slowly until the prisoner was down the ramp. A warm sensation filled the small hand thrust deep into his robe pocket. Stefen felt his heart speed up and his body go rigid with tension. The boy resigned himself to die, knowing what he had to do for the greater good of those close to him. He also knew the price he would pay if he denied those very same people.

The bay was empty. The leader motioned for him to follow. One step and he was on the man's heels, asking if he could see the place where the ship was controlled.

Surprised, the leader smiled back at him and nodded. They walked through corridors of gleaming metal and sparkling-clean white ceilings. Slight indentations marked places where doors slid into the walls. Speakers, unseen in the corridors, announced the stages of unloading and counted out the time, relaying orders back and forth from the ships.

The command area was alive with lights and equipment. The door closed behind them. Padree was hot in his robes. His hands sweated. Awed by the collage of lights, he glanced around and saw no one else in the area.

The signal box tingled in his left hand. Perspiration broke out in a flood over his body. He heard words coming from the man glancing at him and pointing to a series of bright lights running a pattern up a board, then down, over and over. For a moment the lights put him in a trance.

A tingling sensation ran up his arm and alerted his whole body.

An icy gold handle filled Padree's right hand. Slowly, he withdrew it from its sheath, keeping it well hidden in the folds of his robe.

A sudden calm wrought by training and resignation swept over Stefen as he experienced his father's actions. The moment of destiny was at hand.

Nothing could change it.

There was no going back.

It was almost a relief that it had finally arrived. Success carried its own rewards, and defeat would bring him a swift end.

He approached the leader, who continued speaking words that did not register any more. They were unimportant, extraneous. Only his body language warranted attention. There was a streak of triumph in the logic Padree had heard every day of his preparation. They would not expect a child capable, and he would be a man when it was over.

As rehearsed a thousand times, Padree stumbled and fell. Left-handed, he tried to get up, wincing at his right ankle, which would not support him. The leader regarded him suspiciously, but succumbed to the tears gathering in the child's eyes, tears of the abject fear of failure. The fear intensified and kindled a fresh doubt.

When the leader reached down to help, Padree sprang, whipping the knife across the man's exposed throat. Blood spurted, covering his face, pulsating across his robes. He pushed back before the man fell, shook himself and stumbled to the door. The small panel had four buttons instead of three. He looked for the one that started with the symbols associated with the manual lock mechanism and pushed it.

There was a distinctive click.

Not wanting to, knowing he had to, he turned back to the leader twitching on the floor. What he saw made him run, eyes focused on the tremulous hand wrapped around a Lat-kor. Lunging, he grappled with the man. What seemed to last an eternity was over in heartbeats as blood pumped out around them.

After a moment's silence, he reached into his robes and depressed the side of the signal box. All that was left for him to do was wait until the men outside overran the guards. If all else failed, they controlled at least one ship and Padree was guaranteed passage off the penal colony.

He used his robe to wipe the blood from his knife. The fabric was coarse and smeared more than it cleaned. He put it away and went to work on retrieving the weapon lodged in the dead man's hand. The blood was sticky. As though in a final act of defiance, the fingers seemed soldered to it. He pried them away one at a time and examined the crimson-smudged treasure.

When he scooted away from the corpse his robe left a dark trail streaked on the clean white floor. The even lighting made it uglier. He tried to ignore it, knowing it was something he could not afford to dwell on. He flipped the safety off the Lat-kor and crossed his legs, prepared to shoot if the wrong ones came through the door before he received the signal to unlock it.

He fought back tears and steeled himself against the flood of emotions ripe with guilt. It was true. He was no longer a child.

Quaking, Stefen folded his hands. It was hard to accept the idea of a boy no older than he was when Padree died taking on such a black task and accomplishing it so adroitly. The isolation of the boy in the command room felt no less than what he had felt after his father's death. Slowly, it dawned on him that the presence of people did not make the difference in loneliness. It was the relationship with those people which made the difference.

Again, he thought of Lozadar. The outcast was not lonely when with people, even people who were as strange to him as the Leatez and their worship of the Deity. Yet, he was lonely with them and knew he would be even if his senses were restored.

Stymied, he lowered his head and raised his hands. There was an acrid smell captured in the vee of his folded palms. He sniffed, trying to place it. His fingers were sticky and stretched the skin when he pulled them apart. He sniffed again, feeling his stomach climb into his throat.

Timidly, he reached out, hoping he would not find his fears justified.

Tari flinched, undulating rythmically under his touch. He knew she was crying hard.

The sticky feel of her face and matted chunks of her hair were more than he could bear. He wanted to tell her how sorry he was, that he had not meant to harm her.

How could this have happened? There was no memory of hitting her, only the emotion-filled vision and his jealousy of Lozadar. . . .

Frantic, he rose, summoned Andazu and groped through the curtains. He pulled his clothes on, wondering when he had taken them off.

The fenwapter came to his side and guided him out to Asa. He struggled, stomach convulsing, and managed to mount the kervemith. Holding the horn, he steadied as she came to stand.

Andazu bounded up behind him, asking where he wanted to go.

For several heartbeats, he did not know, then decided upon the Forbidden Place. He felt compelled to return. It was the source.

Andazu leaped down and gathered up his packs, then returned.

Asa turned toward the jungle, roaring for her mate to join them.

The Leatez gathered near the firepit watched them go. Tears splattered the ground, shed by men and women whose hopes were disappearing into the jungle. Hands sought the solace of a loved one who would be there when the outworlders came again. They were completely defenseless against them now. The Holy One had come and tasted of the only virgin they could offer and found her lacking.

Tari's sobs poured out of the hut, but no one moved to help her.

Aviea lifted his staff. "Oh, Deity," he began in a strong voice that carried into the jungle, "you test us greatly. Let not the presence of the offensive outcast and his blasphemy be set upon our heads. He will be sent from this holy place of worship. Smile upon us, great Deity, and accept the sacrifice we have made. Send back our Holy One for protection and guidance. Let us enter Passage safe in the Virgin's womb so that we may survive to honor you again."

He lowered his staff and led his people into the sanctuary, where the transmitter waited.

Adru lingered, hearing his sister's cries filled with pain and restrained by the knowledge that she had failed to satisfy the Holy One and no Leatez would look upon her again. He glanced over his shoulder and saw no one watching. Quickly, he darted across the bare expanse and ducked into the hut.

He froze for an instant, forced himself to respond to the sound behind the tapestry and brushed it aside. Tari shook her head, knowing he had just exiled himself from their people for her sake. "Go back before they find you missing," she pleaded through her tears. "I can't bear that guilt too. Please, Adru . . . please, don't do that to me."

"Come on. I'll help you dress. If we can make it to the

166

jungle where Lozadar and Kansi are, we'll be safe. Well, safer than we are here. Aviea is blaming him for the Holy One's departure. I'm sure he is summoning the outworlder lady."

He picked up her dress and helped her get into it. As she tried to stand, he ransacked the hut, taking blankets, the knives from off the center table and the bowls, dumping the contents onto the floor.

Tari held onto the curtain and made her way toward the center. Her left eye was swollen closed from a split in her eyebrow. Discoloration grew pronounced over the entire left side of her face as well as parts of her exposed arms and shoulders.

The drape at the door flew back, jolting Adru. Lozadar and Kansi gaped at the bloodied woman clutching to the curtain for support.

"What in hell's name happened here?" Lozadar reached for Tari as she swayed on her pendulum course towards him.

Adru picked up the outcast's pack and handed it to Kansi. "We've got to leave immediately. I'll explain later."

"She's in no shape to go anywhere. Haven't you got a healer, someone who practices medicine?" He scooped her up and was surprised by how light she was. Beneath the discolorations on her face was a child the same age as Chalate and Corry. It hurt to see the similarities. He wanted vengeance against Stefen for her. "No one has the right to do this to another human being," he muttered. "I don't give a damn how holy he is. God, Kansi! She's just a kid who wanted to please him."

Adru was pale. "Aviea is sending for the outworlders to take you away."

"That's terminal stupidity. He starts up that transceiver and every ship in the quadrant will converge right here."

"I'm sure it is too late to worry about it," Adru said, adjusting the bundle he gathered.

Lazadar looked at him; he seemed older. "Where's Stefen?"

"Gone."

"What do you mean, gone?" Kansi asked, peeking out the door to the right.

"Just what I said. He's gone, and they believe the outcast must be gotten rid of before he will return." To Lozadar, "We must go. If we leave Tari, they'll abandon her. She has been dispossessed because the Holy One did not find her pleasing."

Lozadar swore vehemently, shifted her in his arms and turned to the door.

"It's clear," Kansi whispered. "Hurry before someone comes out of the guard hut. And it's nearly time for meditation change."

They ran in single file to the jungle, keeping the hut between them and the main part of the clearing. Lozadar held Tari close to him, trying to keep her from being jarred more than absolutely necessary. He refused to look at her. She bounced against him like a rag doll.

Lozadar led the way through the jungle, which grew thicker the deeper they penetrated. He did not slow until his lungs were burning and his shoulders ached from Tari's weight.

"Kansi," he panted, "we can't make the high mountain cave. Do you know these mountains at all?"

"No," she breathed back.

"I do." Adru took the lead. The incline to the east was steep and thickly foliated overhead. It was dark before they reached the top and rested.

None of them spoke for a long time, each dealing with the strain of their flight. Kansi finally crawled over to Lozadar and tended Tari. The moons lit the sky and the orbi flowers brightened the jungle. Adru recounted the happenings at the village, ending with his decision to stay with his sister at any cost. It was not an easy thing to leave the security of the people and caverns for one so young, though it was easier than he had once thought it would be.

Lozadar sat against a putch, trying to put some sense into the incident and admiring the boy for his courage. Noting the position of the moons and the need for sanctuary, he asked how Adru had come to know the mountains.

"I thought I would be chosen to go into the jungle." Glancing furtively at Kansi, "I have always had trouble believing Aviea." Head bowed in shame, "When I was very young he frightened me. He does not find carnal satisfaction with Basea."

"Adru! Watch what you say." Kansi beheld her charge in horror.

Indignant, "It's true. He calls it worship. But it is not to the Deity! My meditation training was spent as his gratifier. I have hated him since. He tells us the Virgin is female and the Deity male. But I am male. And he is male. There can be no worship in that." The boy's eyes glazed over and there was no longer a dam holding back the words and emotions held inside for so long.

"Even after meditation training was over he sought me out when I was working in the near jungle. My gatherings were poor because of him. And I could say nothing. I could do nothing. Who would believe me? I would be accused of blasphemy and banned from the village with no place to go during Passage.

"So I prepared. I started going farther and farther. Several times I managed to stay away for the night, exploring the mountains he forbade us to enter."

Tenderly, he picked up Tari's hand. "I couldn't go away and make her worry. Or you, Kansi. And even after I found a place and fixed it up I knew I couldn't confront Aviea without bringing pain or, worse, exile on you, too."

Revolted by Adru's story and its implications, Lozadar's admiration for him continued to grow. He had misjudged the boy as passive and weak because of his appearance—the same soft appearance which Aviea probably found attractive, he concluded.

"Is it far?" Lozadar asked, watching the sky through a hole in the foliate ceiling.

"Into the ravine and halfway up the other side," Adru answered. "We should be moving."

Lozadar wrapped Tari in a blanket and picked her up. Following the boy and Kansi was easier than trying to lead. Adru had a good working knowledge of the patterns and trails wound into the vegetation. They reached the bottom of the ravine as the sun began to turn the east gray.

Overhead, the familiar sounds of engines killed the dawn's vigor. They came in from the east, flying low over the mountains toward the Leatez village.

No one spoke, but each pushed harder up the incline. Rain clouds gathered and emptied steadily upon them, washing out their tracks, but making the scant trail they followed treacherous.

The Deity was directly overhead when the clouds broke and Adru halted. He pulled aside armfuls of orbi vines to reveal a cave large enough for Lozadar to enter standing.

Inside, he set Tari down immediately, fearing he would drop her if he had to carry her another step.

The sounds of engines came again, the pitch slightly lower.

Lozadar ran outside and climbed a putch until he could see the sky. Head shaking, he wondered if humanity suffered insanity by what was carried genetically, or if it was a learned trait.

Chapter 18

CORINDA DEZ KALIEA WALKED UP THE RAMP of the command ship, head bowed, feet scuffing with uncertainty. An attitude bordering acute depression pierced the brief jubilation of knowing Lozadar was alive. "So close and so far . . ." she mumbled.

General Myzillion remained at the base confronting Aviea and Basea. The throng of people he half expected to filter out of the village to satiate their curiosity did not materialize. Questioning the leaders produced no answer to that anomaly. It annoyed him, since both categorically denied being visited by any other ships.

"Tell me, when he left, did he say where he was headed or why?" A rough edge stayed in his voice. He glanced around, looking for something, anything to give him a reason to spend the time it would take to search the surrounding area with armed soldiers. His battle sense denied the indulgence and warned him to leave.

Aviea met his gaze and raised his staff. "He has offended the Holy One of the Deity. He is not wanted here. He has not returned since the Hour of Desolate Desertion. He is the cause for our abandonment. He is the emissary of the Weaker Power."

"I respect your right for worship. However, Bespeaker, this will all resolve itself far more quickly if you could find it in your heart to extend some tolerance to Sire cor Baalan just long enough for us to come for him." Without waiting for an answer, General Myzillion turned up the ramp and waved his hand in the air to make a circle.

Hatches closed. General quarters were sounded.

Before he was halfway up a piercing whine blasted intermittently from the heart of his ship. He ran, futilely glancing over his shoulder at the sky. The ramp retracted under his feet and propelled him forward.

"Battle stations. Battle stations. This is a red alert," droned the computer warning.

General Myzillion stormed the corridor, pushing those crew members aside who did not see him coming. Red-faced, he hurled himself into the lift and slammed the square for the bridge and muttered a priority command to the wall.

Long strides carried him across the clean expanse to his com chair. Corinda stood glued to the side. Unblinking, she watched the monitor screens showing the approach of five enemy ships. The extreme-left picture showed the power shield encasing each ship. It shimmered around the fringes and distorted the speeding metal inside to match the unreality Corinda felt swallowing her. The General's strong voice focused her attention on the bridge.

"Strap yourself into that," he said, shoving her into the com chair. He immediately slammed his fist through the protective casing of the emergency key, the first any commander had utilized in Colonial history, caught two fingers in it, pulled and jumped back. Corinda disappeared behind the walls of a life pod which closed in on her from both the floor and the ceiling. Her stomach lurched. The pod slid down a tube void of light and filled with vertigo. A screen brightened and showed the nude spot on the bridge where the com had been a few seconds earlier.

Hart stood next to a portable command bank usually used by his captain. Since Gevek's death it had remained empty. He shouted orders as the ships lifted from the Leatez clearing to meet the threat above. There was little hope in their plight. The disadvantage belonged to them right down the line.

He sent orders to the three ships and activated the escape pods. The command ship was always the primary target. *Best to size the situation up with prevention than try to pretend it's better than it is,* he reaffirmed, punching in the last of the sequence.

"We are the decoy," he said calmly to his crew. "I want survivors down there to engage in hand-to-hand. You know what's down there and what not to do. Use that knowledge. It's been bought and paid for. Good luck."

The ships were too far away to see their markings. A universal design made it impossible to tell who was at war in the sky. Lozadar counted nine and wondered who held the hammer. They played a waiting game, taunting each other to see who would be the first to break for the void above the planet where the weapons fired for long distances on true lines.

The four lined up in an unusual configuration spearheaded by the command ship. The three behind were close and partially shielded. He had to admire the strategy. Pulled in as they were was risky if they shared shield power, which was the only reason for such a formation.

The five opened fire simultaneously.

The intensity hurt Lozadar's eyes. He looked away, his vision filled by crawling black dots which blotted out what he looked at. Sound told him the score. Reflex sent him looking up. Through the dots he saw several dozen escape capsules descend into the clouds. The three ships unleashed a barrage and sped after the retreating five. A flare preceded the distant sound of another explosion, then another.

Corinda dug her nails into the padding embracing her. Through the portholes raged a nightmare come true. The waiting ended unmercifully.

Daylight split the dark outside. For a flicker of an instant the six layers of deck below and in front of the command area showed. It disintegrated.

The bulkheads collapsed; twigs in a tornado. Sparks replaced the orderly mass of lights along the computer consoles. The surge of turbulent air did not even permit fire or smoke. Chairs, bodies, broken parts of the ship and her crew slammed against the outside of Corinda's capsule.

No one heard her screams or witnessed her struggle to get out of the encasement.

The ship erupted away from her. Blue sky. Black clouds. She was alone—again an unwitting survivor because of the Colonial General.

Lozadar squinted into the clouds for a sign of the capsules. The wreckage from the subsequent blasts would disintegrate before reaching the ground. Debris from the first one rained in the north and west.

He climbed down from his perch, feeling the strain of their flight into the jungle. The scarcity of fotigs registered. He found a stalk with half a dozen still clinging to the end and cut it free. Was the jungle less fruitful here? Or did the seasons coincide with Passage? Dismayed, he dropped to the ground and entered the cave.

"How is she?"

Kansi looked up and drew a blanket over Tari. "She should live. I don't think she has any broken bones. There will be scars. The physical injuries do not worry me. I'm afraid she will go into the death fever."

Fresh, soft lines in her face deepened. She leaned close to him. "Why? You know him. Why did he do this to her? What could she have done to . . ."

"I don't know." He sank to the floor and cracked a fotig.

She settled beside him and took the jagged half he offered. They ate in silence for several minutes, Lozadar stealing glances at Tari as she slept. The bruises were colorful, but did not look as bad with the blood cleaned away.

He leaned back against the wall. The cool stone soothed the heat of anger rippling under his thoughts. The cave was already well stocked with dried batinas, shanuts, fotigs, raisins and what looked like chotiburu jerky in Adru's hand. The boy had planned on surviving and had chosen a good sanctuary, with water running crosswise twenty meters inside.

"I don't think he hurt Tari deliberately, Kansi." The quiet words captured Adru's attention. "She's still alive." As he spoke, the words made sense to him. He wondered where Stefen would go as he tried to outrun himself. "No. I don't believe it was deliberate."

Tari whimpered and opened her eyes. "I'm sorry," she whispered.

Lozadar stretched to his left and held himself up with his elbow. Gently he touched the crown of her head. "What happened, Tari?"

"He hurts inside." She turned away and closed her eyes.

A long silence marked by her even breathing indicated that her fresh sleep had become deep and dream-filled.

"I'm going gathering," Adru said. "We'd better get what's left if we're going to make it through Passage and the cold without growing hungry."

He no longer looked frail and soft. The confidence he

exuded knew the price of survival. A twinkle in his eyes faltered when he bid a quiet farewell to his sister.

Lozadar ate a strip of chotiburu and forced it down with another fotig.

Kansi watched him. She did not speak and waited for him to take the intiative.

"Kansi . . ."

"Don't say it." She moved close to him, shedding her clothes on the way. "Try to make it back before Passage, Lozadar."

He wrapped his arms around her, burying his face in her salt-scented hair. "I'll try. God, but I hate to leave you. You're one in a million."

"Just come back. I'll be waiting."

The faster Asa ran the worse Stefen felt. Foam splashed against his face. He regretted pushing her so hard and let her halt. Slipping to the ground, he could smell the aroma of fresh blood—Asa's, flecking the foam dripping from her fangs.

Miserable, he settled against a putch, head in hands, elbows on knees. This was not the way he wanted it to be. Never would he intentionally hurt Tari or drive Asa beyond exhaustion if he were thinking rationally. It seemed that he no longer knew himself as anything but an extension of Padree and the Lovers. Somewhere along the line the message he was supposed to receive was lost in emotions and the burning need to be unlike his father.

Desperately he wanted some inner light to shine and give him guidance. The isolation of being lost and out of contact with his world was worse than any danger or fear, real or imagined.

During a limbo in which time carried no meaning, he felt Andazu come to his side. Long after the fenwapter ate and slept, Stefen tuned into him, his heart heavy with the loyalty Andazu maintained and the ever-present sorrow for Kachieo's loss. The fenwapter never questioned, never judged. He was always there to help. It shamed Stefen. He deemed himself unworthy.

He touched Andazu and woke him. *Send Esse to find Lozadar. Bring him.*

After the fenwapter left, he thought about the outcast and the gamut of his feelings concerning him. He needed him as a restraint in the presence of people. The idea was demeaning and deplorable. He had to learn how to be with people. Life alone, apart from his own kind, who would so willingly take him in as one of them, was death. Yet he could not risk a repeat of Tari.

The thought of what he had done to her twisted his insides. He wept openly for them both.

The air turned cool, a subtlety Stefen related to the disappearance of the stronger sun. The nights grew shorter as Passage neared. Soon they would have to find shelter for the duration. It would be a lean Passage without adequate food storage or drying preparations. And somehow it did not really matter to him.

The catharsis of tears drained him sufficiently to permit thinking rationally. With the advent of Passage, Esse and Asa needed to be freed to find their own sanctuary. Esse had won a place for them if they returned to the area around the Leatez village. He considered staying with them, then discarded the idea as unfair. Asking the kervemith to restrain themselves after waking from hibernation when they were hungry and food was scarce put too much burden on them. And that unfair he could not be, he decided.

Soon after Lozadar comes they will have to go, he mused. *Soon, before I lose this thread of clear thinking.*

He put his head back against the tree. In a peaceful moment, he imagined the stars looking back through the leaves. All of his life he had taken the violence of Passage and the peace of the growing season for granted. *Yes, they indulged me.* The words of the Deity echoed in his head. *It was not the real world any more than what I live in now is.*

Dispassionately he thought about Padree, seeing him as neither good nor evil, but a man molded by necessity, inner drive and the forces around him. He was his father's son as well as Annalli's. In that light he thought about Padree as a child taking the life of the ship's commander on the prison planet. This he compared with the gentle-souled, loving man who had raised him for ten Passages.

"A man does what he has to do, when he has to do it," Padree used to say over and over. "If he doesn't, he isn't a man."

The rape-murder vision seemed to deny such an easy

solution. He considered it again, trying hard not to judge, wanting desperately to remain impartial.

The scene was vivid and still repugnant. Malodorous smoke burned his sinuses and stung his throat. The frenzy of the battle hung in the air, charging everything with a temporary bloodthirsty insanity. A relief to be alive and whole emanated from the survivors—attackers and defenders alike.

He saw Padree as a man bent upon taking out a blind revenge at the whole of civilization. Time and circumstances hid his original objectives. He became an extension of those drives around him, no longer willing to fight the moral battle of what was just or unjust in the light of the personal values hopelessly lost for that time of his life. Eventually, he abandoned himself to the same volatile forces which had made it mandatory for him to kill as a child. Lacking all conscience, he considered emotion a void he could not afford to tamper with for fear of the price attached. Padree had become a vengeance machine fighting for a cause unknown.

A glimmer of understanding gave Stefen hope for finding the end of his maze. He shifted against the tree and waited for Esse.

There was little point in going on to the Forbidden Place. It held no answers. The key lay elsewhere in the conglomeration of vision packed with emotion, locked inside his head, wrapped in dark riddles and the memories of others transfixed in fragile horrors.

Lozadar took to the trees as soon as he was away from the little stronghold. Often he looked around, memorizing the terrain, the mountains in the distance and the sculpture of the horizons against the clouded sky. Leaving Kansi behind with Tari, who might or might not decide to live, and the youngster, who was emulating the strength of the Holy One more than he knew, did not sit well. The obligation he felt toward Stefen dimmed.

He considered returning to Kansi, rationalizing that her need for him was greater than Stefen's. Stefen had Andazu, the kervemith and Evaladyn's horde if needed.

Swinging down on a nacki vine, he knew the help Stefen required could not be found in the jungle creatures regardless of how well they meant or their diligence.

Halfway back to the settlement he paused, gathered a

couple of nacki fruits and an overripe fotig. These he ate slowly, savoring the moisture of each. Finished, he pushed on, wanting to swing in close to the settlement to see what was happening. The sojourn through the jungle required a great concentration for the speed at which he chose to travel. For the most part, he avoided sharp leaf edges and jagged eyelets where fotig stalks had fallen away, their worth obliterated.

The strong sun had disappeared from the sky leaving the weaker one to taunt the surface. Lozadar was grateful for the light. He was not confident enough to attempt the ever-changing jungle at night. He kept moving, pushing to reach the settlement before the brief dark night found him short of his goal. He used tricks Stefen had taught him. By putting his body on "automatic" and thinking about something else, he skirted the worst of the leaf bunches and chose the strongest vines.

Part of him warned that all hell was going to break loose if he or Stefen was caught. The unpleasant thought invaded his reverie often. He tried to use the flight as a peaceful interlude, knowing he was doing all he could for the present and it still was not enough. Images of Kansi spurred him onward.

How easily he had come to care for her and how different she was from anyone he knew in the Seven! She gave herself to him without ulterior motives. The sex role in their worship of the Virgin and Deity imparted an expertise in her lovemaking which complemented his own and lent a mutual comfort from the first. It was an integral part of her nature, just as breathing was for most women.

He stopped short, realizing he had covered the distance. Through a clump of withering leaves he saw the village.

Three ships sat in the clearing. Their weapons were pointed outward as though they expected a military deluge to pour from the jungle.

The shadows were long, heralding the onslaught of the short night. Even squinting, he could not make out the insignia on the ships from his vantage point. Inwardly he swore. The ground below bore watching for guards from the ships, though he did not think they would venture too far into the jungle.

Aviea and Basea stood in the space between the two

larger firepits. The villagers clustered behind, holding onto each other in obvious fright. The Bespeaker gestured often while speaking. It looked like a futile argument he was having with the uniformed man in the white battle cape.

Lozadar wanted to hear what was being said. He selected a better vantage point. The words did not carry in the silence. While he debated the wisdom of going down to creep along the shadows to one of the huts, a whine came out of the clouds.

Two of the scouters kicked in their engines and ascended, making room for an immense ship preparing to land. As the two smaller craft turned into the fading light their insignia came out of the shadows.

Lozadar's first impulse was to make for the clearing. He stifled it. The House of dez Kaliea would not wreak violence on the peaceful Leatez. He relaxed, glad to have an ally in the neighborhood even if he did not plan to visit.

The larger ship settled, sending dust into the wind. The engines idled as a ramp carrying a man reached out to the dirt.

Lozadar squinted hard. The man was far too thin to be the Coralis Legate even if he were tall enough. He was scarlet from head to toe with the exception of white gloves. The man was familiar, yet Lozadar could not place him. He was of the House of dez Kaliea.

Carefully he thought back to the coronation, trying to put names and faces together. It was an enormous collage.

In the clearing the Leatez were gathered together into a tighter pack and circled by ununiformed men from the main ship. None protested, though occasionally a hysterical wail penetrated the low engine hum. A detachment of ten men, marching in formation in columns of two, went into the sanctuary with their weapons drawn.

Aviea continued to plead, hands gesturing vehemently, head turning often to see his people being herded into the ship. Basea looked resigned and defeated, her aged head bowed, her folded hands close to her drooping breasts.

The scarlet leader raised a gloved hand for silence. Aviea persisted, reached out and grabbed the man in an effort to make him understand something.

Lisan, Lozadar remembered. *That's who it is! But*

179

who the hell are those with him? Why aren't the soldiers of the dez Kaliea House uniformed?

He inspected the ship suspiciously. The design was new, modified to make atmospheric speed slightly better; regular ships had considerable drag, with harsher turns and bends where the body was attached to the landing prods. It was also bigger than any battleship in use, warships being usually medium-sized as the optimum mean. The burnished metal, scarred by heat during repeated entries, looked particularly shiny where the insignia should have been, as though it had been recently removed. Half the ship was exposed to him, and nowhere was there a marking. He wondered if the other side was marked and decided against risking the perimeter again.

Lisan shoved the Bespeaker. The old man stumbled back and fell. Bruskly, he slapped at the place where Aviea had touched him. Left-handed, he summoned the men directly behind him.

Lisan turned toward Basea. Wordless, head bowed, she shuffled toward the ship, faltering with a rigid cringe when a flash of light burst in the Bespeaker's direction.

Swearing under his breath, Lozadar acknowledged the doom of the Leatez. While Aviea might not be the most honorable of men, nor the most trustworthy spiritual adviser, he was a leader and the people responded to him. Whether it was fear or faith binding them did not matter. They were lost now. Even a questionable leader was better than no direction at all for the passive people. Basea was nothing more than a figurehead. The only place she would lead them was the death sleep Kansi spoke of, the death of those unable to see any hope once away from the Village.

Chapter 19

HE WAS BEING WATCHED. HE COULD FEEL IT. Lozadar's heart became a choking lump in his throat. After calculating the distance to the branch below, he turned around to check.

Esse breathed hard without making a sound a dozen meters away.

The magnitude of his relief was so great it nearly cost his footing when the tension fled and collapsed his body.

The kervemith came up behind him on the limb, curious to see what was going on in the Leatez village. It did not take long to satisfy his curiosity—just a few glances in fact. He was ready to leave and nudged Lozadar gently.

Lozadar absently held his left hand up to put an end to the distraction.

Without further protests the remainder of the Leatez followed Basea into the ship. Not once did her head lift. Her lips mumbled the words of a litany taken up by those following her.

The forced evacuation wound up orderly, leaving Lisan dez Kaliea and two of his generals outside the ship to survey the devastation. Soldiers had systematically thrown everything out of the huts and rummaged through the meager booty in search of weapons and souvenirs small enough to fit into a pocket. Torches pulled from smoldering firepits were hurled into the huts. This accomplished, the soldiers returned to the ship.

A trail of smoke wound out of the sanctuary's skylights. Lozadar cringed, remembering the thousands of years of art spanning the countless generations laboring toward its completion. Nauseated, he prayed that they had left the carved door unharmed. But there was not a great deal to burn, and something made the smoke.

Esse licked his hand, taking a layer of skin off with his rough tongue.

Still ignoring the beast, Lozadar pulled his hand down instantly, shook it and rubbed the bright-red welt. As a defense mechanism, he sat, reached back and patted Esse's leg. "Wait, my friend. Watch for a minute. I'm not ready to leave."

It made little difference to the kervemith. His breathing labored from the long search for the outcast. He tossed his head about, looking for food, and saw nothing, but he was not hungry enough to press his rider into an earlier-than-necessary return.

The engines changed pitch. The hum grew louder and higher. Lisan conferred with his generals on the ramp as it retracted, his hands braced on his hips.

"Feel proud, you bastard," Lozadar seethed, squinting intently at the thin man. "Some victory!"

The ship began to lift. Within a few minutes it was completely imbued by a lone cloud. Night took over and hid the last shreds of light from the watching eyes in the jungle.

Lozadar stood, bowed his head and scratched Esse under his jaw. "Let's go make sure that . . . Maybe somebody hid well enough to survive."

Reluctant, Esse held his place.

"Come on, you big baby. We're here now. If I don't check I'll wonder later until it bothers me so much I have to come back. You can stay outside if you want." He leaned to the right, caught a piece of vine and wooed it out of the leaves below until it hung clear. A sharp tug gave him confidence that it would hold him.

He slid to the ground and was swallowed by overwhelming shadow. He blundered through ferns and dangling nacki. The few meters to the jungle edge were a menagerie of hands and fingers, prying, grabbing, poking and scratching at him.

When he emerged into the clearing he looked up to where he thought Esse was. The big kervemith surprised him by being a good thirty meters away and outlined against faint stars in the black sky. Two bounds and the beast was at his side.

"You're going to spoil me if you keep on making it easy for me, Esse."

It felt good to have the company of a friend as he

entered the Leatez clearing. Trouble was the last thing he expected. Esse could detect an engine noise long before the ships were in visual range. They would be easy to avoid in the open with the kervemith.

Feeling a little afraid and not knowing why, Lozadar crossed the expanse. The dying fires were loud, but the sound of his feet on the hard-packed dirt seemed louder. He passed the hut assigned to him and Stefen. The flames had already consumed the interior and brought the roof crashing down.

He held the Lat-kor Stefen had confiscated above the sea. It was a more natural and comfortable weapon then his knife. Beyond the hut the embers of others glowed brightly, but failed to give off much light. The flames were dying quickly, the fuel consumed.

Lozadar picked up a thick log and poked at the center of the firepit. A low flame hovered over a turned chunk and danced blue and orange. A pile of wood stood several paces away. Lozadar tossed a couple of the larger logs in. He fanned it, sending white ash into the air.

He searched for and found a torch snuffed in the soft ash-saturated dirt near the pit. After brushing it clean he lit it. The last bits of dust crackled in a yellow aura.

There were three bodies scattered across the clearing near the sanctuary entrance. Sickened, Lozadar wondered how and when the other two had been killed. No weapons had been fired while he watched. Upon closer inspection he saw that their necks were broken. Their heads, eyes staring at the ground, were turned grotesquely over the left shoulder. It was not an unfamiliar execution. By juggling his hands in the air he reenacted the motions. The killer was left-handed or else the victims would be looking the other way, he concluded. Weak-kneed, he recalled the Chief Protector of the House of dez Kaliea—a lefty.

Eventually he came to stand over Aviea, vowing that if a day of confrontation ever came his way he would kill that skinny dez Kaliea bastard just as cruelly as the old man on the ground was dying. The wound was fatal; a lower-abdomen shot, quarter burst. It would be a while before death claimed the Bespeaker. Possibly he would last until first light.

Lozadar straightened the old man's garb and tried to

make him comfortable—as though such a thing were possible. There was nothing he could do without a med-kit or a mechanic.

Hunkered down on a rock, he watched the aged face try to come to grips with the pain. He seriously contemplated euthanasia. There was little point in the man suffering when death was so certain. Only a small amount of time packed with an enormous amount of pain was left. Aviea clung to consciousness, never quite managing to slip into the absolution of oblivion. His eyes teared when he became aware of Lozadar's presence.

"The Holy One . . . he truly deserted us. . . ." Hard, rasping breathing replaced the words.

Lozadar shook his head, pained by the burden the Leatez tried to bestow upon Stefen's unknowing shoulders. They asked too much from a man who could not help himself, let alone be their savior. It was like asking for a drink and winding up responsible for the whole ocean.

Aviea's eyes widened. ". . . want you, outcast. You. The woman . . ." He turned quiet for a little while. A heavy effort to concentrate changed his face and eased the pain lines around his eyes. Deliberately and at great price, he opened his eyes and spoke to the outcast bending close to his lips. "Your world is false. I wished to be rid of you for the safety of my people."

Fresh blood oozed from the fusion of his robes with his intestines. His face twisted into grotesque wrinkles. He gasped sharply before managing the acceptance of a new pain. "They attacked the woman's ship. Even if they had you . . . they would have taken my people. Oh, Deity. Our people are lost. Guide them. Preserve them . . ." They were words designed for a powerful call, but they came out a muted whisper.

At a loss to offer solace, Lozadar kept quiet. Of course his people would have been taken if Lisan wanted them, with or without pretext. At what point had Corinda given them the sender? Or was it Corinda? The Leatez would never know the difference. It would be advantageous if they decided to level with him and drop the name dez Kaliea.

Running his fingers through his sweaty hair, he did not know what to think.

The single certainty was that once the sender had been

activated it had been a live beacon for any and everybody who wanted to listen and more effective than sub-
liminal advertising. In that light, it did not make sense
unless it was Corinda who had given them the sender
and she had thought her forces were either alone here
or dominated the quadrant. Yet that did not fit. Was she
or was she not a "guest" of the colonials? She was a dez
Kaliea. . . .

He set it aside. For the time being the lack of reason or
logic nudging the pieces together did not matter. He
touched the old man's shoulder, rose and started into
the Sanctuary. More than ever he wanted a look at the
sender. While he did not expect it to be engraved with
the identity of the giver, he hoped there would be something peculiar about it to betray what part of the Seven
Worlds had manufactured it. That wasn't much, but it
was a start.

Esse followed, head swinging from side to side in dis-
comfort. Most of the torches were doused. They lay on
the floor shoved against the hand-polished walls. The
utter disrespect of the invaders roused an anger in
Lozadar as well as a tinge of guilt. These walls of stone
had been smoothed and polished out of love and care,
not because some pompous commander sought busy
work for his crew. This was the equivalent of sacrilege.

Lat-kors had been fired at the bas-relief murals running down the main hall. Gouges marred the smaller
works on the right. Piles of tapestries and stitcheries
were partially burned in one of the side halls.

Ahead, the carved door had not been obliterated by
a Lat-kor. Holes were burned through it. The wood
smoldered around the edges and tried to get a full-fledged
blaze going near the bottom. As old as the wood was, it
should have burned, Lozadar mused.

He pushed the door open, kicked out the fire and entered the Great Hall. Looking around with the eye of a
searcher instead of an appreciating art student, he
sought the transceiver. The Great Hall, where the other
treasures were kept, seemed the right place to start. He
went straight to the throne area. The empty caverns
made the Great Hall feel cold and lonely even with the
fires blazing in their elevated hearths.

He tried to visualize it after a Passage when it was
filled by rejoicing voices singing to their Virgin and Deity,

185

praising the wonders of each and proclaiming their dependency upon them. He visualized Kansi leading the children during their special songs as they dedicated themselves to the service of the Leatez gods.

On hands and knees, he looked under the Bespeaker's throne. There, in the rear, against the solid back, was a transceiver. He reached in and gently slid it out.

Esse lumbered up to the dais and nosed Lozadar.

"Yeah. I'm hurrying. Damn! It's still sending." He debated the risk of turning it off and considered setting a delay command on it. As long as it sent, it would bring ships in from all over the sector.

The kervemith loosed a deafening roar which shook Lozadar and rumbled down the Great Hall.

"Okay. Okay. I'm ready."

Esse roared a second time. When the echo died a sound lingered beyond the door.

For a moment, Lozadar froze, not daring to speculate and knowing there was no time to waste. When he could move, he shoved the sender back under the throne and ran down the firelit aisle. A couple of bounds set Esse at the door beside him. Using a burned-through hole, he peered out.

Nothing was distinguishable in the near-dark. Off in the distance, which was like the opposite end of a mile-long telescope, he saw a soft glow brighter than the firepit could have made. The light was even, brilliant and artificial.

He figured there were still a few minutes left before whoever was out there became curious enough to enter. "Let's get out of here."

The door swung open a quarter of the way. The two slipped noiselessly into the tee and chose the hall on the right. "Has to be another way out of here," he whispered to bolster his courage. To Esse, "How are your instincts when it comes to freedom?"

No response.

He ran down the hall with Esse behind.

Already, cold seeped through the bleak corridors, bathed in shadow with the exception of a dim torch every so often. An illusion of straight-lined halls faded. He ran hard, trying to recall the topography over and around the caverns. The kervemith breathed down his neck, ready to trample him if he stumbled. They shared an urgency to be out of the confining stone tunnels. The walls threatened to squash them like bugs trespassing in a death zone.

It was hard to keep the sensation from turning him around. But there was no going back. The kervemith seemed to know that and slowed, giving ground between himself and the outcast. He sniffed at the air.

Smoke rode in their wake. A distant cacophony wound vicariously through the halls. It filled the small side rooms with their doors ajar to betray a stark solitude.

The air grew stale. It became hard to breathe and less satisfying in the depths of the cavern. This was an area long unused. Lozadar moaned inwardly while running with all the energy he could muster.

He lost track of the turns and angles. The utter absence of light became a natural thing. Esse assumed the guidance role. Lozadar ran just under the beast's jaw, moving, zagging, swaying as the kervemith did.

Abruptly, Esse stopped. Lozadar slammed into a wall. Dazed, moaning, he groped for another avenue.

A crisp echo of hard-heeled boots against the rock floor hammered in the rear.

Frantic, Lozadar spread his arms over the dead end, reaching, feeling for the smallest flaw. He held no illusions of being able to come out on top of the massive sanctuary.

Quite the contrary.

The downward slope had grown steep since the air had reached its present level of impurity. It had settled in the dank place and fermented most of the oxygen molecules away.

He checked the whole wall and found nothing. Defeated, he slumped down, elbows on knees, hands dangling in front. Part of him wanted to know who the searchers were, but not badly enough to go find out.

Lungs aching, throat sore, he pushed to his feet and staggered back the way they had come. Esse remained.

He returned and grabbed handfuls of fur along the kervemith's breast and tugged, nearly falling down with the effort. "Come on. There has to be a way out—somewhere. Nobody builds one-way . . ." The words panted dry on his cracked lips. He half believed the logic, partially because if they stayed in the foul air pocket death was a certainty. Nor was it a pleasant death, but then

187

death was seldom a pleasant affair. The sound of the soldiers urged him onward.

His legs felt cast in lead. Ahead, light flashed off a bend in the walls. As quickly as he could, he followed Esse into a narrow corridor the kervemith decided to squeeze through. As long as they were quiet they were buying time. They kept going, ignoring the men behind once their new path took a safe bend.

The floor changed to rough, unfinished stone. The walls closed in, making it a tight squeeze for Esse. The path took on a steep upward angle. Difficult as it was to travel, it felt good. The direction gave him hope and drew upon reserve energy he did not know he possessed. The air became fresher. Esse, too, prodded him, his claws grating hard on the slippery places when the slant became too great for just his paws to hold him.

Lozadar could smell his own blood coating the corrosive surface. The pain in his feet, knees, hands and elbows registered as a low throb that would blossom later.

The air turned sweet. A couple of times Lozadar thought he felt a breeze, but was afraid to get his hopes up. "Breathing too hard," he whispered, trying to rationalize. He crawled up the last one in a series of small staggered platforms onto a wide ledge. Here the cavern opened up.

He stayed pressed to the wall and slowed to feel his way more carefully. Esse knocked loose rocks off the path. The distant impact made Lozadar more cautious. He moved out of the way for Esse to leap up. He felt the breeze come again.

Grinning, he reached out and found Esse pointed toward him after his jump. "This is it."

He edged forward and down another crude passage to what became a slim eyelet at the end of the path. Esse stayed directly behind, forcing and contorting his bulk through more restrictions which scraped the hide from his ribs. At the eyelet he managed to get his foreshoulders through, but could go no farther.

"Back up. Can you get out?" Lozadar pushed on him. "Work yourself out. I'll go see where this leads. If it's any good, I'll be right back and blast the opening bigger." He turned away. "But I can't blast it unless you're away from it."

He did not have far to go to reach the end of the channel. It veered sharply to the left and ended up outside. The air was delicious and hurt with the big gulps he took. Above were stars, bright and clear in the majesty of their powerful light combining to brighten the mountain and jungle tops. Below was the river. The walls were smooth all the way around. There was no way up, nor any ledges leading off on the sides. Disappointed, he stumbled back to Esse.

Esse retreated from the eyelet. His struggle was punctuated by grunts.

"Relax. It ends at the water. We're an easy fifteen meters above it. There's—"

A blast ripped the cavern. The earth complained and grumbled. Lozadar was hurled backward. He cowered against the walls, trying not to bounce around too much in the quake. He screamed at the kervemith when the eyelet closed. The world crumbled into a million pieces, all of them more sturdy then he.

Chapter 20

STEFEN WOKE, SLEPT OUT BUT NOT RESTED. He could not remember the last time he had felt rested, clean or untroubled. What happened to the days when he had greeted the morning with zeal, enthusiasm, and the full love for life he had grown up knowing? Rubbing his palms together, he could not find a ready answer. Perhaps that was the answer: there were no answers. *That's why a man does what he has to do, even if he doesn't like it,* he mused.

Emotionally he hit a new low by accepting that bit of rationale as a part of him. Somehow, by embracing it as a burden, being the Virgin's Champion made a strange form of sense. But that was not what he objected to. The fight inside of him was gone. Part of him had died to achieve the acquiescence which settled on him.

All things die in their present form, he thought idly. *Some take a long time, some don't. And all things on the Virgin have an integral function in relationship to the whole. I thought myself different. Special. Favored. Unique.*

Yet, although I am all of these to the Lovers, I am the same as the rest. I, too, was created through a set of carefully devised circumstances to serve them.

It no longer seemed an unreasonable thing never to have had a choice in his destiny. It was hard to fathom why it had been such a difficult thing to embrace for so long. What was there to yield?

He rubbed the heavy growth on his face and heard his stomach rumble. He paused, fingers over his eyes, trying to decide how he knew his stomach had made a noise. Was it an internal mechanism as the muscles rolled in spasms? Or had he heard it? Actually heard?

Trembling, afraid to hope, he let himself try to listen to the world around him.

The wind played in the trees; crackling dry nacki leaves rustled against one another; the ferns made a soft whisper waving at the pteridophyte. The noises were ambiguous. The rush of sounds hurt his inner ear. It was a delicious sensation.

Immobile, afraid the sounds were illusion, he listened and poured his entire consciousness into absorbing the whispers of the Virgin. When he felt them memorized once again as an addendum of the savored treasures from his past, he ventured to remove his hands from his face.

He had no hope for the restoration of his sight.

A full return of his senses carried an added responsibility and the necessity to take active charge of the Virgin's destiny as her Champion.

It was dark. Not the same dark which totally encompassed the world of the sightless and sharpened the movements and definitions growing out of the dark. Heart beating wildly with the first surges of elation, he tilted his head all the way back.

Tiny points of light played above the tree branches. They blurred. Tears flowed down his face, and neck and onto his chest.

He cried openly, joyful, fearful tears he did not suspect remained. The awesome task of ridding the Virgin of outworlders who warred with one another seemed impossible without weapons equal to theirs. He had no idea of how to accomplish the task, but knew he would die trying if necessary. The commitment had been made and sealed with his destiny.

It was clearly such a delicate balance that the slightest deviation or outside influence could throw it off. War and machines disrupted the harmony maintaining the surface against the perpetual fight of the natural and physical laws the Deity and Virgin flaunted by her existence. From there, chaos was inevitable. In the realm of the Deity, the world of substance was finite and the sources of energy releases well defined.

The exterior would burn away before the subsequent Passage. Afterward, there would be nothing left but a charred cinder which the two suns would war over. Eventually it would fall the endless fall into the Deity, and obliterated as it entered the solar atmosphere.

It would all happen. Eventually. But now was not the time of joining. Stefen did not question. He merely accepted what knowledge was bestowed on him and worked from there. He did not have the slightest idea of how to go about achieving his goal, but that fact did not worry him too greatly at the present. There was a world to see, listen to and tell he was alive.

Quietly he got to his feet, careful not to disturb Andazu. He looked for Asa, taking in every dim color, minute shape and subtle motion to savor it in case this truly was a dream and never came true. It was too precious to risk losing even a fragment for any reason. He felt whole—not clean, but whole.

He jumped, grabbed a low branch and climbed, using all his senses flagrantly, feeling free in his bondage to the Lovers.

Chief Protector Captain Malchi Oranda of the cor Baalan House was an imposing figure on the bridge of the lead Commander-Flight Mark IV. Circular burn scars on his left cheek lent a more formidable intensity to an appearance already showing the strains of a man determined to rearrange the stars in order to rescue his liege. His distress at finding the traitorous leader of the Colonial Insurrectionists to be a once-trusted battle comrade did not show. Few of Oranda's inner feelings showed at any time, and fewer when he was engaged in a mission.

A small communication capsule lay heavily against the callouses hardening his palm. It was the answer he knew had to lie somewhere within a review of the Insurrectionists' active takeover attempt. The question, asked in whispers across the whole of the Seven Worlds, brought suspicions where trust had once dwelled and made enemies of close friends. Who controlled the Insurrectionists and afforded them access to the capitol house in Antition? The House of cor Baalan had sponsored the Iron General. That mistake could be atoned for later.

He allowed a flicker of relaxation around his mouth that passed for a smile. Uniforms, white and crimson, no uniforms, a rough, desperate task force—that was what he remembered from Chalate and Corry's room. It all fit neatly. While the Colonists would kill the girls, they would not kill Lozadar. There were those among them who would protest too much. He was an excellent bargaining tool, also.

There was a time when the blond giant had laughed and cried as much, possibly even more, as the multitude of friends who loved to be around him. That was long ago, before he had offered his services to the house which had apprehended the Insurrectionists who had slaughtered his wife and two small sons. A debt he felt could never be repaid was incurred when one of the Protectors looked the other way while Malchi Oranda avenged his loved ones. The vindication was performed in a manner which put every Protector in the cor Baalan House on the edge of fear when his perpetually enraged inner anger swelled the surface.

Since that time, his mastery at hiding his emotions had rivaled his devotion to the cor Baalan House. The decasets of restructuring and bone grafting after the palace slaughter had given him plenty of time to analyze the events leading to the fall of Antition.

A small twitch around a scar above his right eyebrow betrayed his concentration on a goal which was futile if his charge was dead. As Protector he needed to see the corpse before admitting the failure and waste of his position. Never would he bow to the end of the cor Baalan lineage, the fine leaders and Rulers, without irrefutable evidence. He needed to believe Lozadar was alive. Without that belief there was no point in living himself, for his only companion would be abject failure.

Three command ships answered to his orders, as well as half a dozen battle ships equipped with ground fighters. The information in the communiqué was correct. This was a strange planet which denied their equipment a life search. But then this system was more than strange. It was a planet designed in Hell and hurled at the universe as an affront to the natural laws.

The traitor they found by following a cross-signal which intersected the homing device directing them through space was well worth the interruption. Seeing the enemy eye to eye gave a new purpose to their quest.

Reasons why the Insurrectionists had gained such a strong foothold since being repelled by the colonies became clearer. With one of the Seven supplying financial backing, they were able to stage more attacks to win supplies, additional ships and power. The opposition had been fed until it was fat enough to attack Antition successfully. The House of cor Baalan believed in the Colonial General. So had Lozadar. And so had Corinda and the dez Kaliea House.

Oranda believed in no one but himself and his liege. Here on the hell planet existed more evidence to support his theory. The evidence of people taken against their will abounded. And the dying Bespeaker cursed the man Oranda brought to confront him with his last breath. It was sickening. Still the traitor denied his actions without offering any explanation.

Oranda stared at the monitor displaying the devastation of the Leatez.

A young officer clad in cor Baalan green saluted, heels clicking. "He is in the big room, sir."

Oranda snapped a return salute. "He has food and water in his reach?"

"Yessir!"

"There's no other way out?"

"No sir. Not that we could find. And if we couldn't find one, neither will he. We checked every corridor and room."

Oranda exhaled. He knew they were too inexperienced to do any serious checking. But he did not want to take a prisoner into battle. He watched the monitors showing the enemy ships gathering above the atmosphere for a diving attack. Better to incarcerate him so he would not know whether to hope for rescue or death when the battle was done. The men he sent into the jungle would never be able to blast him out when the sanctuary was sealed. Each of the cor Baalan Protectors commanding the other ships knew where he was.

"Prepare to lift," he ordered, gazing at Lieutenant Mya's back. The General would not get away, nor would a lucky score by one of his fighters relieve him of his life. He would stand trial in what was left of Antition. And if he didn't? Oranda saw no point in making death an easy thing for his enemy.

"Yessir," came an answer from a row of green uniforms manning the consoles. One turned to face the gaze she felt on her rigid back. The looks they exchanged required no words to enforce their determination.

"Lift and fire."

The Commander-Flight Mark IV rose. A bolt of light shot out of the upper-deck weapons systems.

The serrated overhang protecting the Leatez clearing from the harshest weather out of the east fell, hauling down thousands of tons of rocks and filling the space where the huts and firepits had been. After the dust settled there was no trace left of the Leatez civilization.

Rocks came at Lozadar from all sides, rolling with him, running after him and falling, forever falling. He slammed into the surface of the water with a brutal, unexpected force that ripped the air from his lungs and shoved his backbone into his stomach. He went limp, unable to dodge or fend off boulders and sheets of mountain coming down on him in the water.

As he was driven deeper by the momentum he waited for his life to flash before him. He had heard that it did. It also seemed like a disgusting way to die, considering all the dangers he had faced in Antition and on the Virgin. *Ironic,* he decided. *They've killed me not even knowing I was here.*

He felt lightheaded. Pain crushed his chest. It eased as the vertigo increased. *Where's my damn life?* he mouthed in the water.

The pain returned sharply. His body lurched sideways, propelled through the water by some unseen, powerful force defying the rain of boulders and unaffected by the current.

Reality and illusion became one and the same. If the thing holding him, the thing that had rescued him from the rock shower, did not bring him up to the surface quickly, the rescue would be for nothing. *But who said I was rescued,* he wondered as life events began to materialize.

Lozadar fought to keep his head clear by complimenting himself on the way he was handling the situation of his imminent death. It was far better than he had a right to expect. Perhaps he did not understand it correctly. *No, he understands,* came the voice of the heavy in the two-sided conversation trying to ignore the morose specter rising before him.

God, I've always wanted my own, what are you? A zuriserpant?

His face broke the surface. It hurt to suck in air. He coughed, spat blood and clutched at his ribs where the tentacle slithered away. Through the agony of breathing in good air and coughing up blood and water he tried to meet the stare of the strange eye bent in an elaborate sigmate.

The Seven crescendoed into his mind.

A battle was close. It filled the skies overhead. First light hinted over the east where the river disappeared into stone walls. Flashes of light as the battle raged in the stratosphere splayed the quiet dawn.

The zuriserpant turned languidly into the middle of the river and submerged up to Lozadar's chest. Only his tentacle eye stuck above water.

Although dazed, he knew he did not want to leave the area. He let go and tried to swim for the jagged wall, hoping to climb up to the midsection where he had last seen Esse.

The current was strong. It pulled him downstream and put pressure on his chest. Breathing became more difficult. He rolled onto his back, coughed, and kicked harder to minimize the use of his arms.

The zuriserpant came after him and ungracefully re-seated him. The creature paused. His eye weaved and dipped in confusion.

Lozadar pointed to the section of demolished wall he wanted to climb. Reluctantly the zuriserpant glided crosscurrent toward it. The slow pace was a welcome breather and gave Lozadar time to prepare for the pain he knew the climb would bring.

A frantic thought sent him groping down his right side. The feel of the Lat-kor comforted him and brought an instant relaxation. The climb would be futile if he could not blast a passage clear to get to Esse.

He sighed heavily. They would have to travel the entire length, if not more because of detours, in order to get out. Esse had to be all right. "I sure as hell can't carry him," he mumbled aloud. Jumping into the river was out of the question. The kervemith was a natural enemy of the zuriserpant and not too fond of water. Sometimes all the logical cooperation between the Virgin's species was quite illogical when it came time for a quiet, practical, lifesaving application.

The climb seemed six kilometers straight up and would have been impossible without the battering effects of the wall as it crumbled overhead. The rock pincers he had passed earlier were closer together, making it a tight squeeze for him from the narrow ledge outside. He refused to look down. After the climb, the drop seemed much farther, since he had already survived the plunge once. The ache in his side served as a reminder of how close a call it had been.

Esse whined restlessly in the dark. His great bulk grazed the wall perpendicular to the inner ledge. Parts of it were broken away. Lozadar spoke quiet reassurances.

Getting down from the ledge was difficult. He slid most of the way and left souvenirs of skin and black curses behind. He hurried to the side when Esse started down. The beast's claws screeched against the stone.

The collapse had altered and twisted the shaft to narrow it in more places. Esse forced himself through with a determination that made Lozadar look away. Blood was the lubricant which greased his bulk through. He whined. Jagged layers, turned sideways, gouged away hunks of his flesh.

The sun was well over the horizon when they groped through to the main passage, but none of the Deity's rays found them. Fatigued, Lozadar stumbled beside Esse, banging his shins on rocks and uttering a stream of curses under his breath. His complaints were lost against Esse's restless whines, which did not cease when the beast inhaled.

Walking, searching, he found a torch and lit it by scraping it along a broken holder with a smattering of the Leatez firestarter left on it. The light was a comfort to them both. Esse's whine quieted slightly. The corridor they had run down a short while ago reduced them to a crawl with the rubble choking it. Doors, knocked off their hide hinges, twisted out and lay across the tunnel. Segments of the arched ceiling lay on the floor to deny the durability promised by the architecture.

"Must have been some blast. Wonder why they wanted this place destroyed and who *they* are." Sealing it was something Corinda would think of doing under the circumstances. She wanted everything to be at rest, undisturbed, and peaceful once the gauntlet was passed on or a life lived out to endgame.

The enormous dwelling felt as safe as a tomb. The outside threats were sealed off.

The corridors changed, flaring between arch supports carved into the living rock. The walk became easier and the way less cluttered as they neared the center. Sensing Lozadar's relaxation, Esse quieted and slowed.

As they passed the Great Hall he picked up two torches lying on the floor beside the defiled lady on the door.

Esse went rigid and growled. His fangs were exposed up to the gumline and his horns lowered for battle.

Lozadar's heart pounded faster. His hand closed on the torches. Slowly, he stood, eyes rapidly trying to take in all directions for the best escape route. He risked a glance through the partially opened door. There was nothing unusual. Still . . .

Esse growled low in his throat.

Lozadar calmly switched hands on the torch, lit one of the spares and discarded the other two. In the same motion he unfastened the Lat-kor from his belt.

"Lozadar cor Baalan?" came a bass voice from the opposite side of the door. "Is that you, Lozadar?" There was a deep chuckle void of mirth which followed.

Cautiously, holding his breath, Lozadar moved to the hinged side of the door and gave it a slight push. It swung, still balanced in spite of the damage.

The burned carving paused halfway, giving Lozadar a forty-five-degree angle to search. He reached around and pushed the door again, hard, until it banged on the other side of the wall. His hand felt exposed and vulnerable. Quickly, he pulled back, waited, then leaned a bit closer to the opening.

Initially he saw nothing out of the ordinary. The Great Hall looked just the way it had before they set out on the river path. Squinting, he studied the thrones, then jerked back to the safety of the hallway.

The elevated hearths had lost most of their fire. They needed the loving attention of the Leatez. But beyond them . . . Aviea on his throne? "Okay," he whispered, staring across the open doorway to Esse, "we'll say it is the Bespeaker. That's not his voice."

The second time he leaned toward the door he was reassured by the cool plasti-metal handgrip of his Lat-kor. The interior was darker. The hearths were dying. *For the first time in how many hundred years?* he wondered. It saddened him to see the end of a civilization, particularly one as unimposing upon the rest of the galaxy as this one had been. *Sure it had its flaws,* he conceded, *but what culture doesn't?*

He cleared his throat. "Who calls?" His voice carried throughout the Great Hall and into the corridors. A fine curtain of grit slithered down the wall beside the door.

"Stuhart Myzillion, Colonial War General, excellency."

Lozadar froze. Excellency? He was somebody's excellency? What a ludicrous notion. He wanted to laugh, but could not. The cold of the wall he was pressed against turned the sweat running down his body into ice and imparted nothing to sooth his mind. The full impact of what was his, whether he wanted it or not, on the other worlds, in the capitol house of Antition, cracked at the wall he had built around his inner responsibilities. All those people looking up to him for guidance, waiting for a decision which affected millions of lives and wanting him to pass judgment.

He wanted to yell out that he was not Lozadar cor Baalan!

He was not now—nor had he ever been—Ruler of the Seven Worlds.

He was a space merchant and sometime scouter for the Imperial Navy, just as he had dreamed of being as a child. He was not obligated to the traditional dictates of blood, but married to a woman from the Virgin; a woman he cared for and needed and one who made him feel whole. A woman he would not give up.

"You seek what I am not and can never be, General Myzillion. I am the outcast, set upon the Virgin to die, and bound to Stefen, Judge of Man. The man you seek no longer exists." His voice was steady and imparted more surety than he felt.

"Corinda was right," came a muttering full of self-reproach. There was a pause which seemed like an impasse. "Look, could you give me a hand in here? I'm a bit tied up and there's some unfinished business I'd like to take care of."

Lozadar glanced at Esse, then leaned inside.

Esse growled and took a step toward the door.

Holding the torch in front and to the side, Lozadar entered the Great Hall. He looked for a trap and could not find one.

"Over here." Myzillion was hogtied on his belly and against the wall a few centimeters from the door.

Lozadar glared at the General and saw him as a traitor tied by the knots only the cor Baalan Protectorate utilized. They were distinctive and could not be mistaken. The identity of the man crashed down on him harder than a three-ton boulder. His peace of mind, his future, his whole way of life was in jeopardy of meeting the same end as the Leatez if the man went free. This man knew him well and had been trusted as no other Colonial had ever been.

Pleasurably, his fingers closed around the laser as it rose to point at the Iron General, Stuhart Myzillion.

Chapter 21

IT WAS ALMOST TIME TO WORRY OVER LOZA-dar and Esse's absence. Stefen held off, trying to delay it only to find that delay an impossibility. Streaks of light in the dark sky evidenced aliens at battle. The mere presence of the outworlders was source enough for worry.

He stroked Asa, appreciating the gleam of her silky fur in the gray light. "Let's go. Take us to Esse," he said cheerfully. He slapped her foreshoulder as she rose to continue their slow journey. "Find your mate."

The two packs Stefen wore took some getting used to. Guilt for pushing Asa beyond her limits prevented him from asking her to carry even one of them in addition to her burden of injuries mending painfully. He noted the way she glanced back at him and Andazu, admonishing them for their dilatory pursuit.

He crossed the open spaces on vines, leaped from putch to putch and scrambled over the ground where the lava intruded. The east grew bright with first light. It served as a reminder to the travelers that soon it would be the time of total sunlight over the whole of the Virgin. The power play was about to commence its annual struggle.

Naked fotig stalks, broken, some down into the eyelets, warned those of the surface about the barren land slated ahead. The heavy nacki vines were easier to find in the trees. Their leaves and flowers clung in stages of brown wilt. Fruit rotted in clusters, fell and splattered on the ground. More dropped whenever Stefen's weight shook the weary connecting joints. Seasonal trees had lost whole patches of colorful leaves. The nude branches were black, crooked fingers against the sky and jungle. Wainor bushes had already shed their bright-yellow adornments yet still clung to their shanuts as a bastion against starvation for those on the land.

Hilly terrain kept Stefen guessing at what waited beyond the next crest. It had been a rugged course Asa carried him over. The grueling flight shamed him further when he thought about Tari. There was a great deal he had to say to her now that he could speak. He fervently beseeched the Virgin to restore her health.

Over the top of a rise, swinging across two wide open expanses by the added momentum gained with body contortions, Stefen caught a glimmer of sunlight reflecting off the ground ahead.

He changed course and kept moving and building speed. He sent Asa and the fenwapter on to continue retracing Esse's trail. If there were dangers he did not want them exposed. Neither was capable of full-strength combat. And such loyal friends deserved far better treatment, at least more respect for the fragility of their lives, than he had extended since the last Passage. The kervemith needed no coaxing. She wanted the company of her mate. Andazu was more difficult to persuade and ultimately needed to be ordered to accompany Asa.

Initially, he planned to detour inward close enough to make some kind of identification of whatever soiled the land. As he neared, he realized it was a much smaller object than it seemed. The angle of reflection produced a gross distortion.

He slowed, drawn to the smooth metal until he was all but over it. Above, it had torn a hole in the nacki and putch covering on an oblique eastern entry angle. Now the morning light shot straight on it.

Stefen remained in the trees and circled, wary, curious. There were no visible seams, nor were there portholes on or near the top.

He moved closer to the ground, constantly on guard in case the thing popped open and his enemy came out armed for his destruction. Fleetingly, he wished for Andazu's company. Strange how lonely it felt in possession of all his senses. He recalled thinking their restoration would solve all his problems and absolve his doubts and inadequacies.

Nervous, he smiled at his faulty logic, bent and squinted at the orb. The metal looked to be a different texture and discolored near the base. His descent to bare ground carried no noise. His breathing melted into the morning breeze. The thundering heart trapped between his ears remained quiet to the outside world.

Circling, knife in hand and ready, he listened, smelled and looked for the enemy to show. Crouched, he moved around the capsule until he reached the discolored portion. He tried to look inside, but made out nothing.

He stood debating several minutes, then crouched down on all fours.

Inside in a dim glow cast by a small panel of blinking lights he saw the beautiful mate he had desired—Corinda, woman-to-be of Lozadar. His excitement was so great he thought his heart would burst. Taking hold of himself, he mended the lapse in his defenses. Listening, feeling the ground for signs of approaching life, smelling for a scent of the outworlders, he wondered how she could possibly have been left unguarded, uncared for in the jungle before Passage. It both pleased and angered him.

Poised against the capsule, he tapped the glass with his knife handle.

Corinda dangled in the seat, her head drooped to her right, straight across from Stefen.

He banged harder, concerned about her lack of response.

She stirred slightly.

The expanse created by the capsule bothered him. He banged harder on the hull with the handle. A horrendous clanging noise reverberated throughout the partially defoliated trees. Apprehensively, he scrutinized the land while trying to calculate how far the sound carried. When he returned his attention to the interior, Corinda was staring back at him, mouth opened.

After several exaggerated gestures, he understood her desire for him to go away. He felt bad. How would he be able to persuade her to be his mate if all she wanted him to do was move away?

He sat halfway up a putch, elbow on knees, hands outstretched, and idly shredded a dry nacki flower core.

Below, the capsule came alive. The engine noise was so quiet it did not reach beyond Stefen's perch and then could be heard only with very sensitive ears. Slowly, the pod turned and righted itself. The noise halted.

Stefen waited several hundred heartbeats before the front of the capsule opened a crack. He neither spoke nor moved, content to watch for the time being.

Corinda stepped out clutching a Lat-kor in both hands. Anxiety and fear rode each of the jerky moves she made during a scrutiny of her immediate surroundings. A gash near her right temple was matted with dark hair which belonged on the other side of her head. Clotted blood held it in place.

Brownish flakes crumbled along her neck and the side of her face. They fell as her head turned. The right shoulder, arm and breast area of her shirt were the same dried-blood color.

His first impulse was to call out or swing down on a vine and land in front of her. His heart raced at the thought of touching her, feeling her close, sharing his body while sharing hers.

She held the Lat-kor more securely now and evidenced skill in her stance. Her nervousness and fear did not dull the fact that she was prepared to kill at the slightest provocation. As fearful as she appeared, Stefen did not think it would take much to justify necessity to her. He calmed his physical fervor into a subjective tolerance.

Corinda darted inside the capsule and emerged a few heartbeats later. She was carrying a bulky pack slung over her left shoulder. For an instant, she looked frail and vulnerable and caught up like the rest of them in a web of circumstances she wished never to have happened. Then it was gone. A steel door slammed over her features. Her shoulders straightened. She slipped on the pack and stood tall.

After a hundred heartbeats she reached back into the capsule and pulled out a coil of rope and a knife in a belted sheath.

The coil went over her head and under her arm. It crossed her chest low, pushed by the back pack. Left-handed, she got the belt around her waist and fastened it, glancing down only a couple of times.

Stefen stood also. He knew she could not see him unless she looked directly at him through the break in the leaves he used to watch her. "Corinda of the Seven Worlds, friend of Lozadar the Outcast, you now belong to Stefen, Judge of Man upon the Virgin." He moved down to a vertical branch.

Corinda looked all around. The Lat-kor rose a few centimeters. "I belong to no one unless I choose to. If you're a friend of Lozadar cor Baalan's, produce him and let him tell me who you are."

It was confusing, just as all his dealings with out-worlders were. The emotion in her words went beyond a reaction to being abandoned on a foreign planet. Surely this was not the same gentle-souled woman who had fought with her captors in the clearing to save the yaxura babes. How could it be?

She slapped the hull to close the capsule door, then stomped down the ramp. "If you are man enough to show yourself, then do so. Otherwise, shut up and leave me alone. I have business to attend to."

For the first time Stefen thought he had proof that Lozadar had lied to him. Corinda did not seem to be the sensitive, warm individual the Ruler had glowingly painted. She strapped on a wrist-clamp accessory to the Lat-kor and wore it as a ready-made bracelet. A few deft motions fastened her hair at the back of her neck and tucked her billowy pants into the tops of her high black boots.

She checked a small instrument brought from her pants pocket, turned eastward and began moving.

"I would be very, very careful where I put my foot down if I were you." The taunt was unmistakable. Stefen moved through the trees ahead of her and dropped to the ground on the other side of a grabber-moss patch. He held three fotigs in his hand.

Corinda kept walking, looking around for the source of the voice and maintaining a watch for predators, native and immigrant alike. Sometimes there seemed little difference in the mentality. She saw Stefen at the same time he threw one of the husked fruits at the moss. The swift action appalled her. It could have been her the green death consumed so greedily. Weak-kneed, she returned his gaze.

"I've seen you before." Subdued, she swallowed hard. The tilt of her head and the squint of her eyes betrayed a confusion creeping into her stubbornness.

Again, the quiet moment of indecision lapsed. She turned abruptly and began skirting the moss. A quick assessment of his weapons and the distance between them allowed her to move the Lat-kor a few centimeters from her palm. Her fingers were already experiencing a cramp as they fought to maintain an equal grip on the perspiration-slick handle. Ignoring him, she selected a dangling vine, yanked hard, then pulled, putting all of her weight on it.

It held. Hand over hand, the Lat-kor still within reach, she entwined her right leg and climbed while being transported over the grabber moss.

It took a tremendous effort to quell the fear gnawing at her. It had to be buried along with those very same emotions, for it was not a time for fear or anything else which hindered the cool, logical thinking she needed to have for any chance of survival.

The point of the turmoil caused by the binary star system was close. Consternation forged tiny lines around her mouth and the beginnings of crow's-feet.

It had not seemed far from the Leatez sanctuary in the capsule. Few things seemed far in a ship when all were located on the same planet. But people did. *God, how far away was Lozadar? How long had it been? It felt like a thousand standards. And Stuhart?*

A chilled knife ripped at her breast when she thought of Hart. She faltered in her climb.

Much as she did not want to and as hard as she had tried not to, she loved the man. For a moment, she gazed around and let a hatred of the planet wash over her. The rolling green torment, vined with long living prison bars, death at every turn and marvelous creatures who should indeed have the entire planet to themselves, surrounded her. It *felt* wrong to be here. Sin. That was the feeling. It felt sinful. *Perhaps it is a sin,* she thought dismally. *This place has taken my friend and my lover and shows me nothing but death.*

Her despairing thoughts were cut short by a discovery of wreckage on the ground ahead. She hurried, brushing aside leaves, jumping over vines and debris to get there.

There were signs of a struggle and several bodies recognizable as the bridge crew on duty when the attack began. The scent of burned jungle lingered; substantiation that the battle had been waged on several fronts and there had been more than one victory. Gaping yaxura holes ringed the outer fringes of the jungle. The dirt mounded high against the outer charcoal layers of nearby putch trunks and denuded ground where black sprigs of wainor skeletons looked as though they would crumble at a touch.

She walked in the center of scrape tracks where a yaxura had retreated to an abnormally large hole. She fought back the tears and anger that any of those in Hart's command would be stupid enough to attack the indigenous life. *Don't they ever learn?* she lamented.

A crushing terror stopped her heart. When she could move again she climbed into a tree, held onto vines and smaller branches and made her way to the wreckage. Grabber moss, gaping yaxura holes and bodies made the ground not only dangerous, but vile.

When the limb ended she lunged to the ground leaving skin on the old fotig nodules and gritting her teeth against the pain. She barely missed the grabber patch. She ran to a big man lying face down in the moist soil. The sun caught a hint of red-gold through the fine layer of dirt covering him. "Hart?" she whispered, praying it was not him. Squatting, she flexed her fingers, then roughly turned the man over.

His midsection was burned in a large-burst pattern. The agony on his dirt-crusted face would stay with her forever. Flecks of dirt clung to the whites of his eyes. Blue and expressive, they attested to the horror of death. A dried trickle of blood had run out of his nose, into his wide-open mouth and down his chin, where it mingled with spittle. The stench of death rose from the corpse.

It was not Hart.

Numb, she rose and listened to distant sounds of chirping grow louder in the jungle.

Stefen paralleled her flight and zeroed in on the wreckage. It dismayed him to see her intense concern for the man called Hart.

The branch became slippery as it narrowed. Below, a runner of grabber moss carpeted a stretch.

Corinda turned mechanically toward the other bodies. Crying soundlessly, she moved from one to the next, muttering their names, remembering their families, their smiles and personalities. She searched for Hart among the dead. The cor Baalan green uniforms of those on the perimeter of the slaughter demanded as much attention as a stick jabbed under her fingernail. Her eyes stung, refusing to focus behind a sheet of moisture. She walked into the jungle to compose herself and gather enough courage to look inside the wreckage.

Stefen swung over the side and dropped on top of the wreck. He slid down and looked inside.

Even disabled, it was a prison with its metal walls and spear-shaped ribs supporting the outer skin. None of the panels were alive. The ship reeked of death and violence. The stench offended him. He grabbed a pack similar to the one Corinda wore and left, taking a deep breath of the less tainted air heavy with decaying vegetation and hungry ganids. The whole venture took less than a hundred heartbeats.

"Hold it right there," came a voice from across the torn jungle.

Stefen froze, admonishing himself for not circling to check downwind.

Corinda also turned to stone. Not daring to blink for fear of betraying her presence, she watched Stefen. *Him, they might let go,* she mused. *If they think he's with me, he's dead and so am I, just like Hart and probably Loz.*

A cold determination descended over her with the acknowledgment of Hart's fate. Somehow it did not seem possible something like this could have happened. And in the same light, it was long, long overdue. It was all in vain. She groaned. *No one will know the truth or be able to sort it out from the neat web Lisan's woven over the Colonials. They won't dig in the right cranny. And if they do, they won't believe it. House of dez Kaliea—deals in mass destruction as well as mass production. Hart. Hart, you were right and I couldn't see it for so long. I wish I could tell you. . . .*

Gradually she returned to the situation at hand. Stefen was talking to someone in the jungle. His body glistened with perspiration as he shifted his weight and casually dropped his left hand against his thigh. He flashed one finger, then two fingers. He repeated the action.

Corinda finally ventured to move, mentally kicking herself for the thought lapse. The signal made sense. Carefully, she guided the Lat-kor into her palm and flicked off the safety. Next, she began a slow turn, trying to employ the guerrilla tactics Hart had taught her to blend with her gymnastics. *He was right,* she mused, putting ice over her emotions, *this is the last battleground. It will end here. For us, at least.*

A movement in the jungle became her target. The

white was too white and the scarlet too brilliant to be an indigenous creature's coloring. She held out her arm, steadying her right wrist with her left hand. Tremors were willed into subsidence. *Bastard!* she screamed silently and fired.

A motion on the left, just beyond the open space where Stefen stood, caught her eye. Instantly she took a bead, rolled her thumb over the spreader and fired. A wide beam hit the jungle and torched the whole area.

Stefen found himself staring at the putch branch where the outworlder still had her arms extended and the weapon pointed in his direction. He was not sure, but he thought she was crying.

"Bastards!" The weapon erupted again, sending more of her fury out to the world.

Chapter 22

KANSI CRADLED TARI'S HEAD AGAINST HER shoulder. Her clear alto voice warmed the stone with the Ritual of New Life that she sang with the children at the end of Passage each year. Tari hummed occasionally, but did not sing. They rocked back and forth as one person with a split personality, one aspect trying to find a reason to live in the light of total failure, the other quietly offering reason after reason.

Adru ran into the cavern, ashen and breathless. Doubled over, he gasped deep breaths and tried to speak. Trembling, he reached out to Kansi and motioned toward the entrance.

She responded by sitting Tari up and whispering soothing reassurances to her. The impulse to run out and see what had sent Adru into such a state needed a strong will to squelch.

Kansi peered into the withering jungle ranging the downward slope the cavern was set into. At first she did not see anything unusual. Then came the sounds of running, stopping, running and stopping again.

Her heart beat rapidly. Fear as she had never known gripped her tightly in its palm. She retreated quietly and returned to Adru.

"Do they know we're here?"

Adru took a deep breath and shook his head. "It doesn't matter. They'll find us. They all look alike to me, Kansi." He was on the edge of frenzy, his dark eyes looking for a place to run. "There are all kinds of them out there. Did you smell the fire? They're fighting each other."

A reminder of the insecure adolescent who had roamed the village during the day clung to Adru. His struggle to be a man was obvious. He floundered with a reed container near the food-storage cache and brought out a knife. It made him feel stronger to have it at his side.

Kansi knelt beside Tari and attempted a smile, which came off as a wince. She talked softly and coaxed the girl to her feet. Kansi constantly repeated that she must walk alone.

Kansi didn't know whether it was better to run for it, risking Tari's progress back to the living, or wait and see if they were safe where they were. The idea of being trapped in the back of the cavern with Adru and Tari did not appeal to her. Working silently, she straightened Tari's clothing and fashioned a blanket into a cape around her. Adru followed suit.

Bushes snapped. The outside world lit up in flames. A scream and the sounds of men swearing and puffing assaulted their small shelter. The three Leatez froze where they were.

A man dragging a companion by the arms turned, saw them and stopped. "What in the face of hell is this?"

He resumed pulling the injured man inside before receiving an answer.

One of the two white-and-crimson-uniformed men firing at a target beyond the cavern glanced back and quipped, "Looks like people. Nothin' surprises me here."

Yells were traded back and forth outside. The two stayed quiet at the entrance while the third worked over his injured comrade.

Before Kansi realized it, Tari had left them and was crouched next to the man bleeding heavily from a wound in his upper right thigh. Her smile was radiant, her touch on his pained brow soft and welcome. His response to her was immediate.

As his fellow soldier worked on the wound with the aid of a hissing tube, he watched Tari and found the strength to touch her pale-blond hair. "You're real," he croaked.

The man working on the wound glanced up at Kansi and asked, "Are you from the village in the mountain?"

She nodded and went to Tari, but did not have the heart to take her away from the young man staring at her as though she were all there was between him and death.

"There's a war going out there," said the man as he repacked his little kit with a triangle and cross on it. "The best chance we have is to get back to the village and hope for help to arrive." He met Kansi's eyes for an instant.

He looked weary down to the marrow in his bones. Dark circles framed the hollow recesses of his eyes. "They will try to blast us off this hill. You'd best come with us."

At first she felt afraid. His colors were so similar to those of the men who had taken away the Villagers. But the manner of these men was different. Though it was not a quality easily defined. Following her instincts and thankful for the good fortune of being forced out by a more friendly group of outworlders, she nodded, then gestured to Adru.

Huddled at the entrance, Adru overly protective of Tari and the injured man braced between two of the men, waited for a signal to come from across the hummocky slope.

A shrill whistle preceded a caterwaul from four separate directions.

They ran and tried to spread out as the lead man had instructed them to do.

Smoke and flame erupted all around them. The ground felt hot and unstable, as though it would fall away down to the mantle at any step.

Ahead, Kansi saw a line of men using putch trees as shields. The high branches were on fire and so much fuel for the real inferno at the center. Bits of flaming nacki and small branches fell and kindled the withered, damp debris scattered over the regolith. It was impossible to watch all the dangers at once.

There were yells, horrendous noises of split trees falling and taking great streamers of dark nacki with them. Some lay at acute angles and forever braced by their long branches. The assault on the hillside resulted in perpendicular limbs becoming broken arms hanging from twisted, charred shoulders. It was death.

Kansi ran as hard as she could for the defense line and held tightly to Tari's hand. A brutal yank sent her sprawling. Floundering, she turned back, surprised, to find Tari on the ground. On top of her lay Adru.

Kansi crawled around Tari to the boy. "Oh, Adru!" Her scream pierced the battle and brought two men out from the perimeter. Tari wiggled free, sat up and stared dumbfounded at her brother.

A satisfied expression aged his face. Kansi could not look at the hole in his side, nor did she move when Tari was pulled away. Adru opened his mouth to say something. Before the words came a massive convulsion seized him. When it was over his mouth remained opened and forever soundless.

Men pulled at Kansi and pried her fingers away from the boy. There were hundreds of words, the heat of the fires and the aura of death storming her senses. She gazed at the men watching the jungle. They were from Lozadar's world. A violent, mad world where death ruled.

Abruptly, the jungle became silent.

Lozadar met General Myzillion's unwavering green eyes amid the planes and angles of features sculpted by tinted mud and clumped hair stiffened by mud. The heavy rope attested to the respect his captors had for his size and strength.

Stuhart's eyes remained fixed upon Lozadar as he effected a slight nod in lieu of a respectful bow. "Excellency, we've been looking for you since . . ." His voice faded, then came back strong. ". . . since Antition saw more blood in her streets in one night than in the last three millennia."

"I'd say your men did a good enough job of finding me there," Lozadar said. His eyes narrowed and his finger warred with his mind to pull the trigger.

"It is not as you believe, sire. There were Colonials involved, yes. Uniformed Colonials, or uniformed men. Whichever. The United Colonial Federation was not involved in the movement against the Seven Worlds, nor have we ever taken up arms in any capacity other than as an ally." He tried to roll into a sitting position. Small cracks formed in the dirt dried on his face. "She said you wouldn't believe it unless it came from her. Not any more than the others in Antition. Damn!"

Mustering up his last pleas, he maneuvered around to look directly at Lozadar. "You are the sole surviving Ruler of the Seven Worlds, sire. No one would question your taking a Colonial's life, not even a Colonial War General you had appointed—like me. At least make it a clean shot. Please. It beats the hell out of dying of starvation like a trussed-up animal waiting for slaughter. Your Chief Protector is a dedicated and zealous man, Lozadar cor Baalan." He lowered his gaze, prepared to die. Under his breath he whispered his peace.

Little of what General Myzillion said registered enough

to make sense to Lozadar, nor did he want it to. Here was an enemy: *the Iron General,* a commander in the force which had brutally raped and killed his sisters; *the Iron General,* a man of responsibility. A multitude of ways to kill him ran through Lozadar's mind, each one more hideous than its predecessor.

The Iron General.

His bloodlust for revenge knew no bounds. And Oranda knew this man was responsible. Why else would he have left him to die like this?

There was a time when he had trusted the General with his life, and more. He had trusted him to bring peace and order to the colonies, trusted enough to help him gain admission terms through the Assembly of High Houses of the Seven Worlds. He had been a man trusted to uphold the central government and command his forces for the mutual benefit of the Seven Worlds government and the colonies.

The Iron General—Stuhart Myzillion!

"You bastard," Lozadar seethed, red-faced, wide-eyed and intense. "I trusted you. Do you hear me? I trusted you! And you killed them! My God, Myzillion. Isn't there a grain of decency in you?"

The General looked up, appalled at first, then ready for a rebuttal. "Tell me, sire, what could I possibly have gained by performing the atrocities we both know took place inside the capitol? You were our greatest hope. Our only means for incorporation long before the crown even looked like a reality on your head. You were Lozadar cor Baalan, my friend, before you were my Ruler. What could I have possibly gained for either myself or my cause?

"I hope you will try to answer that before killing me, sire. It would be extremely unfortunate for both of us if my death were a hasty act or the product of a misguided judgment."

He wanted to kill Myzillion, wanted to experience the fulfillment of revenge, and knew this would be his best chance. Stefen would never allow him to leave. There was a life force here, one powerful enough to incapacitate a man to the nth degree and not kill him. Killing was too easy. Irrevocable. Staring at Myzillion, he realized how final the act of a half-nanosecond burst actually was.

He envied him.

If the ropes were shed, Myzillion would be free to live his life just as he had before coming to the Virgin. He could leave and go home. *Home,* Lozadar wailed inwardly, *how do you go home when everyone's dead?*

Slowly, he turned toward the thrones. Aviea glowered down on him with glassy eyes. They were still condescending, judging, accusing him of the horrible fate of the Leatez. And he knew he was guilty.

Another death riding his conscience was intolerable. He could neither leave nor rectify the happenings of Antition. The best he could do was prepare for Passage.

He lowered the Lat-kor and found himself standing at the end of the hearth aisle. Before him Aviea was lashed to the throne. He looked at him for a long time, during which the only sounds in the Great Hall were made by the kervemith's regular breathing and his claws extruding and retracting as he paced the stone floor.

Lozadar did not keep track of time. It was irrelevant. Stuhart Myzillion thought it was at least seven eternities. When the Ruler did speak the sound startled him.

"Tell me, General, why would those who murdered my sisters refer to you as their leader?"

"I have several theories, but they all boil down to one thing. You're leverage. They didn't plan on killing you in Antition, but they wanted you to believe that the Colonial Federation was not allied with the Seven. They are, Lozadar. Solidly."

"Is Oranda coming back?"

"I don't know. He blew the entrances to seal me in." Softer, "I don't know why he didn't kill me outright."

An air of perplexity in the General's tone forced Lozadar to afford the big red head a glance. "Does being tied up like that make you feel powerless? Helpless? Vulnerable? Eager to die? Does it sap your will to live?"

Myzillion looked back at the man standing in shadows across the room for several minutes before answering, "You left out 'afraid and isolated.'"

"Yeah. I guess I did."

He rolled over to the wall and managed to work into a semi-upright position. "Been there?"

"You'd be surprised at how much this place has changed me, Hart." A burst of pained, stilted laughter careened off the artful stone walls. "I took to the Virgin the way an adolescent takes to sex. Mentally, at least. Physi-

218

cally, that's another story—a long one. I spent a lot of time deluding myself that I really wanted to stay here, was entitled to stay here, for the rest of my life." He sauntered back to the Iron General.

"I need a friend, Hart. Lord knows I don't want to believe you were involved." Patting Esse, "I'll cut you loose. You stay with me. The first wrong move you make will be your last. Esse here will tear you apart so fast you'll be dead before you see him coming."

The General looked up without lifting his head. "I believe you. You've got nothing to worry about. If I ever challenged you on the Day of Equality it would be over something on a more personal level, not the government of the Seven or the colonies."

"Ohhh?" He sliced through the wrist rope, leaned farther and cut the bond around Myzillion's ankles. "Such as?"

He banged his boots against the stone to get feeling into his feet. "A woman, perhaps. That's important."

"Corinda?"

Rubbing red-and-purple bruise bracelets, Myzillion met Lozadar's questioning gaze. "What makes you think that wasn't a purely hypothetical statement?"

"Shit. Who else? You haven't met my wife. Everybody else is dead or married."

The first strains of color flooding into Myzillion's cheeks faded. Hope brightened his eyes and the beginnings of a smile showed an even set of teeth. "You're married?"

"Yeah. Well, sort of, but yes, in mind at least and here on the Virgin. Come on. We're going to check this place out. There should be plenty of rations stored for Passage. If it looks okay, we'll blast our way out and get Kansi. After that, General Myzillion, you and I are going to have a long, long talk. Then I'll decide whether or not to kill you."

"I don't suppose you'd care to make a side trip, sire?" He stood and measured himself against the kervemith.

"Where?"

Softly, "Lady Corinda is out there somewhere. Alone —if she's lucky. I think she came down a kilometer and a half west of me, but I can't be sure. I didn't have a chance to look for her before Oranda found us. There was a fight. I got most of my men out and into the jungle before Oranda surrounded the wreck."

They left the Great Hall carrying torches. "I'll tell you, sire—"

"Please. Lozadar. Not sire."

"Sure. In my next life I'm not wearing crimson or scarlet." He glanced over to see how the remark had been taken.

"What's that supposed to mean?"

"Would you believe it if I told you this movement was formed and the Insurrectionists are led by Lisan dez Kaliea and some of the House of dez Kaliea generals?" He held his breath after finishing the accusation.

"Yes, Hart, I'd believe it. That's part of the reason why I probably couldn't kill you. I saw them take the last of the Leatez from here and shoot old Aviea. In this day and age genocide is a little hard to swallow if you choose to believe it.

"How did you happen to be with Corinda?"

"I took her from the palace when I found you already gone and your rooms on fire. I'm sorry about Chalate and Corry." His voice became a whisper. "I saw—"

"Be quiet," he hissed. "Someone's coming."

Esse turned away from the torch Lozadar quickly placed in a wall holder. Stealthily, the two men ducked past a partially open door and into a storeroom. The clack of boots on stone betrayed the interlopers as outworlders. Lozadar felt vulnerable without Esse at his side. Over the booming heels came the muffled scream of someone in pain.

Chapter 23

AGILITY FORTIFIED STEFEN'S INSTINCT FOR self-preservation. He dove into the wreckage, pressed flat to the floor and covered his head with his arms. His eyes were pressed shut. Heat radiated around him. A sinister odor mingled with the smoke. *Outworlders,* he fumed, *are impossible to understand and totally irrational with their code of civilizationalism.* He found delight in the manufacture of a new word—just the kind of word an outworlder would use to confuse him. Like "pragmatist." Mentally, he made a note to ask Lozadar the meaning of that word if he ever saw him again.

He retreated farther into the capsule as the heat intensified. "She has gone wild," he muttered, sliding over the gritty floor.

The jungle outside the ship erupted in flame, the source faster than the eye could register. He tried to make out the fragments of energy disrupting the Virgin. They were too fast to see before the damage was inflicted. Heat pouring in the door blistered the brightly coated interior walls.

Supine, helpless, he wondered if the Lovers had foreseen any such circumstances. The situation was laughable when he managed a detachment from the reality of it. Here he was, Champion of the Virgin, Judge of Man— lying on an outworlder floor while a crazy lady he desired to take as a lifetime mate destroyed his demesne.

The firing stopped.

Stefen waited, unsure whether she had come to her senses or if the weapon was broken. He did not move. The pyre raged outside. The uncertainty of her mind fed his personal insecurity. He stared at the floor. Calling out to her entered his mind, and left hurriedly. The act could set him up like a ganid on a hot iron.

During his incarceration, he thought about his father and mother, for no reason he could fathom. They were just there in his mind, contrasting themselves to each other and to him and the volatile outworlder in the jungle. Time passed quickly.

The Deity looked down from zenith through a hollow in the gathering rain clouds. As though discontent with what lay upon his love's skin, he let the gray billows close like iron doors. Rain pelleted the metal ruins, though not a sound was directly relayed to the interior. A thrumming noise leaked in from the tear where the door had been. The noise cajoled Stefen into looking up.

The jungle smoldered and hissed in the downpour. Stefen slowly pushed to his feet, wary of what lurked outside.

Charcoal-barked putch trees sputtered and crackled. Puddles accumulated around the upheaved ground encircling the wreck. Soil collapsed into the yaxura holes at the fringes of the hacked-out clearing.

Lightning flashed, blinding the unsuspecting for several heartbeats. Irate thunder shook the land, sending weak vines, burned branches and dead leaf coils to the ground. Mud slithered into the yaxura holes, filling them and leveling the jungle as it had done each time it rained for eons.

Stefen waited for another flash.

This one was so brilliant he could see its pattern through his closed eyelids. As soon as it ended he bolted from the wreck, threw himself on the ground and rolled away from the entrance. With the exception of his face, mud covered every centimeter of him. There was no place to hide in the burned out fringes. He hesitated, not wanting to stay on the ground where the grabber moss was camouflaged by the mud. Patches of the deadly green might take hunks out of his body, possibly consuming an entire limb or needling into a vital organ.

He leaped into a tree and was encouraged to move quickly by the heat seeping out of the hissing bark which nipped at his callused feet. He did not travel far before spying Corinda across the way in a small island of green untarnished by the fire.

Cautiously, slowly, he began to circle the ruins, watching her and employing all his senses to detect additional enemies lurking in the vicinity. Where there had been one, there would undoubtedly be others, he decided. They will miss the ones she killed. They will come looking.

Stefen grinned. His eyes narrowed with the conception of a devilish plan to draw additional outworlders to the already devastated sector. Feeling more confident then he had felt for a long time, he closed in on Corinda and willed the yaxura to gather. Somehow, he knew they would answer and do as he bade. It did not matter why the sudden power materialized with certainty clinging to it, just that it happened. He accepted it as a part of his role as the Virgin's Champion. It would not be so otherwise.

Corinda was oblivious to his approach. Her head, bowed for some time, remained low. The tie which had held her hair back lay on the ground nearly buried in the mud. Dark tangles of hair kept the water off her cheeks. She did not seem to notice that it was raining. The Lat-kor hung against her shins as she hugged them, barely moving in a back-and-forth rocking to soothe away an inner worry no one on the outside could touch.

Stefen squatted beside her, ready to grab the Lat-kor if she tried to use it. "We must be moving, Lady Corinda." He leaned to see her face to be sure his words were registering.

The only expression he was able to decipher was one of agony. Her head shook.

"Come. When the rain lets up we will have no cover here. There will be others who will come to see what has happened here. We must be far away by then." He took her shoulders and tried to bring her to her feet. She was a dead weight and did not even glance his way.

"You go do whatever it is that you do here. My war is over. I'm tired, and I'm not used to war. It's too horrible. My friends are gone. My family is either traitors or dead.

"Just let me be. Hart died here," she said more gently, gazing at the mud-freckled wreckage. "It's as good a place as any to—"

"You are coming with me." He jerked her upright, ripped the wrist guard holding the Lat-kor away and hoisted her over his shoulders.

She came to life instantly. "Put me down! Dammit! So help me, I'll kill you if you don't leave me here!" Arms flailing, feet kicking, she was unable to score a good blow against him.

"I have told you, Lady Corinda, we must leave here." Awkwardly, he fixed the Lat-kor in his belt and consequently grasped her tighter than he wanted to. "This is never going to work," he muttered.

"That's right! So put me down and leave me alone." Sobs choked off her words and broke her fight. Limp, she cried openly, her body heaving unevenly in sorrow's wake.

Steven surveyed the demolished land. It reeked of vile desolation. A low rumbling in the distance bowed to the thunder in the sky. Gradually, the rumbling grew stronger, unaffected by the lightning or the ensuing thunder. He held Corinda's hand tightly and shifted her weight across his shoulders. His left arm moved her leg forward by yanking against the crook of her knee.

Yaxura surfaced one by one, sending the jungle into convulsions and the limb Stefen precariously balanced on into shivers. He snatched at a dangling vine to steady them. For a moment he gazed at the underground army. They would do what he wanted without further communication. It was as though they worked for a common goal, as they did in actuality—the preservation of the fragile balance of life on the Virgin.

The beasts drooled an acid which burned the ground even in the downpour. Tiny curls of smoke rose only a few centimeters from the impact points before the rain beat them down to the mud.

Corinda stilled. She came out of her ocean of misery long enough to see what was happening around them. The yaxura surfaced, disappeared and reappeared at regular intervals, their holes unseen even close up. Their great maws hid in the soil. Only a single eye watched the land.

"Are they going to attack us? What's happening to them?" They no longer looked in need of protection as they had in the clearing before Gevek's slaughter.

"More outworlders will come. The yaxura will take care of those who decide to remain." Stefen nodded to the closest beast, who lifted his head and bellowed a return, spraying them with volumes of rich oxygen.

"Please. Put me down. I'll go where you say." Sniffing, she mustered a total composure.

Reluctantly, Stefen set her on the limb beside him. When he straightened and looked into her face, his heart skipped two beats. Not a trace of emotion nor a shred of leftover agony lingered in her expression. Her eyes were just eyes that gave away nothing of the personality dwelling behind them. A chill radiated from her. An aura of death clung to her.

It was inconceivable that a person could be dead and living simultaneously. Corinda was the personification of such a feat. It both awed and scared him. Still, he wanted her as his mate, but knew her quota for love was used up for the time being, perhaps even for all time. The strange feeling made him shudder.

"How will you know you're having them kill the right ones?" she asked evenly, almost in a monotone.

"Outworlders have brought grief during this revolution of the Virgin. To me, the ones worth saving have been saved. The others will perish." A half-smile projected the sinister aspects of the Judge. "During Passage, any foolish enough to remain on her surface will never leave. The Deity will not permit it. He told me so. But you—you are special. You will be my mate."

Mentally, she fumbled over the words while trying to find a deserving reply. Her eyes remained on him until he felt a small wave of gooseflesh crawl over his skin. Eventually, she inspected his body, slowly, and asked him to turn around. The persistent up-and-down movement of her eyes made him uncomfortable. He turned, watching her over his shoulder.

"Nope. It isn't worth it. I don't think I'll be your mate, or anything else of yours. You do realize I'm leaving the first chance I get—with the right people, that is." Fists on hips, she let her weight shift to her right foot. She looked indecisive and more than a person at odds with herself. "If I have to stay alive, then I have things to do and places to go."

The constant change in her perplexed Stefen and brought back memories of Lozadar shortly after he had found him. Did the Virgin affect all outworlders in this way? Or were they like this before they arrived? "I thought you wanted to die."

"I changed my mind. Somehow, I think I might get more enjoyment out of a few others preceding me." She turned toward the jungle beyond the tree center. "You were the man in the trees . . . I remember your eyes. You looked right through me." Shuddering, "I don't suppose you have the control over those beasts down there to keep them from killing people from the Colonial Federation, do you?"

"I have no idea what the Colonial Federation is or how to tell it from the others," he admitted.

"The ones with markings on their uniforms like those dolts who panicked and set the jungle on fire are Colonials." She turned back to where he followed and for a split second flashed a smile. It passed so quickly that the sincerity of it could not be established. "They're the good guys. So are the ones with the cor Baalan crest on green." Her voice faltered. "The cor Baalan forces must be filled with a blind hatred by now and pretty irrational in their revenge."

"Revenge?" *Ahhh. Something I understand.* He grinned.

"I thought you said you knew Lozadar."

"I do. I let him live until he is judged."

He pointed the way east. She nodded and grabbed the vine he had tested. Stefen held on, arms around her, his body straining to forestall a reaction to her. Inwardly, he laughed, no longer interested in the incongruities and inconsistencies woven into his life, content just to live it.

They crossed a burned-out swatch cut in the land and landed in living jungle withering with the season. "I must say, that's damn big of you to permit him to live. Where is he?"

"I . . . I don't exactly know."

"Terrific." The branch she shuffled across with the help of a thinner one growing downward shook under their combined weight. She grabbed a vine, pull-tested and swung over to a sturdier path. "Just how many of these fortunate outworlders are there under your beneficent care?"

He understood the first part of the question and the tone of the second. "Two. Including you."

Eyes rolling skyward and noting that the rain stopped, she muttered, "How? How did I get so lucky? Why does everyone want to save me? I'm worthless. I don't take war well. It thoroughly depresses me into a suicidal state. And fighting scares me to death."

He caught her around the waist, grabbed another nacki and swung them to the next tree, where he paused only long enough for her to grab hold of the next vine. "I decided you were the mate I have been seeking when you saved the yaxura children from death." A quick glance at her, "You are nice to look at."

Behind them the day grew brighter and the dying storm loud. Corinda tried to look back. "Ships," she whispered, half afraid they would hear her. Squinting through the sparse nacki and putch leaves to the bright craft against the low gray clouds, "The dez Kaliea crest . . ." A string of obscenities hissed under the audible range.

"They will be well received." Stefen smiled mischievously.

After several seconds, Corinda smiled back and nodded. "Lisan likes welcoming committees." She hurried down the branch, Stefen behind her, prodding. Ashute dez Kaliea—her father and the Coralis Legate—took shape in her mind as he was the last time she saw him alive. Heavy scarlet robes accentuated his rotund shape and fastened solidly to a large frame possessing a physical strength past its prime, but not so far past that any would be foolish enough to challenge him. Strange how memory highlighted things barely noticeable when the scene was a reality.

Little things, like the way his hair was thinning along his forehead, the lines at the corners of his brown eyes, more going up than down, the precision of his gray-brown eyebrows as they arched thickly into his forehead, stood out in the image. A weight crushed her as she tried to face, for the millionth time, the reality that she would never see him again, the first person she had loved.

The chink in her armor eroded into a crack, splitting her defenses wide and pouring out depression.

She relived his change of expression when the long-bladed knife had thumped into her father's chest. His tunic had turned maroon, almost black, as blood soaked his garments. Again, dread stoked a panic in her. She wanted to run, just as she had in the capitol. Heart thudding, eyes dry, and her mouth stuffed with sand-laced cotton balls instead of teeth, she surged ahead blindly.

Stefen was taken by surprise when she bolted forward, fell from the limb and tumbled to the ground. She scrambled to her feet and ran, hands outstretched, reminding him fleetingly of a time when he had run through the jungle in the same manner. He descended on an angle, paralleling, until he intercepted her.

She was wild, irrational. She looked everywhere except at him.

Inwardly, Corinda found an expression of genuine sorrow, but tears would not pour out to the world. The pain was still too great, the admission of her isolation too imminent, and the enormity of her losses staggering. She let herself run with it this time and allowed it to control every fiber of her being and exhaust itself and her. Evading, shoving it away, pretending it did not exist required too much effort. The blocks erected one at a time to form a bastion against the atrocities of the past were too transparent all of a sudden and required more energy than she had to keep them in place.

She ran into Stefen, colliding with Hart in her head at the same time. Two dozen Colonial soldiers came to a halt, weapons drawn. For a timeless instant, there was a mirror of pain and fear in his face and a revulsion for the tragedy going on all around them. Screams wound through the corridors of the palace. Running feet clattered on the stone floors, fading and growing, only to fade out again.

"Your father?" the General asked.

Even now she could feel the awful truth churn inside her bowels, then the total detachment from her body, from Hart, from her father. How strange she looked; mouth open, eyes bulging out of her head, disheveled hair soaked with the same perspiration beading her face and streaking the court makeup she hated.

"Lozadar?" Hart asked, then shook her. "Have you seen the Ruler?"

Imperceptibly at first, then vehemently, she shook her head.

He passed her off to four men and shouted orders she didn't understand, nor did she want too.

She sank to the ground, feeling a sting in her dry eyes. "Hart? My God, Hart, I didn't even tell you how much I care, how much I love you. I'm sorry. I'm sorry for you, for my father, for . . ." The words faded into the air.

Stefen, muddled by the state of things, held onto her and watched the near jungle.

It turned quiet. Not a stem wearied of holding onto its branch. The clouds waited in the sky. All around them the Virgin seemed to be listening to the ramblings of the woman Stefen wanted as a mate.

Stroking her shoulders and back, he could feel the smoothness of her skin overlying hard muscle. Gently, he touched her chin with his fingertips and drew her around to see him.

The blank expression of her face did not diminish her appeal to him. He leaned close to her and brushed her lips with his.

She did not so much as blink.

228

Chapter 24

"WHERE ARE THE PEOPLE?" DEMANDED AN edgy masculine voice.

"I don't know. They should be here. Maybe they're in the Great Hall."

Lozadar's heart pounded at the sound of Kansi's voice. The Lat-kor in his hand felt good. A quick glance at Hart betrayed the Colonial's uncertainty. He seemed to be listening for something.

A dragging noise grew louder with the pants and groans of tired men. Myzillion peered through a crack in the door, moved sideways and changed his focal point to study the procession in the hall. Finally, he stood, lifted his hand to signal Lozadar to stay put and went out the door, closing it behind before Lozadar could protest.

Lozadar opened the door far enough to catch a narrow glimpse of the corridor. Hart stood silent, not moving so much as his hand. The men in the hallway hushed and turned toward the big red head. After a few seconds, they shifted into ranks.

Lozadar left the room and emerged beside the General.

Kansi ignored the men bowing all around her. She grinned and picked her way through the soldiers bent on one knee at the sight of their Ruler.

She paused, just out of reach, and looked around, for the first time registering the significance of his import to the outworlders with power enough to destroy the stars. Dreams for a man of her own crumbled in the void between them. Head bowed, she stepped back slightly to kneel before him.

"Kansi," he said in a whisper filled with emotion.

When she looked up, his hand was extended to her. She took it and rose, allowing him to guide her to his side. Never in her life could she recall being quite as happy as at that moment. Gladly, she wrapped her arms around his middle and reveled in her intimacy.

"My troops, sire." General Myzillion bowed formally. The clicking of his heels resounded through the cavern.

Esse snorted and crept into the tee from the main hallway.

The men came to their feet, glancing at one another and finally at their General.

Lozadar snarled the little he knew of the kervemith's intonation for reassurance. The beast sniffed the air, turned and disappeared down the hall. "I, ah, you have wounded, Hart. Get them taken care of." To Kansi, "Where's Tari?"

She indicated two men beyond the twenty-plus on one knee. One held Tari, the other used a pair of long sticks lashed as a crutch and held to yet another's shoulder as a stabilizer.

"Adru?"

She could not look at him. She shook her head. Her mouth opened several times. No words found their way to her lips. She turned and embraced him as though they were the only people there.

The General dispatched his troops to the Great Hall and warned them loudly about Esse's rights. Still casting sideways glances at Lozadar and Kansi, he selected two men to return the way they came in and stand watch. Briefly, he disappeared into the Great Hall.

"Kansi," Lozadar whispered, lifting her chin from his chest.

Tears brimmed her eyes. "It was terrible. We were caught in the middle. We couldn't stay there."

"Shh." A series of kisses diverted them both from the tasks ahead. "It's over now." He pulled her so tightly to him that he could feel her ribs against his.

The General cleared his throat and adjusted a Lat-kor with two spare power packs dangling from its handle.

Brushing hair away from her face, Lozadar smiled, happy to see her less worrried and the tease of sensuality present once again. "I have to go. I haven't found Stefen yet, and I must look for Corinda."

Doubtful, "Corinda? A woman?"

His smile became a grin as he nodded. "A very good friend. You'll like her, Kansi." He placed a kiss on her forehead and gathered her close so she could not see his face. "The Leatez are gone. Aviea is dead. His body is in the Great Hall."

They were silent for a short time. The General looked around him as though noticing the stone-sculpted walls.

"Would you like me to talk to Tari?"

She shook her head against him.

"She didn't fail her people. If anything, they failed her. Stefen is not a god with magic answers. Tell her . . . tell her I've gone to find her Holy One and bring him back. And guarantee her that he won't touch her again unless she wants him to." He spat out the last few words with a certainty Tari would worship him as her god for the rest of her life.

She released him enough to lift her head back and take in the fatigue carved into his face. "I love you, Lozadar Outcast. Come back to me."

"You couldn't keep me away."

Unexpectedly, she let go and glanced toward the Great Hall. "They need food, water and herbs to tend their wounds. I will see what I can do to help."

Esse roared in the corridor, inciting a verbal upheaval in the colonial ranks. Lozadar called out to the beast. Simultaneously, General Myzillion shouted orders to his men and selected a leader for the interim of his absence.

Carrying torches, they walked the corridor to the place Kansi had brought the battle-weary soldiers to. Much of the rubble had been forced aside to clear a narrow path. The damage was not as severe as in the corridor leading to the river.

The silence between the two men was unnatural and aided a depression creeping over them. The General cleared his throat and gestured at the mighty beast lumbering through the hall behind them. His green-and-gold head swung from side to side while his ever-active eyes took in every minute cranny in the stone. "How did you housebreak him? Or isn't he?"

"I didn't. I don't. And I'm not going to try." The bitter death toll Lisan had inflicted on the colonials, combined with the fate of the Leatez, hammered deeper into Lozadar with each step.

As though reading his Ruler's thoughts, "Two ships got away. This one was forced down in the mountains near where your, ah, wife was holed up with the boy and the young woman.

"They were followed. The attack was halfhearted, obviously, or they would all be dead. The boy was killed protecting his sister. He shielded her with his body." Head shaking, "Those bastards."

"He was a man, General. Not a boy." Very softly, "Adru was a man."

Myzillion looked suddenly at him, surprised by the vehemence overpowering the sorrow in the Ruler's tone. They walked in silence again and followed a path lit by occasional torches dangling from the remains of wall mounts.

At the end, the two colonials standing watch challenged the General as they approached in the dark. Both men relaxed upon seeing him, but their gaze seldom wandered from the kervemith.

The General gave them a few instructions, to which Lozadar added his own, before the men were given a guard-rotation schedule. Lozadar watched Myzillion with his men and saw the same zealous trust and blind worship with which the Leatez regarded Stefen.

Beyond the dense foliage showing signs of a path beaten through it, rain pounded the jungle. Lozadar stroked Esse and watched the beast test the air. "Think you can take us both on your broad back, fella?" He used his scanty knowledge of the kervemith sounds mixed with a smattering of fenwapter.

Esse lowered himself to the ground. Lozadar took the frontal niche at the beast's neck so his feet could dangle. After a few instructions and a lot of inner doubts, the General climbed up behind him. The military rigidity was more than what had become natural over the years.

In moments the bleak mountain wall pocked by centuries of tenacious vines laboring into small fractures of the weaker sedimentary layers was behind them. Esse flung them at the middle elevation of the jungle. He leaped from putch to putch, barely touchng the thinner branches for more than a quarter heartbeat.

The feeling in the air and on the land was ripe with foreboding. It ate at Lozadar like a cancer feasting on a damaged lung or the ganids consuming a two-days-dead fenwapter. The eerie light cast by both suns on the bright side of the clouds made strange, steamy shadows which lacked a true delineation. The jungle looked more depleted each time Lozadar saw it. The stench of rotting flesh rode the breeze the rain tried to wash clean. But the outworlder bile was not easily cleaned away.

The smell of threatening evil Lozadar knew well. It was the same on the Virgin as in Antition, only now he knew its name and would recognize the malodorous warning. Calmly, he drew the Lat-kor from his waistband and thumbed off the safety.

Uneasy, the General followed suit. "If we do run into trouble, it's going to be harder than hell to shoot from up here."

Esse circumvented the fortress hidden under tons of rock and jungle. The rain eased. Visibility increased. The clearing marked the distance ahead. It brought a renewed sorrow to Lozadar. Rain enhanced the ugly state of the rockfall. Black streaks stained the stone blocks which formed the walls. The area was a blight against the changing foliage dismally standing back.

The fury of the rain had churned the entire open space into an ocean of frothy black mud. Islands of burned reed furniture peeked from disintegrating mounds of black-skeletoned fronds and putch limbs.

Esse hurried away. In moments it was behind them. He roared into the drizzle, then tried to catch the sound. His enduring agility bore them deep into the jungle before the clouds began a slow eastward roll to empty their contents into the ocean. The wind came from the northwest, gentle at first, then blowing into a rage, stripping the dead and dying vegetation from the heights, sending debris scurrying over the ground and feeding the grabber moss with the flurry. The maelstrom flourished and vexed the cloud into boiling shades of gray.

Heat rose out of the ground and taunted the whole world. Between the rain, their perspiration and the glistening kervemith, it was impossible to believe that anything on the surface was dry. The physical misery was hewn deeply into the riders' muscles. The strange light patterns illuminating the congress of gray overhead imparted no hint of what time of the day it was, just that this part of the Virgin was still bathed in light.

Only Esse's continual roar broke the monotony. When a second, faint response came, the beast pushed himself harder. His riders were low on his back and holding on as though their lives depended on their grip—which they did. He took daring chances with the length of the gaps he hurdled over empty spaces to the ground better than fifty meters down.

"Hold on," Lozadar yelled over his shoulder. One glimpse of the fenwapter dropping from a lofty branch onto Asa served as a warning. Andazu chittered excitedly, the tone imploring some unknown desire burning hot within him.

Asa turned as her mate neared and took to the path she had just covered. The guttural cacophony shot with snarls cheered the bleak day. Esse hardly broke stride but slowed to allow her the lead. Yet even as they ran into the wind wisps of burned jungle grew pungent in the air.

Kilometers passed unmarked. The perpetual bounce against the steel-muscled kervemith wore sore spots and bone bruises into the riders. The day had two temperatures: hot and hotter. Steam rose from the ground where moisture collected. It dissipated rapidly in spite of the cloud cover. The Virgin's beasts moved over the land with a certainty unshared by their human companions.

Twice they paused for water; the amount perspired away was phenomenal. Andazu maintained a respectable distance from the new outworlder. He watched, as did Asa, with deep curiosity and guarded trust.

The marked absence of chotiburus and ganids added to the unnatural inhospitality of the heights of the trees where falizians usually nestled. Occasionally one of the green-scaled fliers tipped a thin branch, but none of them stayed for more than a few seconds.

Lozadar continually measured the terrain and committed it to memory. He pondered the swift devastation rampant on the Virgin like a blitzkrieg plague. For the first time in the heights, he could see through the treetops to the southwestern mountains. Spirals of black smoke wound from the volcanic cones to the lifting cloud ceiling.

The disruption of the land paralleled inner changes evolving Lozadar into yet another personality which tried to blend all that he was into solidarity. Had he never come across the Iron General and his men, everything would have remained stable. There would have been a way to work things over, sort them out and rationalize his necessity to remain on the Virgin. After all, Stefen held the power, and the Deity who gave him that power was as real as the kervemith he bounced upon.

Now, he sought a way around the judgment he had

awaited. *Hell,* he mused, *how could I have even considered the possibility of living here without knowing what's going on in the outside worlds? It would be like being sentenced to a penal colony—no, volunteering to live on one without the pleasure of committing the crime...*

He shuddered between bounces and held tighter to Esse's horn.

How could Hart's loyalty have even been in question? Hart. Damn good name for a man who loved the colonies as much as he did.

Before too great a self-chastisement, he remembered the symbols on the ships in the clearing where Kachieo was murdered. The dez Kaliea House had been trusted at one time, too. There were many things to consider before he lined up his forces and loyalties. Sooner or later, probably sooner, there would be a decisive battle. No matter how he sliced the pie, it always looked as if a spaceship was the key. Without one, where was there to go? And how could he begin to fight back at the Insurrectionists and the House of dez Kaliea, with half a millennium of shipbuilding and weapons innovation backing them?

Stefen stroked the side of Corinda's face until her eyes took on some recognition. A flicker of panic came and left. The tears he expected and could feel well up below the surface of her never flowed.

"Where you come from, do they teach you not to listen to your inner needs?"

Her eyes turned to ice, but she did not pull away from him or attempt to sit up.

"There are children of the Weaker Power, demons, inside of you. Passage is very near. Let them go. Release them and be free." As he spoke, he watched her for a change and explored her neck and torso with his left hand. "You will be vulnerable for only a short time and I will be there with you. We can spend Passage learning one another.

"The other worlds will slip out of your memory. The Virgin will help you to forget. I will take good care of you, Corinda." Suddenly, he grinned and radiated a boyish charm in the fresh lines mapping his face, lines not even hinted at last Passage. "If Lozadar lives, I will let him go, send him back. We will capture an outworlder ship and give it to him.

"Yes. That's what we'll do."

Slowly, her head shook.

"What's the matter? I can do it. I know I can. The yaxura will help. So will the others. We will have a good life at the Crystal Curtain." His voice rose with excitement. "We will enjoy a long life there with many friends. They are not what you are used to, but they are far more loyal and trustworthy than the outworlders. And children, Corinda. We can have many children."

She pushed away, trying to sit up, dazed by what she heard and the overall confusion in her mind. "Can't have children now."

Wind broke the sweltering calm hazing the area. A fresh smoky odor found its way through the desolate jungle, clinging to each tree, shrub and fern in its path. A shadow befell Stefen's presence. "What do you mean?"

Awakening from the turmoil inside, Corinda recognized a threat in his voice and tried to counter with poise she did not feel. "I have an implant which has to be removed surgically before—well, before I can have children." She sat up a little straighter and untangled his arms from around her.

"Why would you need that?" There was anger in his tone, as though he dreaded the answer in advance. He grasped her upper arms tightly.

Immediately the cloudy blanket stifling her senses disintegrated. Corinda tried to remember exactly what had been said, and how. A danger she could feel pulsed out of him and into her. Her eyes narrowed a bit and met his. "I could probably figure out what you want me to say and say it. But I'm not going too. Where I come from, every girls visits the med center at puberty and is outfitted with an implant. So are the boys. It's called population control. We're also instructed in sexuality and the arts of lovemaking." She squinted more. "And we're instructed in certain techniques of self-defense should some man think he's going to bestow a favor on us we don't care to enjoy at that time."

They glared at one another for several hundred heartbeats, each sizing the other up. The context of her words came through the tactful phrasing. Inwardly, Stefen shook. For a heartbeat, he remembered Tari and experienced more remorse. Again, he expressed a strong hope to the Deity that Tari was all right. He returned to contemplating the woman before him. It had never occurred during his daydream fantasies that she would not want him as a mate, or that she might not be content to stay on the Virgin with him at the Crystal Curtain. The sense of power experienced a short time ago became dismay. There was no facet in the legacy the Lovers had blessed him with to rectify this contingency.

An ineptitude for dealing with outworlders, others of his species, his kind, nestled uncomfortably in the crucible in his mind. Just when he thought he understood them and their differences from one another, it no longer made sense when applied to him.

"Why?" he asked in a whisper. "Why don't you want me as a mate?"

A memory stabbed her heart with enough pain to make her flinch. "It's not you. I . . . the man I want is dead. He was, or should have been, on that wreckage back there. If he was and my cousin Lisan has him, he's as good as dead. But even if he were alive, and the messenger he sent to Antition successful . . ." Her voice trailed as her eyes closed.

"When all was said and done, I would marry Lozadar." She turned to Stefen, seeking a form of remote understanding. "We do what we must do whether it suits us or not. We advocate personal freedom and have very little of it ourselves. It's the price we pay." A mirthless laugh changed her face. "Rather, it's the price exacted for being born into an archaic ruling system which should have gone out with the trash of the first colony."

Bewildered, "You would take Lozadar as mate and not want him, but someone else?"

"Yes. There was never a doubt. I suppose if things had worked out a little differently, and Hart were not the way he is, we might manage a discreet relationship. Loz would understand." She chuckled sadly. "Loz would. But Hart wouldn't."

"And if there were no ships and if Lozadar the Outcast was dead—what would you do? Would you be my mate then?"

Corinda looked at him coldly, easily reading the workings of his mind through his transparent expression. "No. I would consider myself totally free and would choose no one I did not love. And I would wait. For if Loz is dead, ships from the cor Baalan House would be just as likely to return as they are now. Hart sent for them."

Sighing, Stefen let go of her and stood up to peer into the brownish jungle. "I do not understand."

Cordina rose and brushed the dirt from her clothes. "It's called loyalty to a man and a cause. No matter how we feel about each other, Loz is the Ruler of the Seven Worlds and we believe in him and the future of the colonies wanting to join the Federation. Loz is one of the few men who could pull it all together. That's why he was so dangerous."

A kervemith roar pierced the windy heat, then left a silence.

Chapter 25

STEFEN SNARLED A GREETING WHEN HE picked up the distant sounds of their dozen legs in the heights. They took few precautions for silence.

Andazu chittered and swung down through the lofty branches, mostly using his left hand and feet. The lop-sided motions were becoming smooth with practice. He dropped from fifteen meters up, caught several side branches to slow him, and landed on the ground between Corinda and Stefen.

Corinda froze, entranced by the gibberish being exchanged between the creature and the jungle man. *He said he had friends,* she chided herself, regarding Andazu with fascination. The prosthesis fashioned for his missing paw was ingenious. She stared at it.

The kervemith approached quietly. Both were tired and looked more than ready to prepare for hibernation.

Lozadar called out, waving his left arm furiously. The sight of Corinda, alive and physically well, was enough to bring a sting to his eyes. But Stefen, obviously in possession of all his faculties, was a joy to behold. As soon as Esse leaped to the ground, Lozadar slid from his neck, jubilant. He ran for Stefen, clapping his shoulders in delight, grinning from ear to ear.

"You're okay? You're really okay! Everything works?"

Stefen returned the grin weakly. "Yes." From over Lozadar's shoulder he saw Corinda pale as she turned toward the kervemith.

She met Hart's gaze from atop the beast. Slowly a tear rolled down her cheek, though she did not move toward him. Relief softened everything about her.

"Corinda," the General said, nodding without breaking eye contact.

"H-Hart." She returned the gesture awkwardly. In the strained silence marked by the heavy breathing which

239

swelled and collapsed the kervemith's chests, Corinda willed her gaze away from him and sought Lozadar. A faint smile of triumph flickered across her features, making the single tear on her cheek out of place. "Loz . . ."

He gathered her in his arms and held her, relieved to find her alive, remembering the terror of Antition, the gore and countless liters of blood spilled down the main step of the government's oldest building. The Grevenwald System was marked by the atrocities of its capital. "Why did you come looking for me, Rin? You would have been happier if you hadn't found me. So would Hart." He rubbed his cheek against the crown of her head. The General climbed down from Esse.

Stefen was at a total loss of understanding. The Deity held the Virgin on a tight rein lest she be wooed by the weaker sun. Padree had killed to save Annalli from being bedded by another. Yet, here before his very eyes, Lozadar the Outcast commiserated with his intended mate over her love for the outworlder, Hart. Worse, he cared for another, yet would not take any as true mate save Corinda. Surely Kansi would not agree to that arrangement.

"The Seven and the colonies need you, Loz. People are dying out there by the thousands. Antition was only the beginning." She looked up beyond the stubbly face and into his eyes. "There's so much happening, and I think you're just about the only one who has any chance of stopping it. The Seven and the colonies will listen to you. There is no one else, and they're slaughtering one another now while . . ." She stopped and shook her head. The totality of it was too overwhelming to condense into a few moments.

"I don't think I'm free to leave." Head swinging toward Stefen. "He's just the tip of the iceberg. This place has a . . . an intelligence all its own. It has to do with the sun and this planet and Stefen being the Judge of Man. Take my word for it, it does exist. It is the greatest proof I have ever seen of there being any form or substance to the word 'God.' It is God to this place."

"If you had a free choice, if this place said you could go—Stefen, that is—would you go back to Antition, Loz?" The words came hard as a way evolved for her to find the alternative she wanted for him.

He pondered for a moment, then said, "Told you before. We don't get free choice."

She smiled ruefully and looked down, knowing the bondage enslaving them both. "It was a foolish question."

"Come on. It's a whole lot cooler back at the Sanctuary." He released her and turned her in Hart's direction. A pat on her posterior sent her on her way to the General.

"Tari's there," he said evenly to Stefen. "I think you ought to see her."

Immediately Stefen looked down and played with the fenwapter's claw. "I don't know why I did that to her. She didn't do anything." Glancing up, "Would the Leatez be displeased and disown me as the Holy One if I returned?"

Lozadar failed to answer for several heartbeats. When he spoke, his voice was dangerously quiet and low-toned. "Is that what you're concerned about? Losing your place as their object of worship?"

Stefen shrugged. "I *am* the Holy One. Did I not live in the jungle and walk out of it to them? I did not write their beliefs. They were molded by the Deity and the Virgin."

"Stefen, somewhere this has taken a wrong turn for you. I don't think you understand what was involved.

"You ran out on them. I don't know why, unless it was because of what you did to Tari." Seeing Stefen's head bow, he continued, "They would have let her die in that hut if we hadn't taken her out. They were going to burn it with her in it because she did not please you? My God! You damn near beat her to death.

"What's happening to you, Stefen? I mean, I know if you had wanted to kill her you could have with very little effort. Why?" His voice trailed off as Stefen shook his head from side to side.

Abruptly, Stefen turned away and bellowed. The kervemith leaped into the trees, the smaller female following the male as they climbed. In seconds they were out of sight.

Andazu chittered and called. Stefen turned back to Lozadar. "Tell my people I will return after Passage."

"Your people do not exist anymore. They were taken by our mutual enemy—all of them. Aviea the Bespeaker was slain. The entrance has been sealed. Esse knows the new way in. Tari, Kansi and about twenty-five of General Myzillion's men are there now. They fought in the mountains behind the Sanctuary. Adru was killed protecting Tari.

"She is all that is left of your worshipers, Stefen."

Wordless, Stefen bolted toward the nearest low branch, mounted it and climbed with Andazu. He did not look back as his pace accelerated.

The three outworlders watched in silence for some time after he was gone. Perspiration rolled over them and soaked their already wet clothing. Finally Lozadar turned to the General and pointed to the way they had come.

"It's a long way. The heat gets a hell of a lot worse. So we'd better hurry, because it's going to take us a couple of days to get back."

Corinda caught his arm as he moved to take the lead. "Did they take the sender when they took the people?"

"No." To Hart, "Did Oranda take it when they threw you into the great Hall?"

"I don't think so." He glanced at Corinda and smiled. "There may be hope yet."

"Hope or a quick death," she muttered, releasing Lozadar's arm. "Let's go. We can talk as we walk."

He spent the remainder of the day meditating and running; from whom or what, he was unsure, and it made no difference. Andazu knew his mood and stayed distant and aloof, permitting himself to be seen only when it was absolutely necessary. A tree branch or wilting fern brown with shriveled fronds served as screens. Ominous rumblings deep in the earth were mere echoes of the conflict raging within Stefen.

All that Lozadar had told him about outworlders, their customs, rituals, loyalties and drives, made no sense in the light of Corinda's attitudes. They were the same, but they were different. Very different. Envy for Lozadar turned into hatred. Recriminations followed in abundance.

By the time the Deity had crept behind the horizon and the weaker sun blazed beyond the growing cloud blanket, Stefen settled into a perch where a large branch joined the trunk of an ancient putch. He toyed with the few precious shanuts Andazu had foraged. Never had he stayed out this long into the Passage cycle unprepared. Gazing at the boiling clouds rich with orange-and-blue linings, he contemplated the power inherent in what he saw. He likened the turmoil to his emotions and identified with the struggle of the Weaker Power to possess the forbidden Lady who would not come to him willingly.

When he attempted to speak with the Deity's presence hovering over him, there was no response. An impression of reserve laced with a stern disapproval bordered on contempt.

It stunned him to realize that the Deity did not wholly embrace him as He had when he was in the sense-deprivation state. Failure eased over him. Somewhere he had not lived up to the Deity's expectations.

"Deity," he murmured, imploring, "show me which way to go. Guide me. Tell me. I don't know which way to go. I look at the outworlders and see confusion. They are more complicated than I can understand.

"I see the land, the Virgin, and still do not know my role as Champion. The power you bequeath and rescind is beyond my comprehension. You allow me to gather the yaxura to obliterate the enemy, yet you allow the enemy to take those who would pay homage to me."

You are a man. Not a god. The Leatez are of no concern in the balance of life. They were allotted places to exist in peace so long as they did not disrupt our cycle with machines and weapons of the outworlders. This doctrine was not adhered to. As soon as it was to their advantage, they used the one machine they possessed. It brought devastation and ruin.

Stefen, we care little whether or not you are worshiped, loved or accepted by the people marring the Virgin's vegetation cloak. The important thing is for you to find a way in which to be rid of the dangerous machines and weapons they carry in their ships. Warlike species as they are, they may use their abominations. Already, we fight the effects of the instability they have produced.

It will not take much more to sever the thread woven to keep us stable. And should the Virgin at last become mine, one within the realm of our intelligence and beings . . . A warming sensation changed to one of yearning.

It is yourself and the creatures of the Virgin you are guarding and struggling to save, Stefen. Not us. Our time will come in the scheme of Universal events and evolution. We have waited for the union since the beginning of her time. And we continue to wait, until her children come to fruition or prove totally unworthy of our sacrifice. It is a responsibility that Creators have toward those they create.

"But, Deity, I do not know how to go about accomplishing the riddance of the outworlder plague on the surface. I do not know how to be worthy of the sacrifice you make." In frustration he clenched his fists and locked his jaw.

There is a way, and it is open to you. You are no longer the child of the jungle hiding behind a waterfall, Stefen. You are a man and responsible for your actions and omissions. As yet, you have made little use of the lessons contained in the visions, nor have you derived the benefits from Lozadar you could have. Think of who Padree was, what he became and those who took the ones you would have worship you. They are one and the same, both in species and in origin.

Do what you must do, Stefen. Do what must be done. Beyond this, I will not guide you. You must find your own way, make your own settlements and seek your own peace.

The finality in the Deity's communication set the weight of the world on Stefen's shoulders. It was inconceivable that he should have to be responsible for so much and so many. He contemplated the words, dissecting them, searching for hidden meanings and applications, desperately probing for a direction and gradually realizing as the brilliant Deity rose again that the answers were obvious as long as he did not put himself first.

Andazu had slept fitfully through the time of the weaker sun. Stefen stroked him and handed over a small branch with a few shanuts still attached. The fenwapter refused the food. For the first time since before going to the Forbidden Place, Stefen took a good look at his old friend.

There was nothing in his outward appearance to give away the age and solitude inside the creature. His fur stayed the same pale gray, though perhaps the luster did not seem so bright in the cloud-filtered light. Even in sleep, the raspy intonations of beseeching the Ancients escaped his dark lips. Kachieo's death had taken something out of him which would never be replaced. Suddenly he was reminded of Padree and the way he had seemed to die a day at a time once Annalli passed away. Permanent grief clung to the fenwapter's inner thoughts. Its extent was so vast that it could not be hidden, though he tried whenever Stefen groped for the link.

Andazu turned to put his back toward Stefen.

"It's okay, Andazu. I know you like the outcast and you think I have not been fair to him. You are right. Even so, how can I send him home?" He knew it was more than Lozadar bothering the fenwapter, or else he would not have closed his mind so completely and suddenly. It was most unusual for Andazu to feel strongly against one of his actions. The realization made Stefen contrite.

As one, they made their way eastward. An urgency to find a permanent shelter rode the heat billowing from the ground and being pressed from the sky. Rain fell. It was hot and burned Stefen's exposed flesh. They stayed in the lower branches, where it became a steamy mist coating the trees with slippery peril.

The total fatigue of the season and the physical stress of the kervemith prevented riding. Asa attacked a lone chotiburu in search of its horde shelter with a ferocity that astounded Stefen. Her kill was shared by her mate and no other.

Lightning reached out of the clouds and split the putch they were using in half. They scrambled to get clear of the falling side and avoid being dumped into the grabber moss covering the ground.

Stefen clung to a vine and felt the whoosh of the branch send chaos into the steam behind. Grabber moss splashed along the empty islands of the jungle floor, where it would instantly take hold. Splotches landed on the trunks of putch trees and slid to the ground, already turning brown against the green as it was slowly reabsorbed into the whole of the deadly sea.

The air felt wrong so early in the approach of Passage. Never had the Virgin been so maligned by virulent heat until the time of total light. The struggle between the strong and weak suns which put her in the middle took on a vicious desperation. The heat of her land attested to the constant pull at the core of her being.

The urgency to do something to alleviate her plight presented no solutions to Stefen, only more determination to move over her surface. Hunger growling in his stomach set him looking for any surviving foodstuff in the trees and on the ground. Andazu paced him, remaining removed with his close proximity.

A distant growl intensified, coming from above the clouds, growing louder and louder. It lasted for what seemed like forever. Stefen stared toward the threat he could not see beyond the gray-black barrier raining on him. There were more ships coming than all he had ever seen or imagined existed. And they kept coming and coming.

Explosions ripped the sky apart.

Muted hues of vibrant color assaulted the clouds above the hot rain. Their tantalizing dance cajoled the watchers to peer a little harder. Bright flashes of light shot holes in the gray which mended instantly. The thunder of a thousand volcanoes inundated the land and shook the trees nude of their few leaves.

Pungent fire speared the clouds and ravaged the land.

Stefen witnessed the desecration of his world and felt the certainty of death.

Chapter 26

KILOMETERS EARLIER THE THREE OUT-
worlders had finished sharing all the important pieces of
information each held. The trek demanded a toll which
heightened when energy was diverted to speech. For the
most part, they were able to travel on the ground. The
dead vegetation decayed rapidly in the steambath atmosphere. The only growth thriving under the adverse
turn in the climate was the grabber moss. It looked invit-
ingly lush and green, refreshing in the bleak world suffocating around them.

When the wind died to a steam-filled breeze, the silence was awful. Each move of their arhythmical legs
soaked by perspiration bludgeoned the almost perpetual
day. The time of total dark, which hardly felt like more
than a few minutes, was the most restful period since
they had begun. Food was sparse to nonexistent; what
there was of it rotted on the ground. They shared the rations in Corinda's pack, which Lozadar carried.

Rifts in the earth opened. Steam poured out to further
heat the land. Occasionally the bellowing of a yaxura
carried through the naked specters of browns, blacks and
grays, spurring the travelers on with the edge of agony inherent in the call.

Each carried personal burdens wrought from the free
flow of conversation during their rest. The future looked
bleak. The key they all recognized was the necessity of a
ship. From there, it was a matter of testing the hold
Stefen and his gods held upon the Ruler of the Seven
Worlds. There was more to it for Lozadar. It meant something to pledge his word as a bond. He weighed the pros
and cons, knowing a countless number of lives would be
lost if sanity were not restored to the Seven Worlds
through the Grevenwald System and the capital city of
Antition.

Stefen was a friend—complex, uneducated, wise beyond his years and simple all at the same time. In ways, he regarded Stefen as a younger brother. It surprised him to find this in his analysis of the gamut of feeling ripping his conscience. The grin he attempted became a grimace. Never again would he so unconditionally commit himself to anything or anyone for any reason. It was too damn final and binding.

Corinda fared better than he had thought she would. Perhaps it was her stubborn streak. The thought of being married to that kind of determination was a dismal one. It had advantages. The black lines circling under her eyes spread deeply into her cheeks. Against her colorless pallor, the dark tones aged her beyond their combined years. Belatedly, he noticed the same look dawning over the General as they walked and sometimes stumbled together behind him.

They chose a clear stream as the best place for a respite. The water was warm. It tasted as though it had been stored in an old canteen and aged for several hundred standards. Each took a turn rolling in the narrow trickle to change the moisture content of their clothing and bodies.

Lozadar took a foil of salt tablets out of the pack, dismayed to see how few there were left. He gave the General two, which were immediately consumed. Corinda made a face as she chewed hers. Lozadar took one with an explanation about being used to the heat. While they did not verbally call him a liar, their expressions did.

"Into the trees, troops," Lozadar mumbled, swinging the pack up. Ahead was a sea of grabber moss. It rolled and pitched for as far as they could see. A maze of putch trunks solidified to hide its extent.

"How much farther?" Corinda asked.

Lozadar jumped, grabbed a branch and hauled himself into the tree. He reached down for Corinda as Hart lifted her up. "Not far, Rin. I'm not sure. Maybe we'll get there by dark. Maybe not."

"I'm tired."

"I know. But we can't stop. Sling your leg over and tie on the rope. We're traveling in tandem now."

She moved out of the way promptly in even, energy-conserving motions. Within seconds the General was on the branch and had tied off the last loop of the rope. They

248

moved out across a long branch ensnared by several others at the end. The steamy drizzle started again, just enough to coat everything with a fresh layer of slippery film and limit visibility down to near zero.

They crawled along the paths suspended in colorless monotony. Lozadar led them back in the same direction each time they were forced to detour from the straight line he would have preferred to travel.

Engine noises whined through the mist. Little time was wasted glancing around. It was difficult enough to see the heels of the person in front and follow the unpredictible winds and bends of the trail. The tense moments when vincs became their transportation mode, the safety of the rope abandoned, were becoming more frequent. The growing cacophony in the sky added a ripple of terror to the strained undercurrent strung out by the rope.

They spoke little; the difficulty of being heard made the effort pointless. Light flashed brightly and died an instant later. Sporadic colors clawed their way through the foggy steam lying on the land like translucent lead.

By wordless consent, the pace quickened. The shaking land bore the blame for the tremulous muscles quaking under each of their forced-calm facades. They found the need of assistance, both in receiving and lending it, greater with the contact of a new branch in another tree. The constant threat of being deposed to the death below the mist sapped mental energy.

"If it were dark now, I'd scream and go insane," Corinda muttered at the clouds. Lozadar settled her on a new branch and tied the rope through her belt.

Wind generated by the spacecraft reached them. They sat on their path, hunched forward, and scooted along, unwilling to stop or bow to the gusts unpredictably slamming at them until forced.

For a time, the three huddled against an upright branch. They held to it and each other. The wind lashed the mist into a frenzy, tore away whole limbs from the putch, snapped fern trees like kindling wood and ripped the survival pack off Lozadar's back. The length of the gust denied the ships as the cause. It was something indigenous to the Virgin, one of her atrocities saved only for Passage.

After the limbo clinging to the island safety, the wind lessened and the mist thinned. Slowly, they unwound, each grimacing at the strain deep within their muscles. The war moved away. Not once were they privy to know who battled above the depressing gray cover, or if there had been a victory.

Lozadar moved them onward, always on guard for the wind changes which could send one of them tumbling. It was not until the light poured a diffused pattern through the clouds and evolved to a less powerful intensity that the ships returned. This time, there was no firing. They flew low and disturbed the midworld where the three clung for dear life. The absolute calm that followed was unnatural and carried an ominous portent which stiffened the hair on the back of Lozadar's neck.

They took advantage of the lull to make time, almost carelessly running down the branch trails, crossing expanses all three at a time on a single vine and hurrying toward their destination. Lozadar set a grueling pace. Alone, he could cover at least three or four times the distance in the same amount of time. He urged them on as much as he thought wise, not wanting to frustrate Corinda any further, nor antagonize the General with the same action.

She did better than he had a right to expect, and he knew it. Her natural ability as an athlete gave her an edge and balance. Grudgingly, with a smile, he admitted she was doing much better than he had on the first day.

Night came, forcing them to rest. It lasted long enough to set the aches and stress in their bodies. The heat stabilized. By the time a glimmer of light bit the eastern gray hard enough to illuminate the trail, they were on the move.

The clearing appeared out of nowhere, a welcome sight for Lozadar. It was not until he told Corinda they were nearly home that he felt the moisture crawling down his cheeks from the edges of his eyes. He had not recognized the doubts he had held for their survival and was glad—now.

The shroud closed off a glimpse of the slate-gray mountain jutting like a broken tooth above the clearing. Lozadar led the way down. The two followed, needing no coercion. They ran across the open ground near the protection of the jungle. The distance to the side entrance alternated between being short and impossibly long.

Half an hour later they were passed by the guards into the Sanctuary of the Leatez.

Stefen found a singlemindedness for returning to the Leatez village blinding enough to blot out the light war eating up the skies. Trees fell. Whole volcanic mountains were obliterated by one short burst of the terrible weapons the outworlders wielded indiscriminately. Their fall racked the land in protest at an untimely demise in the midst of companions who would devour the hard rock, melt it down and remold it to form more height. Bolts of blinding destruction mutilated the surface by opening wounds deep into the black rock which oozed noxious smoke and gases.

Andazu paced him, as did the kervemith, sometimes staying behind, most of the time just ahead, calling out when the mist grew too thick. Individually, they rode out the intense winds and exchanged nothing more than a mental nod before resuming the journey. Guided by the fenwapter Stefen traveled during the night.

Several times he thought he heard the outworlders in the distance, but he gave up that notion. Moody as the Virgin was presently, she was most likely playing tricks.

Often he wondered what the outworlder ships were doing. It did not seem possible for them to see what was on the surface. The fog and mists combined to make a hand at arm's length invisible much of the time.

The ships continued to sound. Stefen pressed on, taking chances in the low visibility he would not dream of taking only a day before with clear skies and calm winds.

When quiet sheathed the land, he pushed harder to make the village before dark.

Crippled too extensively for an escape to the black voids of space where an experienced war captain would have little trouble eluding his pursuers, the enormous unmarked ship slipped into the cloud cover and killed its power.

Oranda swore. The thwack of his solid fist crashing on the com chair's panel straightened the backs put to him at the control boards. He ordered his fleet away from 4724Y's atmosphere and behind the largest of her two moons for repair and rest. Playing the Insurrectionists' game in the atmosphere was suicide, he reiterated to himself for the six hundredth time.

He had watched the shifts change three times since last sleeping. He leaned back and sucked in a nonexistent stomach, then pressed the belt-release button to extricate himself from the chair. Heavily, he rose with an eye on the damage-control screen and the lists of time versus parts and labor from the other ships.

If he were not so thoroughly depressed over his error in judgment in assessing who his enemy was and the combined strengths the cor Baalan fleet met, he would have felt more pride in the showing his ships made. To damage the big one was no small feat, he knew.

Walking down the hall to his quarters, he began to feel a little better.

Whatever that damn thing was leading the smaller Scouter XIs, it wouldn't be leaving the hellhole it landed on without extensive repairs.

His cabin door identified him and opened as he approached.

The makings of a grin cracked the set lines of his face for a precious few seconds. That ship was damaged so badly that new parts would be needed from its building place. "Two in one," he said and pulled off his left boot.

Shiny and black, his boots were lined up beside the bed so they could be stepped into quickly in case of an emergency. Oranda stared at his image in a mirror embraced by off-white wall. He needed a shave and some time in the light bath.

"Later," he told the disheveled image, then lay back on his bunk with his fingers laced behind his neck and his right foot resting atop his left.

A thorough assessment of his actions indicated that he had fallen very short of his potential and erred grievously in judgment. It kept him from sleeping.

After a time, he turned onto his left side and depressed four buttons. "Send a message to the Main Colonial Fleet and ask them to block space traffic in and out of here at every jump. Then wake me when the repairs on this ship are advanced sufficiently to return to the planet. We have a lot of unfinished business there."

"Sire." Timidly, the guard touched Lozadar's shoulder. "Sire, I'm sorry to wake you."

252

"Then don't. Let me sleep," he mumbled, rolling over and pulling his blanket up around his neck.

The guard stood over him with an air of uncertainty that filled the room.

Kansi opened her eyes and saw a familiar face of a man who had assisted her in binding up the outworlders' wounds. He looked extremely uncomfortable, as though he would rather have been anywhere but where he was. Softly, he cleared his throat. "Sire, there is a man who says you owe him loyalty waiting at the entrance. We do not know what to do with him. He has the beast who accompanied you before and more with him."

Kansi propped herself on one elbow and managed a sleepy half-smile. "He'll be out soon."

The guard bowed gratefully and left.

The ache running down Lozadar's bones and up his muscles collected inside of his head, rattled around and recycled with a little less intensity. He made himself alert to the bows and salutes of the colonials in the hallways. The walkway had been cleared of most of the rubble and did not need much attention.

Stefen stood like a stone god at the entrance. The kervemith flanked him. Crouched on all fours in front of him was Andazu. There was something different about the fenwapter that took Lozadar a few minutes to place. His jaw was outthrust and his teeth bared.

He waved the guards off as he approached.

They were reluctant to leave the Ruler with the beasts and turned away slowly.

"I'm glad you decided to come," Lozadar said when he was face to face with Stefen.

"There is much to do in a short time. The Virgin is distressed. The unbalance created by the outworlder weapons takes a great toll."

"You know I cannot stop them from here." He met the icy void of Stefen's gaze and stepped back awkwardly. Shrugging off the estrangement he felt, "Come. There is a room which serves as a bathing place a little way down the hall. Esse and Asa will fit in one at a time, if they wish too."

After a marked hesitation, Stefen acquiesced and stepped around Andazu to follow Lozadar. The beasts followed him silently and in single file with a distance between them, as though they anticipated a battle. The

253

abnormal onset of the Passage syndrome left scars on the kervemith. Blood coated their nostrils and mingled with the saliva which perpetually dripped from their fangs.

Moss covered the walls of the common bath. The floor felt abnormally warm underfoot. Stefen removed his packs and knife and climbed in backward in order to watch Lozadar. "I will trade your obligation to forever remain on the Virgin once we have made a final journey together."

Lozadar waited for him to continue and sat calmly on a stone bench.

Asa sauntered up to the water and drank. Esse watched the door.

"I want the Lady Corinda to stay in your place. That will be acceptable." He dipped into the water and massaged the mud from his scalp. When he stood, he shook like a kervemith and flung water in all directions.

Lozadar refolded his arms. This new turn of events did not sit well amid the burdens he had already shouldered.

"She will stay under those terms."

"Then you have already discussed this with her, Stefen?"

He glanced at the ceiling, thinking. "I believe she will accept those terms." Looking directly at Lozadar, "I will ask her in your presence, if it pleases you. One of your people must remove the thing which keeps her from being a whole woman before you are free."

If he were not chagrined by Stefen's proposition, he would have laughed. He met Stefen's gaze for a long time while mulling over his approach. Haltingly, he began by pleading guilty to exploring Stefen's pack. He moved into the area of genetics and his knowledge of Padree. "Corinda is your aunt, your mother's sister. The dez Kaliea line is already too tight. That is one of the many reasons why she was pledged to me. We were able to side-step that issue until I became the Ruler.

"Here?" He gestured to the moss-carpeted walls around them. "Without a medical mechanic? Or a genetic engineer in residence? Stefen, her kids don't stand a chance of surviving."

Stefen trudged out of the water and glared at the Ruler of the Seven Worlds—places so corrupt that children were contaminated before they were born. The truth he could feel emanating from Lozadar stung his soul and depressed him. The bottom fell out of his dreams and clattered silently on the floor between the two men, widening the rift cracking their friendship.

"Gather your things. You may bring any who wish to fight the enemy on the land. We have a battle to attend." The champion's words were soft spoken and even. "Pray that your outworlder ships do not find it necessary to return here, Lozadar. Already the damage they have wrought upon the Virgin is bordering the irreparable."

Chapter 27

IN THE REALM OF THE INCONSTANT, THE limits were perilously finite. The Deity looked on as His beloved Virgin was ravaged by the odious destruction forces brandished by the outworlders. They cared nothing for the devastation they caused to befall her.

The fragile balance holding the Laws of the Universe at bay began to teeter. Were it possible for the Virgin to cry, she would. But all her resources were required to hold her place around the Deity. The forces wrenching at her core increased the nutation of her axis significantly.

They communicated little as they experienced the foreshadow of the holocaust to come.

The Deity's ire was softened by the Virgin's benevolent attitude toward the unknowing outworlders who were killing her physical embodiment. For all their sophisticated knowledge, they did not know peace. The frustrations and injustices suffered by Padree and those like him were understandable, just as were the emotions of those now upon her tender skin who pursued the faction he had started.

The imbalance mushrooming through her sphere increased exponentially.

Her land masses rode uneasily on the molten peridotite of the mantle. The core tried to expand, could not, and began an accelerated heat production under the pressure confining it.

Her time of struggle was seen and felt by the Weaker Power. He exerted more pressures upon her and heightened the battle she waged to stay alive and stable in the realm of the Deity she loved.

The three women, two severely wounded men and two strong guards were left at the Sanctuary. It was quiet after the orderly confusion of departure. From having too much to do, the women had nothing demanding and little to keep them occupied.

Kansi sat beside Tari. The girl possessed an ethereal smile which was brilliant enough to light up the Great Hall all by itself. The Holy One had begged her forgiveness—begged forgiveness! The sound of his voice combined with his touch were the panacea that had restored a vibrant mental health which aided her slowly healing body.

Corinda spent a long time staring at the damaged sender and the fine thread Hart's expert said would blow them all up if changed. She could almost feel the waves it sent out across deep space, calling voicelessly to any who would listen. It had been a hope for salvation during the long, exhausting trek to the Sanctuary. Now it was nothing but another form of death.

The onslaught of an early Passage of unprecedented ferocity sent the kervemiths on the prowl for the shelter of Esse's newly acquired horde. The lair was very close to the Leatez village and high enough to be secluded from them. Inside, most of the beasts were deep in the hibernation slumber which lasted through the worst of Passage. In the far recesses, chotiburus snored uneasily, their fate sealed when the horde gathered them together and shepherded them into the lair.

Bone-weary, Asa selected a place to lie down. Esse surveyed the entire den and took stock of who the next challengers for the position of leader would be by gauging size and approximate age.

Before joining his mate, he stood at the mouth of the lair. The stone layers which once had risen above the entrance to obscure it from the Leatez clearing were now an enormous rubble pile at the base. He could see over the jungle, beyond the rift where the river flowed, to the granite mountains before the clouds swallowed the distance.

It was an excellent choice for the Passage lair. High. Open. Secure for uncounted Passages as though the sedimentary mountains were special to the ruling gods and those who dwelt within were safe from natural harm.

Behind Lozadar were Stefen and Andazu. They hurried through the green tunnels, black-interiored without the sun. General Myzillion and his men followed a few paces back. Each carried a chotiburu-skin pack dipped in a dark pitch to waterproof it. Food, supplies, primitive bandage rolls and ointments were the bulk. The two med-kits from the ships were divided among them to ensure that one accident would not deprive them of a whole kit.

Lozadar led them past the grotto. Water no longer poured out of the side of the mountain. The collapse of the serrated stone canopy had altered its course. During the short time the heat took a toll. Algae grew in the warm pool and floated on the top in brown-tinged green froth. It scummed the sides and reached into the escape stream to small pockets hollowed in the bed.

From there they moved through what remained of the trees to the high walls of the riverbanks. The colonial soldiers were apprehensive as they gazed into the dark water. No longer was it calmly wandering out to the sea because it had no better place to go. It rushed with a fury. The rains draining from the mountains raised the level close to the ledge Lozadar had fallen from. Soon water would pour into the hole and fill the lower recess of the Sanctuary as it probably had done for centuries, then drain during the calmer aftermath of the cold spell.

Stefen stood on the edge of the cliff, arms raised to the dank sky. Gleefully, he summoned the Lords of the Great Sea to serve him. He was exultant when they responded by bucking in the frothy surface below.

Lozadar watched him with a twinge of fear. The maniacal expression Stefen wore was new.

Unexpectedly, Stefen jumped from the cliff. His plunge into the water lasted several seconds before he surfaced on the back of a zuriserpant.

"I was hoping there was a better way," Lozadar mumbled, waving back at Stefen.

One by one, General Myzillion's men followed suit, each more confident when his predecessor succeeded.

Lozadar watched the fenwapter with a newfound dolor. "Andazu. You have changed a great deal since we first met. Is there anything I can do? Is there any way I can help?"

The fenwapter sighed heavily. "Ancients wait close by. Kachieo waits." The words exacted an unexpected penance. His head hung in the direction of the river.

Andazu felt old to Lozadar. His sluggish movements

screamed of a tiredness for living characteristic of those who found despair wherever they looked. His eyes seemed to focus on Stefen. For a moment, Lozadar shared the fenwapter's acute grief for the Champion. It staggered him to think of Stefen sentenced with the fate of the entire planet. No man could shoulder such a burden and discharge it successfully. It was an impossibility, for the salvation, as he saw it, required manipulating people and forces of which Stefen knew little or nothing.

He, too, looked down at Stefen proudly astride a blue-green beauty riding high in the water. He knew better than to doubt what Stefen said concerning the unnecessary use of their weapons. Fragile as the inexplicable balance holding the Virgin in orbit around the Deity was, it could well be that it had existed on the raw edge of extinction from the very beginning. Love, being alone, he could understand. The whole of the Virgin and her creation he could not begin to grasp, but he did find an acceptance of its entirety.

Abruptly, he was staring down at the river and seeing Andazu plummet screeching into the watery abyss. For an instant he thought his sight had failed and the heat had broiled his brain. But when he cleared his eyes, Andazu was atop a zuriserpant. The fear of the great water and the beasts within them had been conquered.

Looking about, perhaps he thought it better to die at sea or in battle on a strange ground than to bear the isolation here, Lozadar mused, aching inside for the fenwapter.

He put it out of mind and jumped, dreading with the certainty of prior experience the impact when he struck the water. Feet first, he drove deep into the layers of of varying temperature current. A zuriserpant wrapped him securely in a tentacle supporting his eye and seated him.

On the surface, Lozadar took stock of their feeble army—twenty soldiers plus himself, the General and Stefen. Between them they possessed six Armcos and sixteen Lat-kors with extra-charge power packs for three. The whole thing felt like a suicide mission designed by Lisan dez Kaliea.

Shades of blue blended into the murky river water. The zuriserpants formed a wedge led by Stefen. They traveled near the surface to hold their riders out of the water. Each showed the tops of six gill sets flapping oxygen back at those at the rear of the solid wedge. Their large tail fins protruded from the water and splashed back and forth against the intentions of the current.

The day no longer indicated where the cycle of light was. As they neared the ocean, it became dark without warning. Andazu chittered wildly and betrayed the tremendous fear eating at him and the hope of a swift death. His zuriserpant wrapped him in a tentacle like a security blanket.

Stefen drove the Lords of the Great Sea without rest from one rendezvous point to the next. Lozadar and the colonials learned to sleep sitting up by holding fast to the zuriserpant's tentacle. The ocean raged a fury taunted by the land. There was no relief anywhere from the increasing heat consuming the Virgin. Seawater merely changed the salty moisture of the tiny army heading for the safe landing site Stefen had camped under on the way to the Forbidden Place.

Before the next dark phase, exchanging exhausted zuriserpants for fresh, willing ones was second nature to the colonials. Only Andazu clung to the old fear of being consumed by the water.

Esse lifted his head from his paws. The sultry mood of the lair sweated the rock overhead. A distant sound piqued his ears.

Alert, he took stock of the horde of strangers he led.

All slept. Even the chotiburus snored at a deeper pitch, resigned to handle their dreaded fate after a good hibernation.

He listened, growling softly in his throat.

The Lieutenant was at an age when her face no longer retained the tight-skinned spirit of the young. Experience carved lines into the unique character which clung to the quality that had made her a beauty for so much of her life. From the distance of the com chair where Captain Malchi Oranda watched her, he still thought her gorgeous.

Protector Lieutenant Mya crossed the open space and stood at the Captain's helm. She glanced in Oranda's direction and traded a silent message and answer in less than a half second. The standards spent side by side had done that for them.

Her smooth alto called out orders and the chant of commands to swing them away from their position behind the moon. The screens filled with angry clouds hugging 4724Y like a fearful child.

The Mark IV plunged toward the surface alone, its mission not one bent upon the destruction of the enemy known to be in hiding. That would come later, after the rest of the ships were fully repaired and their crews refreshed by a minimum of one off-duty free time shift. Mya and Oranda knew the frantic kind of living crammed into those brief hours. Some of their best times had been under those conditions. But there would be more time after the mission was over.

They punctured the upper cloud layer, slowed markedly and zeroed in on their target. The screens betrayed nothing of the surface. Clouds and misty fog clutched at the planet as though evolving molecularly into toxins deadly to the vermin attacking her.

The Mark IV settled at the rear of the clearing where the Leatez had made their home for millennia. Broken rock spoiled the area. Giant slabs were piled against the old entrance and reached up to the small skylights chiseled into the outer fortress wall.

Oranda glanced at the mockup drawing of the interior prepared by one of his men. It blazed on a side screen in colors corresponding to elevation and projected areas of accessibility.

Once the ship settled, the standby thrusters hummed quietly. Lieutenant Mya saluted her superior as he prepared to depart.

Esse stood at the entrance of the lair and watched the ship in the clearing release a score of men and equipment. Curious, he crouched and scooted to the edge, where his forepaws dangled in open air when he lay down again.

Captain Oranda led his engineers to the base of the rubble piling up to the skylights. He felt obligated to lead the way into the Sanctuary. Not enough time had passed for the Colonial War General to die of starvation, though if he had not able to reach the food rooms, he would be weak.

A man and a woman wearing engineering stripes and breathing masks moved to the front of the detail and sprayed the rock pile with a plastic gel to hold the rocks in place without making them smooth. The jet streams arced high in the air and shot through the skylight slits.

When they had finished, they hurriedly returned the canisters to the ship and returned.

Troubled, Esse nudged Asa to rouse her. The ordeal Stefen had subjected her to during his flight required the rest she abandoned herself to in order to heal her completely. The most he could get from her was a nostril-fluttering deep breath.

He returned to the cliff edge. The outworlders were climbing up rocks they had fused together. They disappeared behind a lower cliff.

Bound to the protection of those in Stefen's care, Esse raced along the cliff. His giant form gracefully leaped thirty-meter rifts in the mountain as he descended toward the entrance area.

Noise from every direction assaulted his ears. It was the same high whine that had awakened him.

Small fighter ships rose out of the jungle, each bearing the dez Kaliea emblem which Esse had learned to associate with the enemy. He jumped up to a ledge partially intact and circled over to the next stone ridge.

The ship in the clearing cut loose with a horrendous noise. Unwillingly, Esse spared it a glance. It began to glow. Two of the outworlders not yet climbing the rock ran toward it.

It lifted, leaving those on the ground behind.

Esse was committed and beyond the point of return to the lair. He roared in anguish.

"Move it! Move it! Get up here and slide into the Sanctuary." The captain braced himself at the top and anchored another rope into the solid rock face. He called to the two remaining in the clearing and cursed the fact that youth was wasted on the young. They had the vigor but not the wisdom to survive.

It was a neat trap, one he possibly could have set himself. Twice he had been guilty of underestimating Lisan. For a split second as he helped one of the climbers swing free of the top rocks he realized that he must have partially believed General Myzillion's tale—absurd as it was.

He glanced at his ship.

Mya knew what to do.

A small grimace of satisfaction prevailed.

The six remaining fighters and two scouters converged on the Mark IV.

A sapphire shimmer engulfed the larger ship bearing the cor Baalan crest.

The fighters spaced themselves out, trying to keep the Mark IV on the ground by sheer physical presence.

Lieutenant Mya continued to raise the ship and hold her shields at maximum.

The two from the clearing were scrambling up the rocks to their Captain.

A series of test shots flew at the Mark IV. They were nothing serious, merely a feeling out of defenses and a ploy for the larger ship to diminish her defensive position.

The sapphire screen held easily and shed the blasts. A ricochet slammed into the space between the two climbing the rock. The blast incinerated them and made a lava hole through the rubble and into the Sanctuary itself.

Esse dropped to the ground at the entrance and bellowed at the man standing guard. He moved away. Esse started loping down the corridor, roaring a warning all the way.

Mya continued to lift, undaunted by the pressure of the fighter's shields now touching those of the Mark IV.

Oranda blindly held onto the last rope he had secured in the stone. The fused rock below him fell away into a molten pit. He kicked frantically at the wall, trying to find one good toehold to steady him.

Three bursts centered upon Oranda erupted simultaneously. The northern part of the Sanctuary caved in on itself. Corinda met Kansi's eyes across a table where they were preparing a Leatez stew.

Tari screamed and ran, warning that the danger pressing them on all sides allowed no time to spare if they

264

were to escape. She met Esse, waved her arms and turned the beast to the side, passed him and ran on.

As a child's block tower would crumble to the ground when the bottom one is yanked away, so did the mountain, on a much grander scale.

The ships continued firing upon the Mark IV. The mountain received more of the glancing blows.

Lieutenant Mya watched the quick obliteration of her Captain and friend. She did not so much as blink. Her orders were clear.

Later, alone, perhaps there would be a tear.

A stream of commands gushed out of her mouth.

The Mark IV turned abruptly and cut under the fighters and above the crumbling mountain. The oblique maneuver caught the enemy off guard, and in seconds Mya commanded the upper hand and fired down at the fighters trying to follow.

The sedimentary mountain took the brunt of the misses and deflections. It turned into smoldering pools of liquid rock.

Chapter 28

BLEEDING FROM HIS REAR HAUNCH, ESSE struggled to free himself from the rocks trying to fossilize his bones with the mountain. Straining toward a glimmer of light refracted against a portion of shattered wall, he shifted enough to trigger a slide.

His left fang was broken. The exposed nerve was a constant source of a pain far in excess of his other combined injuries.

Heat seeped through the stone behind him. The perpetual temperature rise imparted an incentive of its own. He struggled harder and was rewarded with the freedom of his right midleg. The new leverage helped to extricate the left one and finally shuffle boulders around sufficently to pull out his rear legs.

Staggering, slipping on his own blood and sweat across the mammoth slabs and man-sized boulders choking the remnant of hallway, Esse blundered forward. He labored to shift the smaller ones and increase the size of daylight winding through the quarried maze.

A roar and a heave threw his weight against a shale slab buttressed between him and freedom.

It grated at both ends, but stood fast.

Eyeing it through a haze of bright red over blue eyes, he dared it to defy him again. He cleared the backway of another boulder, stared at the barrier for a long while, then charged it with his powerful chest. Bones cracked on impact. His roar came out a whine. He teetered, shuffling backward.

He was a kervemith. A leader! He would not die in captivity forged by outworlder hell machines. Rest. He settled down, panting hard, always watching the shale as though he could disintegrate it with the intensity of his gaze.

The rest was short. The heat sweltering at the rear intensified. Low rumbles and the ill boding of the rocks around him set him on his feet.

The conglomerate behind him shifted and began to roll. The land shook like a chotiburu in his locked jaws. One bounce set him on the shale, forcing it, pushing, using the earth's timorous attitude to loosen it.

An open sea of lava churned behind him. It extended all the way to the river. Its width was too vast for him to estimate.

The shale teetered.

Esse shoved it a last time.

A crack started behind him and ran the length of the arched roof.

The shale split. Esse crammed his bulk through the upper opening, using his claws as grapple hooks in the shale in his desperate yen for open space.

Once his head and forepaws were through they served to pull the rest of him out of the quarry.

Slowly, carefully, he made his way through the last partially clear portion of the tunnel.

At the place where the tunnel ended and the jungle had flourished only a short time ago, he found survivors.

Tari lay staring at a rock beside her head. Her blood coated it. The outworlder lady lay beside her. Lifeless. Beyond her, Kansi struggled feebly to dig free.

Esse watched. Immobility bronzed the pain in his fang and muscles. Gingerly, he pawed at the rubble pinning the woman to the ground.

Abruptly, Tari moved. "Who's there?" She squinted hard at Esse, wiggled and brought her hand out from a pile of dirt and rock. She tried to sit and managed to do so only with tremendous effort. After brushing her hand off on the upper rags of her clothing, she rubbed her eyes, continued to squint and shook her head, trying to clear it.

Together, they dug Kansi out. The last portion of the mountain where Esse had been trapped fell into the lava sea.

Tari struggled to her feet, unable to put much weight on her left foot. She held onto Esse and Kansi, her fingers claws in his bloodied coat.

The trio watched the lava. The mountain in its entirety was gone. Those in the Sanctuary, and in the kervemith lair, were also gone. The obliteration was complete, with the exception of the onlookers.

"Come on, we've got to get to the place in the next mountain," Kansi said, grabbing her ribs. She looked at the new landscape, level to the mountain rising with the little stronghold Adru had stocked. It was inconceivable that the land could change so completely, so swiftly.

Tari leaned heavily on the beast and hobbled toward safety. Kansi stopped often and coughed out streams of blood.

Activity in the lava sea abated. The last dregs spilled into the river, where they cooled to form a dam. The violence with which the mountain had disintegrated had flung much of the molten rock into the current to construct a broad base for the barrier. The river battered at it, swirled around the far side and began to rise behind the constriction. It would have sealed itself off if much of the mountain had not been reclaimed by the Virgin herself, ingested and prepared to be regurgitated somewhere else.

Lozadar watched Stefen rise and dip with the lead zuriserpant. Once in a while the land became visible through the mist. Often they were lucky to see the entire wedge and had to rely totally upon the strange, scaled ocean dwellers.

Which of them had experienced the greatest change since the Forbidden Place was a subject open for debate. The primary force behind Lozadar's pendulum swing back to the Seven Worlds was represented by the presence of the Colonial General on his right. The process of rediscovery and the loss of a utopian dream added to the burden of responsibility resting squarely on Lozadar.

It was one way or the other. There was no melding of the two divergent worlds.

The long trek sucked energy from him, mentally and physically. Yet Stefen looked fresher each kilometer, as though he possessed some secret knowledge. While Lozadar contemplated that aspect, a fog so thick he could not see his hand at an arm's length descended over them. Whitecaps were swallowed where they formed. The swells shrinking into the emerald-green sea quelled all sound save that made by the zuriserpants. The ocean turned into a glassy surface pressed shiny by the density of the fog.

The zuriserpants sank lower in the water, arching their backs so their gills and fins made no noise in the abnormal silence.

Lozadar wanted to call out to his comrades. The quality of the mood sitting on the sea did not permit it.

From overhead, muffled by clouds as effective as a cotton padding, came the sounds of ships. Small craft. Fighters and a couple of scouters.

They passed, unseen.

The ominous silence remained, as though the Virgin waited for yet another crisis to end.

It was faint. Time and concentration strengthened it. A low hum in the distance.

A big ship.

Automatically, Lozadar looked up.

The ship retreated the way it had come, leaving the ocean riders to stare at the sultry moisture bearing down on them.

When night came the air felt harder to breathe and the zuriserpants slowed and finally stopped. Individually, the small army ate and rested. A feeling of tension rippled through the men and the zuriserpants.

At first light, General Myzillion slipped into the calm sea and swam to the cliff rising out of the water. One at a time his men followed, making almost no noise.

Lozadar remained beside Stefen. Both watched the attack of the cliff for ten meters. Beyond that the fog was thick again.

The General's men were well trained to survive, regardless of where or under what circumstances. They were colonials and took great pride in overcoming the most adverse conditions.

It was a long way up the face of the cliff to the flat shelf above. Myzillion could hear his men scramble below. The mist became his best ally at the top. It sheltered him from eyes that might be lurking only a few meters away and snuffed any slight mistakes his soggy boots made against the rocks.

He made a quick survey of the area and found its only occupant to be more heat. Hurriedly, he helped his men over the lip and lined them up. There was little time allotted for the distance to the perimeter of the Insurrectionists' base, where they would be joined by a number of the Virgin's creatures. Secretly, Myzillion was glad his men were already familiar with the monsters. With a shade of luck it was one less thing to worry over.

Corinda nagged at the back of his mind. While he needed every man he had for this harebrained scheme of the jungle man's, he wished she were safer than the stone walls made her.

Lozadar rode silently beside Stefen for several kilometers. Gradually, the fog thinned around and behind them. It receded just in front of them as they swung out to sea, then inland.

They sat in the water, waiting for a signal. Thousands of zuriserpants converged on them. Their masses were so great that it appeared to be a forest of tentacled eyes a man could walk across if he could duck the weaving, wandering oculars contorted into a thousand shapes which communicated whole messages.

The sea maintained a quiescence adhered to by the zuriserpants. Those on the land above would not know of their presence until they chose to make it known.

"There will be great sorrow on the Virgin when the battle is over."

Lozadar glanced at Stefan. The Champion looked straight ahead, his chin higher than it had been for a long time.

"The Leatez mountain is dead. Those inside are gone to the Virgin's bowels." He turned to meet Lozadar's inquisition. "I am sorry—for you, for me," nodding to the land, "your friend and Esse." He turned to Andazu. "The kervemith is as you are, my friend. It seems death stalks every corner of the land since the Outworlder has breathed our air."

Stunned, Lozadar demanded to know how he could have learned the fate of the Sanctuary. He did not want to believe such an atrocity could happen.

"Esse. I can hear him in here." He tapped his right temple and looked into the mist. "When we tried to do that, we could not. He is near death, outcast. Tari and Kansi are with him. Kansi, too, falters." Abruptly, he turned on Lozadar. "When this is over today, you go with the other outworlders. There is no future here for

271

you. There may be none for me, either. I would ask one thing of you should we be victorious today."

Lozadar was too grief-stricken to ask questions.

"Keep your wars away from the Virgin, Lozadar, Ruler of the Seven Worlds. We cannot afford them. Our existence, while it may appear similar to yours, is much different. Our adversaries do not harm you. It is strange.

"We live in harmony, but our physical laws are unbalanced. In your realm you have definite checks and balances as safeguards. You know your limitations. So much is taken for granted, but you have no genuine harmony, do you?"

The Ruler met his gaze and saw an aging man.

"There is a reason for this," Stefen continued slowly. "All the worlds over which you rule are dead. They have either been killed by the human conquerors who pillaged the land and slaughtered the world's adornments or they were left abandoned and unwanted by their intelligences before man evolved."

"How do you know this?"

"The Deity chose to tell me. But he did not tell me where they went after they abandoned their orbs to wander in space around an uncaring star."

"If he does tell you, before I go . . ." Lozadar tried to imagine a predecessor species in the Seven.

Stefen smiled instantly. "I will tell you. You have been a friend, Lozadar. A good friend who has perhaps helped me to grow toward my destiny more easily than I could have done alone."

Lozadar fortified his composure. "Don't get maudlin on me. This plan can work, you know."

Stefen did not hear him. His features tightened with a look of intense concentration. Squinting, he peered at the cliffs being exposed by the lifting fog.

The zuriserpants submerged, with the exception of the ones with riders. Andazu's mount hugged the cliff wall and moved north. At some familiar point, the fenwapter would part company with the sea eagerly.

Lozadar wanted to balk aloud. It was suicide for the fenwapter to ascend the face of the cliff alone. In moments there would be a war going on.

"He knows what he does," Stefen said quietly. "It's time. The Virgin is ready. The Deity . . . comes."

Without reason, the world felt different. The full impact of Stefen's words homed in on Lozadar. If he cried out loud, he did not know it. Sweat flowed from every pore in his body. But he felt the loss and knew the grief which spawned an outrage and hatred he wanted to fling at Lisan dez Kaliea. Not as Ruler of the Seven Worlds or Legate of the cor Baalan House, but as Lozadar —a man who hurt from the core of his soul, a man whose best friend and whose newfound love had been forever removed from his embrace.

The old wound of his family and the vision of his sisters—tucked neatly away to keep a tenuous form of sanity while the wound healed—crept out of its corner ripe with vengeance.

Too much time on the Virgin had eradicated the carefully formed facades Lozadar had once mastered. The sorrow stepping on his heart knew no bounds. It radiated away from him, wove cruelly with his hate and fired his anger. A vicious circle, his malignant emotions came to fruition without bonds or inhibitions. Finally, he could see the fate designed for him and him alone.

A hot wind rose out of the sea to create a support for the heavy fog burdening the surface. The yaxura jolted the land and rose from the fetid compost ripening under its source. Several dozen falizians sang in the mist-laced treetops. Shyly, fenwapters collected in the heights, ever watchful of the kervemith stealthily converging on the metallic shapes by way of the lower branches. Grunting chotiburus snorted and loped short-legged jaunts between the gaping chasms of the yaxura.

General Myzillion and his men split forces and covered the base on the rocky sides of the cliff where it fell to the sea on the north and south. They used the rocks and scanty growth clinging to the edge as camouflage. Seaward, Myzillion saw the two mounted zuriserpants resting close together in the water. It gave him an eerie feeling to see them so vulnerable.

The base was quiet for a long time while the jungle creatures converged and the atmosphere thinned.

"Your friend. He will do as I told him?" Stefen repeated the question before receiving a nod as an answer.

Lozadar shook himself physically to regain a grasp of the present reality and situation. On the cliff directly in

273

front, Lisan's ship rose like a charred metallic mountain desecrated by the wrath of nature and the elements. Quiet was an ill sign.

The sea began its age-old business of wave building and cliff erosion. Still, Lozadar felt ready to jump out of his skin with anticipation.

Eight fighters and three scouters, one damaged, kicked in their engines.

Inexplicably, a calm damped the horrendous pounding sensation in Lozadar's throat and head. The source emanated from Stefen. When he looked at his friend, he wished that he had not. The appearance of age and ordeal rested unkindly upon him. Worry marks slashed at his forehead and gouged the sides of his eyes. His hair, ten centimeters long, had a gray cast to it in the daylight. Lozadar remembered how silver it had seemed to be during the brief, dark period of waiting.

Stefen did not acknowledge the scrutiny. Instead, he concentrated upon the ships on the plateau. He sat absolutely straight, as though the mere touch of a finger upon him would shatter his rigid structure into a million pieces.

Thundering, the clouds boiled on top of one another, fighting, and finally rolled away to let a tiny circle of pure sunlight beam through. The circle increased, focused upon the flat cliff top flanked by mountains and the sea. The ire from the sky impended a burst of fury which dwarfed the sounds coming from the ships and banished them into a background cacophony. The light blazed down, growing hotter and hotter.

A flicker of shimmering blue flowed over each of the ships and died.

Openmouthed, the outworlders watched the shields they used in battle and when warp jumping disintegrate. A fresh heat enveloped the land. It did not radiate from the blinding light in the sky, but rather from the ships themselves.

The colonials ducked farther behind the boulders shielding them from the Insurrectionists. The yaxura worked to create mounds. The fenwapters and kervemith impinged on the falizians and abdicated their aggressions. While they shunned the heat, they did not retreat from the line they drew for the defense of the Virgin.

Stefen stood on top of the zuriserpant, arms raised to

274

the light pouring through the prodigious gap in the dark-gray clouds roiling overhead.

The engine noises stopped. Hatches withdrew. Men and women poured out of the smaller ships.

The cloud opening shrank, devoting its tight beam upon the giant ship denuded of the dez Kaliea emblem at the center of the occupation.

Inhabitants of the Virgin charged to wreak their revenge upon the enemy who had disrupted their Passage hibernation, threatened their dens and jeopardized their future and their very survival in the Universe.

The General's men swung into action. From both sides of the enemy encampment they charged in a loose wedge, weapons drawn.

Terrified men and women ran to the jungle, found death waiting in a myriad of grotesque forms and galloped to the sea. Below, thousands of zuriserpants carpeted the aquamarine and white-frothed water. Weapons flared aimlessly.

General Myzillion led his task force in the direction of the nearest scouter, which was large enough to accommodate them all. Two of his men were severely wounded. When two others went to help them, they were waved off. From the ground, they bought the few precious minutes their comrades needed to gain access to the scouter and seal out its former owners. General Myzillion moved on, firing carefully to prevent a premature depletion of his power reserve.

He swore bitterly when a burning pain punctured his left shoulder. Blood oozed out of the deep hole opened to his shoulder bone from his chest. The instinct to clutch at it as though he might somehow be able to seal off the pain with his fingertips was denied. Goaded by a sensation that his time was limited, he kept firing and stumbling toward the open hatch of a fighter.

Engines of both scouters roared into life and immediately lifted into the air.

General Myzillion hurled himself into the hatch, weapon ready to take out any who had managed to endure the heat still clinging to the interior. Stretching with his left hand, he slapped the manual closure switch.

Alone, breathing hard, he rested for a few seconds while the agony ripping at his shoulder toned down to a lower throb.

He crawled for half a dozen meters, then pulled himself to his feet. Using the walls as a support, he dropped the Lat-kor and concentrated on the open door just ahead. His vision faded in and out, antagonizing his lust to achieve his mission.

He fell into the command chair and fumbled the engines to life. He felt the subtle response of the ship as it rose straight up for a hundred meters. He goaded it a bit farther, tilted it downward and peered directly into the belly of Lisan dez Kaliea's Insurrectionist command post.

Unconsciously, Lozadar held his breath. The small fighter teetered in the air, its left thruster noticeably suffering intermittency problems. He quietly berated himself for not taking a stronger stand to be a part of the annihilation of Lisan's headquarters and Lisan himself. Watching like this was too impersonal. His fingers pressed into the flesh of his thighs, vicariously strangling his enemy above.

Myzillion bore down on the metal gargantuan and wrapped his fingers around the edges of a line of numbered buttons on his left. The pain in his arm faded away as he concentrated on the target. Deliberately his fingertips drummed buttons one at a time in rapid succession.

Bursts of energy collided on the monstrosity dominating the plateau. Its repercussions rocked the listing fighter.

The light became brighter.

Stefen called out to the zuriserpants, folded his hands in the air in front of him and pointed his fingers at the voice carried over the sea and onto the land.

The yaxura retreated into the depths for safety.

Falizians flapped their hundreds of wings with such velocity that the putch tips bent and snapped under the wind strain.

Fenwapters and kervemith raced along the branching avenues to the volcano paths.

A few reluctant chotiburus clutched pieces of fleshy bone in their jaws and tried to escape the impending doom of the plateau.

Agog, Lozadar watched the enormous ship take hit after hit from Myzillion's fighter, dead center, unscreened.

Gradually, the big ship began to melt. The liquid metal ran off in layers and dripped at the edges. It hissed on the ground and solidified. No hatch opened. No emergency claxon sounded.

The drippings turned rancid black. The center where Myzillion fired erupted into an inferno whose ire reached back at the lighted circle assaulting it with a relentless power. The impact hurled the tiny fighter into a lateral spin out over the ocean. It disappeared into the clouds.

Lozadar withdrew his fingers from the flesh holes they had gouged in his legs and forced himself to look away from the maelstrom on the land.

Stefen bent his elbows outward, fingers still pointed at the visage of light. Slowly, it retracted. Thunder besieged the clouds as they came together. Bitter revenge filled the humid air.

Exhausted, Stefen collapsed into a sitting position. When he met Lozadar's gaze, he was old, his vitality usurped by the Deity's invasion of his personage. Flesh hung on his face, wrinkled and dry. His eyes possessed a rheumy look. A cataract clouded his left eye. The muscular bronze flesh of his body had turned pale white as the visage of power drained from him. His hands, gnarled and twisted, shook as they grasped at the zuriserpant's tentacle for support.

Lozadar stared. He was out of questions and long out of answers.

A blue vein pulsed in Stefen's temple. He mumbled something into the air.

The two passenger-carrying zuriserpants turned away and swam through an opening aisle in the masses. They moved north, toward the step cliffs which led to the Forbidden Place in the jungle. They had not ventured far before the pounding of the zuriserpant tails in the water created a set of vibrations which brought the cliff down into the sea.

There existed no traces of the outworlders upon the Virgin.

Chapter 29

THE STENCH OF DEATH AND LOSS RODE heavy in the air as the zuriserpants sped across the water. A strength flickered in Lozadar. He thought of all the pain in the Seven Worlds and felt that he bore it in himself. He considered those whom he loved, liked and respected—they were dead. A sensation of desertion twisted at his heart.

So many had believed in his ability to be a good Ruler. That faith needed justification. "The dead should not die in vain," he whispered, remembering something his father had once told him concerning the relationship of life and death.

Time passed at a strange, accelerated rate on the Virgin. He could not look at Stefen without tears coming to his eyes. The man was burned out, used up by the entity he had acquiesced in after so much resistance and pain. The power was never his to use or deny. He served as a tool, a vessel to be utilized, then discarded.

When they reached the step cliffs they parted company with the Lords of the Great Sea.

Stefen did not speak, nor did Lozadar find the temerity to attempt a conversation. He did not know how the Champion kept moving. His back was bent in a slight hunch. Age made his step unsure. The jerky motions of his head in contrast to the uncertainty of his step completed the oldster's image. He did not seem to notice Lozadar's presence.

At the top, Andazu waited. The fenwapter maintained the same reserve as Lozadar. Neither could bring themselves to humiliate Stefen by offering physical aid.

It was close to dark by the time they had reached the Forbidden Place.

Stefen turned to the outcast and took his hand. They exchanged no words. Steam hissed out of unevenly spaced vents surrounding the black obsidian dais. The mist stuffed into the maw was quiet, consoling in a blue tinge.

The Champion looked serene, totally at peace for the first time since Lozadar had met him. He was almost envious.

"Each man has a purpose in life," Stefen said in an old, cracking voice. "I have found and met mine. It is done. My son will have the same purpose." He smiled crookedly. "Perhaps he will live longer and your reign as Ruler will afford him time to seek the surviving Leatez." The smile became a grin. "There are still some hiding on the Virgin."

Before Lozadar could reply, Stefen released his hand and walked into the mist.

Lozadar stared at the brilliant colors for a long time. They glowed softly in the dark.

At first light, Andazu lumbered up to him. Around his neck was an amulet of a lady sitting in a sunburst.

Together, they left the Forbidden Place to her ghosts and returned to the step cliffs of the sea. Andazu moved mechanically down the stone giants to the pounding surf. A lone zuriserpant waited to take him across the ocean and up the river to the place where Tari outwaited Passage with the kervemith leader. Andazu had much to do and teach before he could bow to his Ancients with pride and honor unparalleled by any fenwapter leader in their long history.

Lozadar watched him leave heavy-hearted, yet glad for him. The courage of the fenwapter was something he would remember for as long as he lived.

He sat on the water-polished stone for half the day before he saw the two scouters flanking a limping fighter come out of the clouds. Behind them were the Mark IV's of the house of cor Baalan.

The reign of Lozadar, Ruler of the Allied Worlds, had just begun.